DEATH IN THE AIR

It had become obvious to Toller Maraquine and some others watching on the ground that the airship was heading into danger, but—incredibly—its captain appeared not to notice. "What does the fool think he's doing?" Toller shouted. He took from his pocket the stubby telescope he had carried since childhood and used it to scan the cloud layers. As he had half expected, he was able within seconds to pick out several blurry specks of blue and magenta. Ptertha.

He discerned hurried movements behind the ship's foredeck rails. The airship's envelope rippled and the whole assemblage tilted as the craft slewed to the right, but by then it was actually grazing the cloud, being lost to view now and again as it was engulfed by vaporous tendrils. A wail of terror, fine-drawn by distance and flowing air, reached the hushed watchers along the shore.

Toller guessed that somebody on board the airship had encountered a ptertha and he felt a thrill of dread. It was a fate which had overtaken him many times in bad dreams. Faced by assassins or ferocious animals, a man could—no matter how overwhelming the odds—go down fighting and in that way aspire to a strange reconciliation with death. But when the livid globes came questing and quivering, there was *nothing* that could be done.

BOB SHAW

THE RAGGED ASTRONAUTS

BAEN BOOKS

THE RAGGED ASTRONAUTS

A Baen Book

Baen Publishing Enterprises
260 Fifth Avenue
New York, N.Y. 10001

First paperback printing, May 1988

ISBN: 0-671-65405-5

Cover art by Alan Gutierrez

Library of Congress Cataloging in Publicatoin Data

Shaw, Bob.
  The ragged astronauts.

  I. Title.
PR6069.H364R34 1987   813'.54   87-913
ISBN 0-671-65644-9

Printed in the United States of America

Distributed by
SIMON & SCHUSTER
1230 Avenue of the Americas
New York, N.Y. 10020

Contents

PART I

Shadow at Noon

CHAPTER 1

It had become obvious to Toller Maraquine and some others watching on the ground that the airship was heading into danger, but—incredibly—its captain appeared not to notice.

"What does the fool think he's doing?" Toller said, speaking aloud although there was nobody within earshot. He shaded his eyes from the sun to harden his perception of what was happening. The background was a familiar one to anybody who lived in those longitudes of Land—flawless indigo sea, a sky of pale blue feathered with white, and the misty vastness of the sister world, Overland, hanging motionless near the zenith, its disk crossed again and again by swathes of cloud. In spite of the foreday glare a number of stars were visible, including the nine brightest which made up the constellation of the Tree.

Against that backdrop the airship was drifting in on a light sea breeze, the commander conserving power crystals. The vessel was heading directly towards the shore, its blue-and-grey envelope foreshortened to a circle, a tiny visual echo of Overland. It was making steady progress, but what its captain had apparently failed to appreciate was that the onshore breeze in which he was travelling was very shallow, with a depth of not more than three-hundred feet. Above it and moving in the opposite direction was a westerly wind streaming down from the Haffanger Plateau.

Toller could trace the flow and counterflow of air with precision because the columns of vapour from the pikon reduction pans along the shore were drifting inland only a short distance before rising and being wafted back out to sea. Among those man-made bands of mist were ribbons of cloud from the roof of the plateau—therein lay the danger to the airship.

Toller took from his pocket the stubby telescope he had carried since childhood and used it to scan the cloud layers. As he had half expected, he was able within seconds to pick out

9

several blurry specks of blue and magenta suspended in the matrix of white vapour. A casual observer might have failed to notice them at all, or have dismissed the vague motes as an optical effect, but Toller's sense of alarm grew more intense. The fact that he had been able to spot some ptertha so quickly meant that the entire cloud must be heavily seeded with them, invisibly bearing hundreds of the creatures towards the airship.

"Use a sunwriter," he bellowed with the full power of his lungs. "Tell the fool to veer off, or go up or down, or. . . ."

Rendered incoherent by urgency, Toller looked all about him as he tried to decide on a course of action. The only people visible among the rectangular pans and fuel bins were semi-naked stokers and rakers. It appeared that all of the overseers and clerks were inside the wide-eaved buildings of the station proper, escaping the day's increasing heat. The low structures were of traditional Kolcorronian design—orange and yellow brick laid in complex diamond patterns, dressed with red sandstone at all corners and edges—and had something of the look of snakes drowsing in the intense sunlight. Toller could not even see any officials at the narrow vertical windows. Pressing a hand to his sword to hold it steady, he ran towards the supervisors' building.

Toller was unusually tall and muscular for a member of one of the philosophy orders, and workers tending the pikon pans hastily moved aside to avoid impeding his progress. Just as he was reaching the single-storey building a junior recorder, Comdac Gurra, emerged from it carrying a sunwriter. On seeing Toller bearing down on him, Gurra flinched and made as if to hand the instrument over. Toller waved it away.

"You do it," he said impatiently, covering up the fact that he would have been too slow at stringing the words of a message together. "You've got the thing in your hands—what are you waiting for?"

"I'm sorry, Toller." Gurra aimed the sunwriter at the approaching airship and the glass slats inside it clacked as he began to operate the trigger.

Toller hopped from one foot to the other as he watched for some evidence that the pilot was receiving and heeding the beamed warning. The ship drifted onwards, blind and serene. Toller raised his telescope and concentrated his gaze on the blue-painted gondola, noting with some surprise that it bore the plume-and-sword symbol which proclaimed the vessel to be a royal messenger. What possible reason could the King have for communicating with one of the Lord Philosopher's most remote experimental stations?

After what seemed an age, his enhanced vision enabled him to discern hurried movements behind the ship's foredeck rails. A few seconds later there were puffs of grey smoke along the gondola's left side, indicating that its lateral drive tubes were being fired. The airship's envelope rippled and the whole assemblage tilted as the craft slewed to the right. It was rapidly shedding height during the manoeuvre, but by then it was actually grazing the cloud, being lost to view now and again as it was engulfed by vaporous tendrils. A wail of terror, fine-drawn by distance and flowing air, reached the hushed watchers along the shore, causing some of the men to shift uneasily.

Toller guessed that somebody on board the airship had encountered a ptertha and he felt a thrill of dread. It was a fate which had overtaken him many times in bad dreams. The essence of the nightmare was not in visions of dying, but in the sense of utter hopelessness, the futility of trying to resist once a ptertha had come within its killing radius. Faced by assassins or ferocious animals, a man could—no matter how overwhelming the odds—go down fighting and in that way aspire to a strange reconciliation with death, but when the livid globes came questing and quivering, there was *nothing* that could be done.

"What's going on here?" The speaker was Vorndal Sisstt, chief of the station, who had appeared in the main entrance of the supervisors' building. He was middle-aged, with a round balding head and the severely upright posture of a man who was selfconscious about being below average in height. His neat sun-tanned features bore an expression of mingled annoyance and apprehension.

Toller pointed at the descending airship. "Some idiot has travelled all this distance to commit suicide."

"Have we sent a warning?"

"Yes, but I think it was too late," Toller said. "There were ptertha all round the ship a minute ago."

"This is terrible," Sisstt quavered, pressing the back of a hand to his forehead. "I'll give word for the screens to be hoisted."

"There's no need—the cloud base isn't getting any lower and the globes won't come at us across open ground in broad daylight."

"I'm not going to take the risk. Who knows what the . . . ?" Sisstt broke off and glared up at Toller, grateful for a safe outlet for his emotions. "Exactly when did you become empowered to make executive decisions here? In what I believe to be my station? Has Lord Glo elevated you without informing me?"

"Nobody needs elevation where you're concerned," Toller said, reacting badly to the chief's sarcasm, his gaze fixed on the airship which was now dipping towards the shore.

Sisstt's jaw sagged and his eyes narrowed as he tried to decide whether the comment had referred to his physical stature or abilities. "That was insolence," he accused. "Insolence and insubordination, and I'm going to see that certain people get to hear about it."

"Don't bleat," Toller said, turning away.

He ran down the shallow slope of the beach to where a group of workers had gathered to assist in the landing. The ship's multiple anchors trailed through the surf and up on to the sand, raking dark lines in the white surface. Men grabbed at the ropes and added their weight to counter the craft's skittish attempts to rise on vagrant breezes. Toller could see the captain leaning over the forward rail of the gondola, directing operations. There appeared to be some kind of commotion going on amidships, with several crewmen struggling among themselves. It was possible that somebody who had been unlucky enough to get too close to a ptertha had gone berserk, as occasionally happened, and was being forcibly subdued by his shipmates.

Toller went forward, caught a dripping rope and kept tension on it to help guide the airship to the tethering stakes which lined the shore. At last the gondola's keel crunched into the sand and yellow-shirted men vaulted over the side to secure it. The brush with danger had evidently rattled them. They were swearing fiercely as they pushed the pikon workers aside, using unnecessary force, and began tying the ship down. Toller could appreciate their feelings, and he smiled sympathetically as he offered his line to an approaching airman, a bottle-shouldered man with silt-coloured skin.

"What are you grinning at, dung-eater?" the man growled, reaching for the rope.

Toller withdrew the rope and in the same movement threw it into a loop and snapped it tight around the airman's thumb. "Apologise for that!"

"What the . . . !" The airman made as if to hurl Toller aside with his free arm and his eyes widened as he made the discovery that he was not dealing with a typical science technician. He turned his head to summon help from other airmen, but Toller diverted him by jerking the rope tighter.

"This is between you and me," Toller said quietly, using the power of his upper arms to increase the strain on the line. "Are you going to apologise, or would you like your thumb to wear on a necklet?"

"You're going to be sorry for. . . ." The airman's voice faded and he sagged, white-faced and gasping, as a joint in his thumb made a clearly audible popping sound. "I apologise. Let me go! I apologise."

"That's better," Toller said, releasing the rope. "Now we can all be friends together."

He smiled in mock geniality, giving no hint of the dismay he could feel gathering inside him. It had happened yet again! The sensible response to a ritual insult was to ignore it or reply in kind, but his temper had taken control of his body on the instant, reducing him to the level of a primitive creature governed by reflex. He had made no conscious decision to clash with the airman, and yet would have been prepared to maim him had the apology not been forthcoming. And what made matters worse was the knowledge that he was unable to back down, that the trivial incident might still escalate into something very dangerous for all concerned.

"*Friends*," the airman breathed, clutching his injured hand to

13

his stomach, his face contorted with pain and hatred. "As soon as I can hold a sword again I'll. . . ."

He left the threat unfinished as a bearded man in the heavily embroidered jupon of an aircaptain strode towards him. The captain, who was about forty, was breathing noisily and the saffron material of his jupon had damp brown stains below his armpits.

"What's the matter with you, Kaprin?" he said, staring angrily at the airman.

Kaprin's eyes gave one baleful flicker in Toller's direction, then he lowered his head. "I snared my hand in a line, sir. Dislocated my thumb, sir."

"Work twice as hard with the other hand," the captain said, dismissing the airman with a wave and turning to face Toller. "I'm Aircaptain Hlawnvert. You're not Sisstt. Where is Sisstt?"

"There." Toller pointed at the station chief, who was uncertainly advancing down the slope of the shore, the hem of his grey robe gathered clear of the rock pools.

"So that's the maniac who's responsible."

"Responsible for what?" Toller said, frowning.

"For blinding me with smoke from those accursed stewpots." Hlawnvert's voice was charged with anger and contempt as he swung his gaze to encompass the array of pikon pans and the columns of vapour they were releasing into the sky. "I've been told they're actually trying to make power crystals here. Is that true, or is it just a joke?"

Toller, barely clear of one potentially disastrous scrape, was nonetheless affronted by Hlawnvert's tone. It was the principal regret of his life that he had been born into a philosophy family instead of the military caste, and he spent much of his time reviling his lot, but he disliked outsiders doing the same. He eyed the captain coolly for a few seconds, extending the pause until it was just short of open disrespect, then spoke as though addressing a child.

"Nobody can make crystals," he said. "They can only be grown—if the solution is pure enough."

"Then what's the point of all this?"

"There are good pikon deposits in this area. We are extracting it from the soil and trying to find a way to refine it until it's pure enough to produce a reaction."

"A waste of time," Hlawnvert said with casual assurance, dismissing the subject as he turned away to confront Vorndal Sisstt.

"Good foreday, Captain," Sisstt said. "I'm so glad you have landed safely. I've given orders for our ptertha screens to be run out immediately."

Hlawnvert shook his head. "There's no need for them. Besides, you have already done the damage."

"I. . . ." Sisstt's blue eyes shuttled anxiously. "I don't understand you, Captain."

"The stinking fumes and fog you're spewing into the sky disguised the natural cloud. There are going to be deaths among my crew—and I deem you to be personally responsible."

"But. . . ." Sisstt glanced in indignation at the receding line of cliffs from which, for a distance of many miles, streamer after streamer of cloud could be seen snaking out towards the sea. "But that kind of cloud is a general feature of this coast. I fail to see how you can blame me for. . . ."

"Silence!" Hlawnvert dropped one hand to his sword, stepped forward and drove the flat of his other hand against Sisstt's chest, sending the station chief sprawling on his back, legs wide apart. "Are you questioning my competence? Are you saying I was careless?"

"Of course not." Sisstt scrambled to his feet and brushed sand from his robes. "Forgive me, Captain. Now that you bring the matter to my attention, I can see that the vapour from our pans could be a hazard to airmen in certain circumstances."

"You should set up warning beacons."

"I'll see that it's done at once," Sisstt said. "We should have thought of it ourselves long ago."

Toller could feel a tingling warmth in his face as he viewed the scene. Captain Hlawnvert was a big man, as was normal for one of a military background, but he was also soft and burdened with fat, and even someone of Sisstt's size could have vanquished him with the aid of speed and hate-hardened muscles. In addition, Hlawnvert had been criminally incompetent in his handling of the airship, a fact he was trying to obscure with his bluster, so going against him could have been justified before a tribunal. But none of that mattered to Sisstt. In keeping with his own nature the station chief was fawning over the hand which abused him. Later he would excuse his cowardice with jokes and try to compensate for it by mistreating his most junior subordinates.

In spite of his curiosity about the reason for Hlawnvert's visit, Toller felt obliged to move away, to dissociate himself from Sisstt's abject behaviour. He was on the point of leaving when a crop-haired airman wearing the white insignia of a lieutenant brushed by him and saluted Hlawnvert.

"The crew are ready for your inspection, sir," he said in a businesslike voice.

Hlawnvert nodded and glanced at the line of yellow-shirted men who were waiting by the ship. "How many took the dust?"

"Only two, sir. We were lucky."

"Lucky?"

"What I mean, sir, is that but for your superb airmanship our losses would have been much higher."

Hlawnvert nodded again. "Which two are we losing?"

"Pouksale and Lague, sir," the lieutenant said. "But Lague won't admit it."

"Was the contact confirmed?"

"I saw it myself, sir. The ptertha got within a single pace of him before it burst. He took the dust."

"Then why can't he own up to it like a man?" Hlawnvert said irritably. "A single wheyface like that can unsettle a whole crew." He scowled in the direction of the waiting men, then turned to Sisstt. "I have a message for you from Lord Glo, but there are certain formalities I must attend to first. You will wait here."

The colour drained from Sisstt's face. "Captain, it would be better if I received you in my chambers. Besides, I have urgent. . . ."

"You will wait *here*," Hlawnvert interrupted, stabbing Sisstt's chest with one finger and doing it with such force that he caused the smaller man to stagger. "It will do you good to see what mischief your polluting of the skies has brought about."

In spite of his contempt for Sisstt's behaviour, Toller began to wish he could intervene in some way to end the little man's humiliation, but there was a strict protocol governing such matters in Kolcorronian society. To take a man's side in a confrontation without being invited was to add fresh insult by implying that he was a coward. Going as far as was permissible, Toller stood squarely in Hlawnvert's way when the captain turned to walk to the ship, but the implicit challenge went unnoticed. Hlawnvert side-stepped him, his face turned towards the sky, where the sun was drawing close to Overland.

"Let's get this business over and done with before littlenight," Hlawnvert said to his lieutenant. "We have wasted too much time here already."

"Yes, sir." The lieutenant marched ahead of him to the men who were ranked in the lee of the restlessly stirring airship and raised his voice. "Stand forward all airmen who have reason to believe they will soon be unable to discharge their duties."

After a moment's hesitation a dark-haired young man took two paces forward. His triangular face was so pale as to be almost luminous, but his posture was erect and he appeared to be well in control of himself. Captain Hlawnvert approached him and placed a hand on each shoulder.

"Airman Pouksale," he said quietly, "you have taken the dust?"

"I have, sir." Pouksale's voice was lifeless, resigned.

"You have served your country bravely and well, and your name will go before the King. Now, do you wish to take the Bright Road or the Dull Road?"

"The Bright Road, sir."

"Good man. Your pay will be made up to the end of the voyage and will be sent to your next-of-kin. You may retire."

"Thank you, sir."

Pouksale saluted and walked around the prow of the airship's gondola to its far side. He was thus screened from the view of his former crewmates, in accordance with custom, but the executioner who moved to meet him became visible to Toller, Sisstt and many of the pikon workers ranged along the shore. The executioner's sword was wide and heavy, and its brakka wood blade was pure black, unrelieved by the enamel inlays with which Kolcorronian weapons were normally decorated.

Pouksale knelt submissively. His knees had barely touched the sand before the executioner, acting with merciful swiftness, had dispatched him along the Bright Road. The scene before Toller—all yellows and ochres and hazy shades of blue—now had a focal point of vivid red.

At the sound of the death blow a ripple of unease passed through the line of airmen. Several of them raised their eyes to gaze at Overland and the silent movement of their lips showed they were bidding their dead crewmate's soul a safe journey to the sister planet. For the most part, however, the men stared unhappily at the ground. They had been recruited from the crowded cities of the empire, where there was considerable scepticism about the Church's teaching that men's souls were immortal and alternated endlessly between Land and Overland. For them death meant death—not a pleasant stroll along the mystical High Path linking the two worlds. Toller heard a faint choking sound to his left and turned to see that Sisstt was covering his mouth with both hands. The station chief was trembling and looked as though he could faint at any second.

"If you go down we'll be branded as old women," Toller whispered fiercely. "What's the matter with you?"

"The barbarism." Sisstt's words were indistinct. "The terrible barbarism . . . What hope is there for us?"

"The airman had a free choice—and he behaved well."

"You're no better than. . . ." Sisstt stopped speaking as a commotion broke out by the airship. Two airmen had gripped a third by the arms and in spite of his struggles were holding him in front of Hlawnvert. The captive was tall and spindly, with an incongruously round belly.

". . . couldn't have seen me, sir," he was shouting. "And I was upwind of the ptertha, so the dust couldn't have come anywhere near me. I swear to you, sir—I haven't taken the dust."

Hlawnvert placed his hands on his broad hips and looked up at the sky for a moment, signifying his disbelief, before he spoke. "Airman Lague, the regulations require me to accept your statement. But let me make your position clear. You won't be offered the Bright Road again. At the very first signs of fever or paralysis you will go over the side. Alive. Your pay for the entire voyage will be withheld and your name will be struck from the royal record. Do you understand these terms?"

"Yes, sir. Thank you, sir." Lague tried to fall at Hlawnvert's feet, but the men at his side tugged him upright. "There is nothing to worry about, sir—I haven't taken the dust."

At an order from the lieutenant the two men released Lague and he walked slowly back to rejoin the rank. The line of airmen parted to make room for him, leaving a larger gap than was necessary, creating an intangible barrier. Toller guessed that Lague would find little consolation during the next two days, which was the time it took for the first effects of ptertha poison to become apparent.

Captain Hlawnvert saluted his lieutenant, turning the assembly over to him, and walked back up the slope to Sisstt and Toller. Patches of high colour showed above the curls of his beard and the sweat stains upon his jupon had grown larger. He looked up at the high dome of the sky, where the eastern rim of Overland had begun to brighten as the sun moved behind it, and made an impatient gesture as though commanding the sun to disappear more quickly.

"It's too hot for this kind of vexation," he growled. "I have a long way to go, and the crew are going to be useless until that coward Lague goes over the side. The service regulations will have to be changed if these new rumours aren't quashed soon."

"Ah. . . ." Sisstt strained upright, fighting to regain his composure. "New rumours, Captain?"

"There's a story that some line soldiers down in Sorka died after handling ptertha casualties."

"But pterthacosis isn't transmissible."

"I know that," Hlawnvert said. "Only a spineless cretin would think twice about it, but that's what we get for aircrew these days. Pouksale was one of my few steady men—and I've lost him to that damned fog of yours."

Toller, who had been watching a burial detail gather up Pouksale's remains, felt a fresh annoyance at the repetition of the indictment and his chief's complaisance. "You don't have to keep on blaming our fog, Captain," he said, giving Sisstt a significant glance. "Nobody in authority is disputing the facts."

Hlawnvert rounded on him at once. "What do you mean by that?"

Toller produced a slow, amiable smile. "I mean we all got a clear view of what happened."

"What's your name, soldier?"

"Toller Maraquine—and I'm not a soldier."

"You're not a. . . ." Hlawnvert's look of anger gave way to one of sly amusement. "What's this? What have we here?"

Toller remained impassive as the captain's gaze took in the anomalous aspects of his appearance—the long hair and grey robes of a philosopher combined with the height and blocky musculature of a warrior. His wearing of a sword also set him apart from the rest of his kin. Only the fact that he was free of scars and campaign tattoos distinguished him in physique from a full-blooded member of the military.

He studied Hlawnvert in return, and his antagonism increased as he followed the thought processes so clearly mirrored on the captain's florid face. Hlawnvert had not been able to disguise his alarm over a possible accusation of negligence, and now he was relieved to find that he was quite secure. A few coarse innuendoes about his challenger's pedigree were all the defence he needed in the lineage-conscious hierarchy of Kolcorron. His lips twitched as he tried to choose from the wealth of taunts available to him.

Go ahead, Toller thought, projecting the silent message with all the force of his being. *Say the words which will end your life.*

Hlawnvert hesitated, as though sensing the danger, and again the interplay of his thoughts was clearly visible. He wanted to humiliate and discredit the upstart of dubious ancestry who had dared impugn him, but not if there was serious risk involved. And calling for assistance would be a step towards turning a triviality into a major incident, one which would highlight the very issue he wanted to obscure. At length, having decided on his tactics, he forced a chuckle.

"If you're not a soldier you should be careful about wearing that sword," he said jovially. "You might sit on it and do yourself a mischief."

Toller refused to make things easy for the captain. "The weapon is no threat to *me*."

"I'll remember your name, Maraquine," Hlawnvert said in a low voice. At that moment the station's timekeeper sounded the littlenight horn—tonguing the double note which was used when ptertha activity was high—and there was a general movement of pikon workers towards the safety of the buildings. Hlawnvert turned away from Toller, clapped one arm around Sisstt's shoulders and drew him in direction of the tethered airship.

"You're coming aboard for a drink in my cabin," he said. "You'll find it nice and snug in there with the hatch closed, and you'll be able to receive Lord Glo's orders in privacy."

Toller shrugged and shook his head as he watched the two men depart. The captain's excessive familiarity was a breach of the behavioural code in itself, and his blatant insincerity in embracing a man he had just thrown to the ground was nothing short of an insult. It accorded Sisstt the status of a dog which could be whipped or petted at the whim of its owner. But, true to his colours, the station chief appeared not to mind. A sudden bellowing laugh from Hlawnvert showed that Sisstt had already begun to make his little jokes, laying the groundwork for the version of the encounter he would later pass on to his staff and expect them to believe. *The captain loves people to think he's a real ogre—but when you get to know him as well as I do. . . .*

Again Toller found himself wondering about the nature of Hlawnvert's mission. What new orders could be so urgent and important that Lord Glo had considered it worth sending them by special carrier instead of waiting for a routine transport? Was it possible that something was going to happen to break the deadly monotony of life at the remote station? Or was that too much to hope for?

As darkness swept out of the west Toller looked up at the sky and saw the last fierce sliver of the sun vanish behind the looming immensity of Overland. As the light abruptly faded the cloudless areas of the sky thronged with stars, comets and whorls of misty radiance. Littlenight was beginning, and under its cover the silent globes of the ptertha would soon leave the clouds and come drifting down to ground level in search of their natural prey.

Glancing about him, Toller realised he was the last man out in the open. All personnel connected with the station had retreated indoors and the crew of the airship were safely enclosed in its lower deck. He could be accused of foolhardiness in lingering outside for so long, but it was something he quite often did. The flirtations with danger added spice to his humdrum existence and were a way of demonstrating the essential difference between himself and a typical member of one of the philosophy families. On this occasion his gait was slower and more casual than ever as he walked up the gentle incline to the supervisors' building. It was possible that he was being watched, and his private code dictated that the greater the risk of a ptertha strike the less afraid he should appear to be. On reaching the door he paused and stood quite still for a moment, despite the crawling sensation on his back, before lifting the latch and going inside.

Behind him, dominating the southern sky, the nine brilliant stars of the Tree tilted down towards the horizon.

CHAPTER 2

Prince Leddravohr Neldeever was indulging himself in the one pursuit which could make him feel young again.

As the elder son of the King, and as head of all of Kolcorron's military forces, he was expected to address himself mainly to matters of policy and broad strategy in warfare. As far as individual battles were concerned, his proper place was far to the rear in a heavily protected command post from which he could direct operations in safety. But he had little or no taste for hanging back and allowing deputies, in whose competence he rarely had faith anyway, to enjoy the real work of soldiering. Practically every junior officer and foot soldier had a winestory about how the prince had suddenly appeared at his side in the thick of battle and helped him hew his way to safety. Leddravohr encouraged the growth of the legends in the interests of discipline and morale.

He had been supervising the Third Army's push into the Loongl Peninsula, on the eastern edge of the Kolcorronian possessions, when word had been received of unexpectedly strong resistance in one hilly region. The additional intelligence that brakka trees were plentiful in the area had been enough to lure Leddravohr into the front line. He had exchanged his regal white cuirass for one moulded from boiled leather and had taken personal control of part of an expeditionary force.

It was shortly after dawn when, accompanied by an experienced high-sergeant called Reeff, he bellied his way through forest undergrowth to the edge of a large clearing. This far to the east foreday was much longer than aftday, and Leddravohr knew he had ample reserves of light in which to mount an attack and carry out a thorough mopping-up operation afterwards. It was a good feeling, knowing that yet more enemies of Kolcorron were soon to go down weltering in blood before his own sword. He carefully parted the last leafy screen and studied what was happening ahead.

A circular area some four-hundred yards in diameter had been totally cleared of tall vegetation except for a stand of brakka trees at the centre. About a hundred Gethan tribesmen and women were clustered around the trees, their attention concentrated on an object at the tip of one of the slim, straight trunks. Leddravohr counted the trees and found there were nine—a number which had magical and religious links with the heavenly constellation of the Tree.

He raised his field glasses and saw, as he had expected, that the object surmounting one of the trees was a naked woman. She was doubled over the tip of the trunk, her stomach pressed into the central orifice, and was held immovably in place by cords around her limbs.

"The savages are making one of their stupid sacrifices," Leddravohr whispered, passing his glasses to Reeff.

The sergeant examined the scene for a long moment before returning the glasses. "My men could put the bitch to better uses than that," he said, "but at least it makes things easier for us."

He pointed at the thin glass tube attached to his wrist. Inside it was part of a cane shoot which had been marked with black pigment at regular intervals. A pacebeetle was devouring the shoot from one end, moving at the unchanging rate common to its kind.

"It is past the fifth division," Reef said. "The other cohorts will be in position by now. We should go in while the savages are distracted."

"Not yet." Leddravohr continued watching the tribesmen through his glasses. "I can see two look-outs who are still facing outwards. These people are becoming a bit more wary, and don't forget they have copied the idea of cannon from somewhere. Unless we take them completely by surprise they will have time to fire at us. I don't know about you, but I don't want to breakfast on flying rock. I find it quite indigestible."

Reeff grinned appreciatively. "We'll wait till the tree blows."

"It won't be long—the top leaves are folding." Leddravohr watched with interest as the uppermost of the tree's four pairs of gigantic leaves rose from their normal horizontal position and furled themselves around the trunk. The phenomenon occurred about twice a year throughout a brakka tree's span of maturity in the wild state, but it was one which as a native of Kolcorron he had rarely seen. In his country it was regarded as a waste of power crystals to permit a brakka to discharge itself.

There was a short delay after the top leaves had closed against the trunk, then the second pair quivered and slowly swung upwards. Leddravohr knew that, well below the ground, the partition which divided the tree's combustion chamber was beginning to dissolve. Soon the green pikon crystals which had been extracted from the soil by the upper root system would mingle with the purple halvell gathered by the lower network of roots. The heat and gas thus generated would be contained for a brief period of time—then the tree would blast its pollen into the sky in an explosion which would be heard for miles.

Lying prone on the bed of soft vegetation, Leddravohr felt a pulsing warmth in his groin and realised he was becoming sexually excited. He focused his glasses on the woman lashed to the top of the tree, trying to pick out details of breast or buttock. Until that moment she had been so passive that he had believed her to be unconscious, perhaps drugged, but the movement of the huge leaves farther down the trunk appeared to have alerted her to the fact that her life was about to end, although her limbs were too well bound to permit any real struggle. She had begun twisting her head from side to side, swinging the long black hair which hid her face.

"Stupid bitch," Leddravohr whispered. He had limited his study of the Gethan tribes to an assessment of their military capabilites, but he guessed their religion was the uninspired mishmash of superstitions found in most of the backward countries of Land. In all probability the woman had actually volunteered for her role in the fertility rite, believing that her sacrifice would guarantee her reincarnation as a princess on Overland. Generous dosages of wine and dried mushroom could render such ideas temporarily persuasive, but there was nothing like the imminence of death to induce a more rational mode of thought.

"Stupid bitch she may be, but I wish I had her under me right now," Reeff growled. "I don't know which is going to blow first—that tree or mine."

"I'll give her to you when we have finished our work," Leddravohr said with a smile. "Which half will you take first?"

Reeff produced a nauseated grimace, expressing his admiration for the way in which the prince could match the best of his men in any branch of soldiering, including that of devising obscenities. Leddravohr turned his attention to the Gethan look-outs. His field glasses showed that they were, as he had anticipated, casting frequent glances towards the sacrificial tree, upon which the third pair of leaves had begun to rise. He knew there was a straightforward botanical reason for the tree's behaviour—leaves in the horizontal attitude would have been snapped off by the recoil of the pollination discharge—but the sexual symbolism was potent and compelling. Leddravohr was confident that every one of the Gethan guards would be staring at the tree when the climactic moment arrived. He put his glasses away and took a firm grip on his sword as the leaves clasped the brakka's trunk and, almost without delay, the lowermost pair began to stir. The flailing of the woman's hair was frenetic now and her cries were thinly audible at the edge of the clearing, mingled with the chanting of a single male voice from somewhere near the centre of the tribal assembly.

"Ten nobles extra to the man who silences the priest," Leddravohr said, reaffirming his dislike for all superstition-mongers, especially the variety who were too craven to do their own pointless butchery.

He raised a hand to his helmet and removed the cowl which had concealed its scarlet crest. The young lieutenants commanding the other three cohorts would be watching for the flash of colour as he emerged from the forest. Leddravohr tensed himself for action as the fourth pair of leaves lifted and closed around the brakka's trunk, gentle as a lover's hands. The woman trussed across the tip of the tree was suddenly quiescent, perhaps in a faint, perhaps petrified with dread. An intense pulsing silence descended over the clearing. Leddravohr knew that the partition in the tree's combustion chamber had already given way, that a measure of green and purple crystals had already been mixed, that the energy released by them could be pent up for only a few seconds. . . .

The sound of the explosion, although directed upwards, was appalling. The brakka's trunk whipped and shuddered as the pollinated discharge ripped into the sky, a vaporous column momentarily tinged with blood, concentrically ringed with smoke.

Leddravohr felt the ground lift beneath him as a shock wave raced out through the surrounding forest, then he was on his feet and running. Deafened by the awesome blast of sound, he had to rely on the evidence of his eyes to gauge the degree of surprise in the attack. To the left and right he could see the orange helmet crests of two of his lieutenants, with dozens of soldiers emerging from the trees behind them. Directly ahead of him the Gethans were gazing spellbound at the sacrificial tree, whose leaves were already beginning to unfurl, but they were bound to discover their peril at any second. He had covered almost half the distance to the nearest guard and unless the man turned soon he was going to die without even knowing what had hit him.

The man turned. His face contorted, the mouth curving downwards, as he shouted a warning. He stamped his right foot on something concealed in the grass. Leddravohr knew it was the Gethan version of a cannon—a brakka tube set on a shallow ramp and intended solely for anti-personnel use. The impact of the guard's foot had shattered a glass or ceramic capsule in the breech and mixed its charge of power crystals, but—and this was why Kolcorron had little regard for such weapons—there was an inevitable delay before the discharge. Brief though the period was, it enabled Leddravohr to take evasive action. Shouting a warning to the soldiers behind him, he veered to the right and came at the Gethan from the side just as the cannon exploded and sent its fan-shaped spray of pebbles and rock fragments crackling through the grass. The guard had managed to draw his sword, but his preoccupation with the sacrifice had rendered him untuned and unready for combat. Leddravohr, without even breaking his stride, cut him down with a single slash across the neck and plunged on into the confusion of human figures beyond.

Normal time ceased to exist for Leddravohr as he cut his way towards the centre of the clearing. He was only dimly aware of the sounds of struggle being punctuated by further cannon blasts. At least two of the Gethans he killed were young women, something his men might grumble about later, but he had seen otherwise good soldiers lose their lives through trying to differentiate between the sexes during a battle. Turning a killing stroke into one which merely stunned involved making a decision and losing combat efficiency—and it took only an eyeblink for an enemy blade to find its mark.

Some of the Gethans were trying to make their escape, only to be felled or turned back by the encircling Kolcorronians. Others were making a fight of it as best they could, but their preoccupation with the ceremony had been fatal and they were paying the full price for their lack of vigilance. A group of tribesmen, plait-haired and outlandish in skin mosaics, got among the nine brakka trees and used the trunks as a natural fortification. Leddravohr saw two of his men take serious wounds, but the Gethans' stand was short-lived. They were hampered by lack of room and made easy targets for spearmen from the second cohort.

All at once the battle was over.

With the fading of the crimson joy and the return of sanity Leddravohr's cooler instincts reasserted themselves. He scanned his surroundings to make sure he was in no personal danger, that the only people still on their feet were Kolcorronian soldiers and captured Gethan women, then he turned his gaze to the sky. While in the forest he and his men had been safe from ptertha, but now they were in the open and at some slight risk.

The celestial globe which presented itself to Leddravohr's scrutiny looked strange to a native of Kolcorron. He had grown up with the huge and misty sphere of Overland hanging directly overhead, but here in the Loongl Peninsula the sister world was displaced far to the west. Leddravohr could see clear sky straight above and it gave him an uncomfortable feeling, as though he had left an important flank exposed in a battle plan. No bluish specs were to be seen drifting against the patterns of daytime stars, however, and he decided it was safe to return his attention to the work at hand.

The scene all about him was a familiar one, filled with a medley of familiar sounds. Some of the Kolcorronians were shouting coarse jokes at each other as they moved about the clearing dispatching wounded Gethans and collecting battle trophies. The tribesmen had little that could be considered valuable, but their Y-shaped ptertha sticks would make interesting curios to be shown in the taverns of Ro-Atabri. Other soldiers were laughing and whooping as they stripped the dozen or so Gethan women who had been taken alive. That was a legitimate activity at this stage—men who had fought well were entitled to the prizes of war—and Leddravohr paid only enough attention to satisfy himself that no actual coupling had begun. In this kind of territory an enemy counterattack could be launched very quickly, and a soldier in rut was one of the most useless creatures in the universe.

Railo, Nothnalp and Chravell—the lieutenants who had led the other three cohorts—approached Leddravohr. The leather of Railo's circular shield was badly gashed and there was a reddening bandage on his left arm, but he was fit and in good spirits. Nothnalp and Chravell were cleaning their swords with rags, removing all traces of contamination from the enamel inlays on the black blades.

"A successful operation, if I'm not mistaken," Railo said, giving Leddravohr the informal field salute.

Leddravohr nodded. "What casualties?"

"Three dead and eleven wounded. Two of the wounded were hit by the cannon. They won't see littlenight."

"Will they take the Bright Road?"

Railo looked offended. "Of course."

"I'll speak to them before they go," Leddravohr said. As a pragmatic man with no religious beliefs he suspected his words might not mean much to the dying soldiers, but it was the sort of gesture which would be appreciated by their comrades. Like his practice of permitting even the lowliest line soldier to speak to him without using the proper forms of address, it was one of the ways in which he retained the affection and loyalty of his troops.

29

He kept to himself the intelligence that his motives were entirely practical.

"Do we push straight on the Gethan village?" Chravell, the tallest of the lieutenants, returned his sword to its sheath. "It's not much more than a mile to the north-east, and they probably heard the cannon fire."

Leddravohr considered the question. "How many adults remain in the village?"

"Practically none, according to the scouts. They all came here to see the show." Chravell glanced briefly upwards at the dehumanised tatters of flesh and bone dangling from the tip of the sacrificial tree.

"In that case the village has ceased to be a military threat and has become an asset. Give me a map." Leddravohr took the proffered sheet and went down on one knee to spread it on the ground. It had been drawn a short time previously by an aerial survey team and emphasised the local features of interest to the Kolcorronian commanders—the size and location of Gethan settlements, topography, rivers, and—most important from a strategic point of view—the distribution of brakka among the other types of forestation. Leddravohr studied it carefully, then outlined his plans.

Some twenty miles beyond the village was a much larger community, coded G31, capable of fielding an estimated three-hundred fighting men. The intervening terrain was, to say the least of it, difficult. It was densely wooded and crisscrossed with steep ridges, crevasses and fast-flowing streams—all of which conspired to make it a nightmare for Kolcorronian soldiers whose natural taste was for plains warfare.

"The savages must come to us," Leddravohr announced. "A forced march across that type of ground will tire any man, so the faster they come the better for us. I take it this is a sacred place for them?"

"A holy of holies," Railo said. "It's very unusual to find nine brakka so close together."

"Good! The first thing we do is bring the trees down. Instruct the sentinels to allow some villagers to get close enough to see what is happening, and to let them get away again. And just before littlenight send a detachment to burn the village—just to drive the message home. If we are lucky the savages will be so exhausted when they get here they'll barely have enough strength to run on to our swords."

Leddravohr concluded his deliberately simplistic verbal sketch by laughing and tossing the map back to Chravell. His judgment was that the Gethans of G31, even if provoked into a hasty attack, would be more dangerous opponents than the lowland villagers. The forthcoming battle, as well as providing valuable experience for the three young officers, would let him demonstrate once again that in his forties he was a better soldier than men half his age. He stood up, breathing deeply and pleasurably, looking forward to the remainder of a day which had begun well.

In spite of his relaxed mood, ingrained habit prompted him to check the open sky. No ptertha were visible, but he was alerted by a suggestion of movement in one of the vertical panels of sky seen through the trees to the west. He took out his field glasses, trained them on the adjoining patch of brightness and a moment later caught a brief glimpse of a low-flying airship.

It was obviously heading for the area command centre, which was about five miles away on the western edge of the peninsula. The vessel had been too distant for Leddravohr to be certain, but he thought he had seen a plume-and-sword symbol on the side of the gondola. He frowned as he tried to imagine what circumstance was bringing one of his father's messengers to such an outlying region.

"The men are ready for breakfast," Nothnalp said, removing his orange-crested helmet so that he could wipe perspiration from his neck. "A couple of extra strips of salt pork wouldn't do any harm in this heat."

Leddravohr nodded. "I suppose they've earned that much."

"They'd also like to start on the women."

"Not until we secure the area. Make sure it is fully patrolled, and get the slimers brought forward immediately—I want those trees on the ground fast." Leddravohr moved away from the lieutenants and began a circuit of the clearing. The predominant sound was now that of the Gethan women screaming abuse

31

in their barbaric tongue, but cooking fires were beginning to crackle and he could hear Railo shouting orders at the platoon leaders who were going on patrol.

Near the base of one of the brakka trees was a low wooden platform heavily daubed in green and yellow with the matt pigments used by the Gethans. The naked body of a white-bearded man lay across the platform, his torso displaying several stab wounds. Leddravohr guessed the dead man was the priest who had been conducting the ceremony of sacrifice. His guess was confirmed when he noticed high-sergeant Reeff and a line soldier in conversation close to the primitive structure. The two men's voices were inaudible, but they were speaking with the peculiar intensity which soldiers reserved for the subject of money, and Leddravohr knew a bargain was being struck. He unstrapped his cuirass and sat down on a stump, waiting to see if Reeff was capable of any degree of subtlety. A moment later Reeff put his arm around the other man's shoulders and brought him forward.

"This is Soo Eggezo," Reeff said. "A good soldier. He's the one who silenced the priest."

"Useful work, Eggezo." Leddravohr gazed blandly at the young soldier, who was tongue-tied and obviously overawed by his presence, and made no other response. There was an awkward silence.

"Sir, you generously offered a reward of ten nobles for killing the priest." Reeff's voice assumed a throaty sincerity. "Eggezo supports his mother and father in Ro-Atabri. The extra money would mean a great deal to them."

"Of course." Leddravohr opened his pouch and took out a ten-noble note and extended it to Eggezo. He waited until the soldier's fingers had almost closed on the blue square of woven glass, then he quickly returned it to his pouch. Eggezo glanced uneasily at the sergeant.

"On second thoughts," Leddravohr said, "these might be more . . . convenient." He replaced the first note with two green squares of the five-noble denomination and handed them to Eggezo. He pretended to lose interest as the two men thanked him and hurried away. They went barely twenty paces before stopping for another whispered conversation, and when they parted Reeff was tucking something into a pocket. Leddravohr smiled as he committed Reeff's name to long-term memory. The sergeant was the sort of man he occasionally had use for— greedy, stupid and highly predictable. A few seconds later his interest in Reeff was pushed into the hinterland of his consciousness as a howl of jovial protest from many Kolcorronian throats told him the slimers had arrived to deal with the stand of brakka trees.

Leddravohr rose to his feet, as anxious as anybody to avoid getting downwind of the slimers, and watched the four seminude men emerge from the surrounding forest. They were carrying large gourds slung from padded yokes and they also bore spades and other kinds of digging implements. Their limbs were streaked with the living slime which was the principal tool of their trade. Every artifact they carried was made from glass, stone or ceramic because the slime would quickly have devoured all other materials, especially brakka. Even their breech clouts were woven from soft glass.

"Out of the way, dung-eaters," their round-bellied leader shouted as they marched straight across the clearing to the brakka. His words provoked a barrage of insults from the soldiers, to which the other slimers responded with obscene gestures. Leddravohr moved to keep upwind of the four men, partly to escape the stench they were exuding, but mainly to ensure that none of the slime's airborne spores settled on his person. The only way to rid one's self of even the slightest contamination was by thorough and painful abrasion of the skin.

On reaching the nearest brakka the slimers set down their equipment and began work immediately. As they dug to expose the upper root system, the one which extracted pikon, they kept up their verbal abuse of all soldiers who caught their gaze. They could do so with impunity because they knew themselves to be the cornerstone of the Kolcorronian economy, an outcast elite, and were accorded unique privileges. They were also highly paid for their services. After ten years as a slimer a man could retire to a life of ease—provided he survived the lengthy process of being cleansed of the virulent mucus.

Leddravohr watched with interest as the radial upper roots were uncovered. A slimer opened one of the glass gourds and, using a spatula, proceeded to daub the main roots with the pus-like goo. Cultured from the solvent the brakka themselves had evolved to dissolve their combustion chamber diaphragms, the slime gave out a choking odour like bile-laden vomit mingled, incongruously, with the sweetness of whitefern. The roots, which would have resisted the sharpest blade, swelled visibly as their cellular structure was attacked. Two other slimers hacked through them with slate axes and, working with showy energy for the benefit of their audience, dug further down to reveal the lower root system and the bulbous swelling of the combustion chamber at the base of the trunk. Inside it was a valuable harvest of power crystals which would have to be removed, taking the utmost care to keep the two varieties separated, before the tree could be felled.

"Stand back, dung-eaters," the oldest slimer called out. "Stand back and let. . . ." His voice faded as he raised his eyes and for the first time realised that Leddravohr was present. He bowed deeply, with a grace which went ill with his naked and filth-streaked belly, and said, "I cannot apologise to you, Prince, because of course my remarks were not addressed to you."

"Well put," Leddravohr said, appreciating nimbleness of mind from such an unlikely source. "I'm pleased to learn you don't suffer from suicidal tendencies. What's your name?"

"It is Owpope, Prince."

"Proceed with your labours, Owpope—I never tire of seeing the wealth of our country being produced."

"Gladly, Prince, but there is always a slight risk of a blowout through the side of the chamber when we broach a tree."

"Just exercise your normal discretion," Leddravohr said, folding his arms. His acute hearing picked up a ripple of admiring whispers going through the nearby soldiery, and he knew he had added to his reputation as the prince with the common touch. The word would spread fast—*Leddravohr loves his people so much that he will even converse with a slimer*. The little episode was a calculated exercise in image-building, but in truth he did not feel he was demeaning himself by talking to a man like

Owpope, whose work was of genuine importance to Kolcorron. It was the useless parasites—like the priests and philosophers —who earned his hatred and contempt. They would be the first to be purged out of existence when he eventually became King.

He was settling down to watch Owpope apply an elliptical pattern of slime to the curving base of the brakka trunk when his attention was again caught by a movement in the sky to the west. The airship had returned and was scudding through the narrow band of blue which separated Overland from the jagged wall of trees. Its appearance after such a short time meant that it had not landed at G1, the area command centre. The captain must have communicated with the base by sunwriter and then come directly to the forward zone—which made it almost certain that he was carrying an urgent message to Leddravohr from the King.

Mystified, Leddravohr shaded his eyes from the sun's glare as he watched the airship slow down and manoeuvre towards a landing in the forest clearing.

CHAPTER 3

Lain Maraquine's domicile—known as the Square House—was positioned on Greenmount, a rounded hill in a northern suburb of Ro-Atabri, the Kolcorronian capital.

From the window of his study he had a panoramic view of the city's various districts—residential, commercial, industrial, administrative—as they sifted down to the Borann River and on the far bank gave way to the parklands surrounding the five palaces. The families headed by the Lord Philosopher had been granted a cluster of dwellings and other buildings on this choice site many centuries earlier, during the reign of Bytran IV, when their work was held in much higher regard.

The Lord Philosopher himself lived in a sprawling structure known as Greenmount Peel, and it was a sign of his former importance that all the houses in his bailiwick had been placed in line-of-sight with the Great Palace, thus facilitating communication by sunwriter. Now, however, such prestigious features only added to the jealousy and resentment felt by the heads of other orders. Lain Maraquine knew that the industrial supremo, Prince Chakkell, particularly wanted Greenmount as an adornment to his own empire and was doing everything in his power to have the philosophers deposed and moved to humbler accommodation.

It was the beginning of aftday, the region having just emerged from the shadow of Overland, and the city was looking beautiful as it returned to life after its two-hour sleep. The yellow, orange and red coloration of trees which were shedding their leaves contrasted with the pale and darker greens of trees with different cycles which were coming into bud or were in full foliage. Here and there the brightly glowing envelopes of airships created pastel circles and ellipses, and on the river could be seen the white sails of ocean-going ships which were bringing a thousand commodities from distant parts of Land.

Seated at his desk by the window, Lain was oblivious to the spectacular view. All that day he had been aware of a curious excitement and a sense of expectancy deep within himself. There was no way in which he could be certain, but his premonition was that the mental agitation was leading to something of rare importance.

For some time he had been intrigued by an underlying similarity he had observed in problems fed into his department from a variety of sources. The problems were as routine and mundane as a vintner wanting to know the most economical shape of jar in which to market a fixed quantity of wine, or a farmer trying to decide the best mix of crops for a certain area of land at different times of the year.

It was all a far cry from the days when his forebears had been charged with tasks like estimating the size of the cosmos, and yet Lain had begun to suspect that somewhere at the heart of the commonplace commercial riddles there lurked a concept whose implications were more universal than the enigmas of astronomy. In every case there was a quantity whose value was governed by changes in another quantity, and the problem was that of finding an optimum balance. Traditional solutions involved making numerous approximations or plotting vertices on a graph, but a tiny voice had begun to whisper to Lain and its message was the icily thrilling one that there might be a way of arriving at a *precise* solution algebraically, with a few strokes of the pen. It was something to do with the mathematical notion of limits, with the idea that. . . .

"You'll have to help with the guest list," Gesalla said as she swept into the panelled study. "I can't do any serious planning when I don't even know how many people we are going to have."

A glimmering in the depths of Lain's mind was abruptly extinguished, leaving him with a sense of loss which quickly faded as he looked up at his black-haired solewife. The illness of early pregnancy had narrowed the oval of her face and given her a dark-eyed pallor which somehow emphasised her intelligence and strength of character. She had never looked more beautiful in Lain's eyes, but he still wished she had not insisted on starting the baby. That slender, slim-hipped body did not look to him as though it had been designed for motherhood and he had private fears about the outcome.

"Oh, I'm sorry, Lain," she said, her face showing concern. "Did I interrupt something important?"

He smiled and shook his head, once again impressed by her talent for divining other people's thoughts. "Isn't it early to be planning for Yearsend?"

"Yes." She met his gaze coolly—her way of challenging him to find anything wrong with being efficient. "Now, about your guests. . . ."

"I promise to write out a list before the day is over. I suppose it will be much the same as usual, though I'm not sure if Toller will be home this year."

"I hope he isn't," Gesalla said, wrinkling her nose. "I don't want him. It would be *so* pleasant to have a party without any arguments or fighting."

"He *is* my brother," Lain protested amiably.

"Half-brother would be more like it."

Lain's good humour was threatened. "I'm glad my mother isn't alive to hear that comment."

Gesalla came to him immediately, sat on his lap and kissed him on the mouth, moulding his cheeks with both her hands to coax him into an ardent response. It was a familiar trick of hers, but nonetheless effective. Still feeling privileged even after two years of marriage, he slid his hand inside her blue camisole and caressed her small breasts. After a moment she sat upright and gave him a solemn stare.

"I didn't mean any disrespect to your mother," she said. "It's just that Toller *looks* more like a soldier than a member of this family."

"Genetic flukes sometimes happen."

"And there's the way he can't even read."

"We've been through all this before," Lain said patiently. "When you get to know Toller better you'll see that he is as intelligent as any other member of the family. He *can* read, but he isn't fluent because of some problem with the way he perceives printed words. In any case, most of the military are literate—so your observation is lacking in relevance."

"Well. . . ." Gesalla looked dissatisfied. "Well, why does he have to cause trouble everywhere he goes?"

"Lots of people have that habit—including one whose left nipple is tickling my palm at this moment."

"Don't try to turn my mind to other things—especially at this time of day."

"All right, but why does Toller bother you so much? I mean, we are pretty well surrounded by individualists and near-eccentrics on Greenmount."

"Would you like it better if I were one of those faceless females who have no opinions about anything?" Gesalla was galvanised into springing to her feet, her light body scarcely reacting against his thighs, and an expression of dismay appeared on her face as she looked down into the walled precinct in front of the house. "Were you expecting Lord Glo?"

"No."

"Bad luck—you've got him." Gesalla hurried to the door of the study. "I'm going to vanish before he arrives. I can't afford to spend half the day listening to all that endless humming and hawing—not to mention the smutty innuendoes." She gathered her ankle-length skirts and ran silently towards the rear stairs.

Lain took off his reading glasses and gazed after her, wishing she would not keep reviving the subject of his brother's parentage. Aytha Maraquine, his mother, had died in giving birth to Toller, so if there had been an adulterous liaison she had more than paid for it. Why could Gesalla not leave the matter at that? Lain had been attracted to her for her intellectual independence as well as her beauty and physical grace, but he had not bargained for the antagonism towards his brother. He hoped it was not going to lead to years of domestic friction.

The sound of a carriage door slamming in the precinct drew his attention to the outside world. Lord Glo had just stepped down from the aging but resplendent phaeton which he always used for short journeys in the city. Its driver, holding the two bluehorns in check, nodded and fidgeted as he received a lengthy series of instructions from Glo. Lain guessed that the Lord Philosopher was using a hundred words where ten would have sufficed and he began to pray that the visit would not be too much of an endurance test. He went to the sideboard, poured out two glasses of black wine and waited by the study door until Glo appeared.

"You're very kind," Glo said, taking his glass as he entered and going straight to the nearest chair. Although in his late fifties, he looked much older thanks to his rotund figure and the fact that his teeth had been reduced to a few brownish pegs splayed behind his lower lip. He was breathing noisily after climbing the stairs, his stomach ballooning and collapsing under his informal grey-and-white robe.

"It's always a pleasure to see you, my lord," Lain said, wondering if there was a special reason for the visit and knowing there was little point in his trying to elicit the information too soon.

Glo drank half his wine in one gulp. "Mutual, my boy. Oh! I've got something . . . hmm . . . at least, I *think* I've got something to show you. You're going to like this." He set his glass aside, groped in the folds of his clothing and eventually produced a square of paper which he handed to Lain. It was slightly sticky and mid-brown in colour except for a circular patch of mottled tan in the centre.

"Farland." Lain identified the circle as being a light picture of the only other major planet in the local system, orbiting the sun at some twice the distance of the Land-Overland pair. "The images are getting better."

"Yes, but we still can't make them permanent. That one has faded . . . hmm . . . noticeably since last night. You can hardly see the polar caps now, but last night they were very clear. Pity. Pity." Glo took the picture back and studied it closely, all the while shaking his head and sucking his teeth.

"The polar caps were as clear as daylight. Clear as daylight, I tell you. Young Enteth got a very good confirmation of the angle of . . . ah . . . inclination. Lain, have you ever tried to visualise what it would be like to live on a world whose axis was tilted? There would be a hot period of the year, with long days and short nights, and a cold . . . hmm . . . period, with long days . . . I mean *short* days . . . and long nights . . . all depending on where the planet was in its orbit. The colour changes on Farland show that *all* the vegetation is geared to a single ... hmm ... superimposed cycle."

Lain concealed his impatience and boredom as Glo launched himself upon one of his most familiar set pieces. It was a cruel irony that the Lord Philosopher was becoming prematurely senile, and Lain—who had a genuine regard for the older man—saw it as a duty to give him maximum support, personally and professionally. He replenished his visitor's drink and made appropriate comments as Glo meandered on from elementary astronomy to botany and the differences between the ecology of a tilted world and that of Land.

On Land, where there were no seasons, the very first farmers must have had the task of separating the natural jumble of edible grasses into synchronous batches which matured at chosen times. Six harvests a year was the norm in most parts of the world. Thereafter it had simply been a matter of planting and reaping six adjacent strips to maintain supplies of grain, with no long-term storage problems. In modern times the advanced countries had found it more efficacious to devote whole farms to single-cycle crops and to work in six-farm combines or multiples thereof, but the principle was the same.

As a boy, Lain Maraquine had enjoyed speculating about life on distant planets—assuming they existed in other parts of the universe and were peopled by intelligent beings—but he had quickly found that mathematics offered him greater scope for intellectual adventure. Now all he could wish for was that Lord Glo would either go away and let him get on with his work or proceed to explain his visit. Tuning his thoughts back into the rambling discourse he found that Glo had switched back to the experiments with photography and the difficulties of producing emulsions of light-sensitive vegetable cells which would hold an image for more than a few days.

"Why is it so important to you?" Lain put in. "Anybody in your observatory staff could draw a much better picture by hand."

"Astronomy is only a tiny bit of it, my boy—the aim is to be able to produce totally ... hmm ... accurate pictures of buildings, landscapes, people."

"Yes, but we already have draughtsmen and artists who can do that."

Glo shook his head and smiled, showing the ruins of his teeth, and spoke with unusual fluency. "Artists only paint what they or their patrons believe to be important. We lose so much. The times slip through our fingers. I want every man to be his own artist—then we'll discover our history."

"Do you think it will be possible?"

"Undoubtedly. I foresee the day when everybody will carry light-sensitive material and will be able to make a picture of *anything* in the blink of an eye."

"You can still outfly any of us," Lain said, impressed, feeling he had momentarily been in the presence of the Lord Glo who used to be. "And by flying higher you see farther."

Glo looked gratified. "Never mind that—give me more . . . hmm . . . wine." He watched his glass closely while it was being refilled, then settled back in his chair. "You will never guess what has happened."

"You've impregnated some innocent young female."

"Try again."

"Some innocent young female had impregnated you."

"This is a serious matter, Lain." Glo made a damping movement with his hand to show that levity was out of place. "The King and Prince Chakkell have suddenly wakened up to the fact that we are running short of brakka."

Lain froze in the act of raising his own glass to his lips. "I can't believe this, as you predicted. How many reports and studies have we sent them in the last ten years?"

"I've lost count, but it looks as though they have finally taken some effect. The King has called a meeting of the high . . . hmm . . . council."

"I never thought he'd do it," Lain said. "Have you just come from the palace?"

"Ah . . . no. I've known about the meeting for some days, but I couldn't pass the news on to you because the King sent me off to Sorka—of all places!—on another . . . hmm . . . matter. I just got back this foreday."

"I could use an extra holiday."

"It was no holiday, my boy." Glo shook his large head and looked solemn. "I was with Tunsfo—and I had to watch one of his surgeons perform an autopsy on a soldier. I don't mind admitting I have no stomach for that kind of thing."

"Please! Don't even talk about it," Lain said, feeling a gentle upward pressure on his diaphragm at the thought of knives going through pallid skin and disturbing the cold obscenities beneath. "Why did the King want you there?"

Glo tapped himself on the chest. "Lord Philosopher, that's me. My word still carries a lot of weight with the King. Apparently our soldiers and airmen are becoming . . . hmm . . . demoralised over rumours that it isn't safe to go near ptertha casualties."

"Not safe? In what way?"

"The story is that several line soldiers contracted pterthacosis through handling victims."

"But that's nonsense," Lain said, taking a first sip of his wine. "What did Tunsfo find?"

"It was pterthacosis, all right. No doubt about it. Spleen like a football. Our official conclusion was that the soldier encountered a globe at dead of night and took the dust without knowing it—or that he was telling . . . hmm . . . lies. That happens, you know. Some men can't face up to it. They even manage to convince *themselves* that they're all right."

"I can understand that." Lain drew in his shoulders as though feeling cold. "The temptation must be there. After all, the slightest air current can make all the difference. Between life and death."

"I would prefer to talk about our own concerns." Glo stood up and began to pace the room. "This meeting is very important to us, my boy. A chance for the philosophy order to win the recognition it deserves, to regain its former status. Now, I want you to prepare the graphs in person—make them big and colourful and . . . hmm . . . simple—showing how much pikon and halvell Kolcorron can expect to manufacture in the next fifty years. Five year increments might be appropriate—I leave that to you. We also need to show how, as the requirement for natural crystals decreases, our reserves of home-grown brakka will increase until we. . . ."

"My lord, slow down a little," Lain protested, dismayed to see Glo's visionary rhetoric waft him so far from the realities of the situation. "I hate to appear pessimistic, but there is no guarantee that we will produce *any* usable crystals in the next fifty years. Our best pikon to date has a purity of only one third, and the halvell is not much better."

Glo gave an excited laugh. "That's only because we haven't had the full backing of the King. With proper resources we can solve all the purification problems in a few years. I'm sure of it! Why the King even permitted me to use his messengers to recall Sisstt and Duthoon. They can give up-to-date reports on their progress at the meeting. Hard facts—that what impress the King. Practicalities. I tell you, my boy, the times are changing. I feel sick." Glo dropped back into his chair with a thud which disturbed the decorative ceramics on the nearest wall.

Lain knew he should go forward to offer comfort, but he found himself shrinking back. Glo looked as though he could vomit at any moment, and the thought of being close to him when it happened was too distasteful. Even worse, the meandering veins on Glo's temples seemed in danger of rupturing. What if there actually were a fountaining of red? Lain tried to visualise how he would cope if some of the other man's blood got on to his own person and again his stomach gave a preliminary heave.

"Shall I go and fetch something?" he said anxiously. "Some water?"

"More wine," Glo husked, holding out his glass.

"Do you think you should?"

"Don't be such a prune, my boy—it's the best tonic there is. If you drank a little more wine it might put some flesh on your . . . hmm . . . bones." Glo studied his glass while it was being refilled, making sure he received full measure, and the colour began returning to his face. "Now, what was I talking about?"

"Wasn't it something to do with the impending rebirth of our civilisation?"

Glo looked reproachful. "Sarcasm? Is that sarcasm?"

"I'm sorry, my lord," Lain said. "It's just that brakka

conservation has always been a passion with me—a subject upon which I can easily become intemperate."

"I remember." Glo's gaze travelled the room, noting the use of ceramics and glass for fitments which in almost any other house would have been carved from the black wood. "You don't think you . . . hmm . . . overdo it?"

"It's the way I feel." Lain held up his left hand and indicated the black ring he wore on the sixth finger. "The only reason I have this much is that it was a wedding token from Gesalla."

"Ah yes—Gesalla." Glo bared his divergent teeth in a parody of lecherousness. "One of these nights, I swear, you'll have some extra company in bed."

"My bed is your bed," Lain said easily, aware that Lord Glo never claimed his nobleman's right to take any woman in the social group of which he was dynastic head. It was an ancient custom in Kolcorron, still observed in the major families, and Glo's occasional jests on the subject were merely his way of emphasising the philosophy order's cultural superiority in having left the practice behind.

"Bearing in mind your extreme views," Glo went on, returning to his original subject, "couldn't you bring yourself to adopt a more positive attitude to the meeting? Aren't you pleased about it?"

"Yes, I'm pleased. It's a step in the right direction, but it has come so *late*. You know it takes fifty or sixty years for a brakka to reach maturity and enter the pollinating phase. We'd still be facing that time lag even if we had the capability to grow pure crystals right now—and it's frighteningly large."

"All the more reason to plan ahead, my boy."

"True—but the greater the need for a plan the less chance it has of being accepted."

"That was very profound," Glo said. "Now tell me what it . . . hmm . . . means."

"There was a time, perhaps fifty years ago, when Kolcorron could have balanced supply and demand by implementing just a few commonsense conservation measures, but even then the princes wouldn't listen. Now we're in a situation which calls for really drastic measures. Can you imagine how Leddravohr would react to the proposal that all armament production should be suspended for twenty or thirty years?"

"It doesn't bear thinking about," Glo said. "But aren't you exaggerating the difficulties?"

"Have a look at these graphs." Lain went to a chest of shallow drawers, took out a large sheet and spread it on his desk where it could be seen by Glo. He explained the various coloured diagrams, avoiding abstruse mathematics as much as possible, analysing how the country's growing demands for power crystals and brakka were interacting with other factors such an increasing scarcity and transport delays. Once or twice as he spoke it came to him that here, yet again, were problems in the same general class as those he had been thinking about earlier. Then he had been tantalised by the idea that he was about to conceive of an entirely new way of dealing with them, something to do with the mathematical concept of limits, but now material and human considerations were dominating his thoughts.

Among them was the fact that Lord Glo, who would be the principal philosophy spokesman, had become incapable of following complex arguments. And in addition to his natural disability, Glo was now in the habit of fuddling himself with wine every day. He was nodding a great deal and sucking his teeth, trying to exhibit concerned interest, but the fleshy wattles of his eyelids were descending with increasing frequency.

"So that's the extent of the problem, my lord," Lain said, speaking with extra fervour to get Glo's attention. "Would you like to hear my department's views on the kind of measures needed to keep the crisis within manageable proportions?"

"Stability, yes, stability—that's the thing." Glo abruptly raised his head and for a moment he seemed utterly lost, his pale blue eyes scanning Lain's face as though seeing it for the first time. "Where were we?"

Lain felt depressed and oddly afraid. "Perhaps it would be best if I sent a written summary to you at the Peel, one you could go over at your leisure. When is the council going to meet?"

"On the morning of two-hundred. Yes, the King definitely said two-hundred. What day is this?"

"One-nine-four."

"There isn't much time," Glo said sadly. "I promised the King I'd have a significant . . . hmm . . . contribution."

"You will."

"That's not what I. . . ." Glo stood up, swaying a little, and faced Lain with an odd tremulous smile. "Did you really mean what you said?"

Lain blinked at him, unable to place the question in context properly. "My lord?"

"About my . . . about my flying higher . . . seeing farther?"

"Of course," Lain said, beginning to feel embarrassed. "I couldn't have been more sincere."

"That's good. It means so. . . ." Glo straightened up and expanded his plump chest, suddenly recovering his normal joviality. "We'll show them. We'll show *all* of them." He went to the door, then paused with his hand on the porcelain knob. "Let me have a summary as soon as . . . hmm . . . possible. Oh, by the way, I have instructed Sisstt to bring your brother home with him."

"That's very kind of you, my lord," Lain said, his pleasure at the prospect of seeing Toller again modified by thoughts of Gesalla's likely reaction to the news.

"Not at all. I think we were all a trifle hard on him. I mean, a year in a miserable place like Haffanger just for giving Ongmat a tap on the chin."

"As a result of that tap Ongmat's jaw was broken in two places."

"Well, it was a *firm* tap." Glo gave a wheezing laugh. "And we all felt the benefit of Ongmat being silenced for a while." Still chuckling, he moved out of sight along the corridor, his sandals slapping on the mosaic floor.

Lain carried his hardly-touched glass of wine to his desk and sat down, swirling the black liquid to create light patterns on its surface. Glo's humorous endorsement of Toller's violence was quite typical of him, one of the little ways in which he reminded members of the philosophy order that he was of royal lineage and therefore had the blood of conquerors in his veins. It showed he was feeling better and had recovered his self-esteem, but it did nothing to ease Lain's worries about the older man's physical and mental fitness.

In the space of only a few years Glo had turned into a bumbling and absent-minded incompetent. His unsuitability for his post was tolerated by most department heads, some of whom appreciated the extra personal freedom they derived from it, but there was a general sense of demoralisation over the order's continuing loss of status. The aging King Prad still retained an indulgent fondness for Glo—and, so the whispers went, if philosophy had come to be regarded as a joke it was appropriate that it should be represented by a court jester.

But there was nothing funny about a meeting of the high council, Lain told himself. The person who presented the case for rigorous brakka conservation would need to do it with eloquence and force, marshalling complex arguments and backing them up with an unassailable command of the statistics involved. His stance would be generally unpopular, and would attract special hostility from the ambitious Prince Chakkell and the savage Leddravohr.

If Glo proved unable to master the brief in time for the meeting it was possible he would call on a deputy to speak on his behalf, and the thought of having to challenge Chakkell or Leddravohr—even verbally—produced in Lain a cold panic which threatened to affect his bladder. The wine in his glass was now reflecting a pattern of trembling concentric circles.

Lain set the glass down and began breathing deeply and steadily, waiting for the shaking of his hands to cease.

CHAPTER 4

Toller Maraquine awoke with the knowledge, which was both disturbing and comforting, that he was not alone in bed.

He could feel the body heat of the woman who was lying at his left side, one of her arms resting on his stomach, one of her legs drawn up across his thighs. The sensations were all the more pleasant for being unfamiliar. He lay quite still, staring at the ceiling, as he tried to recall the exact circumstances which had brought female company to his austere apartment in the Square House.

He had celebrated his return to the capital with a round of the busy taverns in the Samlue district. The tour had begun early on the previous day and had been intended to last only until the end of littlenight, but the ale and wine had been persuasive and the acquaintances he met had eventually begun to seem like cherished friends. He had continued drinking right through aftday and well into the night, revelling in his escape from the smell of the pikon pans, and at a late stage had begun to notice the same woman close to him in the throng time after time, much more often than could be accounted for by chance.

She had been tawny-haired and tall, full-breasted, broad of shoulder and hip—the sort of woman Toller had dreamed about during his exile in Haffanger. She had also been brazenly chewing a sprig of maidenfriend. He had a clear memory of her face, which was round and open and uncomplicated, with wine-heightened colouring on the cheeks. Her smile had been very white and marred only by a tiny triangular chip missing from one front incisor. Toller had found her easy to talk to, easy to laugh with, and in the end it had seemed the most natural thing in the world for them to spend the night together. . . .

"I'm hungry," she said abruptly, raising herself into a sitting position beside him. "I want some breakfast."

Toller ran an appreciative eye over her splendidly naked torso and smiled. "Supposing I want something else first?"

She looked disappointed, but only for an instant, then returned his smile as she moved to bring her breasts into contact with his chest. "If you're not careful I'll ride you to death."

"Please try it," Toller said, his smile developing into a gratified chuckle. He drew her down to him. A pleasurable warmth suffused his mind and body as they kissed, but within a moment he became aware of something being wrong, of a niggling sense of unease. He opened his eyes and immediately identified one source of his worry—the brightness of his bedchamber indicated that it was well past dawn. This was the morning of day two-hundred, and he had promised his brother that he would be up at first light to help move some charts and a display easel to the Great Palace. It was a menial task which anybody could have done, but Lain had seemed anxious for him to undertake it, possibly so that he would not be left alone in the house with Gesalla while the lengthy council meeting was in progress.

Gesalla!

Toller almost groaned aloud as he remembered that he had not even seen Gesalla on the previous day. He had arrived from Haffanger early in the morning and after a brief interview with his brother—during which Lain had been preoccupied with his charts—had gone straight out on the drinking spree. Gesalla, as Lain's solewife, was mistress of the household and as such would have expected Toller to pay his respects at the formal evening meal. Another woman might have overlooked his behavioural lapse, but the fastidious and unbending Gesalla was bound to have been furious. On the flight back to Ro-Atabri Toller had vowed that, to avoid causing any tensions in his brother's house, he would studiously keep on the right side of Gesalla—and he had led off by affronting her on the very first day. The flickering of a moist tongue against his own suddenly reminded Toller that his transgressions against domestic protocol had been greater than Gesalla knew.

"I'm sorry about this," he said, twisting free of the embrace, "but you have to go home now."

The woman's jaw sagged. "What?"

"Come on—hurry it up." Toller stood up, swept her clothes into a wispy bundle and pushed them into her arms. He opened a wardrobe and began selecting fresh clothes for himself.

"But what about my breakfast?"

"There's no time—I have to get you out of here."

"That's just great," she said bitterly, beginning to sort through the binders and scraps of near-transparent fabric which were her sole attire.

"I told you I was sorry," Toller said as he struggled into breeches which seemed determined to resist entry.

"A lot of good that. . . ." She paused in the act of gathering her breasts into a flimsy sling and scrutinised the room from ceiling to floor. "Are you *sure* you live here?"

Toller was amused in spite of his agitation. "Do you think I would just pick a house at random and sneak in to use a bed?"

"I thought it was a bit strange last night . . . getting a coach all the way out here . . . keeping so quiet . . . This is Greenmount, isn't it?" Her frankly suspicious stare travelled his heavily muscled arms and shoulders. He guessed the direction in which her thoughts were going, but there was no hint of censure in her expression and he took no offence.

"It's a nice morning for a walk," he said, raising her to an upright position and hastening her—clothing still partially unfastened—towards the room's single exit. He opened the door at the precise instant needed to bring him into confrontation with Gesalla Maraquine, who had been passing by in the corridor. Gesalla was pale and ill-looking, thinner than when he had last seen her, but her grey-eyed gaze had lost none of its force—and it was obvious she was angry.

"Good foreday," she said, icily correct. "I was *told* you had returned."

"I apologise for last night," Toller said. "I . . . I got detained."

"Obviously." Gesalla glanced at his companion with open distaste. "Well?"

"Well what?"

"Aren't you going to introduce your . . . friend?"

51

Toller swore inwardly as it came to him that there was no longer the slightest hope of salvaging anything from the situation. Even allowing for the fact that he had been adrift on a vinous sea when he met his bed partner, how could he have overlooked such a basic propriety as asking her name? Gesalla was the last person in the world to whom he could have explained the mood of the previous evening, and that being the case there was no point in trying to placate her. *I'm sorry about this, dear brother*, he thought. *I didn't plan it this way. . . .*

"The frosty female is my sister-in-law, Gesalla Maraquine," he said, putting an arm around his companion's shoulders as he kissed her on the forehead. "She would like to know your name, and—considering the sport we had during the night—so would I."

"Fera," the woman said, making final adjustments to her garments. "Fera Rivoo."

"Isn't that nice?" Toller smiled broadly at Gesalla. "Now we can all be friends together."

"Please see that she leaves by one of the side gates," Gesalla said. She turned and strode away, head thrown back, each foot descending directly in front of the other.

Toller shook his head. "What do you think was the matter with her?"

"Some women are easily upset." Fera straightened up and pushed Toller away from her. "Show me the way out."

"I thought you wanted breakfast."

"I thought you wanted me to go home."

"You must have misunderstood me," Toller said. "I'd like you to stay, for as long as *you* want. Have you a job to worry about?"

"Oh, I have a very important position in the Samlue market —gutting fish." Fera held up her hands, which were reddened and marked by numerous small cuts. "How do you think I got these?"

"Forget the job," Toller urged, enclosing her hands with his own. "Go back to bed and wait for me there. I'll have food sent to you. You can rest and eat and drink all day—and tonight we'll go on the pleasure barges."

Fera smiled, filling the triangular gap in her teeth with the tip of her tongue. "Your sister-in-law. . . ."

"Is only my sister-in-law. I was born in this house and grew up in it and have the right to invite guests. You are staying, aren't you?"

"Will there be spiced pork?"

"I assure you that entire piggeries are reduced to spiced pork on a daily basis in this house," Toller said, leading Fera back into the room. "Now, you stay here until I get back, then we'll take up where we left off."

"All right." She lay down on the bed, settled herself comfortably on the pillows and spread her legs. "Just one thing before you go."

"Yes?"

She gave him her full white smile. "Perhaps you'd better tell me *your* name."

Toller was still chuckling as he reached the stairs at the end of the corridor and went down towards the central section of the house, from which was emanating the sound of many voices. He found Fera's company refreshing, but her presence in the house might be just too much of an affront to Gesalla to be tolerated for very long. Two or three days would be sufficient to make the point that Gesalla had no right to insult him or his guests, that any effort she made to dominate him—as she did his brother— would be doomed to failure.

When Toller reached the bottom flight of the main staircase he found about a dozen people gathered in the entrance hall. Some were computational assistants; others were domestics and grooms who seemed to have gathered to watch their master set off for his appointment at the Great Palace. Lain Maraquine was wearing the antique-styled formal garment of a senior philosopher—a full-length robe of dove grey trimmed at the hem and cuff with black triangles. Its silky material emphasised the slightness of his build, but his posture was upright and dignified. His face, beneath the heavy sweeps of black hair, was very pale. Toller felt a surge of affection and concern as he crossed the hall—the council meeting was obviously an important occasion for his brother and he was already showing the strain.

"You're late," Lain said, eyeing him critically. "And you should be wearing your greys."

"There was no time to get them ready. I had a rough night."

"Gesalla has just told me what kind of night you had." Lain's expression showed a blend of amusement and exasperation. "Is it true you didn't even know the woman's name?"

Toller shrugged to disguise his embarrassment. "What do names matter?"

"If you don't know that there isn't much point in my trying to enlighten you."

"I don't need you to. . . ." Toller took a deep breath, determined for once not to add to his brother's problems by losing his temper. "Where is the stuff you want me to carry?"

The official residence of King Prad Neldeever was notable more for its size than architectural merit. Successive generations of rulers had added wings, towers and cupolas to suit their individual whims, usually in the style of the day, with the result that the building had some resemblance to a coral or one of the accretive structures erected by certain kinds of insects. An early landscape gardener had attempted to impose a degree of order by planting stands of synchronous parble and rafter trees, but over the centuries they had been infiltrated by other varieties. The palace, itself variegated because of different masonry, was now screened by vegetation equally uneven in colour, and from a distance it could be difficult for the eye to separate one from the other.

Toller Maraquine, however, was untroubled by such aesthetic quibbles as he rode down from Greenmount at the rear of his brother's modest entourage. There had been rain before dawn and the morning air was clean and invigorating, charged with a sunlit spirit of new beginnings. The huge disk of Overland shone above him with a pure lustre and many stars decked the surrounding blueness of the sky. The city itself was an incredibly complex scattering of multi-hued flecks stretching down to the slate-blue ribbon of the Borann, where sails gleamed like lozenges of snow.

Toller's pleasure at being back in Ro-Atabri, at having

escaped the desolation of Haffanger, had banished his customary dissatisfaction with his life as an unimportant member of the philosophy order. After the unfortunate start to the day the pendulum of his mood was on the upswing. His mind was teeming with half-formed plans to improve his reading ability, to seek out some interesting aspect of the order's work and devote all his energies to it, to make Lain proud of him. On reflection he could appreciate that Gesalla had had every right to be furious over his behaviour. It would be no more than a normal courtesy were he to move Fera out of his apartment as soon as he returned home.

The sturdy bluehorn he had been allocated by the stablemaster was a placid beast which seemed to know its own way to the palace. Leaving it to its own devices as it plodded the increasingly busy streets, Toller tried to create a more definite picture of his immediate future, one which might impress Lain. He had heard of one research group which was trying to develop a combination of ceramics and glass threads which would be tough enough to stand in for brakka in the manufacture of swords and armour. It was quite certain that they would never succeed, but the subject was nearer to his taste than chores like the measuring of rainfall, and it would please Lain to know that he was supporting the conservation movement. The next step was to think of a way of winning Gesalla's approval. . . .

By the time the philosophy delegation had passed through the heart of the city and had crossed the river at the Bytran Bridge the palace and its grounds were spanning the entire view ahead. The party negotiated the four concentric bloom-spangled moats, whose ornamentation disguised their function, and halted at the palace's main gate. Several guards, looking like huge black beetles in their heavy armour, came forward at a leisurely pace. While their commander was laboriously checking the visitors' names on his list one of his pikemen approached Toller and, without speaking, began roughly delving among the rolled-up charts in his panniers. When he had finished he paused to spit on the ground, then turned his attention to the collapsed easel which was strapped across the bluehorn's haunches. He tugged at the polished wooden struts so forcibly that the bluehorn sidestepped against him.

"What's the matter with you?" he growled, shooting Toller a venomous look. "Can't you control that fleabag?"

I'm a new person, Toller assured himself, *and I can't be goaded into brawls*. He smiled and said, "Can you blame her for wanting to get near you?"

The pikeman's lips moved silently as he came closer to Toller, but at that moment the guard commander gave the signal for the party to proceed on its way. Toller urged his mount forward and resumed his position behind Lain's carriage. The minor brush with the guard had left him slightly keyed-up but otherwise unaffected, and he felt pleased with the way he had comported himself. It had been a valuable exercise in avoiding unnecessary trouble, the art he intended to practise for the rest of his life. Sitting easily in the saddle, enjoying the rhythm of the bluehorn's stately gait, he turned his thoughts to the business ahead.

Toller had been to the Great Palace only once before, as a small child, and had only the vaguest recollection of the domed Rainbow Hall in which the council meeting was to be held. He doubted that it could be as vast and as awe-inspiring as he remembered, but it was a major function room in the palace and its use as a venue today was significant. King Prad obviously regarded the meeting as being important, a fact which Toller found somewhat puzzling. All his life he had been listening to conservationists like his brother issuing sombre warnings about dwindling resources of brakka, but everyday life in Kolcorron had continued very much as before. It was true that in recent years there had been periods when power crystals and the black wood had been in short supply, and the cost kept rising, but new reserves had always been found. Try as he might, Toller could not imagine the natural storehouse of an entire world failing to meet his people's needs.

As the philosophy delegation reached the elevated ground on which the palace itself was situated he saw that many carriages were gathered on the principal forecourt. Among them was the flamboyant red-and-orange phaeton of Lord Glo. Three men in philosophy greys were standing beside it, and when they noticed Lain's carriage they advanced to intercept it. Toller identified the stunted figure of Vorndal Sisstt first; then Duthoon, leader of the halvell section; and the angular outline of Borreat Hargeth, chief of weapons research. All three appeared nervous and unhappy, and they closed on Lain as soon as he had stepped down from his carriage.

"We're in trouble, Lain," Hargeth said, nodding in the direction of Glo's phaeton. "You'd better take a look at our esteemed leader."

Lain frowned. "Is he ill?"

"No, he isn't ill—I'd say he never felt better in his life."

"Don't tell me he's been. . . ." Lain went to the phaeton and wrenched open the door. Lord Glo, who had been slumped with his head on his chest, jerked upright and looked about him with a startled expression. He brought his pale blue eyes to focus on Lain, then showed the pegs of his lower teeth in a smile.

"Good to see you, my boy," he said. "I tell you this is going to be our . . . hmm . . . day. We're going to carry all before us."

Toller swung himself down from his mount and tethered it to the rear of the carriage, keeping his back to the others to conceal his amusement. He had seen Glo the worse for wine several times before, but never so obviously, so comically incapable. The contrast between Glo's ruddy-cheeked euphoria and the scandalised, ashen countenances of his aides made the situation even funnier. Any notions they had about making a good showing at the meeting were being swiftly and painfully revised. Toller could not help but enjoy another person attracting the kind of censure which so often was reserved for him, especially when the offender was the Lord Philosopher himself.

"My lord, the meeting is due to begin soon," Lain said. "But if you are indisposed perhaps we could. . . ."

"Indisposed! What manner of talk is that?" Glo ducked his head and emerged from his vehicle to stand with unnatural steadiness. "What are we waiting for? Let's take our places."

"Very well, my lord." Lain came to Toller with a hag-ridden expression. "Quate and Locranan will take the charts and easel.

57

I want you to stay here by the carriage and keep an . . . What do you find so amusing?"

"Nothing," Toller said quickly. "Nothing at all."

"You have no idea of what's at stake today, have you?"

"Conservation is important to me, too," Toller replied, making his voice as sincere as possible. "I was only. . . ."

"Toller Maraquine!" Lord Glo came towards Toller with arms outstretched, his eyes bulging with pleasurable excitement. "I didn't know you were here! How are you, my boy?"

Toller was mildly surprised at even being recognised by Glo, let alone being greeted so effusively. "I'm in good health, my lord."

"You look it." Glo reached up and put an arm around Toller's shoulders and swung to face the others. "Look at this fine figure of a man—he reminds me of myself when I was . . . hmm . . . young."

"We should take our places right away," Lain said. "I don't want to hurry you, but. . . ."

"You're quite right—we shouldn't delay our moment of . . . hmm . . . glory." Glo gave Toller an affectionate squeeze, exhaling the reek of wine as he did so. "Come on, Toller—you can tell me what you've been doing with yourself out in Haffanger."

Lain stepped forward, looking anxious. "My brother isn't part of the delegation, my lord. He is supposed to wait here."

"Nonsense! We're all together."

"But he has no greys."

"That doesn't matter if he's in my personal retinue," Glo said with the kind of mildness that brooked no argument. "We'll proceed."

Toller met Lain's gaze and issued a silent disclaimer by momentarily raising his eyebrows as the group moved off in the direction of the palace's main entrance. He welcomed the unexpected turn of events, which had saved him from what had promised to be a spell of utter boredom, but he was still resolved to maintain a good relationship with his brother. It was vital for him to be as unobtrusive as possible during the meeting, and in particular to keep a straight face regardless of what kind of performance Lord Glo might put on. Ignoring the curious glances from passers-by, he walked into the palace with Glo hugging his arm and did his best to produce acceptable small-talk in response to the older man's questioning, even though all his attention was being absorbed by his surroundings.

The palace was also the seat of the Kolcorronian administration and it gave him the impression of being a city within a city. Its corridors and staterooms were populated by sombre-faced men whose manner proclaimed that their concerns were not those of ordinary citizens. Toller was unable even to guess at their functions or the subjects of their low-voiced conversations. His senses were swamped by the sheer opulence of the carpets and hangings, the paintings and sculptures, the complexity of the vaulted ceilings. Even the least important doors appeared to have been carved from single slabs of perette, elvart or glass-wood, each one representing perhaps a year's work for a master craftsman.

Lord Glo seemed oblivious to the atmosphere of the palace, but Lain and the rest of his party were noticeably subdued. They were moving in a tight group, like soldiers in hostile territory. After a lengthy walk they reached an enormous double door guarded by two black-armoured ostiaries. Glo led the way into the huge elliptical room beyond. Toller hung back to give his brother precedence, and almost gasped as he got his first adult glimpse of the famed Rainbow Hall. Its domed roof was made entirely of square glass panels supported on intricate lattices of brakka. Most of the panels were pale blue or white, to represent clear sky and clouds, but seven adjacent curving bands echoed the colours of the rainbow. The light blazing down from the canopy was a mingling, merging glory which made the furnishings of the hall glow with tinted fire.

At the far locus of the ellipse was a large but unadorned throne on the uppermost level of a dais. Three lesser thrones were ranged on the second level for the use of the princes who were expected to be present. In ancient times the princes would all have been sons of the ruler, but with the country's expansion and development it had become expedient to allow some government posts to be filled by collateral descendants. These were numerous, thanks to the sexual license accorded to the nobility, and it was usually possible to allocate important responsibilities to suitable men. Of the current monarchy, only Leddravohr and the colourless Pouche, controller of public finances, were acknowledged sons of the King.

Facing the thrones were seats which had been laid out in radial sections for the orders whose concerns ranged from the arts and medicine to religion and proletarian education. The philosophy delegation occupied the middle sector in accordance with the tradition dating back to Bytran IV, who had believed that scientific knowledge was the foundation upon which Kolcorron would build a future world empire. In subsequent centuries it had become apparent that science had already learned all that was worth learning about the workings of the universe, and the influence of Bytran's thinking had faded, but the philosophy order still retained many of the trappings of its former eminence, in spite of opposition from others of a more pragmatic turn of mind.

Toller felt an ungrudging admiration for Lord Glo as the pudgy little man, large head thrown back and stomach protruding, marched up the hall and took his position before the thrones. The remainder of the philosophy delegation quietly seated themselves behind him, exchanging tentative glances with their opposites in neighbouring sectors. There were more people than Toller had expected—perhaps a hundred in all—the other delegations being augmented by clerks and advisors. Toller, now profoundly grateful for his supernumerary status, slid into the row behind Lain's computational assistants and waited for the proceedings to begin.

There was a murmurous delay punctuated by coughs and occasional nervous laughs, then a ceremonial horn was sounded and King Prad and the three princes entered the hall by way of a private doorway beyond the dais.

At sixty-plus the ruler was tall and lean, carrying his years well in spite of one milk-white eye which he refused to cover. Although Prad was an imposing and regal figure in his blood-coloured robes as he ascended to the high throne, Toller's interest was captured by the powerful, slow-padding form of

Prince Leddravohr. He was wearing a white cuirass made from multiple layers of sized linen moulded to the shape of a perfectly developed male torso, and it was evident from what could be seen of his arms and legs that the cuirass did not belie what it covered. Leddravohr's face was smooth and dark-browed, suggestive of brooding power, and it was obvious from his bearing that he had no wish to be present at the council meeting. Toller knew him to be the veteran of a hundred bloody conflicts and he felt a pang of envy as he noted the obvious disdain with which Leddravohr surveyed the assembly before lowering himself on to the central throne of the second tier. He could daydream about playing a similar role, that of the warrior prince, reluctantly recalled from dangerous frontiers to attend to trivialities of civilian existence.

An official beat on the floor three times with his staff to signal that the council meeting had begun. Prad, who was noted for the informality with which he held court, began to speak at once.

"I thank you for your attendance here today," he said, using the inflections of high Kolcorronian. "As you know, the subject for discussion is the increasing scarcity of brakka and energy crystals—but before I hear your submissions it is my will that another matter be dealt with, if only to establish its relative unimportance to the security of the empire.

"I do not refer to the reports from various sources that pertha have sharply increased in number during the course of this year. It is my considered opinion that the *apparent* increases can be explained by the fact that our armies are, for the first time, operating in regions of Land where—because of the natural conditions—pertha have always been more plentiful. I am instructing Lord Glo to instigate a thorough survey which will provide more reliable statistics, but in any case there is no cause for alarm. Prince Leddravohr assures me that the existing procedures and anti-pertha weapons are more than adequate to deal with any exigency.

"Of more pressing concern to us are rumours that soldiers have died as a result of coming into contact with pertha casualties. The rumours appear to have originated from units of the Second Army on the Sorka front, and they have spread quickly

—as such harmful fictions do—as far as Loongl in the east and the Yalrofac theatre in the west."

Prad paused and leaned forward, his blind eye gleaming. "The demoralising effect of this kind of scaremongering is a greater threat to our national interests than a two-fold or three-fold increase in the ptertha population. All of us in this hall know that pterthacosis *cannot* be passed on by bodily contact or any other means. It is the duty of every man here to ensure that harmful stories claiming otherwise are stamped out with all possible speed and vigour. We must do everything in our power to promote a healthy scepticism in the minds of the proletariat —and I look particularly to teacher, poet and priest in this respect."

Toller glanced to each side and saw the leaders of several delegations nodding as they made notes. It was surprising to him that the King should deal with such a minor issue in person, and for a moment he toyed with the startling idea that there might actually be some kernel of truth in the odd rumours. Common soldiers, sailors and airmen were a stolid lot as a rule—but on the other hand they tended to be ignorant and gullible. On balance, he could see no reason to believe there was anything more to fear from the ptertha than in any previous era in Kolcorron's long history.

". . . principal subject for discussion," King Prad was saying. "The records of the Ports Authority show that in the year 2625 our imports of brakka from the six provinces amounted to only 118,426 tons. It is the twelfth year in succession that the total has fallen. The pikon and halvell yield was correspondingly down. No figures are available for the domestic harvest, but the preliminary estimates are less encouraging than usual.

"The situation is exacerbated by the fact that military and industrial consumption, particularly of crystals, continues to rise. It is becoming obvious that we are approaching a crucial period in our country's fortunes, and that far-reaching strategies will have to be devised to deal with the problem. I will now entertain your proposals."

Prince Leddravohr, who had become restless during his father's summation, rose to his feet at once. "Majesty, I intend no disrespect to you, but I confess to growing impatient with all this talk of scarcity and dwindling resources. The truth of the matter is that there is an abundance of brakka—sufficient to meet our needs for centuries to come. There are great forests of brakka as yet untouched. The *real* shortcoming lies within ourselves. We lack the resolution to turn our eyes towards the Land of the Long Days—to go forth and claim what is rightfully ours."

In the assembly there was an immediate flurry of excitement which Prad stilled by raising one hand. Toller sat up straighter, suddenly alerted.

"I will not countenance any talk of moving against Chamteth," Prad said, his voice harsher and louder than before.

Leddravohr spun to face him. "It is destined to happen sooner or later—so why not sooner?"

"I repeat there will be no talk of a major war."

"In that case, Majesty, I beg your permission to withdraw," Leddravohr said, his manner taking him within a hair-breadth of insolence. "I can make no contribution to a discussion from which plain logic is barred."

Prad gave his head a single birdlike shake. "Resume your seat and curb your impatience—your newfound regard for logic may yet prove useful." He smiled at the rest of the gathering—his way of saying, *Even a king has problems with unruly offspring* —and invited Prince Chakkell to put forward ideas for reducing industrial consumption of power crystals.

Toller relaxed again while Chakkell was speaking, but he was unable to take his eyes off Leddravohr, who was now lounging in an exaggerated posture of boredom. He was intrigued, disturbed and strangely captivated by the discovery that the military prince regarded war with Chamteth as both desirable and inevitable. Little was known about the exotic land which, being on the far side of the world, was untouched by Overland's shadow and therefore had an uninterrupted day.

The available maps were very old and of doubtful accuracy, but they showed that Chamteth was as large as the Kolcorronian empire and equally populous. Few travellers had penetrated to its interior and returned, but their accounts had been unanimous in the descriptions of the vast brakka forests. The reserves had never been depleted because the Chamtethans regarded it as the ultimate sin to interrupt the life cycle of the brakka tree. They drew off limited quantities of crystals by drilling small holes into the combustion chambers, and restricted their use of the black wood to what could be obtained from trees which had died naturally.

The existence of such a fabulous treasurehouse had attracted the interest of Kolcorronian rulers in the past, but no real acquisitive action had ever been taken. One factor was the sheer remoteness of the country; the other was the Chamtethans' reputation as fierce, tenacious and gifted fighters. It was thought that their army was the sole user of the country's supply of crystals, and certainly the Chamtethans were well known for their extensive use of cannon—one of the most extravagant ways ever devised for the expending of crystals. They were also totally insular in their outlook, rejecting all commercial and cultural contact with other nations.

The cost, one way or another, of trying to exploit Chamteth had always been recognised as being too great, and Toller had taken it for granted that the situation was a permanent part of the natural order of things. But he had just heard talk of change —and he had a deep personal interest in that possibility.

The social divisions in Kolcorron were such that in normal circumstances a member of one of the great vocational family of families was not permitted to cross the barriers. Toller, restless and resentful over having been born into the philosophy order, had made many futile attempts to get himself accepted for military service. His lack of success had been made all the more galling by the knowledge that there would have been no obstacle to his joining the army had he been part of the proletarian masses. He would have been prepared to serve as a line soldier in the most inhospitable outpost of the empire, but one of his social rank could be accorded nothing less than officer status—an honour which was jealously guarded by the military caste.

All that, Toller now realised, was concomitant on the affairs of the country following the familiar centuries-old course. A war with Chamteth would force profound changes on Kolcorron, however, and King Prad would not be on the throne for ever. He was likely to be succeeded by Leddravohr in the not-too-distant future—and when that happened the old order would be swept away. It looked to Toller as though his fortunes could be directly affected by those of Leddravohr, and the mere prospect was enough to produce an undertow of dark excitement in his consciousness. The council meeting, which he had expected to be routine and dull, was proving to be one of the most significant occasions of his life.

On the dais the swarthy, balding and paunchy Prince Chakkell was concluding his opening remarks with a statement that he needed twice his present supply of pikon and halvell for quarrying purposes if essential building projects were to continue.

"You appear not to be in sympathy with the stated aims of this gathering," Prad commented, beginning to show some exasperation. "May I remind you that I was awaiting your thoughts on how to reduce requirements?"

"My apologies, Majesty," Chakkell said, the stubbornness of his tone contradicting the words. The son of an obscure nobleman, he had earned his rank through a combination of energy, guile and driving ambition, and it was no secret in the upper echelons of Kolcorronian society that he nursed hopes of seeing a change in the rules of succession which would allow one of his children to ascend the throne. Those aspirations, coupled with the fact that he was Leddravohr's main competitor for brakka products, meant that there was a smouldering antagonism between them, but on this occasion both men were in accord. Chakkell sat down and folded his arms, making it clear that any thoughts he had on the subject of conservation would not be to the King's liking.

"There appears to be a lack of understanding of an extremely serious problem," Prad said severely. "I must emphasise that the country is facing several years of acute shortages of a vital commodity, and that I expect a more positive attitude from my administrators and advisors for the remainder of this meeting. Perhaps the gravity of the situation will be borne home to you if I call upon Lord Glo to report on the progress which has been made thus far with the attempts to produce pikon and halvell by artificial means. Although our expectations are high in this regard, there is—as you will hear—a considerable way to go, and it behoves us to plan accordingly.

"Let us hear what you have to say, Lord Glo."

There was an extended silence during which nothing happened, then Boreatt Hargeth—in the philosophy sector's second row—was seen to lean forward and tap Glo's shoulder. Glo jumped to his feet immediately, obviously startled, and somebody across the aisle on Toller's right gave a low chuckle.

"Pardon me, Majesty, I was collecting my thoughts," Glo said, his voice unnecessarily loud. "What was your . . . hmm . . . question?"

On the dais Prince Leddravohr covered his face with one splayed hand to mime embarrassment and the same man on Toller's right, encouraged, chuckled louder. Toller turned in his direction, scowling, and the man—an official in Lord Tunsfo's medical delegation—glanced at him and abruptly ceased looking amused.

The King gave a tolerant sigh. "My question, if you will honour us by bringing your mind to bear on it, was a general one concerning the experiments with pikon and halvell. Where do we stand?"

"Ah! Yes, Majesty, the situation is indeed as I . . . hmm . . . reported to you at our last meeting. We have made great strides . . . unprecedented strides . . . in the extraction and purification of both the green and the purple. We have much to be proud of. All that remains for us to do at this . . . hmm . . . stage is to perfect a way of removing the contaminants which inhibit the crystals from reacting with each other. That is proving . . . hmm . . . difficult."

"You're contradicting yourself, Glo. Are you making progress with purification or are you not?"

"Our progress has been excellent, Majesty. As far as it goes, that is. It's all a question of solvents and temperatures and . . . um . . . complex chemical reactions. We are handicapped by not having the proper solvent."

"Perhaps the old fool drank it all," Leddravohr said to Chakkell, making no attempt to modulate his voice. The laughter which followed his words was accompanied by a frisson of unease—most of those present had never seen a man of Glo's rank so directly insulted.

"Enough!" Prad's milk-white eye narrowed and widened several times, a warning beacon. "Lord Glo, when I spoke to you ten days ago you gave me the impression that you could begin to produce pure crystals within two or three years. Are you now saying differently?"

"He doesn't know *what* he's saying," Leddravohr put in, grinning, his contemptuous stare raking the philosophy sector. Toller, unable to react in any other way, spread his shoulders to make himself as conspicuous as possible and sought to hold Leddravohr's gaze, and all the while an inner voice was pleading with him to remember his new vows, to use his brains and stay out of trouble.

"Majesty, this is a matter of great . . . hmm . . . complexity," Glo said, ignoring Leddravohr. "We cannot consider the subject of power crystals in isolation. Even if we had an unlimited supply of crystals this very day . . . There is the brakka tree itself, you see. Our plantations. It takes six centuries for the seedlings to mature and. . . ."

"You mean six decades, don't you?"

"I believe I said decades, Majesty, but I have another proposal which I beg leave to bring to your attention." Glo's voice had developed a quaver and he was swaying slightly. "I have the honour to present for your consideration a visonary scheme, one which will shape the ultimate future of this great nation of ours. A thousand years from now our descendants will look back on your reign with wonder and awe as they. . . ."

"Lord Glo!" Prad was incredulous and angry. "Are you ill or drunk?"

"Neither, Majesty."

"Then stop prating about visions and answer my question concerning the crystals."

Glo seemed to be labouring for breath, his plump chest swelling to take up the slack in his grey robe. "I fear I may be indisposed, after all." He pressed a hand to his side and dropped into his chair with an audible thud. "My senior mathematician,

Lain Maraquine, will present the facts on my . . . hmm . . . behalf."

Toller watched with growing trepidation as his brother stood up, bowed towards the dais, and signalled for his assistants, Quate and Locranan, to bring his easel and charts forward. They did so and erected the easel with a fumbling eagerness which prolonged what should have been the work of a moment. More time was taken up as the chart they unrolled and suspended had to be coaxed to remain flat. On the dais even the insipid Prince Pouche was beginning to look restless. Toller was concerned to see that Lain was trembling with nervousness.

"What is your intention, Maraquine?" the King said, not unkindly. "Am I to revisit the classroom at my time of life?"

"The graphics are helpful, Majesty," Lain said. "They illustrate the factors governing the. . . ." The remainder of his reply drifted into inaudibility as he indicated key features on the vivid diagrams.

"Can't hear you," Chakkell snapped irritably. "Speak up!"

"Where are your manners?" Leddravohr said, turning to him. "What way is that to address such a shy young maiden?" A number of men in the audience, taking their cue, guffawed loudly.

This shouldn't be happening, Toller thought as he rose to his feet, the blood roaring in his ears. The Kolcorronian code of conduct ruled that to step in and reply to a challenge—and an insult was always regarded as such—issued to a third party was to add to the original slur. The imputation was that the insulted man was too cowardly to defend his own honour. Lain had often claimed that it was his duty as a philosopher to soar above all such irrationalities, that the ancient code was more suited to quarrelsome animals than thinking men. Knowing that his brother would not and could not take up Leddravohr's challenge, knowing further that he was barred from active intervention, Toller was taking the only course open to him. He stood up straight, differentiating himself from the seated nonparticipants all around, waiting for Leddravohr to notice him and interpret his physical and mental stance.

"That's enough, Leddravohr." The King slapped the arms of

his throne. "I want to hear what the wrangler has to say. Go ahead, Maraquine."

"Majesty, I. . . ." Lain was now quivering so violently that his robe was fluttering.

"Try to put yourself at ease, Maraquine. I don't want a lengthy discourse—it will suffice for you to tell me how many years will elapse, in your expert opinion, before we can produce pure pikon and halvell."

Lain took a deep breath, fighting to control himself. "It is impossible to make predictions in matters like this."

"Give me your personal view. Would you say five years?"

"No, Majesty." Lain shot a sideways glance at Lord Glo and managed to make his voice more resolute. "If we increased our research expenditure tenfold . . . and were fortunate . . . we might produce some usable crystals twenty years from now. But there is no guarantee that we will ever succeed. There is only one sane and logical course for the country as a whole to follow and that is to ban the felling of brakka entirely for the next twenty or thirty years. In that way. . . ."

"I *refuse* to listen to any more of this!" Leddravohr was on his feet and stepping down from the dais. "Did I say maiden? I was wrong—this is an old woman! Raise your skirts and flee from this place, old woman, and take your sticks and scraps with you." Leddravohr strode to the easel and thrust the palm of his hand against it, sending it clattering to the floor.

During the clamour which followed, Toller left his place and walked forwards on stiffened legs to stand close to his brother. On the dais the King was ordering Leddravohr back to his seat, but his voice was almost lost amid angry cries from Chakkell and in the general commotion in the hall. A court official was hammering on the floor with his staff, but the only effect was to increase the level of sound. Leddravohr looked straight at Toller with white-flaring eyes, but appeared not to see him as he wheeled round to face his father.

"I act on your behalf, Majesty," he shouted in a voice which brought a ringing silence to the hall. "Your ears shall not be defiled any further with the kind of spoutings we have just heard from the so-called thinkers among us."

"I am quite capable of making such decisions for myself," Prad replied sternly. "I would remind you that this is a meeting of the high council—not some brawling ground for your muddied soldiery."

Leddravohr was unrepentant as he glanced contemptuously at Lain. "I hold the lowliest soldier in the service of Kolcorron in greater esteem than this whey-faced old woman." His continued defiance of the King intensified the silence under the glass dome, and it was into that magnifying hush that Toller heard himself drop his own challenge. It would have been a crime akin to treason, and punishable by death, for one of his station to take the initiative and challenge a member of the monarchy, but the code permitted him to move indirectly within limits and seek to provoke a response.

"'Old woman' appears to be a favourite epithet of Prince Leddravohr's," he said to Vorndal Sisstt, who was seated close to him. "Does that mean he is always very prudent in his choice of opponents?"

Sisstt gaped up at him and shrank away, white-faced, anxiously dissociating himself as Leddravohr turned to find out who had spoken. Seeing Leddravohr at close quarters for the first time, Toller observed that his strong-jawed countenance was unlined, possessed of a curious statuesque smoothness, almost as if the muscles were nerveless and immobile. It was an inhuman face, untroubled by the ordinary range of expression, with only the eyes to signal what was going on behind the broad brow. In this case Leddravohr's eyes showed that he was more incredulous than angry as he scrutinised the younger man, taking in every detail of his physique and dress.

"Who are you?" Leddravohr said at last. "Or should I say, what are you?"

"My name is Toller Maraquine, Prince—and I take pride in being a philosopher."

Leddravohr glanced up at his father and smiled, as if to demonstrate that when he saw it as his filial duty he could endure extreme provocation. Toller did not like the smile, which was accomplished in an instant, effortless as the twitching back of a drape, affecting no other part of his face.

"Well, Toller Maraquine," Leddravohr said, "it is very fortunate that personal weapons are never worn in my father's household."

Leave it at that, Toller urged himself. *You've made your point and—against all the odds—you're getting away with it.*

"Fortunate?" he said pleasantly. "For whom?"

Leddravohr's smile did not waver, but his eyes became opaque, like polished brown pebbles. He took one step forward and Toller readied himself for the shock of physical combat, but in that moment the glass axis of the confrontation was snapped by pressure from an unexpected direction.

"Majesty," Lord Glo called out, lurching to his feet, looking ghastly but speaking in surprisingly fluent and resonant tones. "I beg you—for the sake of our beloved Kolcorron—to listen to the proposal of which I spoke earlier. Please do not let my brief indisposition stand in the way of your hearing of a scheme whose implications go far beyond the present and near future, and in the long run will concern the very existence of our great nation."

"Hold still, Glo." King Prad also rose to his feet and pointed at Leddravohr with the index fingers of both hands, triangulating on him with all the force of his authority. "Leddravohr, you will now resume your seat."

Leddravohr eyed the King for a few seconds, his face impassive, then he turned away from Toller and walked slowly to the dais. Toller was startled as he felt his brother grip his arm.

"What are you trying to do?" Lain whispered, his frightened gaze hunting over Toller's face. "Leddravohr has killed people for less."

Toller shrugged his arm free. "I'm still alive."

"And you had no right to step in like that."

"I apologise for the insult," Toller said. "I didn't think one more would make any difference."

"You know what I think of your childish. . . ." Lain broke off as Lord Glo came to stand close beside him.

"The boy can't help being impetuous—I was the same at his age," Glo said. The brilliance from above showed that every pore on his forehead was separately domed with sweat. Beneath

71

the ample folds of his robe his chest swelled and contracted with disturbing rapidity, pumping out the smell of wine.

"My lord, I think you should sit down and compose yourself," Lain said quietly. "There is no need for you to be subjected to any more of. . . ."

"No! You're the one who must sit down." Glo indicated two nearby seats and waited until Lain and Toller had sunk into them. "You're a good man, Lain, but it was very wrong of me to burden you with a task for which you are constitutionally . . . hmm . . . unsuited. This is a time for boldness. Boldness of vision. That is what earned us the respect of the ancient kings."

Toller, rendered morbidly sensitive to Leddravohr's every movement, noticed that on the dais the prince was concluding a whispered conversation with his father. Both men sat down, and Leddravohr immediately turned his brooding gaze in Toller's direction. At a barely perceptible nod from the King an official pounded the floor with his staff to quell the low-key murmurings throughout the hall.

"Lord Glo!" Prad's voice was now ominously calm. "I apologise for the discourtesy shown to members of your delegation, but I also add that the council's time should not be wasted on frivolous suggestions. Now, if I grant you permission to lay before us the essentials of your grand scheme, will you undertake to do so quickly and succinctly, without adding to my tribulations on a day which has already seen too many?"

"Gladly!"

"Then proceed."

"I am about to do so, Majesty." Glo half turned to look at Lain, gave him a prolonged wink and began to whisper. "Remember what you said about my flying higher and seeing farther? You're going to have cause to reflect on those words, my boy. Your graphs were telling a story that even you didn't understand, but I. . . ."

"Lord Glo," Prad said, "I am waiting."

Glo gave him an elaborate bow, complete with the hand flourishes appropriate to the use of the high tongue. "Majesty, the philosopher has many duties, many responsibilities. Not only must his mind encompass the past and the present, it must illuminate the multiple pathways of the future. The darker and more . . . hmm . . . hazardous those pathways may be, the higher. . . ."

"Get on with it, Glo!"

"Very well, Majesty. My analysis of the situation in which Kolcorron finds itself today shows that the difficulties of obtaining brakka and power crystals are going to increase until . . . hmm . . . only the most vigorous and far-sighted measures will avert national disaster." Glo's voice shook with fervour.

"It is my considered opinion that, as the problems which beset us grow and multiply, we must expand our capabilities accordingly. If we are to maintain our premier position on Land we must turn our eyes—not towards the petty nations on our borders, with their meagre resources—but towards the sky!

"The entire planet of Overland hangs above us, waiting, like a luscious fruit ready for the picking. It is within our powers to develop the means to go there and to. . . ." The rest of Glo's sentence was drowned in a swelling tide of laughter.

Toller, whose gaze had been locked with Leddravohr's, turned his head as he heard angry shouts from his right. He saw that, beyond Tunsfo's medical delegation, Lord Prelate Balountar had risen to his feet and was pointing at Glo in accusation, his small mouth distorted and dragged to one side with intensity of emotion.

Borreat Hargeth leaned over from the row behind Toller and gripped Lain's shoulder. "Make the old fool sit down," he urged in a scandalised whisper. "Did you know he was going to do this?"

"Of course not!" Lain's narrow face was haggard. "And how can I stop him?"

"You'd better do something before we're all made to look like idiots."

". . . long been known that Land and Overland share a common atmosphere," Glo was declaiming, seemingly oblivious to the commotion he had caused. "The Greenmount archives contain detailed drawings for hot air balloons capable of ascending to . . ."

"In the name of the Church I command you to cease this

73

blasphemy," Lord Prelate Balountar shouted, leaving his place to advance on Glo, head thrust forward and tilting from side to side like that of a wading bird. Toller, who was irreligious by instinct, deduced from the violence of Balountar's reaction that the churchman was a strict Alternationist. Unlike many senior clerics, who paid lip service to their creed in order to collect large stipends, Balountar really did believe that after death the spirit migrated to Overland, was reincarnated as a newborn infant and eventually returned to Land in the same way, part of a never-ending cycle of existence.

Glo made a dismissive gesture in Balountar's direction. "The main difficulty lies with the region of neutral . . . hmm . . . gravity at the midpoint of the flight where, of course, the density differential between hot and cold air can have no effect. That problem can be solved by fitting each craft with reaction tubes which. . . ."

Glo was abruptly silenced when Balountar closed the distance between them in a sudden rush, black vestments flapping, and clamped a hand over Glo's mouth. Toller, who had not expected the cleric to use force, sprang from his chair. He grabbed both of Balountar's bony wrists and brought his arms down to his sides. Glo clutched at his own throat, gagging. Balountar tried to break free, but Toller lifted him as easily as he would have moved a straw dummy and set him down several paces away, becoming aware as he did so that the King had again risen to his feet. The laughter in the hall died away to be replaced by a taut silence.

"*You!*" Balountar's mouth worked spasmodically as he glared up at Toller. "You touched me!"

"I was acting in defence of my master," Toller said, realising that his reflex action had been a major breach of protocol. He heard a muffled retching sound and turned to see that Glo was being sick with both hands cupped over his mouth. Black wine was gouting through his fingers, disfiguring his robe and spattering on the floor.

The King spoke loudly and clearly, each word like the snapping of a blade. "Lord Glo, I don't know which I find more offensive—the contents of your stomach or the contents of your mind. You and your party will leave my presence immediately,

74

and I warn you here and now that—as soon as more pressing matters have been dealt with—I am going to think long and hard about your future."

Glo uncovered his mouth and tried to speak, the brown pegs of his teeth working up and down, but was able to produce nothing more than clicking sounds in his throat.

"Remove him from my sight," Prad said, turning his hard eyes on the Lord Prelate. "As for you, Balountar, you are to be rebuked for mounting a physical attack on one of my ministers, no matter how great the provocation. For that reason, you have no redress against the young man who restrained you, though he does appear somewhat lacking in discretion. You will return to your place and remain there without speaking until the Lord Philosopher and his cortege of buffoons have withdrawn."

The King sat down and stared straight ahead while Lain and Borreat Hargeth closed upon Glo and led him away towards the hall's main entrance. Toller walked around Vorndal Sisstt, who had knelt to wipe the floor with the hem of his own robe, and helped Lain's two assistants to gather up the fallen easel and charts. As he stood up with the easel under his arm it occurred to him that Prince Leddravohr must have received an unusually powerful reprimand to induce him to remain so quiet. He glanced towards the dais and saw that Leddravohr, lounging in his throne, was staring at him with an intent unwavering gaze. Toller, oppressed by collective shame, looked elsewhere immediately, but not before he had seen Leddravohr's smile twitch into existence.

"What are you waiting for?" Sisstt mumbled. "Get that stuff out of here before the King decides to have us flayed."

The walk through the corridors and high chambers of the palace seemed twice as long as before. Even when Glo had recovered sufficiently to shake off helping hands, Toller felt that news of the philosophers' disgrace had magically flown ahead of them and was being discussed by every low-voiced group they passed. From the start he had felt that Lord Glo was going to be unable to function well at the meeting, but he had not anticipated being drawn into a débâcle of such magnitude. King Prad was famed for the informality and tolerance with which he conducted royal business, but Glo had managed to transgress to such an extent that the future of the entire order had been called into question. And furthermore, Toller's embryonic plan to enter the army by someday finding favour with Leddravohr was no longer tenable—the military prince had a reputation for never forgetting, never forgiving.

On reaching the principal courtyard Glo thrust out his stomach and marched jauntily to his phaeton. He paused beside it, turned to face the rest of the group and said, "Well, that didn't go too badly, did it? I think I can truthfully say that I planted a seed in the King's . . . hmm . . . mind. What do you say?"

Lain, Hargeth and Duthoon exchanged stricken glances, but Sisstt spoke up at once. "You're absolutely right, my lord."

Glo nodded approval at him. "That's the only way to advance a radical new idea, you know. Plant a seed. Let it . . . hmm . . . germinate."

Toller turned away, suddenly in fresh danger of laughing aloud in spite of all that had happened to him, and carried the easel to his tethered bluehorn. He strapped the wooden framework across the beast's haunches, retrieved the rolled charts from Quate and Locranan, and prepared to depart. The sun was little more than halfway between the eastern rim of Overland—the ordeal by humiliation had been mercifully brief—and there was time for him to claim a late breakfast as the first step in salvaging the rest of the day. He had placed one foot in the stirrup when his brother appeared at his side.

"What is it that afflicts you?" Lain said. "Your behaviour in the palace was appalling—even by your own standards."

Toller was taken aback. "*My* behaviour!"

"Yes! Within the space of minutes you made enemies of two of the most dangerous men in the empire. How do you do it?"

"It's very simple," Toller said stonily. "I comport myself as a man."

Lain sighed in exasperation. "I'll speak to you further when we get back to Greenmount."

"No doubt." Toller mounted the bluehorn and urged it forward, not waiting for the coach. On the ride back to the Square House his annoyance with Lain gradually faded as he considered his brother's unenviable position. Lord Philosopher Glo was bringing the order in disrepute, but as a royal he could only be deposed by the King. Attempting to undermine him would be treated as sedition, and in any case Lain had too much personal loyalty to Glo even to criticise him in private. When it became common knowledge that Glo had proposed trying to send ships to Overland all those connected with him would become objects of derision—and Lain would suffer everything in silence, retreating further into his books and graphs while the philosophers' tenure at Greenmount grew steadily less secure.

By the time he had reached the multi-gabled house Toller's mind was tiring of abstracts and becoming preoccupied with the fact that he was hungry. Not only had he missed breakfast, he had eaten virtually nothing on the previous day, and now there was a raging emptiness in his stomach. He tethered the bluehorn in the precinct and, without bothering to unload it, walked quickly into the house with the intention of going straight to the kitchen.

For the second time that morning he found himself unexpectedly in the presence of Gesalla, who was crossing the entrance hall towards the west salon. She turned to him, dazzled by the light from the archway, and smiled. The smile lasted only a moment, as long as it took for her to identify him against the glare, but its effect on Toller was odd. He seemed to see Gesalla for the first time, as a goddess figure with sun-bright eyes, and in the instant he felt an inexplicable and poignant sense of waste, not of material possessions but of all the potential of life itself. The sensation faded as quickly as it had come, but it left him feeling sad and strangely chastened.

"Oh, it's you," Gesalla said in a cold voice. "I thought you were Lain."

Toller smiled, wondering if he could begin a new and more constructive relationship with Gesalla. "A trick of the light."

"Why are you back so early?"

"Ah . . . the meeting didn't go as planned. There was some trouble. Lain will tell you all about it—he's on his way home now."

Gesalla tilted her head and moved until she had the advantage of the light. "Why can't you tell me? Was it something to do with you?"

"With *me*?"

"Yes. I advised Lain not to let you go anywhere near the palace."

"Well, perhaps he's getting as sick as I am of you and your endless torrents of advice." Toller tried to stop speaking, but the word fever was upon him. "Perhaps he has begun to regret marrying a withered twig instead of a real woman."

"Thank you—I'll pass your comments on to Lain in full." Gesalla's lips quirked, showing that—far from being wounded —she was pleased at having invoked the kind of intemperate response which could result in Toller being banished from the Square House. "Do I take it that your concept of a real woman is embodied in the whore who is waiting in your bed at this moment?"

"You can take. . . ." Toller scowled, trying to conceal the fact that he had completely forgotten about his companion of the night. "You should guard your tongue! Felise is no whore."

Gesalla's eyes sparkled. "Her name is Fera."

"Felise or Fera—she isn't a whore."

"I won't bandy definitions with you," Gesalla said, her tones now light, cool and infuriating. "The cook told me you left instructions for your . . . guest to be provided with all the food she wished. And if the amounts she has already consumed this foreday are any yardstick, you should think yourself fortunate that you don't have to support her in marriage."

"But I do!" Toller saw his chance to deliver the verbal thrust and took it on the reflex, with heady disregard for the consequences. "I've been trying to tell you that I gave Fera gradewife status before I left here this morning. I'm sure you will soon learn to enjoy her company about the house, and then we can all be friends together. Now, if you will excuse me. . . ."

He smiled, savouring the shock and incredulity on Gesalla's face, then turned and sauntered towards the main stair, taking care to hide his own numb bemusement over what a few angry seconds could do to the course of his life. The last thing he wanted was the responsibility of a wife, even of the fourth grade, and he could only hope that Fera would refuse the offer he had committed himself to making.

CHAPTER 5

General Risdel Dalacott awoke at first light and, following the routine which had rarely varied in his sixty-eight years of life, left his bed immediately.

He walked around the room several times, his step growing firmer as the stiffness and pain gradually departed from his right leg. It was almost thirty years since the aftday, during the first Sorka campaign, when a heavy Merrillian throwing spear had smashed his thigh bone just above the knee. The injury had troubled him at intervals ever since, and the periods when he was free of discomfort were becoming shorter and quite infrequent.

As soon as he was satisfied with the leg's performance he went into the adjoining toilet chamber and threw the lever of enamelled brakka which was set in one wall. The water which sprayed down on him from the perforated ceiling was hot— a reminder that he was not in his own spartan quarters in Trompha. Putting aside irrational feelings of guilt, he took maximum enjoyment from the warmth as it penetrated and soothed his muscles.

After drying himself he paused at a wall-mounted mirror, which was made of two layers of clear glass with highly different refractive indices, and took stock of his image. Although age had had its inevitable effect on the once-powerful body, the austere discipline of his way of life had prevented fatty degeneration. His long, thoughtful face had become deeply lined, but the greyness which had entered his cropped hair scarcely showed against its fair coloration, and his overall appearance was one of durable health and fitness.

Still serviceable, he thought. *But I'll do only one more year. The army has taken too much from me already.*

While he was donning his informal blues he turned his thoughts to the day ahead. It was the twelfth birthday of his grandson, Hallie, and—as part of the ritual which proved he was ready to enter military academy—the boy was due to go alone against ptertha. The occasion was an important one, and Dalacott vividly remembered the pride he had felt on watching his own son, Oderan, pass the same test. Oderan's subsequent army career had been cut short by his death at the age of thirty-three—the result of an airship crash in Yalrofac—and it was Dalacott's painful duty to stand in for him during the day's celebrations. He finished dressing, left the bedroom and went downstairs to the dining room where, in spite of the earliness of the hour, he found Conna Dalacott seated at the round table. She was a tall, open-faced woman whose form was developing the solidity of early middle age.

"Good foreday, Conna," he said, noting that she was alone. "Is young Hallie still asleep?"

"On his twelfth?" She nodded towards the walled garden, part of which was visible through the floor-to-ceiling window. "He's out there somewhere, practising. He wouldn't even look at his breakfast."

"It's a big day for him. For us all."

"Yes." Something in the timbre of Conna's voice told Dalacott that she was under a strain. "A wonderful day."

"I know it's distressing for you," he said gently, "but Oderan would have wanted us to make the most of it, for Hallie's sake."

Conna gave him a calm smile. "Do you still take nothing but porridge for breakfast? Can't I tempt you with some whitefish? Sausage? A forcemeat cake?"

"I've lived too long on line soldier's rations," he protested, tacitly agreeing to restrict himself to small-talk. Conna had maintained the villa and conducted her life ably enough without his assistance in the ten years since Oderan's death, and it would be presumptuous of him to offer her any advice at this juncture.

"Very well," she said, beginning to serve him from one of the covered dishes on the table, "but there'll be no soldier's rations for you at the littlenight feast."

"Agreed!" While Dalacott was eating the lightly salted porridge he exchanged pleasantries with his daughter-in-law, but the seething of his memories continued unabated and—as had been happening more often of late—thoughts of the son he had lost evoked others of the son he had never claimed. Looking back over his life he had, once again, to ponder the ways in which the major turning points were frequently unrecognisable as such, in which the inconsequential could lead to the momentous.

Had he not been caught off his guard during the course of a minor skirmish in Yalrofac all those years ago he would not have received the serious wound in his leg. The injury had led to a long convalescence in the quietness of Redant province; and it was there, while walking by the Bes-Undar river, he had chanced to find the strangest natural object he had ever seen, the one he still carried everywhere he went. The object had been in his possession for about a year when, on a rare visit to the capital, he had impulsively taken it to the science quarter on Greenmount to find out if its strange properties could be explained.

In the event, he had learned nothing about the object and a great deal about himself.

As a dedicated career soldier he had taken on a solewife almost as a duty to the state, to provide him with an heir and to minister to his needs between campaigns. His relationship with Toriane had been pleasant, even and warm; and he had regarded it as fulfilling—until the day he had ridden into the precinct of a square house on Greenmount and had seen Aytha Maraquine. His meeting with the slender young matron had been a blending of green and purple, producing a violent explosion of passion and ecstasy and, ultimately, an intensity of pain he had not believed possible. . . .

"The carriage is back, Grandad," Hallie cried, tapping at the long window. "We're ready to go to the hill."

"I'm coming." Dalacott waved to the fair-haired boy who was dancing with excitement on the patio. Hallie was tall and sturdy, well able to handle the full-size ptertha sticks which were clattering on his belt.

"You haven't finished your porridge," Conna said as he stood up, her matter-of-fact tone not quite concealing the underlying emotion.

"You know, there is absolutely no need for you to worry," he said. "A ptertha drifting over open ground in clear daylight poses no threat to anybody. Dealing with it is child's play, and in any case I'll be staying close to Hallie at all times."

"Thank you." Conna remained seated, staring down at her untouched food, until Dalacott had left the room.

He went out to the garden which—as was standard in rural areas—had high walls surmounted by ptertha screens which could be closed together overhead at night and in foggy conditions. Hallie came running to him, recreating the image of his father at the same age, and took his hand. They walked out to the carriage, in which waited three men, local friends of the family, who were required as witnesses to the boy's coming-of-age. Dalacott, who had renewed their acquaintanceship on the previous evening, exchanged greetings with them as he and Hallie took their places on the padded benches inside the big coach. The driver cracked his whip over his team of four bluehorns and the vehicle moved off.

"Oho! Have we a seasoned campaigner here?" said Gehate, a retired merchant, leaning forward to tap a Y-shaped ptertha stick he had noticed among the normal Kolcorronian cruciforms in Hallie's armoury.

"It's Ballinnian," Hallie said proudly, stroking the polished and highly decorated wood of the weapon, which Dalacott had given him a year earlier. "It flies farther than the others. Effective at thirty yards. The Gethans use them as well. The Gethans and the Cissorians."

Dalacott returned the indulgent smiles the boy's show of knowledge elicited from the other men. Throwing sticks of one form or another had been in use since ancient times by almost every nation on Land as a defence against ptertha, and had been chosen for their effectiveness. The enigmatic globes burst as easily as soap bubbles once they got to within their killing radius of a man, but before that they showed a surprising degree of resilience. A bullet, an arrow or even a spear could pass through a ptertha without causing it any harm—the globe would only quiver momentarily as it repaired the punctures in its transparent skin. It took a rotating, flailing missile to disrupt a ptertha's structure and disperse its toxic dust into the air.

The bolas made a good ptertha killer, but it was hard to master and had the disadvantage of being too heavy to be carried in quantity, whereas a multi-bladed throwing stick was flat, comparatively light and easily portable. It was a source of wonder to Dalacott that even the most primitive tribesmen had learned that giving each blade one rounded edge and one sharp edge produced a weapon which sustained itself in the air like a bird, flying much farther than an ordinary projectile. No doubt it was that seemingly magical property which induced people like the Ballinnians to lavish such care on the carving and embellishment of their ptertha sticks. By contrast, the pragmatic Kolcorronians favoured a plain expendable weapon of the four-bladed pattern which was suitable for mass production because it was made of two straight sections glued together at the centre.

The carriage gradually left the grain fields and orchards of Klinterden behind and began climbing the foothills of Mount Pharote. Eventually it reached a place where the road petered out on a grassy table, beyond which the ground ascended steeply into mists which had not yet been boiled off by the sun.

"Here we are," Gehate said jovially to Hallie as the vehicle creaked to a halt. "I can't wait to see what sport that fancy stick of yours will produce. Thirty yards, you say?"

Thessaro, a florid-faced banker, frowned and shook his head. "Don't egg the boy into showing off. It isn't good to throw too soon."

"I think you'll find he knows what to do," Dalacott said as he got out of the carriage with Hallie and looked around. The sky was a dome of pearly brilliance shading off into pale blue overhead. No stars could be seen and even the great disk of Overland, only part of which was visible, appeared pale and insubstantial. Dalacott had travelled to the south of Kail province to visit his son's family, and in these latitudes Overland was noticeably displaced to the north. The climate was more temperate than that of equatorial Kolcorron, a factor which —combined with a much shorter littlenight—made the region one of the best food producers in the empire.

"Plenty of ptertha," Gehate said, pointing upwards to where purple motes could be seen drifting high in the air currents rolling down from the mountain.

"There's always plenty of ptertha these days," commented Ondobirtre, the third witness. "I'll swear they are on the increase—no matter what anybody says to the contrary. I heard that several of them even penetrated the centre of Ro-Baccanta a few days ago."

Gehate shook his head impatiently. "They don't go into cities."

"I'm only telling what I heard."

"You're too credulous, my friend. You listen to too many tall stories."

"This is no time for bickering," Thessaro put in. "This is an important occasion." He opened the linen sack he was carrying and began counting out six ptertha sticks each to Dalacott and the other men.

"You won't need those, Grandad," Hallie said, looking offended. "I'm not going to miss."

"I know that, Hallie, but it's the custom. Besides, some of the rest of us might be in need of a little practice." Dalacott put an arm around the boy's shoulders and walked with him to the mouth of an alley created by two high nets. They were strung on parallel lines of poles which crossed the table and went up the slope beyond to disappear into the mist ceiling. The system was a traditional one which served to guide ptertha down from the mountain in small numbers. It would have been easy for the globes to escape by floating upwards, but a few always followed such an alley to its lower end as though they were sentient creatures motivated by curiosity. Quirks of behaviour like that were the main reason for the belief, held by many, that the globes possessed some degree of intelligence, although Dalacott had always remained unconvinced in view of their complete lack of internal structure.

"You can leave me now, Grandad," Hallie said. "I'm ready."

"Very well, young man." Dalacott moved back a dozen paces to stand line abreast with the other men. It was the first time he had ever thought of his grandson as being anything more than a boy, but Hallie was entering his trial with courage and dignity, and would never again be quite the same person as the child who had played in the garden only that morning. It came to

Dalacott that at breakfast he had given Conna the wrong assurances—she had known only too well that her child was never coming back to her. The insight was something Dalacott would have to note in his diary at nightfall. Soldiers' wives were required to undergo their own trials, and the adversary was time itself.

"I knew we wouldn't have to wait very long," Ondobirtre whispered.

Dalacott transferred his attention from his grandson to the wall of mist at the far end of the netted enclosure. In spite of his confidence in Hallie, he felt a spasm of alarm as he saw that two ptertha had appeared simultaneously. The livid globes, each a full two yards in diameter, came drifting low and weaving, becoming harder to see clearly as they moved down the slope to where the background was grass. Hallie, who had a four-bladed stick in his hand, altered his stance slightly and made ready to throw.

Not yet, Dalacott commanded in his thoughts, knowing that the presence of a second ptertha would increase the temptation to try destroying one at maximum range. The dust released by a bursting ptertha lost its toxicity almost as soon as it was exposed to air, so the minium safe range for a kill could be as little as six paces, depending on wind conditions. At that distance it was virtually impossible to miss, which meant that the ptertha was no match at all for a man with a cool head, but Dalacott had seen novices suddenly lose their judgment and coordination. For some there was a strange mesmeric and unmanning quality about the trembling spheres, especially when on nearing their prey they ceased their random drifting and closed in with silent, deadly purpose.

The two floating towards Hallie were now less than thirty paces away from him, sailing just above the grass, blindly questing from one net to the other. Hallie brought his right arm back, making tentative wrist movements, but refrained from throwing. Watching the solitary, straight-backed figure holding his ground as the ptertha drew ever closer, Dalacott experienced a mixture of pride, love and pure fear. He held one of his own sticks at the ready and prepared to dart forward. Hallie moved closer to the net on his left, still withholding his first strike.

"Do you see what the little devil is up to?" Gehate breathed. "I do believe he's. . . ."

At that moment the aimless meanderings of the ptertha brought them together, one behind the other, and Hallie made his throw. The blades of the cruciform weapon blurred as it flew straight and true, and an instant later the purple globes no longer existed.

Hallie became a boy again, just long enough to make one exultant leap into the air, then he resumed his watchful stance as a third ptertha emerged from the mist. He unclipped another stick from his belt, and Dalacott saw that it was the Y-shaped Ballinnian weapon.

Gehate nudged Dalacott. "The first throw was for you, but I think this one is going to be for my benefit—to teach me to keep my mouth shut."

Hallie allowed the globe to get no closer than thirty paces before he made his second throw. The weapon flitted along the alley like a brilliantly coloured bird, almost without sinking, and was just beginning to lose stability when it sliced into the ptertha and annihilated it. Hallie was grinning as he turned to the watching men and gave them an elaborate bow. He had claimed the necessary three kills and was now officially entering the adult phase of his life.

"The boy had some luck that time, but he deserved it," Gehate said ungrudgingly. "Oderan should have been here."

"Yes." Dalacott, racked by bitter-sweet emotions, contented himself with the monosyllabic response, and was relieved when the others moved away—Gehate and Thessaro to embrace Hallie, Ondobirtre to fetch the ritual flask of brandy from the carriage. The group of six, including the hired driver, came together again when Ondobirtre distributed tiny hemispherical glasses whose rims had been fashioned unevenly to represent vanquished ptertha. Dalacott kept an eye on his grandson while he had his first sip of ardent spirits, and was amused when the boy, who had just overcome a mortal enemy, pulled a grotesque face.

"I trust," Ondobirtre said as he refilled the adults' glasses, "that all present have noticed the unusual feature of this morning's outing?"

Gehate snorted. "Yes—I'm glad you didn't attack the brandy before the rest of us got near it."

"That's not it," Ondobirtre said gravely, refusing to be goaded. "Everybody thinks I'm an idiot, but in all the years we've been watching this kind of thing has anybody seen a day when three globes showed up before the bluehorns had stopped farting after the climb? I'm telling you, my shortsighted friends, that the ptertha are on the increase. In fact, unless I'm getting winedreams, we have a couple more visitors."

The company turned to look at the space between the nets and saw that two more ptertha had drifted down from the obscurity of the cloud ceiling and were nuzzling their way along the corded barriers.

"They're mine," Gehate called as he ran forward. He halted, steadied himself and threw two sticks in quick succession, destroying both the globes with ease. Their dust briefly smudged the air.

"There you are!" Gehate cried. "You don't need to be built like a soldier to be able to defend yourself. I can still teach you a thing or two, young Hallie."

Hallie handed his glass back to Ondobirtre and ran to join Gehate, eager to compete with him. After the second brandy Dalacott and Thessaro also went forward and they made a sporting contest of the destruction of every globe which appeared, only giving up when the mist rose clear of the top end of the alley and the ptertha retreated with it to higher altitudes. Dalacott was impressed by the fact that almost forty had come down the alley in the space of an hour, considerably more than he normally would have expected. While the others were retrieving their sticks in preparation for leaving, he commented on the matter to Ondobirtre.

"It's what I've been saying all along," said Ondobirtre, who had been steadily drinking brandy all the while and was growing pale and morose. "But everybody thinks I'm an idiot."

By the time the carriage had completed the journey back to Klinterden the sun was nearing the eastern rim of Overland, and the littlenight celebration in honour of Hallie was about to begin.

The vehicles and animals belonging to the guests were gathered in the villa's forecourt, and a number of children were at play in the walled garden. Hallie, first to jump down from the carriage, sprinted into the house to find his mother. Dalacott followed him at a more sedate pace, the pain in his leg having returned during the long spell in the carriage. He had little enthusiasm for large parties and was not looking forward to the remainder of the day, but it would have been discourteous of him not to stay the night. It was arranged that a military airship would pick him up on the following day for the flight back to the Fifth Army's headquarters in Trompha.

Conna greeted him with a warm embrace as he entered the villa. "Thank you for taking care of Hallie," she said. "Was he as superb as he claims?"

"Absolutely! He made a splendid showing." Dalacott was pleased to see that Conna was now looking cheerful and self-possessed. "He made Gehate sit up and take notice, I can tell you."

"I'm glad. Now, remember what you promised me at breakfast. I want to see you *eating*—not just picking at your food."

"The fresh air and exercise have made me ravenous," Dalacott lied. He left Conna as she was welcoming the three witnesses and went into the central part of the house, which was thronged with men and women who were conversing animatedly in small groups. Grateful that nobody appeared to have noticed his arrival, he quietly took a glass of fruit juice from the table set out for the children and went to stand by a window. From the vantage point he could see quite a long way to the west, over vistas of agricultural land which at the limits of vision shaded off into a low range of blue-green hills. The strip fields clearly showed progressions of six colours, from the pale green of the freshly planted to the deep yellow of mature crops ready for harvesting.

As he was watching, the hills and most distant fields blinked with prismatic colour and abruptly dimmed. The penumbral band of Overland's shadow was racing across the landscape at orbital speed, closely followed by the blackness of the umbra itself. It took only a fraction of a minute for the rushing wall of darkness to reach and envelop the house—then littlenight had begun. It was a phenomenon Dalacott had never tired of watching. As his eyes adjusted to the new conditions the sky seemed to blossom with stars, hazy spirals and comets, and he found himself wondering if there could be—as some claimed—other inhabited worlds circling far-off suns. In the old days the army had absorbed too much of his mental energy for him to think deeply on such matters, but of late he had found a spare comfort in the notion that there might be an infinity of worlds, and that on one of them there might be another Kolcorron identical to the one he knew in every respect save one. Was it possible that there was another Land on which his lost loved ones were still alive?

The evocative smell of freshly-lit oil lanterns and candles took his thoughts back to the few treasured nights he had spent with Aytha Maraquine. During the heady hours of passion Dalacott had known with total certainty that they would overcome all difficulties, surmount all the obstacles that lay in the way of their eventual marriage. Aytha, who had solewife status, would have had to endure the twin disgraces of divorcing a sickly husband and of marrying across the greatest of all social divisions, the one which separated the military from all other classes. He had been faced with similar impediments, with an added problem in that by divorcing Toriane—daughter of a military governor—he would have been placing his own career in jeopardy.

None of that had mattered to Dalacott in his fevered monomania. Then had come the Padalian campaign, which should have been brief but which in the event had entailed his being separated from Aytha for almost a year. Next had come the news that she had died in giving birth to a male child. Dalacott's first tortured impulse had been to claim the boy as his own, and in that way keep faith with Aytha, but the cool voices of logic and self-interest had intervened. What was the point in posthumously smirching Aytha's good name and at the same time prejudicing his career and bringing unhappiness to his family? It would not even benefit the boy, Toller, who would be best left to grow up in the comfortable circumstances of his maternal kith and kin.

In the end Dalacott had committed himself to the course of rationality, not even trying to see his son, and the years had slipped by and his abilities had brought him the deserved rank of general. Now, at this late stage of his life, the entire episode had many of the qualities of a dream and might have lost its power to engender pain—except that other questions and doubts had begun to trouble his hours of solitude. All his protestations notwithstanding, had he really intended to marry Aytha? Had he not, in some buried level of his consciousness, been relieved when her death had made it unnecessary for him to make a decision one way or the other? In short, was he—General Risdel Dalacott—the man he had always believed himself to be? Or was he a . . . ?

"*There* you are!" Conna said, approaching him with a glass of wheat wine which she placed firmly in his free hand while depriving him of the fruit juice. "You'll simply have to mingle with the guests, you know. Otherwise it will look as though you consider yourself too famous and important to acknowledge my friends."

"I'm sorry." He gave her a wry smile. "The older I get the more I look into the past."

"Were you thinking about Oderan?"

"I was thinking about many things." Dalacott sipped his wine and went with his daughter-in-law to make smalltalk with a succession of men and women. He noticed that very few of them had army backgrounds, possibly an indication of Conna's true feelings about the organisation which had taken her husband and was now turning its attention to her only child. The strain of manufacturing conversation with virtual strangers was considerable, and it was almost with relief that he heard the summons to go to the table. It was his duty now to make a short formal speech about his grandson's coming-of-age; then he would be free to fade into the background to the best of his ability. He walked around the table to the single high-backed chair which had been decked with blue spearflowers in Hallie's honour and realised he had not seen the boy for some time.

"Where's our hero?" a man called out. "Bring on the hero!"

"He must have gone to his room," Conna said. "I'll fetch him."

She smiled apologetically and slipped away from the company. There was delay of perhaps a minute before she reappeared in the doorway, and when she did so her face was strangely passive, frozen. She pointed at Dalacott and turned away again without speaking. He went after her, telling himself that the icy sensation in his stomach meant nothing, and walked along the corridor to Hallie's bedroom. The boy was lying on his back on his narrow couch. His face was flushed and gleaming with sweat, and his limbs were making small uncoordinated movements.

It can't be, Dalacott thought, appalled, as he went to the couch. He looked down at Hallie, saw the terror in his eyes, and knew at once that the twitching of his arms and legs represented strenuous attempts to move normally. Paralysis and fever! *I won't allow this*, Dalacott shouted inwardly as he dropped to his knees. *It isn't permitted!*

He placed his hand on Hallie's slim body, just below the ribcage, immediately found the telltale swelling of the spleen, and a moan of pure grief escaped his lips.

"You promised to look after him," Conna said in a lifeless voice. "He's only a baby!"

Dalacott stood up and gripped her shoulders. "Is there a doctor here?"

"What's the use?"

"I know what this looks like, Conna, but at no time was Hallie within twenty paces of a globe and there was no wind to speak of." Listening to his own voice, a stranger's voice, Dalacott tried to be persuaded by the stated facts. "Besides, it takes two days for pterthacosis to develop. It simply can't happen like this. Now, is there a doctor?"

"Visigann," she whispered, brimming eyes scanning his face in search of hope. "I'll get him." She turned and ran from the bedroom.

"You're going to be all right, Hallie," Dalacott said as he knelt again by the couch. He used the edge of a coverlet to dab perspiration from the boy's face and was dismayed to find that he could actually feel heat radiating from the beaded skin. Hallie gazed up at him mutely, and his lips quivered as he tried to smile. Dalacott noticed that the Ballinnian ptertha stick was lying on the couch. He picked it up and pressed it into Hallie's hand, closing the boy's nerveless fingers around the polished wood, then kissed him on the forehead. He prolonged the kiss, as though trying to siphon the consuming pyrexia into his own body, and only slowly became aware of two odd facts—that Conna was taking too long to return with the doctor, and that a woman was screaming in another part of the house.

"I'll come back to you in just a moment, soldier," he said. He stood up, tranced, made his way back to the dining room and saw that the guests were gathered around a man who was lying on the floor.

The man was Gehate—and from his fevered complexion and the feeble pawing of his hands it was evident that he was in an advanced stage of pterthacosis.

While he was waiting for the airship to be untethered, Dalacott slipped his hand into a pocket and located the curious nameless object he had found decades earlier on the banks of the Bes-Undar. His thumb worked in a circular pattern over the nugget's reflective surface, polished smooth by many years of similar frictions, as he tried to come to terms with the enormity of what had happened in the past nine days. The bare statistics conveyed little of the anguish which was withering his spirit.

Hallie had died before the end of the littlenight of his coming of age. Gehate and Ondobirtre had succumbed to the terrifying new form of pterthacosis by the end of that day, and on the following morning he had found Hallie's mother dead of the same cause in her room. That had been his first indication that the disease was contagious, and the implications had still been reverberating in his head when news had come of the fate of those who had been present at the celebration.

Of some forty men, women and children who had been in the villa, no fewer than thirty-two—including all the children—had been swept away during the same night. And still the tide of death had not expended its fell energies. The population of the hamlet of Klinterden and surrounding district had been reduced from approximately three-hundred to a mere sixty within three days. At that point the invisible killer had appeared to lose its virulence, and the burials had begun.

The airship's gondola lurched and swayed a little as it was freed from its constraints. Dalacott moved closer to a port hole and, for what he knew would be the last time, looked down on the familiar pattern of red-roofed dwellings, orchards and striated fields of grain. Its placid appearance masked the profound changes which had taken place, just as his own unaltered physical aspect disguised the fact that in nine days he had grown old.

The feeling—the drear apathy, the failure of optimism—was new to him, but he had no difficulty in identifying it because, for the first time ever, he could see cause to envy the dead.

PART II

The Proving Flight

CHAPTER 6

The Weapons Research Station was in the south-western outskirts of Ro-Atabri, in the old manufacturing district of Mardavan Quays. The area was low-lying, drained by a hesitant and polluted watercourse which discharged into the Borann below the city. Centuries of industrial usage had rendered the soil of Mardavan Quays sterile in some places, while in others there were great stands of wrongly-coloured vegetation nourished by unknown seepings and secretions, products of ancient cesspools and spoilheaps. Factories and storage buildings were copiously scattered on the landscape, linked by deep-rutted tracks, and half-hidden among them were groups of shabby dwellings from whose windows light rarely shone.

The Research Station did not look out of place in its surroundings, being a collection of nondescript workshops, sheds and shabby single-storey offices. Even the station chief's office was so grimy that the typical Kolcorronian diamond patterns of its brickwork were almost totally obscured.

Toller Maraquine found the station a deeply depressing place in which to work. Looking back to the time of his appointment, he could see that he had been childishly naïve in his visualisation of a weapons research establishment. He had anticipated perhaps a breezy sward with swordsmen busy testing new types of blades, or archers meticulously assessing the performance of laminated bows and novel patterns of arrowheads.

On arrival at the Quays it had taken him only a few hours to learn that there was very little genuine research on weapons being carried out under Borreat Hargeth. The name of the section disguised the fact that most of its funds were spent on trying to develop materials which could be substituted for brakka in the manufacture of gears and other machine components. Toller's work mainly consisted of mixing various fibres and powders with various types of resin and using the composite

97

to cast various shapes of test specimens. He disliked the choking smell of the resins and the repetitious nature of the task, especially as his instincts told him the project was a waste of time. None of the composite materials the station produced compared well with brakka, the hardest and most durable substance on the planet—and if nature had been obliging enough to supply an ideal material what was the point in searching for another?

Apart from the occasional grumble to Hargeth, however, Toller worked steadily and conscientiously, determined to prove to his brother that he was a responsible member of the family. His marriage to Fera also had something to do with his newfound steadiness, which was an unexpected benefit from an arrangement he had plunged into for the sole purpose of confounding his brother's wife. He had offered Fera the fourth grade—temporary, non-exclusive, terminable by the man at any time—but she had had the nerve to hold out for third grade status, which was binding on him for six years.

That had been more than fifty days ago, and Toller had hoped that by this time Gesalla would have softened in her attitude to both him and Fera, but if anything the triangular relationship had deteriorated. Irritant factors were Fera's monumental appetite and her capacity for indolence, both of which were an affront to the primly sedulous Gesalla, but Toller was unable to chastise his wife for refusing to amend her ways. She was claiming her right to be the person she had always been, regardless of whom she displeased, just as he was claiming the right to reside in the Maraquine family home. Gesalla was ever on the look-out for a pretext on which to have him dismissed from the Square House, and it was sheer stubbornness on his part which kept him from finding accommodation elsewhere.

Toller was pondering on his domestic situation one foreday, wondering how long the uneasy balance could be maintained, when he saw Hargeth coming into the shed where he was weighing out chopped glass fibres. Hargeth was a lean fidgety man in his early fifties and everything about him—nose, chin, ears, elbows, shoulders—seemed to be sharp-cornered. Today he appeared more restless than usual.

"Come with me, Toller," he said. "We have need of those muscles of yours."

Toller put his scoop aside. "What do you want me to do?"

"You're always complaining about not being able to work on engines of war—and now is your opportunity." Hargeth led the way to a small portable crane which had been erected on a patch of ground between two workshops. It was of conventional rafter wood construction except that the gear wheels, which would have been brakka in an ordinary crane, had been cast in a greyish composite produced by the research station.

"Lord Glo is arriving soon," Hargeth said. "He wants to demonstrate these gears to one of Prince Pouche's financial inspectors, and today we are going to have a preliminary test. I want you to check the cables, grease the gears carefully and fill the load basket with rocks."

"You spoke of a war engine," Toller said. "This is just a crane."

"Army engineers have to build fortifications and raise heavy equipment—so this is a war engine. The Prince's accountants must be kept happy, otherwise we lose funding. Now go to work—Glo will be here within the hour."

Toller nodded and began preparing the crane. The sun was only halfway to its daily occlusion by Overland, but there was no wind to scoop the heat out of the low-lying river basin and the temperature was climbing steadily. A nearby tannery was adding its stenches to the already fume-laden air of the station. Toller found himself longing for a pot of cool ale, but the Quays district boasted of only one tavern and it had such a verminous aspect that he would not consider sending an apprentice for a sample of its wares.

This is a miserly reward for a life of virtue, he thought disconsolately. *At least at Haffanger the air was fit to breathe.*

He had barely finished putting rocks into the crane's load basket when there came the sounds of harness and hoofbeats. Lord Glo's jaunty red-and-orange phaeton rolled through the station's gates and came to a halt outside Hargeth's office, looking incongruous amid the begrimed surroundings. Glo stepped down from the vehicle and had a long discussion with his driver before turning to greet Hargeth, who had ventured out to meet him. The two men conversed quietly for a minute, then came towards the crane.

Glo was holding a kerchief close to his nose, and it was obvious from his heightened colouring and a certain stateliness of his gait that he had already partaken generously of wine. Toller shook his head in a kind of amused respect for the single-mindedness with which the Lord Philosopher continued to render himself unfit for office. He stopped smiling when he noticed that several passing workers were whispering behind their hands. Why could Glo not place a higher value on his own dignity?

"There you are, my boy!" Glo called out on seeing Toller. "Do you know that, more than ever, you remind me of myself as a . . . hmm . . . young man?" He nudged Hargeth. "How is that for a splendid figure of a man, Borreat? That's how I used to look."

"Very good, my lord," Hargeth replied, noticeably unimpressed. "These wheels are the old Compound 18, but we have tried low-temperature curing on them and the results are quite encouraging, even though this crane is more-or-less a scale model. I'm sure it's a step in the right direction."

"I'm sure you're right, but let me see the thing at . . . hmm . . . work."

"Of course." Hargeth nodded to Toller, who began putting the crane through its paces. It was designed for operation by two men, but he was able to hoist the load on his own without undue effort, and directed by Hargeth he spent a few minutes rotating the jib and demonstrating the machine's load-placing accuracy. He was careful to make the operation as smooth as possible, to avoid feeding shocks into the gear teeth, and the display ended with the crane's moving parts in apparently excellent condition. The group of computational assistants and labourers who had gathered to watch the proceedings began to drift away.

Toller was lowering the load to its original resting when, without warning, the pawl with which he was controlling the descent sheared through several teeth on the main ratchet in a burst of staccato sound. The laden basket dropped a short distance before the cable drum locked, and the crane—with

Toller still at the controls—tilted dangerously on its base. It was saved from toppling when some of the watching labourers threw their weight on to the rising leg and brought it to the ground.

"My congratulations," Hargeth said scathingly as Toller stepped clear of the creaking structure. "How did you manage to do that?"

"If only you could invent a material stronger than stale porridge there'd be no. . . ." Toller broke off as he looked beyond Hargeth and saw that Lord Glo had fallen to the ground. He was lying with his face pressed against a ridge of dried clay, seemingly unable to move. Fearful that Glo might have been struck by a flying gear tooth, Toller ran and knelt beside him. Glo's pale blue eye turned in his direction, but still the rotund body remained inert.

"I'm not drunk," Glo mumbled, speaking from one side of his mouth. "Get me away from here, my boy—I think I'm halfway to being dead."

Fera Rivoo had adapted well to her new style of life in Greenmount Peel, but no amount of coaxing on Toller's part had ever persuaded her to sit astride a bluehorn or even one of the smaller whitehorns which were often favoured by women. Consequently, when Toller wanted to get away from the Peel with his wife for fresh air or simply a change of surroundings he was forced to go on foot. Walking was a form of exercise and travel for which he cared little because it was too tame and dictated too leisurely a pace of events, but Fera regarded it as the only way of getting about the city districts when no carriage was available to her.

"I'm hungry," she announced as they reached the Plaza of the Navigators, close to the centre of Ro-Atabri.

"Of course you are," Toller said. "Why, it must be almost an hour since your second breakfast."

She dug an elbow into his ribs and gave him a meaningful smile. "You want me to keep my strength up, don't you?"

"Has it occurred to you that there might be more to life than sex and food?"

"Yes—wine." She shaded her eyes from the early foreday sun and surveyed the nearest of the pastry vendors' stalls which were dotted along the square's perimeter. "I think I'll have some honeycake and perhaps some Kailian white to wash it down with."

Still uttering token protests, Toller made the necessary purchases and they sat on one of the benches which faced the statues of illustrious seafarers of the empire's past. The plaza was bounded by a mix of public and commercial buildings, most of which exhibited—in various shades of masonry and brick—the traditional Kolcorronian pattern of interlocked diamonds. Trees in contrasting stages of their maturation cycle and the colourful dress of passers-by added to the sunlit chiaroscuro. A westerly breeze was keeping the air pleasant and lively.

"I have to admit," Toller said, sipping some cool light wine, "that this is much better than working for Hargeth. I've never understood why scientific research work always seems to involve evil smells."

"You poor delicate creature!" Fera brushed a crumb from her chin. "If you want to know what a *real* stink is like you should try working in the fish market."

"No, thanks—I prefer to stay where I am," Toller replied. It was about twenty days since the sudden onset of Lord Glo's illness, but Toller was still appreciative of the resultant change in his own circumstances and employment. Glo had been stricken with a paralysis which affected the left side of his body and had found himself in need of a personal attendant, preferably one with an abundance of physical strength. When Toller had been offered the position he had accepted at once, and had moved with Fera to Glo's spacious residence on the western slope of Greenmount. The new arrangement, as well as providing a welcome relief from Mardavan Quays, had resolved the difficult situation in the Maraquine household, and Toller was making a conscientious effort to be content. A restless gloominess sometimes came upon him when he compared his menial existence to the kind of life he would have preferred, but it was something he always kept to himself. On the positive side, Glo had proved a considerate employer and as soon as he had regained a measure of his strength and mobility had made as few demands as possible on Toller's time.

"Lord Glo seemed busy this morning," Fera said. "I could hear that sunwriter of his clicking and clacking no matter where I went."

Toller nodded. "He's been talking a great deal with Tunsfo lately. I think he's worried about the reports from the provinces."

"There isn't really going to be a plague, is there, Toller?" Fera drew her shoulders forward in distaste, deepening the cleft in her bosom. "I can't bear having sick people around me."

"Don't worry! From what I hear they wouldn't be around you very long—about two hours seems to be the average."

"Toller!" Fera gazed at him in open-mouthed reproach, her tongue coated with a fine slurry of honeycake.

"There's nothing for you to fret about," Toller said reassuringly, even though—as he had gathered from Glo—something akin to a plague had begun simultaneously in eight widely separated places. Outbreaks had first been reported from the palatine provinces of Kail and Middac; then from the less important and more remote regions of Sorka, Merrill, Padale, Ballin, Yalrofac and Loongl. Since then there had been a lull of a few days, and Toller knew the authorities were hoping against hope that the calamity had been of a transient nature, that the disease had burned itself out, that the mother country of Kolcorron and the capital city would remain unaffected. Toller could understand their feelings, but he saw little grounds for optimism. If the ptertha had increased their killing range and potency to the awesome extent suggested by the dispatches, they were in his opinion bound to make maximum use of their new powers. The respite that mankind was enjoying could mean that the ptertha were behaving like an intelligent and ruthless enemy who, having successfully tested a new weapon, had retired only to regroup and prepare for a major onslaught.

"We should think about returning to the Peel soon." Toller drained his porcelain cup of wine and placed it under the bench for retrieval by the vendor. "Glo wants to bathe before little-night."

"I'm glad I won't have to help."

"He has his own kind of courage, you know. I don't think I could endure the life of a cripple, but I have yet to hear him utter a single word of complaint."

"Why do you keep talking about sickness when you know I don't like it?" Fera stood up and smoothed the wispy plumage of her clothing. "We have time to walk by the White Fountains, haven't we?"

"Only for a few minutes." Toller linked arms with his wife and they crossed the Plaza of the Navigators and walked along the busy avenue which led to the municipal gardens. The fountains sculpted in snowy Padalian marble were seeding the air with a refreshing coolness. Groups of people, some of them accompanied by children, were strolling amid the islands of bright foliage and their occasional laughter added to the idyllic tranquillity of the scene.

"I suppose this could be regarded as the epitome of civilised life," Toller said. "The only thing wrong with it—and this is strictly my own point of view—is that it is much too. . . ." He stopped speaking as the braying note of a heavy horn sounded from a nearby rooftop and was quickly echoed by others in more distant parts of the city.

"Ptertha!" Toller swung his gaze upwards to the sky.

Fera moved closer to him. "It's a mistake, isn't it, Toller? They don't come into the city."

"We'd better get out of the open just the same," Toller said, urging her towards the buildings on the north side of the gardens. People all about him were scanning the heavens, but—such was the power of conviction and habit—only a few were hurrying to take cover. The ptertha were an implacable natural enemy, but a balance had been struck long ago and the very existence of civilisation was predicated on the ptertha's behaviour patterns remaining constant and foreseeable. It was quite unthinkable that the blindly malevolent globes could make a sudden radical change in their habits—in that respect Toller was at one with the people around him—but the news from the provinces had implanted the seeds of unease deep in his consciousness. If the ptertha could change in one way—why not in another?

A woman screamed some distance to Toller's left, and the single inarticulate pulse of sound framed the real world's answer to his abstract musings. He looked in the direction of the scream and saw a single ptertha descend from the sun's cone of brilliance. The blue-and-purple globe sank into a crowded area at the centre of the gardens, and now men were screaming too, counterpointing the continuing blare of the alarm horns. Fera's body went rigid with shock as she glimpsed the ptertha in the last second of its existence.

"Come on!" Toller gripped her hand and sprinted towards the peristyled guildhalls to the north. In his pounding progress across the open ground he had scant time in which to look out for other ptertha, but it was no longer necessary to search for the globes. They could be readily seen now, drifting among the rooftops and domes and chimneys in placid sunlight.

There could only have been a few citizens of the Kolcorronian empire who had never had a nightmare about being caught on exposed ground amid a swarm of ptertha, and in the next hour Toller not only experienced the nightmare to the full but went beyond it into new realms of dread. Displaying their terrifying new boldness, the ptertha were descending to street level all over the city—silent and shimmering—invading gardens and precincts, bounding slowly across public squares, lurking in archways and colonnades. They were being annihilated by the panic-stricken populace, and it was here that the terms of the ancient nightmare became inadequate for the actuality— because Toller knew, with a bleak and wordless certainty, that the invaders represented the new breed of ptertha.

They were the plague-carriers.

In the long-running debate about the nature of the ptertha, those who spoke in support of the idea that the globes possessed some qualities of mind had always pointed to the fact that they judiciously avoided cities and large towns. Even in sizable swarms the ptertha would have been swiftly destroyed on venturing into an urban environment, especially in conditions of good visibility. The argument had been that they were less concerned with self-preservation than with avoiding wasting their numbers in futile attacks—clear evidence of mentation

—and the theory had had some validity when the ptertha's killing range was limited to a few paces.

But, as Toller had intuited at once, the livid globes drifting down in Ro-Atabri were plague-carriers.

For every one of them destroyed, many citizens would be lost to the new kind of poisonous dust which killed at great range, and the horror did not stop there—because the grim new rules of conflict decreed that each direct victim of a ptertha encounter would, in the brief time remaining to them, contaminate and carry off to the grave perhaps dozens of others.

An hour elapsed before the wind conditions changed and brought the first attack on Ro-Atabri to an end, but—in a city where every man, woman and child was suddenly a potential mortal enemy and had to be treated as such—Toller's nightmare was able to continue for much, much longer. . . .

A rare band of rain had swept over the region during the night and now, in the first quiet minutes after sunrise, Toller Maraquine found himself looking down from Greenmount on an unfamiliar world. Patches and streamers of ground-hugging mist garlanded the vistas below, in places obscuring Ro-Atabri more effectively than the blanket of ptertha screens which had been thrown over the city since the first attack, almost two years earlier. The triangular outline of Mount Opelmer rose out of an aureate haze to the east, its upper slopes tinted by the reddish sun which had just climbed into view.

Toller had awakened early and, driven by the restlessness which recently had been troubling him more and more, had decided to get up and walk alone in the grounds of the Peel.

He began by pacing along the inner defensive screen and checking that the nets were securely in place. Until the onslaught of the plague only rural habitations had needed ptertha barriers, and in those days simple nets and trellises had been adequate —but all at once, in town and country alike, it had become necessary to erect more elaborate screens which created a thirty-yard buffer zone around protected areas. A single layer of netting still sufficed for the roofs of most enclosures, because the ptertha toxins were borne away horizontally in the wind, but it was vital that the perimeters should be double screens, widely separated and supported by strong scaffolding.

Lord Glo had gratified Toller by giving him, in addition to his normal duties, the responsible and sometimes dangerous task of overseeing the construction of the screens for the Peel and some other philosophy buildings. The feeling that he was at last doing something important and useful had made him less unruly, and the risks of working in the open had provided satisfactions of a different kind. Borreat Hargeth's only significant contribution to the anti-ptertha armoury had been the development of an odd-looking L-shaped throwing stick which flew faster and farther than the standard Kolcorronian cruciform, and in which in the hands of a good man could destroy globes at more than forty yards. While supervising screen construction Toller had perfected his skill with the new weapon, and prided himself on having lost no workers directly to the ptertha.

That phase of his life had drawn to its ordained close, however, and now—in spite of all his efforts—he was burdened with a sense of having been caught like a fish in the very nets he had helped to construct. Considering that more than two thirds of the empire's population had been swept away by the virulent new form of pterthacosis, he should have been counting himself fortunate to be alive and healthy, with food, shelter and a lusty woman to share his bed—but none of those considerations could offset the gnawing conviction that his life was going to waste. He instinctively rejected the Church's teaching that he had an endless succession of incarnations ahead of him, alternating between Land and Overland; he had been granted only one life, one precious span of existence, and the prospect of squandering what remained of it was intolerable.

Despite the buoyant freshness of the morning air, Toller felt his chest begin to heave and his lungs to labour as though with suffocation. Close to sudden irrational panic, desperate for a physical outlet for his emotions, he reacted as he had not done since his time of exile on the Loongl peninsula. He opened a gate in the Peel's inner screen, crossed the buffer zone and went through the outer screen to stand on the unprotected slope of Greenmount. A strip of pasture—deeded to the philosophy order long ago—stretched before him for several furlongs, its lower end slanting down into trees and mist. The air was almost completely still, so there was little chance of encountering a stray globe, but the symbolic act of defiance had an easing effect on the psychological pressure which had been building within him.

He unhooked a ptertha stick from his belt and was preparing to walk farther down the hill when his attention was caught by a movement at the bottom edge of the pasture. A lone rider was emerging from the swath of woodland which separated the philosophers' demesne from the adjacent city district of Silarbri. Toller brought out his telescope, treasured possession, and with its aid determined that the rider was in the King's service and that he bore on his chest the blue-and-white plume-and-sword symbol of a courier.

His interest aroused, Toller sat down on a natural bench of rock to observe the newcomer's progress. He was reminded of a previous time when the arrival of a royal messenger had heralded his escape from the miseries of the Loongl research station, but on this occasion the circumstances were vastly different. Lord Glo had been virtually ignored by the Great Palace since the débâcle in the Rainbow Hall. In the old days the delivery of a message by hand could have implied that it was privy, not to be entrusted to a sunwriter, but now it was difficult to imagine King Prad wanting to communicate with the Lord Philosopher about anything at all.

The rider was approaching slowly and nonchalantly. By taking a slightly more circuitous route he could have made the entire journey to Glo's residence under the smothering nets of the city's ptertha screens, but it looked as though he was enjoying the short stretch of open sky in spite of the slight risk of having a ptertha descend on him. Toller wondered if the messenger had a spirit similar to his own, one which chafed under the stringent anti-ptertha precautions which enabled what was left of the population to continue with their beleaguered existences.

The great census of 2622, taken only four years earlier, had established that the empire's population consisted of almost two million with full Kolcorronian citizenship and some four million with tributary status. By the end of the first two plague years the total remaining was estimated at rather less than two million. A minute proportion of those who survived did so because, inexplicably, they had some degree of immunity to the secondary infection, but the vast majority went in continual fear for their lives, emulating the lowliest vermin in their burrows. Unscreened dwellings had been fitted with airtight seals which were clamped over doors, windows and chimney openings during ptertha alerts, and outside the cities and townships the ordinary people had deserted their farms and taken to living in woodlands and forests, the natural fortresses which the globes were unable to penetrate.

As a result agricultural output had fallen to a level which was insufficient even for the greatly reduced needs of a depleted population, but Toller—with the unconscious egocentricity of the young—had little thought to spare for the statistics which told of calamities on a national scale. To him they amounted to little more than a shadow play, a vaguely shifting background to the central drama of his own affairs, and it was in the hope of learning something to his personal advantage that he stood up to greet the arriving king's messenger.

"Good foreday," he said, smiling. "What brings you to Greenmount Peel?"

The courier was a gaunt man with a world-weary look to him, but he nodded pleasantly enough as he reined his bluehorn to a halt. "The message I bear is for Lord Glo's eyes only."

"Lord Glo is still asleep. I am Toller Maraquine, Lord Glo's personal attendant and a hereditary member of the philosophy order. I have no wish to pry, but my lord is not a well man and he would be displeased were I to awaken him at this hour except for a matter of considerable urgency. Let me have the gist of your message so that I may decide what should be done."

"The message tube is sealed." The courier produced a mock-rueful smile. "And I'm not supposed to be aware of its contents."

Toller shrugged, playing a familiar game. "That's a pity—I was hoping that you and I could have made our lives a little easier."

"Fine grazing land," the courier said, turning in the saddle to appraise the pasture he had just ridden through. "I imagine his lordship's household has not been greatly affected by the food shortages. . . ."

"You must be hungry after riding all the way out here," Toller said. "I would be happy to set you down to a hero's breakfast, but perhaps there is no time. Perhaps I have to go immediately and rouse Lord Glo."

"Perhaps it would be more considerate to allow his lordship to enjoy his rest." The courier swung himself down to stand beside Toller. "The King is summoning him to a special meeting in the Great Palace, but the appointment is four days hence. It scarcely seems to be a matter of great urgency."

"Perhaps," Toller said, frowning as he tried to evaluate the surprising new information. "Perhaps not."

CHAPTER 7

"I'm not at all sure that I'm doing the right thing," Lord Glo said as Toller Maraquine finished strapping him into his walking frame. "I think it would be much more prudent—not to mention being more fair to you—if I were to take one of the servants to the Great Palace with me and . . . hmm . . . leave you here. There is enough work to be done around the place, work which would keep you out of trouble."

"It has been two years," Toller replied, determined not to be excluded. "And Leddravohr has had so much on his mind that he has probably forgotten all about me."

"I wouldn't count on it, my boy—the prince has a certain reputation in these matters. Besides, if I know you, you're quite likely to give him a reminder."

"Why would I do something so unwise?"

"I've been watching you lately. You're like a brakka tree which is overdue for a blow-out."

"I don't do that sort of thing any more." Toller made the protest automatically, as he had often done in the past, but it came to him that he had in fact changed considerably since his first encounter with the military prince. His occasional periods of restlessness and dissatisfaction were proof of the change, because of the way in which he dealt with them. Instead of working himself up to a state in which the slightest annoyance was liable to trigger an outburst, he had learned—like other men—to divert or sublimate his emotional energies. He had schooled himself to accept an accretion of minor joys and satisfactions in place of that single great fulfilment which was yearned for by so many and destined for so few.

"Very well, young man," Glo said as he adjusted a buckle. "I'm going to trust you, but please remember that this is a uniquely important occasion and conduct yourself accordingly. I will hold you to your word on this point. You realise, of course, why the King has seen fit to . . . hmm . . . summon me?"

"Is it a return to the days when we were consulted on the great imponderables of life? Does the King want to know why men have nipples but can't suckle?"

Glo sniffed. "Your brother has the same unfortunate tendency towards coarse sarcasm."

"I'm sorry."

"You're not, but I'll enlighten you just the same. The idea I planted in the King's mind two years ago has finally borne fruit. Remember what you said about my flying higher and seeing . . . ? No, that was Lain. But here's something for you to . . . hmm . . . think about, young Toller. I'm getting on in years and haven't much longer to go—but I'll wager you a thousand nobles that I will set foot on Overland before I die."

"I would never challenge your word on any subject," Toller said diplomatically, marvelling at the older man's talent for self-deception. Anybody else, with the possible exception of Vorndal Sisstt, would have remembered the council meeting with shame. So great was the philosophers' disgrace that they would surely have been deposed from Greenmount had the monarchy not been preoccupied with the plague and its consequences—yet Glo still nurtured his belief that he was highly regarded by the King and that his fantasising about the colonisation of Overland could be taken seriously. Since the onset of his illness Glo had shunned alcohol, and was able to comport himself better as a result, but his senility remained to distort his view of reality. Toller's private guess was that Glo had been summoned to the palace to account for the continuing failure to produce the efficacious long-range anti-ptertha weapon which was vital if normal agriculture were to resume.

"We've got to make haste," Glo said. "Can't risk being late on our day of triumph." With Toller's help he donned his formal grey robe, working it down over the cane framework which enabled him to stand on his own. His formerly rotund body had shrunk to a loose-skinned slightness, but he had left his clothing unaltered to accommodate and hide the frame, hoping to disguise the extent of his disability. It was one of the human foibles which had earned him Toller's sympathy.

112

"We'll get you there in good time," Toller said reassuringly, wondering if he should be trying to prepare Glo for the possible ordeal that lay ahead.

The drive to the Great Palace took place in silence, with Glo nodding ruminatively to himself now and then as he rehearsed his intended address.

It was a moist grey morning, the gloom of which was deepened by the anti-ptertha screens overhead. The level of illumination had not been reduced a great deal in those streets where it had been sufficient to put up a roof of netting or lattices supported on canes which ran horizontally from eave to eave. But where there were roofs and parapets of different heights in proximity to each other it had been necessary to erect heavy and complicated structures, many of which were clad with varnished textiles to prevent air currents and downdraughts from carrying ptertha dust through countless apertures in buildings which were designed for an equatorial climate. Many of the once-glittering avenues in the heart of Ro-Atabri now had a cavernous dimness to them, the city's architecture having been clogged and obscured and rendered claustrophobic by the defensive shroud.

The Bytran Bridge, the main river crossing on the way south, had been completely sheathed with timber, giving it something of the appearance of a giant warehouse, and from there a tunnel-like covered way crossed the moats and led to the Great Palace, which was now draped and tented. Toller's first intimation that the meeting was going to be different from that of two years earlier came when he noticed the lack of carriages in the principal courtyard. Apart from a handful of official equippages, only his brother's lightweight brougham—acquired after the banning of team-drawn vehicles—waited near the entrance. Lain was standing alone by the brougham with a slim roll of paper under his arm. His narrow face looked pale and tired under the sweeps of black hair. Toller jumped down and assisted Glo to leave his carriage, discreetly taking his full weight until he had steadied himself.

"You didn't tell me this was going to be a private audience," Toller said.

Glo gave him a look of humorous disdain, momentarily appearing his old self. "I can't be expected to tell you everything, young man—it's important for the Lord Philosopher to be aloof and . . . hmm . . . enigmatic now and again." Leaning heavily on Toller's arm, he limped towards the carved arch of the entrance, where they were joined by Lain.

During the exchange of greetings Toller, who had not seen his brother for some forty days, was concerned at Lain's obvious debility. He said, "Lain, I hope you're not working too hard."

Lain made a wry grimace. "Working too hard and sleeping too little. Gesalla is pregnant again and it's affecting her more than the last time."

"I'm sorry." Toller was surprised to hear that, after her miscarriage of almost two years ago, Gesalla was still determined on motherhood. It indicated a maternal instinct which he had trouble in reconciling with the rest of her character. Apart from the single curious shift in his perception of Gesalla on his return from the disastrous council meeting, he had always seen her as being too dry, too well-ordered and too fond of her personal autonomy to enjoy rearing children.

"By the way, she sends her regards," Lain added.

Toller smiled broadly to signal his disbelief as the three men proceeded into the palace. Glo directed them through the muted activity of the corridors to a glasswood door which was well away from the administrative areas. The black-armoured ostiaries on duty were a sign that the King was within. Toller felt Glo's body stiffen with exertion as he strove to present a good appearance, and he in turn tried to look as though he was giving Glo only minimal assistance as they entered the audience chamber.

The apartment was hexagonal and quite small, lighted by a single window, and the only furnishings were a single hexagonal table and six chairs. King Prad was already seated opposite the window and by his side were the princes Leddravohr and Chakkell, all of them informally attired in loose silks. Prad's sole mark of distinction was a large blue jewel which was suspended from his neck by a glass chain. Toller, who had a strong desire for the occasion to pass off smoothly for the sake of his brother and Lord Glo, avoided looking in Leddravohr's direction. He kept his eyes down until the King signalled for Glo and Lain to be seated, then he gave all his attention to getting Glo into a chair with a minimum of creaking from his frame.

"I apologise for this delay, Majesty," Glo said when finally at ease, speaking in high Kolcorronian. "Do you wish my attendant to retire?"

Prad shook his head. "He may remain for your comfort, Lord Glo—I had not appreciated the extent of your incapacity."

"A certain recalcitrance of the . . . hmm . . . limbs, that is all," Glo replied stoically.

"Nevertheless, I am grateful for the effort you made to be here. As you can see, I am dispensing with all formality so that we may have an unimpeded exchange of ideas. The circumstances of our last meeting were hardly conducive to free discussion, were they?"

Toller, who had positioned himself behind Glo's chair, was surprised by the King's amiable and reasonable tones. It seemed as though his own pessimism had been ill-founded and that Glo was to be spared fresh humiliation. He looked directly across the table for the first time and saw that Prad's expression was indeed as reassuring as it could be on features that were dominated by one inhuman, marble-white eye. Toller's gaze, without his conscious bidding, swung towards Leddravohr and he experienced a keen psychic shock as he realised that the prince's eyes had been drilling into him all the while, projecting unmistakable malice and contempt.

I'm a different person, Toller told himself, checking the reflexive defiant spreading of his shoulders. *Glo and Lain are not going to be harmed in any way by association with me.*

He lowered his head, but not before he had glimpsed Leddravohr's smile flick into being, the effortless snake-fast twitch of his upper lip. Toller was unable to decide on a course of action or inaction. It appeared that all the things they whispered about Leddravohr were true, that he had an excellent memory for faces and an even better one for insults. The immediate difficulty for Toller lay in that, determined though he was not to cross Leddravohr, it was out of the question for him to stand with his head lowered for perhaps the whole foreday. Could he find a pretext to leave the room, perhaps something to do with . . . ?

"I want to talk about flying to Overland," the King said, his words a conceptual bomb-blast which blew everything else out of Toller's consciousness. "Are you, in your official capacity as Lord Philosopher, stating that it can be done?"

"I am, Majesty." Glo glanced at Leddravohr and the dark-jowled Chakkell as though daring them to object. "We can fly to Overland."

"How?"

"By means of very large hot air balloons, Majesty."

"Go on."

"Their lifting power would have to be augmented by gas jets—but it is providential that in the region where the balloons would practically cease to function the jets would be their most effective." Glo was speaking strongly and without hesitations, as he could sometimes do when inspired. "The jets would also serve to turn the balloons over at the midpoint of the flight, thus enabling them to descend in the normal manner.

"I repeat, Majesty—we can fly to Overland."

Glo's words were followed by an air-whispering silence during which Toller, bemused with wonder, looked down at his brother to see if—as before—the talk of flying to Overland had come as a shock to him. Lain appeared nervous and ill at ease, but not at all surprised. He and Glo must have been in collaboration, and if Lain believed that the flight could be made—then it could be made! Toller felt a stealthy coolness spread down his spine to the accompaniment of what for him was a totally new intellectual and emotional experience. *I have a future*, he thought. *I have discovered why I am here.* . . .

"Tell us more, Lord Glo," the King said. "This hot air balloon you speak of—has it been designed?"

"Not only has it been designed, Majesty—the archives show that an example was actually fabricated in the year 2187. It was successfully flown several times that year by a philosopher called Usader, and it is believed—although the records are . . . hmm . . . vague on this point—that in 2188 he actually attempted the Overland flight."

"What happened to him?"

"He was never heard of again."

"That hardly inspires confidence," Chakkell put in, speaking for the first time. "It's hardly a record of achievement."

"That depends on one's viewpoint." Glo refused to be discouraged. "Had Usader returned a few days later one might be entitled to describe his flight as a failure. The fact that he did *not* return could indicate that he had succeeded."

Chakkell snorted. "More likely that he died!"

"I'm not claiming that such an ascent would be easy or without its share of . . . hmm . . . risks. My contention is that our increased scientific knowledge could reduce the risks to an acceptable level. Given sufficient determination—and the proper financial and material resources—we can produce ships capable of flying to Overland."

Prince Leddravohr sighed audibly and shifted in his chair, but refrained from speaking. Toller guessed that the King had placed powerful restraints on him before the meeting began.

"You make it all sound rather like an aftday jaunt," King Prad said. "But isn't it a fact that Land and Overland are almost five-thousand miles apart?"

"The best triangulations give a figure of 4,650 miles, Majesty. Surface to surface, that is."

"How long would it take to fly that distance?"

"I regret I cannot give a definite answer to that question at this stage."

"It's an important question, isn't it?"

"Undoubtedly! The speed of ascent of the balloon is of fundamental importance, Majesty, but there are many variables to be . . . hmm . . . considered." Glo signalled for Lain to open his roll of paper. "My chief scientist, who is a better mathematician than I, has been working on the preliminary calculations. With your consent, he will explain the problem."

Lain spread out a chart with trembling hands, and Toller was relieved to see that he had had the foresight to draw it on a limp cloth-based paper which quickly lay flat. Part of it was taken up by a scale diagram which illustrated the sister worlds and their spatial relationships; the remainder was given over to detailed sketches of pear-shaped balloons and complicated gondolas. Lain swallowed with difficulty a couple of times and Toller grew tense, fearing that his brother was unable to speak.

"This circle represents our own world . . . with its diameter of 4,100 miles," Lain finally articulated. "The other, smaller circle represents Overland, whose diameter is generally accepted as being 3,220 miles, at its fixed point above our equator on the zero meridian, which passed through Ro-Atabri."

"I think we all learned that much basic astronomy in our infancy," Prad said. "Why can't you say how long the journey from the one to the other will take?"

Lain swallowed again. "Majesty, the size of the balloon and the weight of the load we attach to it will influence the free ascent speed. The difference in temperature between the gases inside the balloon and the surrounding atmosphere is another factor, but the most important governing factor is the amount of crystals available to power the jets.

"Greater fuel economy would be achieved by allowing the balloon to rise to its maximum height—slowing down all the while—and not using the jets until the gravitational pull of Land had grown weak. That, of course, would entail lengthening the transit time and therefore increasing the weight of food and water to be carried, which in turn would. . . ."

"Enough, enough! My head swims!" The King held out both his hand, fingers slightly crooked as though cradling an invisible balloon. "Settle your mind on a ship which will carry, say, twenty people. Imagine that crystals are reasonably plentiful. Now, how long will it take that ship to reach Overland? I don't expect you to be precise—simply give me a figure which I can lodge in my cranium."

Lain, paler than ever, but with growing assurance, ran a fingertip down some columns of figures at the side of his chart. "Twelve days, Majesty."

"At last!" Prad glanced significantly at Leddravohr and Chakkell. "Now—for the same ship—how much of the green and purple will be required?"

Lain raised his head and stared at the King with troubled eyes. The King gazed back at him, calmly and intently, as he waited for his answer. Toller sensed that wordless communication was taking place, that something beyond his understanding was happening. His brother seemed to have transcended all his nervousness and irresolution, to have acquired a strange authority which—for the moment, at least—placed him on a level with the ruler. Toller felt a surge of family pride as he saw that the King appeared to acknowledge Lain's new stature and was prepared to give him all the time he needed to formulate his reply.

"May I take it, Majesty," Lain said at length, "that we are talking about a one-way flight?"

The King's white eye narrowed. "You may."

"In that case, Majesty, the ship would require approximately thirty pounds each of pikon and halvell."

"Thank you. You're not going to quibble over the fact that a higher proportion of halvell gives the best result in sustained burning?"

Lain shook his head. "Under the circumstances—no."

"You are a valuable man, Lain Maraquine."

"Majesty, I don't understand this," Glo protested, echoing Toller's own puzzlement. "There is no conceivable reason for providing a ship with only enough fuel for one transit."

"A single ship, no," the King said. "A small fleet, no. But when we are talking about. . . ." He turned his attention back to Lain. "How many ships would you say?"

Lain produced a bleak smile. "A thousand seems a good round figure, Majesty."

"A *thousand!*" There was a creaking sound from Glo's cane frame as he made an abortive attempt to stand up, and when he spoke again an aggrieved note had crept into his voice. "Am I the only person here who is to be kept in ignorance of the subject under discussion?"

The King made a placating gesture. "There is no conspiracy, Lord Glo—it's merely that your chief scientist appears to have the ability to read minds. It would please me to learn how he divined what was in my thoughts."

Lain stared down at his hands and spoke almost abstractedly, almost as though musing aloud. "For more than two-hundred days I have been unable to obtain any statistics on agricultural output or ptertha casualties. The official explanation was that the provincial administrators were too severely overworked to prepare their returns—and I have been trying to persuade myself that such was the case—but the indicators were already there, Majesty. In a way it is a relief to have my worst fears confirmed. The only way to deal with a crisis is to face up to it."

"I agree with you," Prad said, "but I was concerned with avoiding a general panic, hence the secrecy. I had to be certain."

"Certain?" Gło's large head turned from side to side. "Certain? Certain?"

"Yes, Lord Glo," the King said gravely. "I had to be certain that our world was coming to an end."

On hearing the bland statement Toller felt a unique emotional pang. Any fear which might have been part of it fled at once before curiosity and an overwhelming, selfish and gloating sense of privilege. The most momentous events in history were being staged for his personal benefit. For the first time in his life, he was in love with the future.

". . . as though the ptertha were encouraged by the events of the past two years, in the manner of a warrior who sees that his foe is weakening," the King was saying. "Their numbers are increasing—and who is to say that their foul emissions will not become even more deadly? It has happened once, and it can happen again.

"We in Ro-Atabri have been comparatively fortunate thus far, but throughout the empire the people are dying from the insidious new form of pterthacosis in spite of all our efforts to fend the globes off. And the newborn, upon whom our future depends, are the most vulnerable. We might be facing the prospect of slowly dwindling into a pitiful, doomed handful of sterile old men and women—were it not for the looming spectre of famine. The agricultural regions are becoming incapable of producing food in the quantities which are necessary for the upkeep of our cities, even allowing for our vastly reduced urban populations."

The King paused to give his audience a thin sad smile. "There are some among us who maintain that there is still room for hope, that fate may yet relent and wheel against the ptertha —but Kolcorron did not become great by supinely trusting to chance. That attitude is foreign to our national character. When forced to yield ground in a battle, we withdraw to a secure redoubt where we can gather our strength and determination to surge forth again and overwhelm our enemies.

"In the present case, as befits the ultimate conflict, there is the ultimate redoubt—and its name is Overland.

"It is my royal decree that we shall prepare to withdraw to Overland—not in order to cower away from our enemy, but to grow numerous and powerful again, to gain time in which to devise means of destroying the ptertha in their loathsome entirety, and finally—regardless of how long it may take—to return to our home world of Land as a glorious and invincible army which will triumphantly lay claim to all that is naturally and rightfully ours."

The King's oratory, enhanced by the formalism of the high tongue, had carried Toller along with it, opening up new perspectives in his mind, and it was with some surprise that he realised no response was forthcoming from either his brother or Glo. The latter was so immobile that he might have been dead, and Lain continued to stare down at his hands as he twisted the brakka ring on his sixth finger. Toller wondered, with a twinge of guilt, if Lain was thinking of Gesalla and the baby which would be born into turbulent times.

Prad ended the silence by choosing, oddly in Toller's view, to address himself to Lain. "Well, wrangler? Have you another demonstration of mind reading for us?"

Lain raised his head and eyed the King steadily. "Majesty, even when our armies were at their most powerful, we avoided going against Chamteth."

"I resent the implications of that remark," Prince Leddravohr snapped. "I demand that. . . ."

"Your *promise*, Leddravohr!" The King rounded angrily on his son. "I would remind you of your promise to me. Be patient! Your time is at hand."

Leddravohr raised both hands in a gesture of resignation as he settled back in his chair, and now his brooding gaze was fixed on Lain. The spasm of alarm Toller felt over his brother's welfare was almost lost in the silent clamour of his reaction to the mention of Chamteth. Why had he been so slow to appreciate that an interplanetary migration fleet, if it were ever constructed, would require power crystals on such a vast scale that its needs could be met from only one scource? If the King's awesome plans also included going to war against the enigmatic and insular Chamtethans, then the near future was going to be even more turbulent than Toller could readily visualise.

Chamteth was a country so huge that it could be reached just as readily by travelling east or west into the Land of the Long Days, that hemisphere of the world which was not swept by Overland's shadow and where there was no littlenight to punctuate the sun's progress across the sky. In the distant past several ambitious rulers had tried probing into Chamteth and the outcome had been so convincing, so disastrous that Chamteth had virtually been erased from the national consciousness. It existed, but—as with Overland—its existence had no relevance to the quotidian affairs of the empire.

Until now, Toller thought, striving to rebuild his picture of the universe. *Chamteth and Overland are linked . . . bonded . . . to take one is to take the other. . . .*

"War against Chamteth has become inevitable," the King said. "Some are of the opinion that it always has been inevitable. What do you say, Lord Glo?"

"Majesty, I. . . ." Glo cleared his throat and sat up straighter. "Majesty, I have always regarded myself as a creative thinker, but I freely admit that the grandeur and scope of your vision have taken my . . . hmm . . . breath away. When I originally proposed flying to Overland I envisaged despatching a small number of pathfinders, followed by the gradual establishment of a small colony. I had not dreamed of migration on the scale you are contemplating, but I can assure you that I am equal to the responsibilities involved. The designing of a suitable ship and the planning of all the necessary. . . ." Glo stopped speaking as he saw that Prad was shaking his head.

"My dear Lord Glo, you are not a well man," the King said,

"and I would be less than fair to you if I permitted you to expend what remains of your strength on a task of such magnitude."

"But, Majesty. . . ."

The King's face hardened. "Do not interrupt! The extremity of our situation demands equally extreme measures. The entire resources of Kolcorron must be reorganised and mobilised, and therefore I am dissolving all the old dynastic family structures. In their place—as of this moment—is a single pyramid of authority. Its executive head is my son, Prince Leddravohr, who will control and coordinate every aspect—military and civil—of our national affairs. He is seconded by Prince Chakkell, who will be responsible to him for the construction of the migration fleet."

The King paused, and when he spoke again his voice had none of the attributes of humanity. "Be it understood that Prince Leddravohr's authority is absolute, that his power is unlimited, and that to go counter to his wishes in any respect is a crime equivalent to high treason."

Toller closed his eyes, knowing that when he opened them again the world of his childhood and youth would have passed into history, and that in its place would be a dangerous new cosmos in which his tenure might be all too brief.

CHAPTER 8

Leddravohr was mentally tired after the meeting and had been hoping to relax during dinner, but his father—with the abundant cerebral energy which characterises some elderly men—talked all the way through the meal. He switched rapidly and effortlessly from military strategy to food rationing schemes to the technicalities of interworld flight, displaying his fascination with detail, trying to explore mutually incompatible probabilities. Leddravohr, who had no taste for juggling with abstracts, was relieved when the meal was finished and his father moved out to the balcony for a final cup of wine before retiring to his private quarters.

"Damn this glass," Prad said, tapping the transparent cupola which enclosed the balcony. "I used to enjoy taking the air here at night. Now I can scarcely breathe."

"Without the glass you wouldn't be breathing at all." Leddravohr flicked his thumb, indicating a group of three ptertha drifting overhead across the glowing face of Overland. The sun had gone down and now the sister world was entering the gibbous phases of its illumination, casting its mellow light over the southern reaches of the city, Arle Bay and the deep indigo expanses of the Gulf of Tronom. The light was good enough to read by and would steadily increase in strength as Overland, keeping pace with the rotation of Land, swung towards its point of opposition with the sun. Although the sky had darkened only to a rich mid-blue the stars, some of which were bright enough to be visible in full daylight, formed blazing patterns from Overland's rim down to the horizon.

"Damn the ptertha, too," Prad said. "You know, son, one of the greatest tragedies of our past is that we never learned where the globes come from. Even if they are spawned somewhere in the upper atmosphere, it might have been possible at one time to

124

track them down and destroy them at source. It's too late now, though."

"What about your triumphant return from Overland? Attacking the ptertha from above?"

"Too late for me, I mean. History will remember me for the outward flight only."

"Ah, yes—history," Leddravohr said, once again wondering at his father's preoccupation with the pale and spurious immortality offered by books and graven monuments. Life was a transient thing, impossible to extend beyond its natural term, and time spent in trying to do so was a squandering of the very commodity one was seeking to preserve. Leddravohr's own belief was that the only way to cheat death, or at least reconcile oneself to it, was to achieve every ambition and sate every appetite, so that when the time came the relinquishing of life was little more than discarding an empty gourd.

His single overriding ambition had been to extend his future kingship to every quarter of Land—including Chamteth—but that was now denied him by a connivance of fate. In its place was the prospect of a hazardous and *unnatural* flight into the sky, followed by little more than a tribal existence on an unknown world. He was angry about that, filled with a gnawing canker of rage unlike anything he had ever known, and somebody would have to pay. . . .

Prad sipped pensively at his wine. "Have you prepared all your dispatches?"

"Yes—the messengers leave at first light." Leddravohr had spent all his free time after the meeting personally writing orders to the five generals he wanted for his staff. "I instructed them to use continuous thrust, so we should have distinguished company quite soon."

"I take it you have chosen Dalacott."

"He's still the best tactician we have."

"Aren't you afraid that his edge might be blunted?" Prad said. "He must be seventy now, and being down in Kail when the plague broke out there can't have done him much good. Didn't he lose a daughter and a grandchild on the very first day?"

"Something like that," Leddravohr replied carelessly. "*He* is still healthy, though. Still of value."

"He must have the immunity." Prad's face became more animated as he fastened on to yet another of his talking points. "You know, Glo sent me some very interesting statistics at the beginning of the year. They were collated by Maraquine. They showed that the incidence of plague deaths among military personnel—which you would expect to be high because of their exposure—is actually somewhat lower than for the population in general. And, significantly, long-serving soldiers and airmen are the least likely to succumb. Maraquine suggested that years of being near ptertha kills and absorbing minute traces of the dust might train the body to resist pterthacosis. It's an intriguing thought."

"Father, it's a totally useless thought."

"I wouldn't say that. If the offspring of immune men and women were also immune, from birth, then you could breed a new race for whom the globes were no threat."

"And what good would that be to you and me?" Leddravohr said, disposing of the argument to his own satisfaction. "No, as far as I'm concerned Glo and Maraquine and their ilk are ornaments we can well do without. I look forward to the day when. . . ."

"*Enough!*" His father was suddenly King Prad Neldeever, ruler of the empire of Kolcorron, tall and rigid, with one terrible blind eye and one equally fearsome all-seeing eye which knew everything Leddravohr would have wished to keep secret. "Ours will not be the house which is remembered for turning its back on learning. You will give me your word that you will not harm Glo or Maraquine."

Leddravohr shrugged. "You have my word."

"That came easily." His father stared at him for a moment, dissatisfied, then said, "Neither will you touch Maraquine's brother, the one who now attends to Glo."

"That oaf! I have more important things with which to occupy my mind."

"I know. I have given you unprecedented powers because you have the qualities necessary to bring a great endeavour to a successful conclusion, and that power is not to be abused."

"Spare me all this, father," Leddravohr protested, laughing to conceal his resentment at being admonished like a wilful child. "I intend to treat our philosophers with all the consideration they deserve. Tomorrow I'm going to Greenmount for two or three days—to learn all I need to know about their skyships —and if you care to make enquiries you'll hear that I am emanating nothing but courtesy and love."

"Don't overdo it." Prad drained his cup with a flourish, set it down on the wide stone balustrade and prepared to leave. "Good night, son. And remember—the future watches."

As soon as the King had departed Leddravohr exchanged his wine for a glass of fiery Padalian brandy and returned to the balcony. He sat down on a leather couch and gazed moodily at the southern sky where three great comets plumed the star fields. *The future watches!* His father was still cherishing the notion of going down in history as another King Bytran, blinding himself to the probability that there would be no historians to record his achievements. The story of Kolcorron was drawing to a bizarre and ignominious end just when it should have been entering the most glorious era of all.

And I'm the one who is losing most, Leddravohr thought. *I'm never going to be a real King.*

As he continued drinking brandy, and the night grew steadily brighter, it came to Leddravohr that there was an anomaly in the contrast between his attitude and that of his father. Optimism was the prerogative of the young, and yet the King was looking to the future with confidence; pessimism was a trait of the old, and yet it was Leddravohr who was gloomy and prey to grim forebodings. Why?

Was it that his father was too wrapped up in his enthusiasm for all things scientific to concede that the migration was impossible? Leddravohr took stock of his thoughts and was forced to discard the theory. At some stage in the day-long meeting he had been persuaded by the drawings, the graphs and the chains of figures, and now he believed that a skyship could reach the sister world. What, then, was the underlying cause of the malaise which had entered his soul? The future was not completely black, after all—there was the final war with Chamteth to anticipate.

As Leddravohr tilted his head back to finish a glass of brandy his gaze drifted towards the zenith—and suddenly he had his answer. The great disk of Overland was now almost fully illuminated and its face was just starting to show the prismatic changes which heralded its nightly plunge into the shadow of Land. Deepnight—that period when the world experienced real darkness—was beginning, and it had its counterpart in Leddravohr's mind.

He was a soldier, professionally immune to fear, and that was why he had been so slow to acknowledge or even identify the emotion which had lurked in his consciousness for most of the day.

He was afraid of the Overland flight!

What he felt was not straightforward apprehension over the undeniable risks involved—it was pure, primitive and unmanning terror at the very idea of ascending thousands of miles into the unforgiving blueness of the sky. The force of his dread was such that when the awful moment for embarkation arrived he might be unable to control himself. He, Prince Leddravohr Neldeever, might break down and cower away like a frightened child, possibly having to be carried bodily on to the skyship in full view of thousands. . . .

Leddravohr jumped to his feet and hurled his glass away, smashing it on the balcony's stone floor. There was a hideous irony in the fact that his introduction to fear should have taken place not on the field of battle, but in the quietness of a small room, at the hands of stammering nonentities, with their scribbles and scratchings and their casual visions of the unthinkable.

Breathing deeply and steadily as an aid to regaining mastery of his emotions, Leddravohr watched the blackness of deepnight envelope the world, and when he finally retired to bed his face had regained its sculpted composure.

CHAPTER 9

"It's getting late," Toller said. "Perhaps Leddravohr isn't coming."

"We'll just have to wait and see." Lain smiled briefly and returned his attention to the papers and mathematical instruments on his desk.

"Yes." Toller studied the ceiling for a moment. "This isn't a sparkling conversation, is it?"

"It isn't any kind of conversation," Lain said. "What's happening is that I'm trying to work and you keep interrupting."

"Sorry." Toller knew he should leave the room, but he was reluctant to do so. It was a long time since he had been in the family home, and some of his clearest boyhood memories were of coming into this familiar room—with its perette wood panels and glowing ceramics—and of seeing Lain at the same desk, going about the incomprehensible business of being a mathematician. Toller's instincts told him that he and his brother were reaching a watershed in their lives, and he had a longing for them to share an hour of companionship while it was still possible. He had been vaguely embarrassed about his feelings and had not tried putting them into words, with the negative result that Lain was ill at ease and puzzled by his continuing presence.

Resolving to be quiet, Toller went to one of the stacks of ancient manuscripts which had been brought from the Greenmount archives. He picked up a leatherbound folio and glanced at its title. As usual the words appeared as linear trains of letters with elusive content until he used a trick which Lain had once devised for him. He covered the title with his palm and slowly slid his hand to the right so that the letters were revealed to him in sequence. This time the printed symbols yielded up their meaning: *Aerostatic Flights to the Far North*, by Muel Webrey, 2136.

That was as far as Toller's interest in a book normally went, but balloon ascents had not been far from his mind since the momentous meeting of the previous day, and his curiosity was further stirred by the realisation that the book was five centuries old. What had it been like to fly across the world in the days before Kolcorron had arisen to unify a dozen warring nations? He sat down and opened the book near the middle, hoping Lain would be impressed, and began to read. Some unfamiliar spellings and grammatical constructions made the text more oblique than he would have liked, but he persevered, sliding his hand across paragraph after paragraph which, disappointingly, had more to do with ancient politics than aviation. He was beginning to lose momentum when his attention was caught by a reference to ptertha: "*. . . and far to our left the pink globes of the ptertha were rising*".

Toller frowned and ran his finger across the adjective several times before raising his head. "Lain, it says here that ptertha are pink."

Lain did not look up. "You must have misread it. The word is 'purple'."

Toller studied the adjective again. "No, it says pink."

"You have to allow a certain amount of leeway in subjective descriptions. Besides, the meanings of words can shift over a long period of time."

"Yes, but. . . ." Toller felt dissatisfied. "So you don't think the ptertha used to be a diff—"

"Toller!" Lain threw down his pen. "Toller, don't think I'm not glad to see you—but why have you taken up residence in my office?"

"We never talk," Toller said uncomfortably.

"All right, what do you want to talk about?"

"Anything. There may not be much . . . time." Toller sought inspiration. "You could tell me what you're working on."

"There wouldn't be much point. You wouldn't understand it."

"Still we'd have been talking," Toller said, rising to his feet and returning the old book to the stacks. He was walking to the door when his brother spoke.

"I'm sorry, Toller—you're quite right." Lain smiled an apology. "You see, I started this essay more than a year ago, and I want to finish it before I get diverted to other matters. But perhaps it isn't all that important."

"It must be important if you've been working on it all that time. I'll leave you in peace."

"Please don't go," Lain said quickly. "Would you like to see something truly wonderful? Watch this!" He picked up a small wooden disk, laid it flat on a sheet of paper and traced a circle around it. He slid the disk sideways, drew another circle which kissed the first and then repeated the process, ending with three circles in a line. Placing a finger at each end of the row, he said, "From here to here is exactly three diameters, right?"

"That's right," Toller said uneasily, wondering if he had missed something.

"Now we come to the amazing part." Lain made an ink mark on the edge of the disk and placed it vertically on the paper, carefully ensuring that the mark was at an outermost edge of the three circles. After glancing up at Toller to make sure he was paying proper attention, Lain slowly rolled the disk straight across the row. The mark on its rim described a lazy curve and came down precisely on the outermost edge of the last circle.

"Demonstration ended," Lain announced. "And that's part of what I'm writing about."

Toller blinked at him. "The circumference of a wheel being equal to three diameters?"

"The fact that it is *exactly* equal to three diameters. That demonstration was quite crude, but even when we go to the limits of measurement the ratio is exactly three. Does that not strike you as being rather astonishing?"

"Why should it?" Toller said, his puzzlement growing. "If that's the way it is, that's the way it is."

"Yes, but why should it be *exactly* three? That and things like the fact that we have twelve fingers make whole areas of calculation absurdly easy. It's almost like an unwarranted gift from nature."

"But . . . But that's the way it *is*. What else could it be?"

"Now you're approaching the theme of the essay. There may be some other . . . *place* . . . where the ratio is three-and-a-quarter, or perhaps only two-and-a-half. In fact, there's no reason why it shouldn't be some completely irrational number which would give mathematicians headaches."

"Some other place," Toller said. "You mean another world? Like Farland?"

"No." Lain gave him a look which was both frank and enigmatic. "I mean another totality—where physical laws and constants differ from those we know."

Toller stared back at his brother as he strove to penetrate the barrier which had slid into place between them. "It is all very interesting," he said. "I can see why the essay has taken you so long."

Lain laughed aloud and came round the desk to embrace Toller. "I love you, little brother."

"I love you."

"Good! I want you to keep that in mind when Leddravohr arrives. I'm a committed pacifist, Toller, and I eschew all violence. The fact that I am no match for Leddravohr is an irrelevance—I would behave towards him in exactly the same way were our social status and physiques transposed. Leddravohr and his kind are part of the past, whereas we represent the future. So I want you to swear that no matter what insult Leddravohr offers me, you will stay apart and leave the conduct of my affairs strictly to me."

"I'm a different person now," Toller said, stepping back. "Besides, Leddravohr might be in a good mood."

"I want your word, Toller."

"You have it. Besides, it's in my own interests to keep on the right side of Leddravohr if I want to be a skyship pilot." Toller was belatedly shocked by the content of his own words. "Lain, why are we taking all this so calmly? We have just been told that the world as we know it is coming to an end . . . and that some of us have to try reaching another planet . . . yet we're all going about our ordinary business as though everything was normal. It doesn't make sense."

"It's a more natural reaction than you might think. And don't forget the migration flight is only a contingency at this stage—it might never happen."

"The war with Chamteth is going to happen."

"That is the King's responsibility," Lain said, his voice suddenly brusque. "It can't be laid at my door. I have to get on with my work now."

"I should see how my lord is faring." As Toller walked along the corridor to the main stair he again wondered why Leddravohr had chosen to come to the Square House instead of visiting Glo at the much larger Greenmount Peel. The sunwriter message from the palace had baldly stated that the Princes Leddravohr and Chakkell would arrive at the house before littlenight for initial technical briefings, and the infirm Glo had been obliged to journey out to meet them. It was now well into aftday and Glo would be growing tired, his strength further sapped by the effort of trying to hide his disability.

Toller descended to the entrance hall and turned left into the dayroom where he had left Glo in the temporary care of Fera. The two had a very comfortable relationship because of—Toller suspected—rather than in spite of her lowly origin and unpolished manner. It was another of Glo's little affectations, a way of reminding those around him that there was more to him than the cloistered philosopher. He was seated at a table reading a small book, and Fera was standing by a window gazing out at the mesh-mosaic of the sky. She was wearing a simple one piece garment of pale green cambric which showed off her statuesque form.

She turned on hearing Toller enter the room and said, "This is boring. I want to go home."

"I thought you wanted to see a real live prince at close quarters."

"I've changed my mind."

"They're bound to be here soon," Toller said. "Why don't you be like my lord and pass the time by reading?"

Fera mouthed silently, carefully forming the swear words so that there would be no doubt about what she thought of the idea. "It wouldn't be so bad if there was even some food."

"But you ate less than an hour ago!" Toller ran a humorously

133

critical eye over his gradewife's figure. "No wonder you're getting fat."

"I'm not!" Fera slapped her belly inwards and contracted her stomach, an action which caused a voluptuous ballooning of her breasts. Toller viewed the display with affectionate appreciation. It was a frequent source of wonder to him that Fera, in spite of her appetite and habit of spending entire days lolling in bed, looked almost exactly as she had done two years earlier. The only noticeable change was that her chipped tooth had begun to turn grey. She devoted much time to rubbing it with white powders, supposed to contain crushed pearls, which she obtained from the Samlue market.

Lord Glo looked up from his book, his clapped-in face momentarily enlivened. "Take the woman upstairs," he said to Toller. "That's what I'd do were I five years younger."

Fera correctly assessed his mood and produced the expected ribaldry. "*I* wish you were five years younger, my lord—merely mounting the stairs would be enough to finish my husband."

Glo gave a gratified whinny.

"In that case, we'll do it right here," Toller said. He darted forward, put his arms around Fera and drew her close to him, half-seriously simulating passion. There was an undeniable element of providing sexual titillation for Glo in what he and Fera were doing, but such was the relationship the three had built up that the overriding motif was one of companionship and friendly clowning. After a few seconds of intimate contact, however, Toller felt Fera move against him with a hint of genuine purpose.

"Do you still have the use of your old bedroom?" she whispered, pressing her lips to his ear. "I'm beginning to feel like. . . ." She stopped speaking and although she remained in his arms he knew that somebody had entered the room.

He turned and saw Gesalla Maraquine regarding him with cool disdain, the familiar expression she seemed to reserve just for him. Her dark filmy clothing emphasised her slimness. It was the first time they had met in almost two years and he was struck by the fact that, as with Fera, her appearance had not altered in any significant way. The sickness associated with her second pregnancy—which had caused her to miss the littlenight meal

—had invested her pale features with a near-numinous dignity which somehow made him feel that he was a stranger to all that was important in life.

"Good aftday, Gesalla," he said. "I see you haven't lost your knack of materialising at precisely the wrong moment." Fera slipped away from him. He smiled and looked down at Glo, expecting his moral support, but Glo indulged in playful treachery by gazing fixedly at his book, pretending to be so lost in it that he had been unaware of what Toller and Fera were doing.

Gesalla's grey eyes considered Toller briefly while she decided if he merited a reply, then she turned her attention to Glo. "My lord, Prince Chakkell's equerry is in the precinct. He reports that the Princes Chakkell and Leddravohr are on their way up the hill."

"Thank you, my dear." Glo closed his book and waited until Gesalla had left the room before baring the ruins of his lower teeth at Toller. "I thought you weren't . . . hmm . . . afraid of that one."

Toller was indignant. "Afraid? Why should I be afraid?"

"Huh!" Fera had returned to her position by the window. "What was wrong with it?"

"What are you talking about?"

"You said she came in at the wrong moment. What was wrong with it?"

Toller was staring at her, exasperated and speechless, when Glo tugged his sleeve to signal that he wanted to get to his feet. In the entrance hall there were footfalls and the sound of a man's voice. Toller helped Glo to stand up and lock the verticals of his cane frame. They walked together into the hall, with Toller inconspicuously taking much of Glo's weight. Lain and Gesalla were being addressed by the equerry, who was aged about forty and had tallowy skin and out-turned liver-coloured lips. His dark green tunic and breeches were foppishly decorated with lines of tiny crystal beads and he wore the narrow sword of a duellist.

"I am Canrell Zotiern, representing Prince Chakkell," he announced with an imperiousness which would have been better suited to his master. "Lord Glo and members of the Maraquine family—no others—will stand here in line facing the door and will await the arrival of the prince."

Toller, who was shocked by Zotiern's arrogance, assisted Glo to the indicated place beside Lain and Gesalla. He glanced at Glo, expecting him to issue the proper reprimand, but the older man seemed too preoccupied with the laboured mechanics of walking to have noticed anything amiss. Several of the household servants watched silently from the door leading to the kitchens. Beyond the archway of the main entrance the mounted soldiers of Chakkell's personal guard disturbed the flow of light into the hall. Toller became aware that the equerry was looking at him.

"You! The body servant!" Zotiern called out. "Are you deaf? Get back to your quarters."

"My personal attendant is a Maraquine, and he remains with me," Glo said steadily.

Toller heard the exchange as across a tumultuous distance. The crimson drumming was something he had not experienced in a long time, and he was dismayed to find that his cultivated immunity to it was proved illusory. *I'm a different person*, he told himself, while a prickly chill moved across his brow. *I AM a different person.*

"And I have a warning for you," Glo went on, speaking in high Kolcorronian and dredging up something of his old authority as he confronted Zotiern. "The unprecedented powers the King has accorded Leddravohr and Chakkell do not, as you appear to think, extend to their lackeys. I will tolerate no further violations of protocol from you."

"A thousand apologies, my lord," Zotiern said, insincere and unperturbed, consulting a list he had taken from his pocket. "Ah, yes—Toller Maraquine . . . and a spouse named Fera." He swaggered closer to Toller. "While the subject of protocol is in the air, Toller Maraquine, where is this spouse of yours? Don't you know that all female members of the household should be presented?"

"My wife is at hand," Toller said coldly. "I will. . . ." He broke off as Fera, who must have been listening, appeared at the door of the dayroom. Moving with uncharacteristic demureness and timidity, she came towards Toller.

"Yes, I can see why you wanted to keep this one hidden," Zotiern said. "I must make a closer inspection on behalf of the prince."

As Fera was passing him he halted her by the expedient of grasping a handful of her hair. The drumming in Toller's brain crashed into silence. He thrust out his left hand and hit Zotiern on the shoulder, knocking him off-balance. Zotiern went down sideways, landing on his hands and knees, and immediately sprang up again. His right hand was going for his sword and Toller knew that by the time he fully regained his feet the blade would be unsheathed. Propelled by instinct, rage and alarm, Toller went in on his opponent and struck him on the side of the neck with all the power of his right arm. Zotiern spun away, limbs flailing the air like the blades of a ptertha stick, crashed to the floor and slid several yards on the polished surface. He ended up lying on his back, unmoving, his head angled close to one shoulder. Gesalla gave a clear, high scream.

"What happens here?" The angry shout came from Prince Chakkell, who had just come through the entrance closely followed by four of his guard. He strode to Zotiern, bent over him briefly—his sparsely covered scalp glistening—and raised his eyes towards Toller, who was frozen in the attitude of combat.

"You! *Again!*" Chakkell's swarthy countenance grew even darker. "What's the meaning of this?"

"He insulted Lord Glo," Toller said, meeting the prince's gaze directly. "He also insulted me and molested my wife."

"That is correct," Glo put in. "Your man's behaviour was quite inexcus—"'

"Silence! I've had my fill of this doltish upstart!" Chakkell swung his arm, signalling his guards to move in on Toller. "Kill him!"

The soldiers came forward, drawing their black swords. Toller backed away, thinking of his own blade which he had left at home, until his heel touched the wall. The soldiers formed a semicircle and closed in on him, eyes slitted and intent beneath the rims of their brakka helmets. Beyond them Toller could see Gesalla hiding in Lain's embrace; the grey-robed Glo rooted to the spot, his hand raised in ineffectual protest; and Fera watching him through latticed fingers. Until that moment the guards had remained equally distant from him, but now the one on the right was taking the initiative and the point of his sword was describing eager little circles as he prepared for the first thrust.

Toller braced himself against the wall and made ready to launch himself forward beneath the thrust when it came, determined to inflict some degree of injury on his executioners rather than simply be cut down by them. The hovering sword tip steadied, purposefully, and its message for Toller was that time was at an end. Heightened perception of everything in his surroundings brought him the awareness that another man was entering the hall, and even in the desperate extremity he was able to feel a pang of regret that the newcomer was Prince Leddravohr, arriving just in time to savour his death. . . .

"Stand away from that man!" Leddravohr commanded. His voice was not unduly loud, but the four guards responded at once by stepping back from Toller.

"What the . . . !" Chakkell wheeled on Leddravohr. "Those men are in my personal guard and they take orders only from me."

"Is that so?" Leddravohr said calmly. He aimed a finger at the soldiers and slowly swung it to indicate the opposite side of the hall. The soldiers went with the line of it, as though controlled by invisible rods, and took up new positions.

"But you don't understand," Chakkell protested. "The Maraquine lout has killed Zotiern."

"It shouldn't have been possible—Zotiern was armed and the Maraquine lout wasn't. This is part of the price you pay, my dear Chakkell, for surrounding yourself with strutting incompetents." Leddravohr went closer to Zotiern, looked down at him and gave a low chuckle. "Besides, he isn't dead. He is damaged beyond repair, mind you, but he isn't quite dead. Isn't that so, Zotiern?" Leddravohr augmented the question by nudging the fallen man with his toe.

Zotiern's mouth emitted a faint bubbling sound and Toller

saw that his eyes were still open, frantic and staring, although his body remained inert.

Leddravohr flicked his smile into existence for Chakkell's benefit. "As you think so highly of Zotiern, we'll do him the honour of sending him off along the Bright Road. Perhaps he would even have chosen it himself were he still able to speak." Leddravohr glanced at the four watchful soldiers. "Take him outside and see to it."

The soldiers, obviously relieved at being able to escape Leddravohr's presence, saluted hastily before swooping on Zotiern and carrying him outside to the precinct. Chakkell made as if to follow, then turned back. Leddravohr gave him a mock-affectionate slap on the shoulder, dropped a hand to his sword and padded across the hall to stand before Toller.

"You seem obsessed with placing your life in danger," he said. "Why did you do it?"

"Prince, he insulted Lord Glo. He insulted me. And he molested my wife."

"Your wife?" Leddravohr turned and looked at Fera. "Ah, yes. And *how* did you overcome Zotiern?"

Toller was puzzled by Leddravohr's tone. "I punched him."

"Once?"

"There was no need to do it again."

"I see." Leddravohr's inhumanly smooth face was enigmatic. "Is it true that you have made several attempts to enter military service?"

"It is true, Prince."

"In that case I have good news for you, Maraquine," Leddravohr said. "You are now *in* the army. I promise you that you will have many opportunities to satisfy your troublesome warlike urges in Chamteth. Report to the Mithold Barracks at dawn."

Leddravohr turned away without waiting for a reply and began a murmured conversation with Chakkell. Toller remained as he was, his back still pressed to the wall, as he tried to control the seething of his thoughts. Despite his ungovernable temper he had taken human life only once before, when he had been set upon by thieves in a dark street in the Flylien district of

Ro-Atabri and had left two of them dead. He had not even seen their faces and the incident had left him unaffected, but in the case of Zotiern he could still feel the appalling crunch of vertebrae and still could see the terrified eyes. The fact that he had not killed the man outright only made the event more traumatic —Zotiern had had a subjective eternity, helpless as a broken insect, in which to anticipate the final sword thrust. Toller had been floundering, trying to come to terms with his emotions, when Leddravohr had delivered his verbal bombshell, and now the universe was a chaos of tumbling fragments.

"Prince Chakkell and I will retire to a separate room with Lain Maraquine," Leddravohr announced. "We are not to be disturbed."

Glo signalled for Toller to come to his side. "We have everything ready for you, Prince. May I suggest that . . . ?"

"Suggest nothing, Lord Cripple—your presence is not required at this stage." Leddravohr's face was expressionless as he looked at Glo, as though he were not even worthy of contempt. "You will remain here in case I have reason to summon you later—though I confess I find it difficult to imagine your ever being of any value to anybody." Leddravohr directed his cold gaze at Lain. "Where?"

"This way, Prince." Lain spoke in a low voice and he was visibly quaking as he moved towards the stair. He was followed by Leddravohr and Chakkell. As soon as they had passed out of sight on the upper floor Gesalla fled from the hall, leaving Toller alone with Glo and Fera. Only a few minutes had passed since they had been together in the dayroom, and yet they now breathed different air, inhabited a different world. Toller sensed he would not feel the full impact of the change until later.

"Help me back to my . . . hmm . . . seat, my boy," Glo said. He remained silent until installed in the same chair in the dayroom, then looked up at Toller with a shamefaced smile. "Life never ceases to be interesting, does it?"

"I'm sorry, my lord." Toller tried to find appropriate words. "There was nothing I could do."

"Don't fret. You came out of it well—though I fear it wasn't in

Leddravohr's mind to do you a favour when he inducted you into his service."

"I don't understand it. When he was walking towards me I thought he was going to kill me himself."

"I'll be sorry to lose you."

"What about me?" Fera said. "Has anybody thought about what's going to happen to me?"

Toller recalled his earlier exasperation with her. "You may not have noticed, but we have all been given other things to think about."

"There is no need for you to worry," Glo said to her. "You may remain at the Peel for as long as you . . . hmm . . . wish."

"Thank you, my lord. I wish I could go there now."

"So do I, my dear, but I'm afraid it's out of the question. None of us is free to leave until dismissed by the prince. That is the custom."

"Custom!" Fera's dissatisfied gaze travelled the room before settling on Toller. "Wrong moment!"

He turned his back on her, unwilling to confront the enigma of the feminine mind, and went to stand at a window. *The man I killed needed to be killed*, he told himself, *so I'm not going to brood about it*. He turned his thoughts to the mystery of Leddravohr's behaviour. Glo was quite right—the prince had not acted out of benignancy when summarily making him a soldier. There was little doubt that he hoped for Toller to be killed in battle, but why had he not seized the opportunity to take revenge in person? He could easily have sided with Chakkell over the death of the equerry and that would have been the end of the matter. Leddravohr was capable of spinning out the destruction of someone who had crossed him so that he could derive maximum satisfaction from it, but surely that would be placing too much importance on an obscure member of a philosophy family.

The thought of his own background reminded Toller of the astonishing fact that he was now in the army, and the realisation struck him with as much or more force than Leddravohr's original pronouncement. It was ironic that the ambition he had cherished for much of his life should have been achieved in such a bizarre fashion and just at a time when he was beginning to put such ideas behind him. What was going to happen to him after he reported to the Mithold Barracks in the morning? It was disconcerting to find that he had no coherent vision of his future, that beyond the coming night the pattern broke up into shards . . . bitty reflections . . . Leddravohr . . . the army . . . Chamteth . . . the migration flight . . . Overland . . . the unknown swirling into the unknown. . . .

A gentle snore from behind him told Toller that Glo had gone to sleep. He left it to Fera to ensure that Glo was comfortable and continued staring through the window. The enveloping ptertha screens interfered with the view of Overland, but he could see the progression of the terminator across the great disk. When it reached the halfway mark, dividing the sister world into hemispheres of equal size but unequal brightness, the sun would be on the horizon.

A short time before that point was reached Prince Chakkell emerged from the lengthy conference and departed for his residence in the Tannoffern Palace, which lay to the east of the Great Palace. Now that the main streets of Ro-Atabri were virtually tunnels it would have been possible for him to stay longer in the Square House, but Chakkell was known for his devotion to his wife and children. After he and his retinue had left there was complete silence in the precinct, a reminder that Leddravohr had come to the meeting unaccompanied. The military prince was noted for travelling everywhere alone— partly, it was said, because of his impatience with attendants, but mainly because he scorned the use of guards. He was confident in his belief that his reputation and his own battle sword were all the protection he needed in any city of the empire.

Toller had hoped that Leddravohr would leave soon after Chakkell, but hour after hour went by with no sign of the discussion coming to an end. It appeared that Leddravohr was determined to absorb as much aeronautical knowledge as was possible in a very short time.

The weight-driven glasswood clock on the wall was showing the hour of ten when a servant arrived with platters of simple food, mainly fishcakes and bread. There was also a note of apology from Gesalla, who was too ill to perform the normal duties of hostess. Fera had been waiting for a substantial spread and was theatrically shocked when Glo explained that no formal meal could be served unless Leddravohr chose to go to table. She ate most of what was available single-handed, then dropped into a chair in a corner and pretended to sleep. Glo alternated between trying to read in the unsatisfactory light from the sconces and staring grimly into the distance. Toller received the impression that his self-esteem had been irreparably damaged by Leddravohr's casual cruelty.

It was almost the eleventh hour when Lain walked into the room. He said, "Please return to the hall, my lord."

Glo raised his head with a start. "So the prince has finally decided to leave."

"No." Lain seemed slightly bewildered. "I think the prince is going to do me the honour of staying the night in my home. We must present ourselves now. You and your wife as well, Toller."

Toller was at a loss to explain Leddravohr's unusual decision as he raised Glo to his feet and helped him to leave the room. In normal times and circumstances it would indeed have been a great honour for a royal to sleep in the Square House, especially as the palaces were within easy reach, but Leddravohr hardly wanted to be gracious. Gesalla was already waiting near the foot of the stair, holding herself tall and straight in spite of her obvious weakness. The others formed a line with her—Glo at the centre, flanked by Lain and Toller—and waited for Leddravohr to appear.

There was a delay of several minutes before the military prince came to the head of the stair. He was eating the leg of a roast quickfowl, and added to the discourtesy by continuing to gnaw at the bone in silence until it was stripped of all flesh. Toller began to get sombre premonitions. Leddravohr threw the bone to the floor, wiped his lips with the back of a hand and slowly came down the stairs. He was still wearing his sword—another incivility—and his smooth face showed no sign of tiredness.

"Well, Lord Glo, it appears I have needlessly kept you here all day." Leddravohr's tone made it clear that he was not apologising. "I have learned most of what I need to know and will be able to finish here in the morning. Many other matters demand my attention, so to avoid wasting time in travelling back and forth to the palace I will sleep here tonight. You will be in attendance at the sixth hour. I take it you *can* bestir yourself by that time?"

"I shall be here at the sixth hour, Prince," Glo said.

"That is good to know," Leddravohr replied, jovially sarcastic. He strolled along the line, paused when he reached Toller and Fera, and produced the instantaneous smile which had nothing to do with humour. Toller faced him as woodenly as possible, his foreboding turning into a certainty that a day which had begun badly was going to end badly. Leddravohr turned off his smile, walked back to the stair and began to ascend. Toller was beginning to wonder if his premonitions could have been groundless when Leddravohr halted on the third step.

"What is this?" he mused, keeping his back to the attentive group. "My brain is weary, and yet my body craves activity. There is a decision to be made here—shall I have a woman, or shall I not?"

Toller, already knowing the answer to Leddravohr's rhetorical question, brought his mouth close to Fera's ear. "This is my fault," he whispered. "Leddravohr hates better than I knew. He wants to use you as a weapon against me, and there is nothing we can do about it. You'll just have to go with him."

"We'll see," Fera said, her composure unaffected.

Leddravohr drummed his fingers on the balustrade, prolonging the moment, then turned to face the hall. "You," he said, pointing at Gesalla. "Come with me."

"But . . . !" Toller took one step forward, breaking the line, his body a pounding column of blood. He gazed in helpless outrage at Gesalla as she touched Lain's hand and walked towards the stair with a strange floating movement as though tranced and not really aware of what was happening. Her beautiful face was almost luminescent in its pallor. Leddravohr went ahead of her and the two were lost in the flickering dimness of the upper floor.

Toller wheeled on his brother. "That's your wife—and she's pregnant!"

"Thank you for that information," Lain said in a dead voice, regarding Lain with dead eyes.

"But this is all *wrong!*'

"It's the Kolcorronian way." Incredibly, Lain was able to fashion his lips into a smile. "It is part of the reason we are despised by every other nation in the world."

"Who cares about the other . . . ?" Toller became aware that Fera, hands on hips, was staring at him with undisguised fury. "What's the matter with you?"

"Perhaps if you had stripped me naked and thrown me at the prince things would have worked out more to your liking," Fera said in a low hard voice.

"What do you mean?"

"I mean you couldn't wait to see me go with him."

"You don't understand," Toller protested. "I thought Leddravohr wanted to punish *me*."

"That's exactly what he. . . ." Fera broke off to glance at Lain, then returned her attention to Toller. "You're a fool, Toller Maraquine. I wish I had never met you." She spun on her heel, suddenly haughty in a way he had never seen before, walked quickly back into the dayroom and slammed the door.

Toller gaped after her for a moment, baffled, then paced an urgent circle around the hall and came back to Lain and Glo. The latter, looking more exhausted and frail than ever, had clasped Lain's hand.

"What would you like me to do, my boy?" he said gently. "I could return to the Peel if you want the privacy."

Lain shook his head. "No, my lord. It is very late. If you will do me the honour of staying here I will have a suite prepared for you."

"Very well." As Lain left to instruct the servants Glo turned his large head in Toller's direction. "You're not helping your brother with all your running about like a caged animal."

"I don't understand him," Toller muttered. "Somebody should *do* something."

"What would you . . . hmm . . . suggest?"

"I don't know. *Something.*"

"Would it improve Gesalla's lot if Lain were to get himself killed?"

"Perhaps," Toller said, refusing to entertain logic. "She could at least be proud of him."

Glo sighed. "Help me to a chair, and then fetch me a glass of something with heat in it. Kailian black."

"Wine?" Toller was surprised despite his mental turmoil. "You want wine?"

"You said somebody should do something, and that's what I'm going to do," Glo said evenly. "You will have to dance to your own music."

Toller help Glo to a high-backed chair at the side of the hall and went to obtain a beaker of wine, his mind oppressed with the problem of how to reconcile himself to the intolerable. The mode of thought was unnatural for him and it seemed a long time before inspiration came. *Leddravohr is only playing with us*, he decided, seizing the thread of hope. *Gesalla can't be to the taste of one who is accustomed to trained courtesans. Leddravohr is only detaining her in his room, laughing at us. In fact, he can express his contempt all the better by scorning to touch any of our women. . . .*

In the hour that followed Glo drank four large bumpers of wine, rendering himself crimson of face and almost totally helpless. Lain had retired to the solitude of his study, still betraying no trace of emotion, and Toller was dejected when Glo announced his desire to go to bed. He knew he would not sleep and had no desire to be alone with his thoughts. He half carried Glo to the assigned suite and helped him through all the tedious procedures of toilet and getting to bed, then came into the long transverse corridor which linked the principal sleeping quarters. There was a whisper of sound to his left.

He turned and saw Gesalla walking towards him on the way to her own rooms. Her black garments, long and drifting, and blanched face gave her a spectral appearance, but her bearing was erect and dignified. She was the same Gesalla Maraquine he had always known—cool, private and indomitable—and at the sight of her he experienced a pang of mingled concern and relief.

"Gesalla," he said, moving towards her, "are you . . . ?"

146

"Don't come near me," she snapped with a look of slit-eyed venom and walked past him without altering her step. Dismayed by the sheer loathing in her voice, he watched until she had passed out of view, then his gaze was drawn to the pale mosaic floor. The trail of bloody footprints told a story more dreadful than any he had tried to banish from his mind.

Leddravohr, oh Leddravohr, oh Leddravohr, he chanted inwardly. *We are wedded now, you and I. You have given yourself to me . . . and only a death will set us apart.*

CHAPTER 10

The decision to attack Chamteth from the west was taken for geographical reasons.

At the western limits of the Kolcorronian empire, somewhat north of the equator, was a chain of volcanic islets which ended in a low-lying triangle of land about eight miles on a side. Known as Oldock, the uninhabited island had several features which were of strategic importance to Kolcorron. One was that it was close enough to Chamteth to form an excellent jumping-off point for a sea-borne invasion force; another was that it was thickly covered with rafter and tallon trees, two species which grew to a great height and offered good protection against ptertha.

The fact that Oldock and the whole Fairondes chain lay in a prevailing westerly air stream was also advantageous to Kolcorron's five armies. Although the troop ships were slowed down and airships forced to make extensive use of their jets, the steady wind blowing across open seas had a greater effect on the ptertha, making it almost impossible for them to get within range of their prey. Telescopes showed the livid globes swarming in high-altitude contraflows but they were for the most part swept away to the east when they tried to penetrate lower levels of the atmosphere. When planning the invasion the Kolcorronian high command had allowed for up to one sixth of their personnel being lost to ptertha, whereas the actual casualties were negligible.

As the armies progressed westward there was a gradual but perceptible change in the patterns of night and day. Foreday grew shorter and aftday longer as Overland drifted away from the zenith and approached the eastern horizon. Eventually foreday was reduced to a brief dazzle of prismatics as the sun crossed the narrow gap between the horizon and Overland's disk, and soon after that the sister world was nesting on Land's eastern rim. Littlenight became a short extension of night, and there was a heightened sense of expectancy among the invaders as the celestial evidence told them they were entering the Land of the Long Days.

The establishment of a beachhead on Chamteth itself was another phase of the operation in which considerable losses had been expected, and the Kolcorronian commanders could scarcely believe their good fortune when they found the tree-covered strands unwatched and undefended.

The three widely separated invasion prongs met no resistance whatsoever, converging and consolidating without a single casualty apart from the accidental fatalities and injuries which are inevitable when large masses of men and matériel enter an alien territory. Almost at once brakka groves were found among the other types of forestation, and within a day bands of naked slimers were at work behind the advancing military. The sacks of green and purple crystals gutted from the brakka were loaded on to separate cargo ships—large quantities of pikon and halvell were never transported together—and in an incredibly short time the first steps had been taken to initiate a supply chain reaching all the way back to Ro-Atabri.

Aerial reconnaissance was ruled out for the time being, because airships were too conspicuous, but with ancient maps to guide them the invaders were able to push westwards at a steady pace. The terrain was swampy in places, infested with poisonous snakes, but presented no serious obstacles to well trained soldiers whose morale and physical condition were at a high level.

It was on the twelfth day that a scout patrol noticed an airship of unfamiliar design scudding silently across the sky ahead of them.

By that time the vanguard of the Third Army was emerging from the waterlogged littoral and was reaching higher ground characterised by a series of drumlins running from north to south. Trees and other kinds of vegetation were more sparse here. It was the type of ground on which an unopposed army could have made excellent progress—but the first of the Chamtethan defenders were lying in wait.

They were swarthy men, long-muscled and black-bearded, wearing flexible armour made from small flakes of brakka sewn together like fish scales, and they fell on the invaders with a ferocity which even the most seasoned Kolcorronians had never encountered before. Some of them appeared to be suicide groups, sent in to cause maximum damage and disarray, creating diversions which enabled others to set up attacks using a variety of long-range weapons—cannon, mortars and mechanical catapults which hurled pikon-halvell bombs.

The Kolcorronian crack troops, veterans of many frontier engagements, destroyed the Chamtethans in the course of a diffuse, multi-centred battle which lasted almost the entire day. It was found that fewer than a hundred men had died, compared with more than twice that number of the enemy, and when the following day had passed without further incident the spirits of the invaders were again at a peak.

From that stage onwards, with secrecy no longer possible, the line soldiers were preceded by an air cover of bombers and surveillance ships, and the men on the ground were reassured by the sight of the elliptical craft patterning the sky ahead.

Their commanders were less complacent, however, knowing they had encountered only a local defence force, that intelligence concerning the invasion had been flashed to the heart of Chamteth, and that the might of a huge continent was being drawn up against them.

CHAPTER 11

General Risdel Dalacott uncorked the tiny poison bottle and smelled its contents.

The clear fluid had a curious aroma, honeyed and peppery at the same time. It was a distillation of extracts of maidenfriend, the herb which when chewed regularly by women prevented them from conceiving children. In its concentrated form it was even more inimical to life, providing a gentle, painless and absolutely certain escape from all the troubles of the flesh. It was greatly treasured among those of the Kolcorronian aristocracy who had no taste for the more honourable but very bloody traditional methods of committing suicide.

Dalacott emptied the bottle into his cup of wine and, after only the slightest hesitation, took a tentative sip. The poison was scarcely detectable and might even have been said to have improved the rough wine, adding a hint of spicy sweetness to it. He took another sip and set the cup aside, not wishing to slip away too quickly. There was a final self-imposed duty he had yet to perform.

He looked around his tent, which was furnished with only a narrow bed, a trunk, his portable desk and some folding chairs on straw matting. Other officers of staff rank liked to surround themselves with luxury to ease the rigours of campaign, but that had never been Dalacott's way. He had always been a soldier and had lived as a soldier should, and the reason he was choosing to die by poison instead of the blade was that he no longer regarded himself as worthy of a soldier's death.

It was dim inside the tent, the only light coming from a single military field lantern of the type which fuelled itself by attracting oilbugs. He lit a second lantern and placed it on his desk, still finding it a little strange that such measures should be necessary for reading at night. This far west in Chamteth, across the Orange River, Overland was out of sight beneath the horizon

151

and the diurnal cycle consisted of twelve hours of uninterrupted daylight followed by twelve hours of unrelieved darkness. Had Kolcorron been in this hemisphere its scientists
would probably have devised an efficient lighting system long
ago.

Dalacott raised the lid of his desk and took out the last volume
of his diary, the one for the year 2629. It was bound in limp green
leather and had a separate sheet for each day of the year.
He opened the book and slowly turned its pages, compacting
the entire Chamteth campaign into a matter of minutes, picking
out the key events which—insensibly at first—had led to his
personal disintegration as a soldier and as a man. . . .

DAY 84. *Prince Leddravohr was in a strange mood at the staff
conference today. I sensed that he was keyed-up and elated, in
spite of the news of heavy losses on the southern front. Time and
time again he made reference to the fact that ptertha appear to be
so few in this part of Land. He is not given to confiding his
innermost thoughts, but by piecing together fragmentary and
oblique remarks I received the impression that he entertained
visions of persuading the King to abandon the whole idea of
migrating to Overland.*

*His rationale seemed to be that such desperate measures would
be unnecessary if it were established that, for some unguessable
reason, conditions in the Land of the Long Days were unfavour-
able to ptertha. That being the case, it would only be necessary for
Kolcorron to subjugate Chamteth and transfer the seat of power
and the remaining population to this continent—a much more
logical and natural process than trying to reach another
planet. . . .*

DAY 93. *The war is going badly. These people are determined,
brave and gifted fighters. I cannot bring myself to contemplate the
possibility of our eventual defeat, but the truth is that we would
have been severely tested in going against Chamteth even in the
days when we could have fielded close on a million fully trained
men. Today we have only a third of that number, an uncomfortably high proportion of them raw conscripts, and we are going to*

need luck in addition to all our skill and courage if the war is to be successfully prosecuted.

An important factor in our favour is that this country is so rich in resources, particularly in brakka and edible crops. The sound of brakka pollination discharges is constantly being mistaken by my men for enemy cannon fire or bombs, and we have an abundance of power crystals for our heavy weaponry. There is no difficulty in keeping the armies well fed, in spite of the Chamtethans' efforts to burn the crops they are forced to abandon.

The Chamtethan women, and even quite small children, will indulge in that form of destruction if left to their own devices. With our manpower stretched to the limit, we are unable to divert combat troops into guard duties and for that reason Leddravohr has decreed that we take no prisoners, regardless of age or sex.

It is sound military thinking, but I have been sickened by the amount of butchery I have witnessed of late. Even the most hardened of the soldiery go about their business with set grey faces, and in the encampments at night there is a contrived and unnatural quality to the little merriment that one overhears.

This is a seditious thought, one I would not express anywhere except in the privacy of these pages, but it is one thing to spread the benefits of the empire to unenlightened and squabbling tribes —and quite another to undertake the annihilation of a great nation whose sole offence was to husband its resources of brakka.

I have never had time for religion, but now—for the first time—I am beginning to comprehend the meaning of the word "sin". . . .

Dalacott paused in his reading and picked up the enamelled cup of wine. He stared into its beaded depths for a moment, resisting the urge to drink deeply, then took a controlled sip. So many people seemed to be calling to him from the far side of that barrier which separated the living from the dead—his wife Toriane, Aytha Maraquine, his son Oderan, Conna Dalacott and little Hallie. . . .

Why had he been chosen to go on and on for more than seventy years, with the false blessing of the immunity, when others could have made much better use of the gift of life?

Without any conscious thought on his part, Dalacott's right hand slipped into a pocket and located the curious object he had found on the banks of the Bes-Undar all those years ago. He stroked his thumb in a circular motion over its mirrorlike surface as he again began to turn the pages of his diary.

DAY 102. *How does one account for the machinations of fate?*

This morning, after having put off doing so for many days, I began signing the sheaf of award citations on my desk and discovered that my own son—Toller Maraquine—is serving as an ordinary soldier in one of the regiments directly under my control!

It appears that he has been recommended for valour disks no less than three times in spite of the brevity of his service and lack of formal training. In theory a conscript, as he must be, should not be spending so much time in the front line, but perhaps the Maraquine family has used its intimate connections with the court to enable Toller to advance his belated military career. This is something I must enquire into if I ever have some freedom from the pressures of my command.

Truly these are changed times, when the military caste not only calls upon outsiders to swell its ranks, but catapults them into the utmost danger and what passes for glory.

I will do my best to see my son, if it can be arranged without exciting suspicion in him and comment from others. A meeting with Toller would be the one gleam of brightness in the deepnight of this criminal war.

DAY 103. *A company of the 8th Battalion was completely overrun in a surprise attack today in sector C11. Only a handful of men escaped the slaughter and many of those were so severely wounded that there was no option for them but the Bright Road. Disasters like that are becoming almost commonplace, so much so that I find myself more preoccupied with the reports which arrived this morning suggesting that our respite from the ptertha will soon come to an end.*

Telescopic observations from airships as far east from here as the Loongl Peninsula revealed some days ago that large numbers of ptertha were drifting south across the equator. The sightings have been patchy, because we have few ships in the Fyallon Ocean at present, but the opinion of scientists seems to be that the ptertha were moving south to take advantage of a "wind cell" which would carry them west for a great distance and then north again into Chamteth.

I have never subscribed to the theory that the globes possess a rudimentary intelligence, but if they really are capable of such behaviour—i.e. making use of global weather patterns—the conclusion that they have a malign purpose is almost inescapable. Perhaps, like ants and some similar creatures, their kind as a whole has some form of composite mind, although individuals are quite incapable of mentation.

DAY 106. Leddravohr's dream of a Kolcorron free from the scourge of the ptertha has come to an abrupt end. The globes have been sighted by fleet auxiliaries of the First Army. They are approaching the south coast in the Adrian region.

There has also been a curious report, as yet unconfirmed, from my own theatre.

Two line soldiers in a forward area claim that they saw a ptertha which was pale pink. According to their story the globe came to within forty or so paces of their position, but showed no inclination to draw nearer and eventually rose and drifted away to the west. What is one to make of such strange accounts? Could it be that two battle-weary soldiers are conniving to obtain a few days of interrogation in the safety of the base camp?

DAY 107. Today—although I take little pride or pleasure in the accomplishment—I justified Prince Leddravohr's confidence in my abilities as a tactician.

The splendid achievement, perhaps the culmination of my military career, began with my making the kind of mistake which would have been avoided by a green lieutenant straight out of academy.

It all began in the eighth hour when I became impatient with Captain Kadal over his tardiness in taking a stretch of open ground in sector D14. His reason for hanging back in the security of the forest was that his hastily prepared aerial map showed the territory to be traversed by several streams, and he believed them to be deep gullies capable of concealing sizable numbers of the enemy. Kadal is a competent officer, and I should have left him to scout the ground in his own way, but I feared that numerous setbacks were making him timorous, and I was overcome by a foolhardy desire to set an example to him and the men.

Accordingly, I took a sergeant and a dozen mounted soldiers and rode forward with them in person. The terrain was well suited to the bluehorns and we covered the ground quickly. Too quickly!

At a distance of perhaps a mile from our lines the sergeant became visibly uneasy, but I was too puffed up with success to pay him any heed. We had crossed two streams which were, as indicated on the map, too shallow to provide any kind of cover, and I became inflamed with a vision of myself casually presenting the whole area to Kadal as a prize I had won on his behalf with my boldness.

Before I knew it we had advanced close on two miles and even in my fit of megalomania I was beginning to hear the nagging voice of common sense warning me that enough was enough, especially as we had crossed a vestigial ridge and were no longer in sight of our own lines.

That was when the Chamtethans made their appearance.

They sprang up from the ground on both sides as if by magic, though of course there was no sorcery involved—they had been hiding in the very gullies whose existence I had blithely set out to disprove. There were at least two-hundred, looking like black reptiles in their brakka armour. Had their force been composed solely of infantry we could have outrun them, but a good quarter of their number were mounted and were already racing to block off our retreat.

I became aware of my men staring at me expectantly, and the fact that there was no sign of reproach in their eyes made my personal position all the worse. I had thrown away their lives with my overweening pride and stupidity, and all they asked of me in that terrible moment was a decision as to where and how they should die!

I looked all about and saw a tree-covered mound several

furlongs ahead of us. It would afford some protection and there was a possibility that from high up in one of the trees we would be able to get a sunwriter message back to Kadal and call for help.

I gave the necessary order and we rode with all speed to the mound, fortuituously surprising the Chamtethans, who had expected us to flee in the opposite direction. We reached the trees well ahead of our pursuers, who in any case were in no particular hurry. Time was on their side, and it was all too clear to me that even if we did succeed in communicating with Kadal it would be to no avail.

While one of the men was beginning to climb a tree with the sunwriter slung on his belt I used my field glasses in an attempt to locate the Chamtethan commander, to see if I could divine his intention. If he was cognisant of my rank he might try to take me alive—and that was something I could not have permitted. It was while sweeping the line of Chamtethan soldiers with the powerful glasses that I saw something which, even at that time of high peril, produced in me a spasm of dread.

Ptertha!

Four of the purple-tinted globes were approaching from the south, borne on the light breeze, skimming over the grass. They were plainly visible to the enemy—I saw several men point at them—but to my surprise no defensive action was taken. I saw the globes come closer and closer to the Chamtethans and—such is the power of reflex—I had to stifle the urge to shout a warning. The foremost of the globes reached the line of soldiers and abruptly ceased to exist, having burst among them.

Still no defensive or evasive action was taken. I even saw one soldier casually slash at a ptertha with his sword. In a matter of seconds the four globes had disintegrated, shedding their charges of deadly dust among the enemy, who appeared to be quite uncaring.

If what had happened up to that point was surprising, the aftermath was even more so.

The Chamtethans were in the process of spreading out to form a circle around our inadequate little fortress when I saw the beginnings of a commotion among their ranks. My glasses showed that some of the black-armoured soldiers had fallen. Already! Their comrades were kneeling beside them to render aid and—within the space of several breaths—they too were sprawling and writhing on the ground!

The sergeant came to my side and said, "Sir, the corporal says he can see our lines. What message do you want to send?"

"Wait!" I elevated my glasses slightly to take in the middle distance and after a moment picked out other ptertha weaving and wavering above the grasslands. "Instruct him to inform Captain Kadal that we have encountered a large detachment of the enemy, but that he is to remain where he is. He is not to advance until I send a further command."

The sergeant was too well disciplined to venture a protest, but his perplexity was evident as he hurried away to transmit my orders. I resumed my surveillance of the Chamtethans. By that time there was a general awareness that something was terribly amiss, evidenced by the manner in which the soldiers were running here and there in panic and confusion. Men who had begun to advance on our position turned and—not understanding that their sole hope of survival lay in fleeing the scene—rejoined the main body of their force. I watched with a clammy coldness in my gut as they too began to stagger and fall.

There were gasps of wonderment from behind me as my own men, even with unaided vision, took in the fact that the Chamtethans were swiftly being destroyed by some awesome and invisible agency. In a frighteningly short space of time every last one of the enemy had gone down, and nothing was moving on the plain save groups of bluehorns which had begun to graze unconcernedly among the bodies of their masters. (Why is it that all members of the animal kingdom, apart from types of simian, are immune to ptertha poison?)

When I had taken my fill of the dread scene I turned and almost laughed aloud as I saw that my men were gazing at me with a mixture of relief, respect and adoration. They had believed themselves doomed, and now—such are the workings of the common soldier's mind—their gratitude for being spared was being focussed on me, as though their deliverance had been won through some masterly strategy on my part. They seemed to have no thought at all for the wider implications of what had occurred.

Three years earlier Kolcorron had been brought to its knees by a sudden malevolent change in the nature of our age-old foe, the ptertha, and now it appeared that there had been another and greater escalation of the globes' evil powers. The new form of pterthacosis—for nothing else could have struck down the Chamtethans—which killed a man in seconds instead of hours was a grim portent of dark days ahead of us.

I relayed a message to Kadal, warning him to keep within the forest and to be on the alert for ptertha, then returned to my vigil. The glasses showed some ptertha in groups of two or three drifting on the southerly breeze. We were reasonably safe from them, thanks to the protection of the trees, but I waited for some time and made sure the sky was absolutely clear before giving the order to retrieve our bluehorns and to return to our own lines at maximum speed.

DAY 109. *It transpires that I was quite wrong about a new and intensified threat from the ptertha.*

Leddravohr has arrived at the truth by a characteristically direct method. He had a group of Chamtethan men and women tied to stakes on a patch of open ground, and beside them he placed a group of our own wounded, men who had little hope of recovery. Eventually they were found by drifting ptertha, and the outcome was witnessed through telescopes. The Kolcorronians, in spite of their weakened condition, took two hours to succumb to pterthacosis—but the hapless Chamtethans died almost immediately.

Why does this strange anomaly exist?

One theory I have heard is that the Chamtethans as a race have a certain inherited weakness which renders them highly vulnerable to pterthacosis, but I believe that the real explanation is the much more complicated one advanced by our medical advisors. It depends on there being two distinct varieties of ptertha—the blackish-purple type known of old to Kolcorron, which is highly venomous; and a pink type indigenous to Chamteth, which is harmless or relatively so. (The sighting of a pink globe in this area turns out to have been duplicated many times elsewhere.)

The theory further states that in centuries of warfare against the ptertha, in which millions of the globes have been destroyed, the entire population of Kolcorron has been exposed to microscopic quantities of the toxic dust. This has given us some slight degree of tolerance for the poison, increased our resistance to it, by a mechanism similar to the one which ensures that some diseases can be contracted only once. The Chamtethans, on the other hand, have no resistance whatsoever, and an encounter with a poisonous ptertha is even more catastrophic for them than it is for us.

One experiment which would go a long way towards proving the second theory would be to expose groups of Kolcorronians and Chamtethans to pink ptertha. No doubt Leddravohr will duly arrange for the experiment to be carried out if we enter a region where the pink globes are plentiful.

Dalacott broke off from his reading and glanced at the time-piece strapped to his wrist. It was of the type based on a toughened glass tube, preferred by the military in the absence of a compact and reliable chronometer. The pace beetle inside it was nearing the eighth division of the graduated cane shoot. The time of his final appointment was almost at hand.

He took a further measured sip of his wine and turned to the last entry in the diary. It had been made many days earlier, and after its completion he had abandoned the habit of a lifetime by ceasing to record each day's activities and thoughts.

In a way that had been a symbolic suicide, preparing him for tonight's actuality. . . .

DAY 114. *The war is over.*

The ptertha plague has done our work for us.

In the space of only six days since the purple ptertha made their appearance in Chamteth the plague has raged the length and breadth of the continent, sweeping away its inhabitants in their millions. A swift and casual genocide!

We no longer have to progress on foot, fighting our way yard by yard against a dedicated enemy. Instead, we advance by airship, with our jets on continuous thrust. Travelling in that manner uses up large quantities of power crystals—both in the propulsion tubes and the anti-ptertha cannon—but such considerations are no longer important.

We are the proud possessors of an entire continent of mature brakka and veritable mountains of the green and purple. We share our riches with none. Leddravohr has not rescinded his order to take no prisoners, and the isolated handfuls of bewildered and demoralised Chamtethans we encounter are put to the sword.

I have flown over cities, towns and villages and farmlands where nothing lives except for wandering domestic animals. The architecture is impressive—clean, well-proportioned, dignified —but one has to admire it from afar. The stench of rotting corpses reaches high into the sky.

We are soldiers no longer.

We are the carriers of pestilence.

We ARE pestilence.

I have nothing more to say.

CHAPTER 12

The night sky, although it had much less overall brightness than in Kolcorron, was spanned by a huge spiral of misty light, the arms of which sparkled with brilliant stars of white, blue and yellow. That wheel was flanked by two large elliptical spirals, and the rest of the celestial canopy was generously dappled with small whirlpools, wisps and patches of radiance, plus the glowing plumes of a number of comets. Although the Tree was not visible, the sky was overlaid with a field of major stars whose intensity made them seem closer than all the other heavenly objects, imparting a sense of depth to the display.

Toller was only accustomed to seeing those configurations when Land was at the opposite side of its path around the sun, at which time they were dominated and dimmed by the great disk of Overland. He stood unmoving in the dusk, watching starry reflections tremble on the broad quiet waters of the Orange River. All about him the myriad subdued lights of the Third Army's headquarters glowed through the tree lanes of the forest, the days of open encampments having passed with the advent of the ptertha plague.

One question had been on his mind all day: *Why should General Dalacott want a private interview with me?*

He had spent several days of idleness at a transit camp twenty miles to the west—part of an army which, suddenly, had no work to do—and had been trying to adapt to the new pace of life when the battalion commander had ordered him to report to headquarters. On arrival he had been examined briefly by several officers, one of whom he thought might be Vorict, the adjutant-general. He had been told that General Dalacott wished to present him with valour disks in person. The various officers had plainly been puzzled by the unusual arrangement, and had discreetly pumped Toller for information before accepting that he was as unenlightened about the matter as they.

162

A young captain emerged from the nearby administrative enclosure, approached Toller through the spangled dimness and said, "Lieutenant Maraquine, the general will see you now."

Toller saluted and went with the officer to a tent which, unexpectedly, was quite small and unadorned. The captain ushered him in and quickly departed. Toller stood at attention before a lean, austere-looking man who was seated at a portable desk. In the weak light from two field lanterns the general's cropped hair could either have been white or blond, and he looked surprisingly young for a man with fifty years of distinguished service. Only his eyes seemed old, eyes which had seen more than was compatible with the ability to dream.

"Sit down, son," he said. "This is a purely informal meeting."

"Thank you, sir." Toller took the indicated chair, his mystification growing.

"I see from your records that you entered the army less than a year ago as an ordinary line soldier. I know these are changed times, but wasn't that unusual for a man of your social status?"

"It was specially arranged by Prince Leddravohr."

"Is Leddravohr a friend of yours?"

Encouraged by the general's forthright but amiable manner, Toller ventured a wry smile. "I cannot claim that honour, sir."

"Good!" Dalacott smiled in return. "So you achieved the rank of lieutenant in less than a year through your own efforts."

"It was a field commission, sir. It may not be given full endorsement."

"It will." Dalacott paused to sip from an enamelled cup. "Forgive me for not offering you refreshment—this is an exotic brew and I doubt if it would be to your taste."

"I'm not thirsty, sir."

"Perhaps you would like these instead." Dalacott opened a compartment in his desk and took out three valour disks. They were circular flakes of brakka inlaid with white and red glass. He handed them to Toller and sat back to view his reactions.

"Thank you." Toller fingered the disks and put them away in a pocket. "I'm honoured."

"You disguise the fact quite well."

Toller was embarrassed and disconcerted. "Sir, I didn't intend any. . . ."

"It's all right, son," Dalacott said. "Tell me, is army life not what you expected?"

"Since I was a child I have dreamed of being a warrior, but. . . ."

"You were prepared to wipe an opponent's blood from your sword, but you didn't realise there would be smears of his dinner as well."

Toller met the general's gaze squarely. "Sir, I don't understand why you brought me here."

"I think it was to give you this." Dalacott opened his right hand to reveal a small object which he dropped on to Toller's palm.

Toller was surprised by its weight, by the massy impact of it on his hand. He held the object closer to the light and was intrigued by the colour and lustre of its polished surface. The colour was unlike any he had seen before, white but somehow more than white, resembling the sea when the sun's rays were obliquely reflected from it at dawn. The object was rounded like a pebble, but might almost have been a miniature carving of a skull whose details had been worn away by time.

"What is it?" Toller said.

Dalacott shook his head. "I don't know. Nobody knows. I found it in Redant province many years ago, on the banks of the Bes-Undar, and nobody has ever been able to tell me what it is."

Toller closed his fingers around the warm object and found his thumb beginning to move in circles on the slick surface. "One question leads to another, sir. Why do you want *me* to have this?"

"Because—" Dalacott gave him a strange smile—"you might say it brought your mother and I together."

"I see," Toller said, speaking mechanically but not untruthfully as the general's words washed through his mind and, like a strong clear wave altering the aspect of a beach, rearranged memory fragments into new designs. The patterns were unfamiliar and yet not totally strange, because they had been inherent in the old order, needing only a single rippling disturbance to make them apparent. There was a long silence broken only by a faint popping sound as an oilbug blundered against a lamp's flame tube and slid down into the reservoir. Toller gazed solemnly at his father, trying to conjure up some appropriate emotion, but inside him there was only numbness.

"I don't know what to say to you," he admitted finally. "This has come so . . . late."

"Later than you think." Again, Dalacott's expression was unreadable as he raised the cup of wine to his lips. "I had many reasons—some of them not altogether selfish—for not acknowledging you, Toller. Do you bear me any ill will?"

"None, sir."

"I'm glad." Dalacott rose to his feet. "We will not meet again, Toller. Will you embrace me . . . once . . . as a man embraces his father?"

"Father." Toller stood up and clasped his arms around the sword-straight, elderly figure. During the brief period of contact he detected a curious hint of spices on his father's breath. He glanced down at the cup waiting on the desk, made a half-intuitive mental leap, and when they parted to resume their seats there was a prickling in his eyes.

Dalacott seemed calm, fully composed. "Now, son, what comes next for you? Kolcorron and its new ally—the ptertha —have achieved their glorious victory. The soldiers' work is all but done, so what have you planned for your future?"

"I think I wasn't intended to have a future," Toller said. "There was a time when Leddravohr would have slain me in person, but something happened, something I don't understand. He placed me in the army and I believe it was his intention that the Chamtethans would do his work at a remove."

"He has a great deal to occupy his thoughts and absorb his energies, you know," the general said. "An entire continent now has to be looted, merely as a preliminary to the building of Prad's migration fleet. Perhaps Leddravohr has forgotten you."

"I haven't forgotten him."

"Is it to the death?"

"I used to think so." Toller thought of bloody footprints on pale mosaic, but the vision had become obscured, overlaid by hundreds of images of carnage. "Now I doubt if the sword is the answer to anything."

"I'm relieved to hear you say that. Even though Leddravohr's heart is not really in the migration plan, he is probably the best man to see it through to a successful conclusion. It is possible that the future of our race rests on his shoulders."

"I'm aware of that possibility, father."

"And you also feel you can solve your own problems perfectly well without my advice." There was a wry twist to the general's lips. "I think I would have enjoyed having you by me. Now, what about my original question? Have you no thought at all for your future?"

"I would like to pilot a ship to Overland," Toller said. "But I think it is a vain ambition."

"Why? Your family must have influence."

"My brother is the chief advisor on the design of the skyships, but he is almost as unpopular with Prince Leddravohr as I am."

"Is it something you genuinely desire to do, this piloting of a skyship? Do you actually *want* to ascend thousands of miles into the heavens? With only a balloon and a few cords and scraps of wood to support you?"

Toller was surprised by the questions. "Why not?"

"Truly, a new age brings forth new men," Dalacott said softly, apparently speaking to himself, then his manner became brisk. "You must go now—I have letters to write. I have some influence with Leddravohr, and a great deal of influence with Carranald, the head of Army Air Services. If you have the necessary aptitudes you will pilot a skyship."

"Again, father, I don't know what to say." Toller stood up, but was reluctant to leave. So much had happened in the space of only a few minutes and his inability to respond was filling him with a guilty sense of failure. How could he meet and say goodbye to his father in almost the same breath?

"You are not required to say anything, son. Only accept that I loved your mother, and. . . ." Dalacott broke off, looking surprised, and scanned the interior of the tent as though suspecting the presence of an intruder.

Toller was alarmed. "Are you ill?"

"It's nothing. The night is too long and dark in this part of the world."

"Perhaps if you lay down," Toller said, starting forward.

General Risdel Dalacott halted him with a look. "Leave me now, lieutenant."

Toller saluted correctly and left the tent. As he was closing the entrance flap he saw that his father had picked up his pen and had already begun to write. Toller allowed the flap to fall and the triangle of wan illumination—an image seeping through the gauzy folds of probability, of lives unlived and of stories never to be told—swiftly vanished. He began to weep as he moved away through the star-canopied dimness. Deep wells of emotion were at last being tapped, and his tears were all the more copious for having come too late.

CHAPTER 13

Night, as always, was the time of the ptertha.

Marnn Ibbler had been in the army since he was fifteen years old, and—like many long-serving soldiers—had developed a superb personal alarm system which told him when one of the globes was near. He was rarely conscious of maintaining vigilance, but at all times he had a full-circle awareness of his surroundings, and even when exhausted or drunk he knew as if by instinct when ptertha were drifting in his vicinity.

Thus it was that he became the first man to receive any inkling of yet another change in the nature and ways of his people's ancient enemy.

He was on night guard at the Third Army's great permanent base camp at Trompha in southern Middac. The duty was undemanding. Only a few ancillary units had been left behind when Kolcorron had invaded Chamteth; the base was close to the secure heartland of the empire, and nobody but a fool ventured abroad at night in open countryside.

Ibbler was standing with two young sentries who were complaining bitterly and at great length about food and pay. He secretly agreed with them about the former—never in his experience had army rations been so meagre and hard to stomach—but, as old soldiers do, he persistently capped every grievance of theirs with hardship stories from early campaigns. They were close to the inner screen, beyond which was a thirty-yard buffer zone and an outer screen. The fertile plains of Middac were visible through the open meshworks, stretching away to the western horizon, illuminated by a gibbous Overland.

There was supposed to be no movement in the outer gloaming—discounting the near-continuous flickering of shooting stars—so when Ibbler's finely attuned senses detected a subtle shifting of shade upon shade he knew at once that it was a ptertha. He did not even mention the sighting to his companions

—they were safe behind the double barrier—and he continued the conversation as before, but a part of his consciousness was now engaged elsewhere.

A moment later he noticed a second ptertha, then a third, and within a minute he had picked out eight of the globes, all forming a single cluster. They were riding out on a gentle north-west breeze, and they faded from his vision some distance to his right where parallax merged the vertical strands of the mesh into a seemingly close-woven fabric.

Ibbler, watchful but still unconcerned, waited for the ptertha, to reappear in his field of view. On encountering the outer screen the globes, obeying the dictates of the air current, would nuzzle their way southwards along the camp's perimeter and eventually, having found no prey, would break free and float off towards the south-west coast and the Otollan Sea.

On this occasion, however, they seemed to be behaving unpredictably.

When minutes had passed without the globes becoming visible, Ibbler's young companions noticed that he had dropped out of the conversation. They were amused when he explained what was in his thoughts, deciding that the ptertha—assuming they had existed outside Ibbler's imagination—must have entered a rising air stream and gone over the camp's netted roofs. Anxious to avoid being classed as a nervous old woman, Ibbler allowed the matter to rest, even though it was rare for the ptertha to fly high when they were near humans.

On the following morning five diggers were found dead of pterthacosis in their hut. The soldier who blundered in on them also died, as did two others he ran to in his panic before the isolation drills were brought into force and all those thought to be contaminated were despatched along the Bright Road by archers.

It was Ibbler who noticed that the diggers' hut was close to and downwind of the point where the group of ptertha would have reached the perimeter on the night before. He secured an interview with his commanding officer and put forward the theory that the ptertha had destroyed themselves against the outer screen as a group, producing a cloud of toxic dust so concentrated that it was effective beyond the standard thirty-yard safety margin. His words were noted with considerable scepticism, but within days the phenomenon they described had actually been witnessed at several locations.

None of the subsequent outbreaks of the ptertha plague was as well-contained as at Trompha, and many hundreds had died before the authorities realised that the war between the people of Kolcorron and the ptertha had entered a new phase.

The general population of the empire felt the effect in two ways. Buffer zones were doubled in size, but there was no longer any guarantee of their efficacy. A light, steady breeze was the weather condition most feared, because it could carry invisible wisps of the ptertha toxin a long way into a community before the concentration fell below lethal levels. But even in gusty and variable wind a large enough cluster of ptertha could lay the stealthy hand of death on a sleeping child, and by morning an entire family or group household would be affected.

The second factor which accelerated the shrinkage of population was the further drop in agricultural output. Regions which had known food shortages began to experience outright famine. The traditional system of continuous harvesting now worked against the Kolcorronians because they had never developed any great expertise in the long-term storage of grain and other edible crops. Meagre reserves of food rotted or became pest-ridden in hastily improvised granaries, and diseases unconnected with the ptertha took their toll of human life.

The work of transferring huge quantities of power crystals from Chamteth to Ro-Atabri continued throughout the worsening crisis, but the military organisations did not go unscathed. Not only were the five armies stood down in Chamteth—they were denied transportation to Kolcorron and the home provinces, and were ordered to take up permanent residence in the Land of the Long Days, where the ptertha—as though sensing their vulnerability—swarmed in ever-increasing numbers. Only those units concerned with gutting the brakka forests and shipping out the cargoes of green and purple crystals remained under the protective umbrella of Leddravohr's high command.

And Prince Leddravohr himself changed.

In the beginning he had accepted the responsibility for the Overland migration almost solely because of loyalty to his father, offsetting his private reservations against the opportunity to conduct an all-out war against Chamteth. Throughout all his preparation for the building of the fleet of skyships he had nourished deep within him the belief that the unappealing venture would never come to fruition, that some less radical solution to Kolcorron's problems would be found, one which was more in keeping with the established patterns of human history.

But above all else he was a realist, a man who understood the vital importance of balancing ambition and ability, and when he foresaw the inevitable outcome of the war against the ptertha he shifted his ground.

The migration to Overland was now part of his personal future and those about him, sensing his new attitude, understood that nothing would be allowed to stand in its way.

CHAPTER 14

"But today of all days!" Colonel Kartkang said forcibly. "I suppose you realise your take-off is scheduled for the tenth hour?"

He was lightly-built for a member of the military caste, with a round face and a mouth so wide that there was a visible gap between each of his smallish teeth. A talent for administration and an unfailing eye for detail had brought him his appointment as head of Skyship Experimental Squadron, and he clearly disliked the idea of permitting a test pilot to leave the base shortly before the most important proving flight in his programme.

"I'll be back long before that time, sir," Toller said. "You know I wouldn't take the slightest risk in this matter."

"Yes, but . . . Do you know that Prince Leddravohr plans to watch the ascent in person?"

"All the more reason for me to be back in good time, sir. I don't want to risk high treason."

Kartkang, still not easy in his mind, squared a sheaf of papers on his desk. "Was Lord Glo important to you?"

"I was prepared to risk my life in his service."

"In that case I suppose you had better pay your last respects," Kartgang said. "But keep it in mind about the prince."

"Thank you, sir." Toller saluted and left the office, his mind a battleground for incompatible emotions. It seemed cruelly ironic, almost proof of the existence of a malign deity, that Glo was to be buried on the very day that a skyship was setting out to prove the feasibility of flying to Overland. The project had been conceived in Glo's brain and had brought him ridicule and disgrace at first, followed by ignominious retirement, and just as he was about to receive personal vindication his beleaguered body had failed him. There would be no plump-bellied statue in the grounds of the Great Palace, and it was doubtful if Glo's name would even be remembered by the nation he had helped to establish on another world. Everything should have been very different.

Visions of the migration fleet touching down on Overland brought a resurgence of the icy excitement which Toller had been living with for days. He had been in the grip of his monomania for so long, working with total commitment towards selection for the first interplanetary mission, that he had somehow lost sight of its astonishing realities. His impatience had slowed the passage of time so much that he had unconsciously begun to believe his goal would forever remain ahead of him, flickering beyond reach like a mirage, and now—with shocking suddenness—the present had collided with the future.

The time of the great voyage was at hand, and during it many things would be learned, not all of them to do with the technicalities of interplanetary flight.

Toller left the S.E.S. administration complex and climbed a wooden stair to the surface of the plain which extended north of Ro-Atabri as far as the foothills of the Slaskitan Mountains. He requisitioned a bluehorn from the stablemaster and set off on the two-mile ride to Greenmount. The varnished linen of the tunnel-like covered way glowed in the foreday sunlight, surrounding him with a yellowish directionless light, and the trapped air was muggy, heavy with the smell of animal droppings. Most of the traffic was heading out from the city, flatbed carts laden with gondola sections and jet cylinders of brakka.

Toller made good time to the eastern junction, entered the tube leading towards Greenmount and soon reached an area protected by the older open-mesh screens of the Ro-Atabri suburbs. He rode through a moraine of abandoned dwellings on the exposed flank of the hill, eventually reaching the small private cemetery adjoining the colonnaded west wing of Greenmount Peel.

Several groups of mourners were already in attendance, and among them he saw his brother and the slender grey-clad figure of Gesalla Maraquine. It was the first time he had seen her since the night she had been abused by Leddravohr, more than a year earlier, and his heart jolted uncomfortably as he realised he was at a loss as to how to conduct himself with her.

He dismounted, straightened the embroidered blue jupon of his skycaptain's uniform and walked towards his brother and his wife, still feeling oddly nervous and self-conscious. On seeing him approach Lain gave him the calm half-smile, indicative of family pride tinged with incredulity, which he had used of late when they met at technical briefings. Toller took pleasure in having surprised and impressed his older brother with his single-minded assault on every obstacle, including reading difficulties, on his way to becoming a skyship pilot.

"This is a sad day," he said to Lain.

Gesalla, who had not been aware of his approach, spun round, one hand flying to her throat. He nodded courteously to her and withheld a verbal greeting, leaving it to her to accept or decline the conversational initiative. She returned his nod, silently but with no visible evidence of her old antipathy and he felt slightly reassured. In his memory her face had been pared by pregnancy sickness, but now her cheeks were more fully curved and touched with pink. She actually looked younger than before and the sight of her filled his eyes.

He became aware of the pressure of Lain's gaze and said, "Why couldn't Glo have had more time?"

Lain shrugged, an unexpectedly casual gesture for one who had been so close to the Lord Philosopher. "Have you had confirmation about the ascent?"

"Yes. It's at the tenth hour."

"I know that. I mean, are you definitely going?"

"Of course!" Toller glanced up at the netted sky and the nacreous morning crescent of Overland. "I'm all set to tackle Glo's invisible mountains."

Gesalla looked amused and interested. "What does that mean?"

"We know the atmosphere thins out between the two worlds," Toller said. "The rate of attenuation has been roughly measured by sending up gas balloons and observing their expansion through calibrated telescopes. It is something which has to be verified by the proving flight, of course, but we believe the air is plenteous enough to sustain life, even at the midpoint."

"Listen to the newly-fledged expert," Lain said.

"I've had the best teachers," Toller replied, unoffended, turning his attention back to Gesalla. "Lord Glo said the flight was comparable to climbing to the peak of one invisible mountain and descending from another."

"I never gave him credit for being a poet," Gesalla said.

"There are many things for which he will never receive credit."

"Yes—like taking in that gradewife of yours when you went off to play soldiers," Lain put in. "Whatever became of her, anyway?"

Toller gazed at his brother for a moment, puzzled and saddened by the hint of malice in his tone. Lain had asked him the same question some time ago, and now it seemed he was bringing up the subject of Fera for no other reason than that it had always been a sore point with Gesalla. Was it possible that Lain was jealous of his "little brother" having earned a place on the proving flight, the greatest scientific experiment of the age?

"Fera soon got bored with life in the Peel and went back into the city to live," Toller said. "I presume she is in good circumstances—I *hope* she is—but I haven't tried to find out. Why do you ask?"

"Ummm . . . Idle curiosity."

"Well, if your curiosity extends as far as my term in the army I can assure you that the word 'play' is highly inappropriate. I . . . ."

"Be quiet, you two," Gesalla said, placing a hand on each man's arm. "The ceremony begins."

Toller fell silent in a fresh confusion of emotions as the burial party arrived from the direction of the house. In his will Glo had stated his preference for the shortest and simplest ceremony that could be accorded a Kolcorronian aristocrat. His cortege consisted only of Lord Prelate Balountar, followed by four dark-robed suffragens bearing the cylindrical block of white gypsum in which Glo's body had already been encased. Balountar, with head thrust forward and black vestments draping a bony figure, resembled a raven as he slow-marched to the circular hole which had been bored into the bedrock of the cemetery.

He intoned a short prayer, consigning Lord Glo's discarded shell to the parent body of the planet for reabsorption, and calling for his spirit to be given a safe passage to Overland, followed by a fortuitous rebirth and a long and prosperous life on the sister world.

Toller was troubled by guilt as he watched the lowering of the cylinder and the sealing of the hole with cement poured from a decorated urn. He wanted to be torn by sadness and grief on parting with Glo for ever, but his wayward consciousness was dominated by the fact that Gesalla—who had never touched him before—had allowed her hand to remain resting on his arm. Did it signal a change in her attitude towards him, or was it incidental to some twist in her relationship with Lain, who in turn had been acting strangely? And underlying everything else in Toller's mind was the pounding realisation that he was soon to ascend so far into the sky's blue dome that he would pass beyond the reach of even the most powerful telescopes.

He was relieved, therefore, when the brief ceremony drew to a close and the knots of mourners—most of them blood relatives —began to disperse.

"I must return to the base now," he said. "There are many things yet to be. . . ." He left the sentence unfinished as he noticed that the Lord Prelate had separated himself from his entourage and was approaching the trio. Assuming that Balountar's business had to be with Lain, Toller took a discreet step backwards. He was surprised when Balountar came straight to him, close-set eyes intent and furious, and flicked him on the chest with loosely dangling fingers.

"I remember you," he said. "Maraquine! You're the one who laid hands on me in the Rainbow Hall, before the King." He flicked Toller again, clearly intending the gesture to be offensive.

"Well, now that you have evened the score," Toller said easily, "may I be of service to you, my lord?"

"Yes, you can rid yourself of that uniform—it is an offence to the Church in general and to me in particular."

"In what way does it offend?"

"In *every* way! The very colour symbolises the heavens, does it not? It flaunts your intention to defile the High Path, does it not? Even though your evil ambition will be thwarted, Maraquine, those blue rags are an affront to every right-thinking citizen of this country."

"I wear this uniform in the service of Kolcorron, my lord. Any objections you have to that should be presented directly to the King. Or to Prince Leddravohr."

"Huh!" Balountar stared venomously for a moment, his face working with frustrated rage. "You won't get away with it, you know. Even though the likes of you and your brother turn your backs on the Church, in all your sophistry and arrogance, you will learn to your cost that the people will stand for just so much. You'll see! The great blasphemy, the great *evil*, will not go unpunished." He spun and strode away to the cemetery gate, where the four suffragens were waiting.

Toller watched him depart and turned to the others with raised eyebrows. "The Lord Prelate appears to be unhappy."

"There was a time when you would have crushed his hand for doing that." Lain imitated Balountar's gesture, flicking limp fingers against Toller's chest. "Do you no longer see red so easily?"

"Perhaps I have seen too much red."

"Oh, yes. How could I have forgotten?" The mockery in Lain's voice was now unmistakable. "This is your new role, isn't it? The man who has drunk too deeply from the cup of experience."

"Lain, I have no inkling of what I have done to earn your displeasure, and even though I'm saddened by it I have no time now to enquire into the matter." Toller nodded to his brother and bowed to Gesalla, whose concerned gaze was switching between the two. He was about to leave when Lain, eyes deepening with tears, abruptly spread his arms in an embrace which brought his brother and wife together.

"Don't take any foolish risks up there in the sky, little brother," Lain whispered. "It's your family duty to come back safely, so that when the time of the migration arrives we can all fly to Overland together. I won't entrust Gesalla to any but the very best pilot. Do you understand?"

Toller nodded, not attempting to speak. The feel of Gesalla's gracile body against his own was asexual, as it had to be, but there was a *rightness* to it, and with his brother completing the psychic circuit there was a sense of comfort and healing, of vital energies being augmented rather than dissipated.

When Toller broke free of the embrace he felt light and strong, fully capable of soaring to another world.

CHAPTER 15

"We have sunwriter reports from as far away as fifty miles upwind," said Vato Armduran, the S.E.S. chief engineer. "The look-outs say there is very little ptertha activity—so you should be all right on that score—but the wind speed is rather higher than I would have wished."

"If we wait for perfect conditions we'll *never* go." Toller shaded his eyes from the sun and scanned the blue-white dome of the sky. Wisps of high cloud had overpainted the brighter stars without screening them from view, and the broad crescent of illumination on Overland's disk established the time as mid-foreday.

"I suppose that's true, but you're going to have trouble with false lift when you clear the enclosure. You'll need to watch out for it."

Toller grinned. "Isn't it a little late for lessons in aero-dynamics?"

"It's all very well for you—I'm the one who's going to have to do all the explaining if you kill yourself," Armduran said drily. He was a spiky haired man whose flattened nose and sword-scarred chin gave him something of the appearance of a retired soldier, but his practical engineering genius had led to his personal appointment by Prince Chakkell. Toller liked him for his caustic humour and lack of condescension towards less gifted subordinates.

"For your sake, I'll try not to get killed." Toller had to raise his voice to overcome the noise in the enclosure. Members of the inflation crew were busily cranking a large fan whose gears and wooden blades emitted a continuous clacking sound as they forced unheated air into the skyship's balloon, which had been laid out downwind of the gondola. They were creating a cavity within the envelope so that hot gas from the power crystal burner could later be introduced without it having to impinge directly on

179

the lightweight material. The technique had been developed to avoid burn damage, especially to the base panels around the balloon mouth. Overseers were bellowing orders to the men who were holding up the sides of the gradually swelling balloon and paying out attachment lines.

The square, room-sized gondola was lying on its side, already provisioned for the flight. In addition to food, drink and fuel it contained sandbags equivalent to the weight of sixteen people which, when taken with the weight of the test crew, brought the load up to the operational maximum. The three men who were to fly with Toller were standing by the gondola, ready to leap on board on command. He knew the ascent had to begin within a matter of minutes, and the emotional turmoil connected with Lain and Gesalla and Glo's burial was steadily fading to a murmur in lower levels of his consciousness. In his mind he was already voyaging in the ice-blue unknown, like a migrating soul, and his preoccupations were no longer those of an ordinary Land-bound mortal.

There was a sound of hoofbeats nearby and he turned to see Prince Leddravohr riding into the enclosure, followed by an open carriage in which sat Prince Chakkell, his wife Daseene and their three children. Leddravohr was dressed as for a military ceremony, wearing a white cuirass. The inevitable battle sword was at his side and a long throwing knife was sheathed on his left forearm. He dismounted from his tall bluehorn, head turning as he took in every detail of the surrounding activity, and padded towards Toller and Armduran.

Toller had not seen him at all during his time in the army and only at a distance since returning to Ro-Atabri, and he noted that the prince's glossy black hair was now tinged with grey at the temples. He was also a little heavier, but the weight appeared to have been added in an even subcutaneous layer all over his body, doing little more than blur the muscle definition and render the statuesque face smoother than ever. Toller and Armduran saluted as he approached.

Leddravohr nodded in acknowledgement. "Well, Maraquine, you have become an important man since last we met. I trust it has made you somewhat easier to live with."

"I don't class myself as important, Prince," Toller said in a carefully neutral voice, trying to gauge Leddravohr's attitude.

"But you *are!* The first man to take a ship to Overland! It's a great honour, Maraquine, and you have worked hard for it. You know, there were some who felt that you were too young and inexperienced for this mission, that it should have been entrusted to an officer with a long Air Service career behind him, but I overruled them. You obtained the best results in the training courses, and you're not encumbered with an aircaptain's obsolete skills and habits, and you are a man of undoubted courage—so I decreed that the captaincy of the proving flight should be yours.

"What do you think of that?"

"I'm deeply grateful to you, Prince," Toller said.

"Gratitude isn't called for." Leddravohr's old smile, the smile which had nothing to do with amity, flickered on his face for an instant and was gone. "It is only just that you should receive the fruits of your labours."

Toller understood at once that nothing had changed, that Leddravohr was still the deadly enemy who never forgot or forgave. There was a mystery surrounding the prince's apparent forbearance of the last year, but no doubt at all that he still hungered for Toller's life. *He hopes the flight will fail! He hopes he is sending me to my death!*

The intuition gave Toller a sudden new insight into Leddravohr's mind. Analysing his own feelings towards the prince he now found nothing but a cool indifference, with perhaps the beginnings of pity for a creature so imprisoned by negative emotion, awash and drowning in its own venom.

"I'm grateful nevertheless," Toller said, relishing the private double meaning of his words. He had been apprehensive about coming face to face with Leddravohr again, but the encounter had proved that he had transcended his old self, truly, once and for all. From now on his spirit would soar as far above Leddravohr and his kind as the skyship was soon to do over the continents and oceans of Land, and that was genuine cause for rejoicing.

Leddravohr scanned his face for a moment, searchingly, then

transferred his attention to the skyship. The inflation crew had progressed to the stage of raising the balloon up on the four acceleration struts which constituted the principal difference between it and a craft designed for normal atmospheric flight. Now three-quarters full, the balloon sagged among the struts like some grotesque leviathan deprived of the support of its natural medium. The varnished linen skin flapped feebly in the mild air currents coming through the perforations in the enclosure wall.

"If I'm not mistaken," Leddravohr said, "it is time for you to join your ship, Maraquine."

Toller saluted him, squeezed Armduran's shoulder and ran to the gondola. He gave a signal and Zavotle, co-pilot and recorder for the flight, swung himself on board. He was closely followed by Rillomyner, the mechanic, and the diminutive figure of Flenn, the rigger. Toller went in after them, taking his position at the burner. The gondola was still on its side, so he had to lie on his back against a woven cane partition to operate the burner's controls.

The trunk of a very young brakka tree had been used in its entirety to form the main component of the burner. On the left side of the bulbous base was a small hopper filled with pikon, plus a valve which admitted the crystals to the combustion chamber under pneumatic pressure. On the opposite side a similar device controlled the flow of halvell, and both valves were operated by a single lever. The passageways in the right-hand valve were slightly enlarged, automatically providing the greater proportion of halvell which had been found best for providing sustained thrust.

Toller pumped the pneumatic reservoir by hand, then signalled to the inflation supervisor that he was ready to begin burning. The noise level in the enclosure dropped as the fan crew ceased cranking and pulled their cumbersome machine and its nozzle aside.

Toller advanced the control lever for about a second. There was a hissing roar as the power crystals combined, firing a burst of hot miglign gas into the balloon's gaping mouth. Satisfied with the burner's performance, he instigated a series of blasts—

keeping them brief to reduce the risk of heat damage to the balloon fabric—and the great envelope began to distend and lift clear of the ground. As it gradually rose to the vertical position the crew holding the balloon's crown lines came walking in and attached them to the gondola's load frame, while others rotated the gondola until it was in the normal attitude. All at once the skyship was ready to fly, only held down by its central anchor.

Mindful of Armduran's warning about false lift, Toller continued burning for another full minute, and as the hot gas displaced more and more unheated air through the balloon mouth the entire assemblage began to strain upwards. Finally, too intent on his work to feel any sense of occasion, he pulled the anchor link and the skyship left the ground.

It rose quickly at first, then the curved crown of the balloon entered the wind above the enclosure walls, generating such a fierce extra lift that Rillomyner gasped aloud as the ship accelerated skywards. Toller, undeceived by the phenomenon, fired a long blast from the burner. In a few seconds the balloon had fully entered the airstream and was travelling with it, and as the relative airflow across the top dropped to zero the extra lift also disappeared.

At the same time, a rippling distortion caused by the initial impact of the wind expelled some gas back out through the mouth of the balloon, and now the ship was actually losing height as it was borne away to the east at some ten miles an hour. The speed was not great compared to what other forms of transport could achieve, but the airship was designed for vertical travel only and any contact with the ground at that stage was likely to be disastrous.

Toller fought the unintentional descent with prolonged burns. For a tense minute the gondola headed straight for the line of elvart trees at the eastern edge of the airfield as though attached to an invisible rail, then the balloon's buoyancy began to reassert itself. The ground slowly sank away and Toller was able to rest the burner. Looking back towards the line of enclosures, some of which were still under construction, he was able to pick out the white gleam of Leddravohr's cuirass among the hundreds of spectators, but—already—the prince seemed to be part of his past, his psychological importance diminishing with perspective.

"Would you like to make a note?" Toller said to Ilven Zavotle. "It appears that the maximum wind speed for take off with full load is in the region of ten miles an hour. Also, those trees should go."

Zavotle glanced up briefly from the wicker table at his station. "I'm already doing it, captain." He was a narrow-headed youngster with tiny clenched ears and a permanent frown, as fussy and fastidious in his ways as a very old man, but already a veteran of several test flights.

Toller glanced around the square gondola, checking that all was well. Mechanic Rillomyner had slumped down on the sandbags in one of the passenger compartments, looking pale of face and distinctly sorry for himself. Ree Flenn, the rigger, was perched like some arboreal animal on the gondola's rail, busily shortening the tether on one of the free-hanging acceleration struts. Toller's stomach produced a chill spasm as he saw that Flenn had not secured his personal line to the rail.

"What do you think you're doing, Flenn?" he said. "Get your line attached."

"I can work better without it, captain." A grin split the rigger's bead-eyed, button-nosed face. "I'm not afraid of heights."

"Would you *like* something to be afraid of?" Toller spoke mildly, almost courteously, but Flenn's grin faded at once and he snapped his karabiner on to the brakka rail. Toller turned away to hide his amusement. Capitalising on his dwarfish stature and comic appearance, Flenn habitually breached discipline in ways which would have earned the lash for other men, but he was highly expert at his work and Toller had been glad to accept him for the flight. His own background inclined him to be sympathetic towards rebels and misfits.

By now the ship was climbing steadily above the western suburbs of Ro-Atabri. The city's familiar configurations were blurred and dulled by the blanket of anti-ptertha screens which had spread over it like some threaded mould, but the vistas of Arle Bay and the Gulf were as Toller remembered them from childhood aerial excursions. Their nostalgic blue faded into a purple haze near the horizon above which, subdued by sunlight, shone the nine stars of the Tree.

Looking down, Toller was able to see the Great Palace, on the south bank of the Borann, and he wondered if King Prad could be at a window at that very moment, gazing up at the fragile assemblage of fabric and wood which represented his stake in posterity. Since appointing his son to the position of absolute power the King had become a virtual recluse. Some said that his health had deteriorated, others that he had no heart for skulking like a furtive animal in the shrouded streets of his own capital city.

Surveying the complex and variegated scene beneath him, Toller was surprised to discover that he felt little emotion. He seemed to have severed his bonds with the past by taking the first step along the five-thousand-mile high road to Overland. Whether he would in fact reach the sister planet on a later flight and begin a new life there was a matter for the future—and his present was bounded by the tiny world of the skyship. The microcosm of the gondola, only four good paces on a side, was destined to be his whole universe for more than twenty days, and he could have no other commitments. . . .

Toller's meditation came to an abrupt end when he noticed a purplish mote drifting against the white-feathered sky some distance to the north-west.

"On your feet, Rillomyner," he called out. "It's time you started earning your pay on this trip."

The mechanic stood up and came out of the passenger compartment. "I'm sorry, captain—the way we took off did something to my gut."

"Get on to the cannon if you don't want to be really sick," Toller said. "We might be having a visitor soon."

Rillomyner swore and lurched towards the nearest cannon. Zavotle and Flenn followed suit without needing to be ordered. There were two of the anti-ptertha guns mounted on each side of the gondola, their barrels made of thin strips of brakka bonded into tubes by glass cords and resin. Below each weapon was a magazine containing glass power capsules and a supply of the latest type of projectile—hinged bundles of wooden rods which opened radially in flight. They demanded better accuracy than the older scattering weapons, but compensated with improved range.

Toller remained at the pilot's station and fired intermittent bursts of heat into the balloon to maintain the rate of climb. He was not unduly concerned about the lone ptertha and had issued his warning as much to rouse Rillomyner as anything else. As far as was known, the globes depended on air currents to transport them over long distances, and only moved horizontally of their own volition when close to their prey. How they obtained impulsion over the final few yards was still a mystery, but one theory was that a ptertha had already begun the process of self-destruction at that stage by creating a small orifice in its surface at the point most distant from the victim. Expulsion of internal gases would propel the globe to within the killing radius before the entire structure disintegrated and released its charge of toxic dust. The process remained a matter for conjecture because of the impossibility of studying ptertha at close range.

In the present case the globe was about four-hundred yards from the ship and was likely to stay at that distance because the positions of both were governed by the same air-flow. Toller knew, however, that the one component of their motion over which the ptertha had good control was in the vertical dimension. Observation through calibrated telescopes showed that a ptertha could govern its attitude by increasing or decreasing its size, thus altering its density, and Toller was interested in carrying out a double experiment which might be of value to the migration fleet.

"Keep your eye on the globe," he said to Zavotle. "It seems to be keeping on a level with us, and if it is that proves it can sense our presence over that distance. I also want to find out how high it will go before giving up."

"Very good, captain." Zavotle raised his binoculars and settled down to studying the ptertha.

Toller glanced around his circumscribed domain, trying to imagine how much more cramped its dimensions would seem with a full complement of twenty people on board. The passenger accommodation consisted of two narrow compartments, at opposite sides of the gondola for balance, bounded by chest-high partitions. Nine or so people would be crammed into each, unable either to lie down properly or move around, and by the end of the long voyage their physical condition was likely to be poor.

One corner of the gondola was taken up by the galley, and the diagonally opposite one by the primitive toilet, which was basically a hole in the floor plus some sanitation aids. The centre of the floor was occupied by the four crew stations surrounding the burner unit and the downward facing drive jet. Most of the remaining space was filled by the pikon and halvell magazines, which were also at opposite sides of the gondola, with the food and drink stores and various equipment lockers.

Toller could foresee the interplanetary crossing, like so many other historic and glorious adventures, being conducted in squalor and degradation, becoming a test of physical and mental endurance which not all would survive.

In contrast to the meanness and compression of the gondola, the upper element of the skyship was awesomely spacious, rarified, a giant form almost without substance. The linen panels of the envelope had been dyed dark brown to absorb the sun's heat and thereby gain extra lift, but when Toller looked up into it through the open mouth he could see light glowing through the material. The seams and horizontal and vertical load tapes appeared as a geometric web of black lines, emphasising the vastness of the balloon's curvatures. Up there was the gossamer dome of a cloud-borne cathedral. impossible to associate with the handiwork of mere weavers and stitchers.

Satisfied that the ship was stable and ascending steadily, Toller gave the order for the four acceleration struts to be drawn in and attached by their lower ends to the corners of the gondola. Flenn completed the task within a few minutes, imparting to the balloon/gondola assemblage the slight degree of structural stiffness needed to cope with the modest forces which would act on it when the drive or attitude jets were in use.

Attached to a lashing hook at the pilot's station was the rip line, dyed red, which ran up through the balloon to a crown panel which could be torn out for rapid deflation. As well as being a safety device it served as a rudimentary climb speed indicator, becoming slack when the crown was depressed by a strong vertical air flow. Toller fingered the line and estimated that they were ascending at about twelve miles an hour, aided by the fact that the miglign gas was slightly lighter than air even when unheated. Later he would almost double that speed by using the drive jet when the ship entered the regions of low gravity and attenuated air.

Thirty minutes into the flight the ship was high above the summit of Mount Opelmer and had ceased its eastward drift. The garden province of Kail stretched to the southern horizon, its strip farms registering as a shimmering mosaic, with each tessera striated in six different shades varying from yellow to green. To the west was the Otollan Sea and to the east was the Mirlgiver Ocean, their curving blue reaches flecked here and there by sailing ships. The ochraceous mountains of Upper Kolcorron filled the view to the north, their ranges and folds compacted by perspective. A few airships gleamed like tiny elliptical jewels as they plied the trade lanes far below.

From an altitude of some six miles the face of Land looked placid and achingly beautiful. Only the relative scarcity of airships and sailing craft indicated that the entire prospect, apparently drowsing in benign sunlight, was actually a battleground, an arena in which mankind had fought and lost a deadly duel.

Toller, as had become his habit when deep in thought, located the curiously massive object given to him by his father and rubbed his thumb over its gleaming surface. In the normal course of history, he wondered, how many centuries would men have waited before essaying the voyage to Overland? Indeed, would they ever have done so had they not been fleeing from the ptertha?

The thought of the ancient and implacable enemy prompted him to cast around and check on the position of the solitary globe he had detected earlier. Its lateral separation from the ship had not changed and, more significantly, it was still matching the rate of climb. Was that proof of sentience and purpose? If so, why had the ptertha as a species singled out man as the focus of its hostility? Why was it that every other creature on Land, with the exception of the Sorka gibbon, was immune to pterthacosis?

As though sensing Toller's renewed interest in the globe, Zavotle lowered his binoculars and said, "Does it look bigger to you, captain?"

Toller picked up his own glasses and studied the purple-black smudge, finding that its transparency defied his attempts to define its boundaries. "Hard to say."

"Littlenight will be here soon," Zavotle commented. "I don't relish the idea of having that thing hanging around us in the dark."

"I don't think it can close in—the ship is almost the same shape as a ptertha, and our response to a crosswind will be roughly similar."

"I hope you're right," Zavotle said gloomily.

Rillomyner looked round from his post at a cannon and said, "We haven't eated since dawn, captain." He was a pale and pudgy young man with an enormous appetite for even the vilest food, and it was said that he had actually gained weight since the beginning of the shortages by scavenging all the substandard food rejected by his workmates. In spite of a show of diffidence, he was a good mechanic and intensely proud of his skills.

"I'm glad to hear your gut is back to its normal condition," Toller said. "I would hate to think I had done it some permanent mischief with my handling of the ship."

"I didn't mean to criticise the take-off, captain—it's just that I have always been cursed with this weak stomach."

Toller clicked his tongue in mock sympathy and glanced at Flenn. "You'd better feed this man before he becomes faint."

"Right away, captain." As Flenn was getting to his feet his shirt parted at the chest and the green-striped head of a carble peered out. Flenn hastily covered the furry creature with his hand and pushed it back into concealment.

"What have you got there?" Toller snapped.

"Her name is Tinny, captain." Flenn brought the carble out and cradled it in his arms. "There was nobody I could leave her with."

Toller sighed his exasperation. "This is a scientific mission, not a . . . Do you realise that most commanders would put that animal over the side?"

"I swear she won't be any trouble, captain."

"She'd better not. Now get the food."

Flenn grinned and, agile as a monkey, disappeared into the galley to prepare the first meal of the voyage. He was small enough to be completely hidden by the woven partition which was chest high to the rest of the crew. Toller settled down to refining his control over the ship's ascent.

Deciding to increase speed, he lengthened the burns from three to four seconds and watched for the time-lagged response of the balloon overhead. Several minutes went by before the extra lift he was generating overcame the inertia of the many tons of gas inside the envelope and the rip line became noticeably slacker. Satisfied with a new rate of climb of around eighteen miles an hour, he concentrated on making the burner rhythm—four seconds on and twenty off—part of his awareness, something to be paced by the internal clocks of his heart and lungs. He needed to be able to detect the slightest variation in it even when he was asleep and being spelled at the controls by Zavotle.

The food served up by Flenn was from the limited fresh supplies and was better than Toller had expected—strips of reasonably lean beef in gravy, pulse, fried grain-cakes and beakers of hot green tea. Toller stopped operating the burner while he ate, allowing the ship to coast upwards in silence on stored lift. The heat emanating from the black combustion chamber mingled with the aromatic vapours issuing from the galley, turning the gondola into a homely oasis in a universe of azure emptiness.

Partway through the meal littlenight came sweeping from the west, a brief flash of rainbow colours preceding a sudden darkness, and as the crew's eyes adjusted the heavens blazed into life all around them. They reacted to the unearthliness of their situation by generating an intense camaraderie. There was an unspoken conviction that lifelong friendships were being formed, and in that atmosphere every anecdote was interesting, every boast believable, every joke profoundly funny. And even when the talk eventually died away, stilled by strangeness, communication continued on another plane.

Toller was set apart to some extent by the responsibilities of command, but he was warmed nonetheless. From his seated position the rim of the gondola was at eye level, which meant there was nothing to be seen beyond it but enigmatic whirlpools of radiance, the splayed mist-fans of comets, and stars and stars and ever more stars. The only sound was the occasional creak of a rope, and the only sensible movement was where the meteors scribed their swift-fading messages on the blackboard of night.

Toller could easily imagine himself adrift in the beaconed depths of the universe, and all at once, unexpectedly, there came the longing to have a woman at his side, a female presence which would somehow make the voyage meaningful. It would have been good to be with Fera at that moment, but her essential carnality would scarcely have been in accord with his mood. The right woman would have been one who was capable of enhancing the mystical qualities of the experience. Somebody like. . . .

Toller reached out with his imagination, blindly, wistfully. For an instant the feel of Gesalla Maraquine's slim body against his own was shockingly real. He leapt to his feet, guilty and confused, disturbing the equilibrium of the gondola.

"Is anything wrong, captain?" Zavotle said, barely visible in the darkness.

"Nothing. A touch of cramp, that's all. You take over the burner for a while. Four-twenty is what we want."

Toller went to the side of the gondola and leaned on the rail. *What is happening to me now?* he thought. *Lain said I was playing a role—but how did he know? The new cool and imperturbable Toller Maraquine . . . the man who has drunk too deeply from the cup of experience . . . who looks down on princes . . . who is undaunted by the chasm between the worlds . . . and who, because his brother's solewife does no more than touch his arm, is immediately smitten with adolescent fantasies about her! Was Lain, with that frightening perception of his, able to see me for the betrayer that I am? Is that why he seemed to turn against me?*

The darkness below the skyship was absolute, as though Land had already been deserted by all of humanity, but as Toller gazed down into it a thin line of red, green and violet fire appeared on the western horizon. It widened, growing increasingly brilliant, and suddenly a tide of pure light was sweeping across the world at heart-stopping speed, recreating oceans and land masses in all their colour and intricate detail. Toller almost flinched in expectation of a palpable blow as the speeding terminator reached the ship, engulfing it in fierce sunlight, and rushed on to the eastern horizon. The columnar shadow of Overland had completed its daily transit of Kolcorron, and Toller felt that he had emerged from yet another occultation, a littlenight of the mind.

Don't worry, beloved brother, he thought. *Even in my thoughts I'll never betray you. Not ever!*

Ilven Zavotle stood up at the burner and looked out to the north-west. "What do you think of the globe now, captain? Is it bigger or closer? Or both?"

"It might be a little closer," Toller said, glad to have an external focus for this thoughts, as he trained his binoculars on the ptertha. "Can you feel the ship dancing a little? There could be some churning of warmer and cooler air as littlenight passes, and it might have worked out to the globe's advantage."

"It's still on a level with us—even though we changed our speed."

"Yes. I think it wants us."

"I know what *I* want," Flenn announced as he slipped by Toller on his way to the toilet. "I'm going to have the honour of being the first to try out the long drop—and I hope it all lands right on old Puehilter." He had nominated an overseer whose petty tyrannies had made him unpopular with the S.E.S. flight technicians.

Rillomyner snorted in approval. "That'll give him something worth complaining about, for once."

"It'll be worse when you go—they're going to have to evacuate the whole of Ro-Atabri when you start bombing them."

"Just take care you don't fall down the hole," Rillomyner growled, not appreciating the reference to his dietary foibles. "It wasn't designed for midgets."

Toller made no comment about the exchange. He knew the two were testing him to see what style of command he was going to favour on the voyage. A strict interpretation of flight regulations would have precluded any badinage at all among his crew, let alone grossness, but he was solely concerned with their qualities of efficiency, loyalty and courage. In a couple of hours the ship would be higher than any had gone before—if one discounted the semi-mythical Usader of five centuries earlier —entering a region of strangeness, and he could foresee the little group of adventurers needing every human support available to them.

Besides, the same subject had given rise to a thousand equally coarse jokes in the officers' quarters, ever since the utilitarian design of the skyship gondola had become common knowledge. He himself had derived a certain amusement from the frequency with which ground-based personnel had reminded him that the toilet was not to be used until the prevailing westerlies had carried the ship well clear of the base. . . .

The bursting of the ptertha took Toller by surprise.

He was gazing at the globe's magnified image when it simply ceased to exist, and in the absence of a contrasting background there was not even a dissipating smudge of dust to mark its location. In spite of his confidence in their ability to deal with the threat, he nodded in satisfaction. Sleep was going to be difficult enough during the first night aloft without having to worry about capricious air currents bringing the silent enemy to within its killing radius.

"Make a note that the ptertha has just popped itself out of existence," he said to Zavotle, and—expressing his relief— added a personal comment. "Put down that it happened about four hours into the flight . . . just as Flenn was using the toilet . . . but that there is probably no connection between the two events."

Toller awoke shortly after dawn to the sound of an animated discussion taking place at the centre of the gondola. He raised himself to a kneeling position on the sandbags and rubbed his arms, uncertain as to whether the coolness he could feel was external or an aftermath of sleep. The intermittent roar of the burner had been so intrusive that he had achieved only light dozes, and now he felt little more refreshed than if he had been on duty all night. He walked on his knees to the opening in the passenger compartment's partition and looked out at the rest of the crew.

"You should have a look at this, captain," Zavotle said, raising his narrow head. "The height gauge actually does work!"

Toller insinuated his legs into the cramped central floorspace and went to the pilot's station, where Flenn and Rillomyner were standing beside Zavotle. At the station was a lightweight table, attached to which was the height gauge. The latter consisted of nothing more than a vertical scale, from the top of which a small weight was suspended by a delicate coiled spring made from a hair-like shaving of brakka. On the previous morning, at the beginning of the flight, the weight had been opposite to the lowest mark on the scale—but now it was several divisions higher.

Toller stared hard at the gauge. "Has anybody interfered with it?"

"Nobody has touched it," Zavotle assured him. "It means that everything they told us must be true. Everything is getting lighter as we go higher! We're getting lighter!"

"That's to be expected," Toller said, unwilling to admit that in his heart he had never quite accepted the notion, even when Lain had taken time to impress the theory on him in private tutorials.

"Yes, but it means that in three or four days from now we won't weigh anything at all. We'll be able to float around in the air like . . . like . . . ptertha! It's all *true*, captain!"

"How high does it say we are?"

"About three-hundred-and-fifty miles—and that agrees well with our computations."

"I don't feel any different," Rillomyner put in. "I say the spring has tightened up."

Flenn nodded. "Me too."

Toller wished for time in which to arrange his thoughts. He went to the side of the gondola and experienced a whirling moment of vertigo as he saw Land as he had never seen it before—an immense circular convexity, one half in near-darkness, the other a brilliant sparkling of blue ocean and subtly shaded continents and islands.

Things would be quite different if you were lifting off from the centre of Chamteth and heading out into open space, Lain's voice echoed in his mind. *But when travelling between the two worlds you will soon reach a middle zone—slightly closer to Overland than to Land, in fact—where the gravitational pull of each planet cancels out the other. In normal conditions, with the gondola being heavier than the balloon, the ship has pendulum stability —but where neither has any weight the ship will be unstable and you will have to use the lateral jets to control its attitude.*

Lain had already completed the entire journey in his mind, Toller realised, and everything he had predicted would come to pass. Truly, they were entering a region of strangeness, but the intellects of Lain Maraquine and other men like him had already marked the way, and they had to be trusted. . . .

"Don't get so excited that you lose the burn rhythm," Toller said calmly, turning to Zavotle. "And don't forget to check the height gauge readings by measuring the apparent diameter of Land four times a day."

He directed his gaze at Rillomyner and Flenn. "And as for you two—why did the Squadron take the trouble to send you to special classes? The spring has *not* altered in strength. We're getting lighter as we get higher, and I will treat any disputing of that fact as insubordination. Is that clear?"

"Yes, captain."

Both men spoke in unison, but Toller noticed a troubled look in Rillomyner's eyes, and he wondered if the mechanic was going to have difficulty in adjusting to his increasing weightlessness. *This is what the proving flight is for*, he reminded himself. *We are testing ourselves as much as the ship*.

By nightfall the weight on the height gauge had risen to near the halfway mark on the scale, and the effects of reduced gravity were apparent, no longer a matter for argument.

When a small object was allowed to drop it fell to the floor of the gondola with evident slowness, and all members of the crew reported curious sinking sensations in their stomachs. On two occasions Rillomyner awoke from sleep with a panicky shout, explaining afterwards that he had been convinced he was falling.

Toller noticed the dreamlike ease with which he could move about, and it came to him that it would soon be advisable for the crew to remain tethered at all times. The idea of an unnecessarily vigorous movement separating a man from the ship was one he did not like to contemplate.

He also observed that, in spite of its decreased weight, the ship was tending to rise more slowly. The effect had been accurately predicted—a result of the fading weight differential between the hot gas inside the envelope and the surrounding atmosphere. To maintain speed he altered the burn rhythm to four-eighteen, and then to four-sixteen. The pikon and halvell hoppers on the burner were being replenished with increasing frequency and, although there were ample reserves, Toller began to look forward to reaching the altitude of thirteen-hundred miles. At that point the ship's weight, decreasing by squares, would be only a fourth of normal, and it would become more economical to change over to jet power until the zone of zero gravity had been passed.

The need to interpret every action and event in the dry languages of mathematics, engineering and science conflicted with Toller's natural response to his new environment. He found he could spend long periods leaning on the rim of the gondola, not moving a muscle, mesmerised, all physical energies annulled by pure awe. Overland was directly above him, but screened from view by the patient, untiring vastness of the balloon; and far below was the home world, gradually becoming a place of mystery as its familiar features were blurred by a thousand miles of intervening air.

By the third day of the ascent the sky, although retaining its normal coloration above and below, was shading on all sides of the ship into a deeper blue which glistered with ever-increasing numbers of stars.

When Toller was lost in his tranced vigils the conversation of the crew members and even the roar of the burner faded from his consciousness, and he was alone in the universe, sole possessor of all its scintillant hoards. Once during the hours of darkness, while he was standing at the pilot's station, he saw a meteor strike across the sky *below* the ship. It traced a line of fire from what seemed to be one edge of infinity to the other, and minutes after its passing there came a single pulse of low-frequency sound—blurred, dull and mournful—causing the ship to give a tentative heave which drew a murmur of protest from one of the sleeping men. Some instinct, a kind of spiritual acquisitiveness, prompted Toller to keep the knowledge of the event from the others.

As the ascent continued Zavotle was kept busy with his copious flight records, many of the entries concerned with physiological effects. Even at the summit of the highest mountain on Land there was no discernible drop in air pressure, but on previous high-altitude sorties by balloon some crew members had reported a hint of thinness to the air and the need to breathe more deeply. The effect had been slight and the best scientific estimate was that the atmosphere would continue to support life midway between the two planets, but it was vital that the predication should be verified.

Toller was almost comforted by the feel of his lungs working harder during the third day—more evidence that the problems of interworld flight had been correctly foreseen—and he was therefore less than happy when an unexpected phenomenon forced itself on his attention. For some time he had been aware of feeling cold, but had dismissed the matter from his thoughts. Now, however, the others in the gondola were complaining almost continuously and the conclusion was inescapable— as the ship gained altitude the surrounding air was growing colder.

The S.E.S. scientists, Lain Maraquine included, had been of the opinion that there would be an increase in temperature as the ship entered rarified air which would be less able to screen it from the sun's rays. As a native of equatorial Kolcorron, Toller had never experienced really severe coldness, and he had thought nothing of setting off on the interplanetary voyage clad in only a shirt, breeches and sleeveless jupon. Now, although not actually shivering, he was continuously aware of the increasing discomfort and a dismaying thought was beginning to lurk in his mind—that the entire flight might have to be abandoned for the lack of a bale of wool.

He gave permission for the crew to wear all their spare clothing under their uniforms, and for Flenn to brew tea on demand. The latter decision, far from improving the situation, led to a series of arguments. Time after time Rillomyner insisted that Flenn, acting out of malice or ineptitude, was either infusing the tea before the water had boiled properly or was allowing it to cool before serving it around. It was only when Zavotle, who had also been dissatisfied, kept a critical eye on the brewing process that the truth emerged—the water had begun to boil before it had reached the appropriate temperature. It was hot, but not "boiling" hot.

"I'm worried about this finding, captain," Zavotle said as he completed the relevant entry in the log. "The only explanation I can think of is that as the water gets lighter it boils at a progressively lower temperature. And if that *is* the case, what is going to happen to us when the weight of everything fades away to nothing? Is the spit going to boil in our mouths? Are we going to piss steam?"

"We would be obliged to turn back before you had to suffer that indignity," Toller said, showing his displeasure at the other man's negative attitude, "but I don't think it will come to that. There must be some other reason—perhaps something to do with the air."

Zavotle looked dubious. "I don't see how air could affect water."

"Neither do I—so I'm not wasting time on useless speculation," Toller said curtly. "If you want something to occupy your mind take a close look at the height gauge. It says we're eleven-hundred miles up—and if that is correct we have been seriously underestimating our speed all day."

Zavotle studied the gauge, fingered the rip line and looked up into the balloon, the interior of which was growing dim and mysterious with the onset of dusk. "Now *that* could be something to do with the air," he said. "I think that what you have discovered is that thinner air would depress the crown of the envelope less at speed and make it seem that we're going slower than we actually are."

Toller considered the proposition and smiled. "You worked that out—and I didn't—so give yourself credit for it in the record. I'd say you're going to be the senior pilot on your next flight."

"Thanks, captain," Zavotle said, looking gratified.

"It's no more than you deserve." Toller touched Zavotle on the shoulder, making tacit reparation for his irritability. "At this rate we'll have passed the thirteen-hundred mark by dawn —then we can take a rest from the burner and see how the ship handles on the jet."

Later, while he was settling down on the sandbags to sleep, he went over the exchange in his mind and identified the true cause of the ill temper he had vented on Zavotle. It had been the accumulation of unforeseen phenomena—the increasing coldness, the odd behaviour of the water, the misleading indication of the balloon's speed. It had been the growing realisation that he had placed too much faith in the predictions of scientists. Lain, in particular, had been proved wrong in three different respects, and if his vaulting intellect had been defeated so soon—on the very edge of the region of strangeness—nobody could know what lay in store for those setting out along the perilous fractured glass bridge to another world.

Until that moment, Toller discovered, he had been naively optimistic about the future, convinced that the proving flight would lead to a successful migration and the foundation of a colony in which those he cared about would lead lives of endless fulfilment. It was chastening to realise that the vision had been largely based on his own egotism, that fate had no obligation to honour the safe conducts he had assigned to people like Lain and Gesalla, that events could come to pass regardless of his considering them unthinkable.

All at once the future had clouded over with uncertainty and danger.

And in the new order of things, Toller thought as he drifted into sleep, one had to learn to interpret a new kind of portent. Day-to-day trivia . . . the degree of slackness in a cord . . .

bubbles in a pot of water . . . These were niggardly omens . . .
whispered warnings, almost too faint to hear. . . .

By morning the height gauge was showing an altitude of fourteen-hundred miles, and its supplementary scale indicated that
gravity was now less than a quarter of normal.

Toller, intrigued by the lightness of his body, tested the
conditions by jumping, but it was an experiment he tried only
once. He rose much higher than he had intended and for a
moment as he seemed to hang in the air there was a terrible
feeling of having parted from the ship for ever. The open
gondola, with its chest-high walls, was revealed as a flimsy edifice
whose pared-down struts and wicker panels were quite inadequate for their purpose. He had time to visualise what would
happen if a floor section gave way when he landed on it, plunging
him into the thin blue air fourteen-hundred miles above the
surface of the world.

It would take a long time to fall that distance, fully conscious,
with nothing to do but watch the planet unfurl hungrily below
him. Even the bravest man would eventually have to begin
screaming. . . .

"We seem to have lost a good bit of speed during the night,
captain," Zavotle reported from the pilot's station. "The rip line
is getting quite taut—though, of course, you can't rely on it
much any more."

"It's time for the jet, anyway," Toller said. "From now on,
until turn-over, we'll use the burner only enough to keep the
balloon inflated. Where's Rillomyner?"

"Here, captain." The mechanic emerged from the other
passenger compartment. His pudgy figure was partially doubled
over, he was clutching the partitions and his gaze was fixed on the
floor.

"What's the matter with you, Rillomyner? Are you sick?"

"I'm not sick, captain. I . . . I just don't want to look outside."

"Why not?"

"I can't do it, captain. I can feel myself being drawn over the
side. I think I'm going to float away."

"You know that's nonsense, don't you?" Toller thought of his own moment of unmanning fear and was inclined towards sympathy. "Is this going to affect your work?"

"No, captain. The work would help."

"Good! Carry out a full inspection of the main jet and the laterals, and make *very* sure we have a smooth injection of crystals—we can't afford to have any surges at this stage."

Rillomyner directed a salute towards the floor and slouched away to fetch his tools. There followed an hour of respite from the full burn rhythm while Rillomyner checked the controls, some of which were common to the downward-facing jet. Flenn prepared and served a breakfast of gruel studded with small cubes of salt pork, all the while complaining about the cold and the difficulty he was having in keeping the galley fire going. His spirits improved a little when he learned that Rillomyner was not going to eat, and as a change from lavatorial humour he subjected the mechanic to a barrage of jokes about the dangers of wasting away to a shadow.

True to his earlier boast, Flenn seemed quite unaffected by the soul-withering void which glimmered through chinks in the decking. At the end of the meal he actually chose to sit on the gondola wall, with one arm casually thrown around an acceleration strut, as he goaded the unhappy Rillomyner. Even though Flenn had tethered himself, the sight of him perched on the sky-backed rim produced such icy turmoil in Toller's gut that he bore the arrangement for only a few minutes before ordering the rigger to descend.

When Rillomyner had finished his work and retired to lie down on the sandbags, Toller took up his position at the pilot's station. He entered the new mode of propulsion by firing the jet in two-second bursts at wide intervals and studying the effects on the balloon. Each thrust brought creaks from the struts and rigging, but the envelope was affected much less than in experimental firings at low altitudes. Encouraged, Toller varied the timings and eventually settled on a two-four rhythm which acted in much the same manner as continuous impulsion without building up excessive speed. A short blast from the burner every second or third minute kept the balloon inflated and the crown from sagging too much as it nosed through the air.

"She handles well," he said to Zavotle, who was industriously writing in the log. "It looks as though you and I are going to have an easy run for the next day or two—until the instability sets in."

Zavotle tilted his narrow head. "It's easier on the ears, too."

Toller nodded his agreement. Although the jet was firing for a greater proportion of every minute than the burner had been doing, its exhaust was not being directed into the great echo chamber of the balloon. The sound of it was flatter and less obtrusive, quickly absorbed by the surrounding oceans of stillness.

With the ship behaving so docilely and according to plan Toller began to feel that his forebodings of the night had been nothing more than a symptom of his growing tiredness. He was able to dwell on the incredible idea that in a mere seven or eight days, all being well, he was due to have a close look at another planet. The ship could not actually touch down on Overland, because doing so would involve pulling out the rip panel, and with no inflation facilities it would be unable to depart again. But it was to go within a few yards of the surface, dispelling the last traces of mystery about conditions on the sister planet.

The thousands of miles of air separating the two worlds had always made it difficult for astronomers to say much more than that there was an equatorial continent spanning the visible hemisphere. It had always been assumed, partly on religious grounds, that Overland closely resembled Land, but there remained the possibility that it was inhospitable, perhaps because of surface features beyond the resolving power of telescopes. And there was the further possibility—an article of faith for the Church, a moot case for philosophers—that Overland was already inhabited.

What would the Overlanders look like? Would they be builders of cities? And how would they react on seeing a fleet of strange ships float down from the sky?

Toller's musing was interrupted by the realisation that the coldness in the gondola had intensified in a matter of minutes. Simultaneously, he was approached by Flenn, who had the pet carble clutched to his chest and was visibly shivering. The little man's face was tinged with blue.

"This is killing me, captain," he said, trying to force his customary grin. "The cold has got worse all of a sudden."

"You're right." Toller felt a stirring of alarm at the idea of having crossed an invisible danger line in the atmosphere, then inspiration came to him. "It's since we eased off on the burner. The blow-back of miglign was helping to keep us warm."

"There was something else," Zavotle added. "The air streaming down over the hot envelope would have helped as well."

"Damn!" Toller frowned up into the geometric traceries of the balloon. "This means we'll have to put more heat in there. We have plenty of green and purple—so that's all right—but there's going to be a problem later on."

Zavotle nodded, looking gloomy. "The descent."

Toller gnawed his lip as, yet again, difficulties unforeseen by the earthbound S.E.S. scientists confronted him. The only way for the hot-air craft to lose altitude was through shedding heat—suddenly a vital commodity as far as the crew were concerned—and to make matters worse the direction of the air flow would be reversed during the descent, carrying the reduced amount of warmth upwards and away from the gondola. The prospect was that they would have to endure days in conditions very much worse than those of the present—and there was a genuine possibility that death would intervene.

A dilemma had to be resolved.

Was the fact that so much depended on the outcome of the proving flight an argument for going on and on, even at the risk of passing an imperceptible point of no return? Or was there a higher obligation to be prudent and turn back with their hard-won store of knowledge?

"This is your lucky day," Toller said to Rillomyner, who was watching him from his usual recumbent position in a passenger compartment. "You wanted work to occupy your mind, and now you've got it. Find a way of diverting some heat from the burner exhaust back down into the gondola."

The mechanic sat up with a startled expression. "How could we do it, captain?"

"I don't know. It's your job to work out things like that. Rig up a scoop or something, and start right now—I'm tired of seeing you lie around like a pregnant gilt."

Flenn's eyes gleamed. "Is that any way to talk to our passenger, captain?"

"You've spent too much time on your backside, as well," Toller told him. "Have you needles and thread in your kit?"

"Yes, captain. Big needles, little needles, enough threads and twines to rig a sailing ship."

"Then start emptying sandbags and making over-suits out of the sacking. We'll also need gloves."

"Leave it to me, captain," Flenn said. "I'll fit us all out like kings." Obviously pleased at having something constructive to do, Flenn tucked the carble into his clothing, went to his locker and began rummaging in its various compartments. He was whistling in shivery vibrato.

Toller watched him for a moment, then turned to Zavotle, who was blowing into his hands to keep them warm. "Are you still worrying about relieving yourself in weightless conditions?"

Zavotle's eyes became wary. "Why do you ask, captain?"

"You should be—it looks like a toss-up as to whether you produce steam or snow."

Shortly before littlenight on the fifth day of the flight the gauge registered a height of 2,600 miles and a gravity value of zero.

The four members of the crew were tied into their wicker chairs around the power unit, their feet outstretched towards the warm base of the jet tube. They were muffled in crude garments of ragged brown sacking which disguised their human form and concealed the heaving of their chests as they laboured to deal with the thin and gelid air. Within the gondola the only signs of movement were the vapour featherings of the men's breath; and on the outside meteors flickered in deep blue infinities, briefly and randomly linking star to star.

"Well, here we are," Toller said, breaking a lengthy silence. "The hardest part of the flight is behind us, we have coped with every unpleasant surprise the heavens could throw at us, and we are still in good health. I'd say we are entitled to drink the brandy with the next meal."

There was another protracted silence, as though thought itself had been chilled into sluggishness, and Zavotle said, "I'm still worried about the descent, captain—even with the heater."

"If we survived this far we can go on." Toller glanced at the heating device which Rillomyner had designed and installed with some assistance from Zavotle. It consisted of nothing more than an elongated S-shape of brakka tubing sections jointed with glass cord and fireclay. Its top end curved over into the mouth of the burner and its bottom end was secured to the deck beside the pilot's station. A small proportion of each blast on the burner was channelled back down through the tube to send scorching miglign gas billowing through the gondola, making an appreciable difference to the temperature levels. Although the burner would necessarily be used less during the descent, Toller believed the heat drawn off from it would be sufficient for their needs in the two severest days.

"It's time for the medical report," he said, signalling for Zavotle to make notes. "How does everybody feel?"

"I still feel like we're falling, captain." Rillomyner was gripping the sides of his chair. "It's making me queasy."

"How could we fall if we have no weight?" Toller said reasonably, ignoring the fluttering lightness in his own stomach. "You'll have to get used to it. How about you, Flenn?"

"I'm all right, captain—heights don't bother me." Flenn stroked the green-striped carble which was nestling on his chest with only its head protruding through a vent in his outer garment. "Tinny is all right, as well. We help keep each other warm."

"I suppose I'm in reasonable condition, considering." Zavotle made an entry in the log, writing clumsily with gloved hand, and raised his reproachful gaze to Toller. "Shall I put you down as being in fine fettle, captain? Best of health?"

"Yes, and all the sarcasm in the world won't get me to change my decision—I'm turning the ship over immediately after little-night." Toller knew the co-pilot was still clinging to his opinion, voiced earlier, that they should delay turning the ship over for a full day or even longer after passing the zero gravity point. The reasoning was that doing so would get them through the region of greatest cold more quickly and with lost heat from the balloon protecting them from the chill. Toller could see some merit in the idea, but he would have exceeded his authority by putting it into practice.

As soon as you pass the midpoint Overland will begin attracting you towards it, Lain had impressed upon him. *The pull will be very slight at first, but it will quickly build up. If you augment that pull with the thrust from the drive jet you will soon exceed the design speed of the ship—and that must never be allowed to happen.*

Zavotle had argued that the S.E.S. scientists had not anticipated the life-threatening coldness, nor had they allowed for the fact that the thin air of the mid-passage exerted less force on the envelope, thus increasing the maximum safe speed. Toller had remained adamant. As captain of the ship he had considerable discretionary powers, but not when it was a case of challenging basic S.E.S. directives.

He had not admitted that his determination had been reinforced by an instinctive distaste for flying the ship upside down. Although during training he had been privately sceptical about the notion of weightlessness, he fully understood that as soon as the ship had passed the midpoint it would have entered the gravitational domain of Overland. In one sense the journey would have been completed, because—barring an act of human will translated into mechanical action—the destinies of the ship and its crew could no longer be affected by their home world. They would have been cast out, redefined as aliens by the terms of celestial physics.

Toller had decided that postponing the attitude reversal until littlenight had passed would use up all the leeway he had in the matter. Throughout the ascent Overland, though screened from view by the balloon, had steadily increased in apparent size and littlenight had grown longer accordingly. The approaching one would last more than three hours, and by the time it had ended the ship would have begun falling towards the sister planet. Toller found the progressive change in the patterns of night and day a powerful reminder of the magnitude of the voyage he had undertaken. There was no surprise as far as the intellect of the grown man was concerned, but the child in him was bemused and awed by what was happening. Night was becoming shorter as littlenight grew, and soon the natural order of things would be reversed. Land's night would have dwindled to become Overland's littlenight. . . .

While waiting for darkness to arrive, Toller and the others investigated the miracle of weightlessness. There was a rare fascination in suspending small objects in the air and watching them hold their positions, in defiance of all of life's teachings, until the next blast from the drive jet belatedly caused them to sink.

It is almost as if the jet somehow restores a fraction of their natural weight, ran Zavotle's entry in the log, *but of course that is a fanciful way of regarding the phenomenon. The real explanation is that they are invisibly fixed in place, and that the thrust from the jet enables the ship to overtake them.*

Littlenight came more suddenly than ever, wrapping the gondola in jewelled and fire-streaked blackness, and for its duration the four conversed in muted tones, recreating the mood of their first starlit communion of the flight. The talk ranged from gossip about life in the S.E.S. base to speculation about what strange things might be found on Overland, and once there was even an attempt to foresee the problems of flying to Farland, which could be observed hanging in the west like a green lantern. Nobody felt disposed, Toller noticed, to dwell on the fact that they were suspended between two worlds in a fragile open-topped box, with thousands of miles of emptiness lapping at the rim.

He also noticed that the crew had stopped addressing him as captain for the time being, and he was not displeased. He knew there was no lessening of his necessary authority—it was an unconscious acknowledgement of the fact that four ordinary men were venturing into the extraordinary, the region of strangeness, and that in their mutual need for each other they were equal. . . .

One prismatic flash brought the daytime universe back into existence.

"Did you mention brandy, captain?" Rillomyner said. "It has

just occurred to me that some internal warmth might fortify this cursed delicate stomach of mine. The medicinal properties of brandy are well known."

"We'll have the brandy with the next meal." Toller blinked and looked about him, re-establishing connections with history. "Before that the ship gets turned over."

Earlier he had been pleased to discover that the ship's predicted instability in and close to the weightless zone was easy to overcome and control with the lateral jets. Occasional half-second bursts had been all that was necessary to keep the edge of the gondola in the desired relationship with the major stars. Now, however, the ship—or the universe—had to be stood on its head. He pumped the pneumatic reservoir to full pressure before feeding crystals to the east-facing jet for a full three seconds. The sound from the miniature orifice was devoured by infinity.

For a moment it seemed that its puny output would have no effect on the mass of the ship, then—for the first time since the beginning of the ascent—the great disk of Overland slid fully into view from behind the curvature of the balloon. It was lit by a crescent of fire along one rim, almost touching the sun.

At the same time Land rose above the rim of the gondola wall on the opposite side, and as air resistance overcame the impulsion from its jet the ship steadied in an attitude which presented the crew with a vision of two worlds.

By turning his head one way Toller could see Overland, mostly in blackness because of its proximity to the sun; and in the other direction was the mind-swamping convexity of the home world, serene and eternal, bathed in sunshine except at its eastern rim, where a shrinking curved section still lay in little-night. He watched in rapt fascination as Overland's shadow swung clear of Land, feeling himself to be at the fulcrum of a lever of light, an intangible engine which had the power to move planets.

"For pity's sake, captain," Rillomyner cried hoarsely, "put the ship to rights."

"You're in no danger." Toller fired the lateral jet again and

Land drifted majestically upwards to be occulted by the balloon as Overland sank below the edge of the gondola. The rigging creaked several times as he used the opposing lateral to balance the ship in its new attitude. Toller permitted himself a smile of satisfaction at having become the first man in history to turn a skyship over. The manoeuvre had been carried out quickly and without mishap—and from that point on the natural forces acting on the ship would do most of his work for him.

"Make a note," he said to Zavotle. "Midpoint successfully negotiated. I foresee no major obstacles in the descent to· Overland."

Zavotle freed his pencil from its restraining clip. "We're still going to freeze, captain."

"That isn't a major obstacle—if necessary we'll burn some green and purple right here on the deck." Toller, suddenly exhilarated and optimistic, turned to Flenn. "How do you feel? Can your head for heights cope with our present circumstances?"

Flenn grinned. "If it's food you want, captain, I'm your man. I swear my arsehole has cobwebs over it."

"In that case, see what you can do about a meal." Toller knew the order would be particulary welcome because for more than a day the crew had opted to go without food or drink to obviate the indignity, discomfort and sheer unpleasantness of using the toilet facilities in virtual weightlessness.

He watched benignly as Flenn pushed the carble back into its warm sanctuary inside his clothing and untied himself from his chair. The little man was obviously struggling for breath as he swung his way into the galley, but the black cabochons of his eyes were glinting with good humour. He reappeared just long enough to hand Toller the single small flask of brandy which had been included in the ship's provisions, then there followed a long period during which he could be heard working with the cooking equipment, panting and swearing all the time. Toller took a sip of the brandy and had given the flask to Zavotle when it dawned on him that Flenn was trying to prepare a hot meal.

"You don't need to heat anything," he called out. "Cold jerky and bread will be enough."

"It's all right, captain," came Flenn's breathless reply. "The charcoal is still lit . . . and it's only a matter of . . . fanning it hard enough. I'm going to serve you . . . a veritable banquet. A man needs a good . . . *Hell!*"

Concurrent with the last word there was a clattering sound. Toller turned towards the galley in time to see a burning piece of firewood rise vertically into the air from behind the partition. Lazily spinning, wrapped in pale yellow flame, it sailed upwards and glanced off a sloping lower panel of the balloon. Just when it seemed that it had been deflected harmlessly away into the blue it was caught by an air current which directed it into the narrowing gap between an acceleration strut and the envelope. It lodged in the juncture of the two, still burning.

"It's mine!" Flenn shouted. "I'll get it!"

He appeared on the gondola wall at the corner, unhooking his tether, and went up the strut at speed, using only his hands in a curious weightless scramble. Toller's heart and mind froze over as he saw brownish smoke puff out from the varnished fabric of the balloon. Flenn reached the burning stick and grasped it with a gloved hand. He hurled the stick away with a lateral sweep of his arm and suddenly he too was separated from the ship, tumbling in thin air. Hands clawing vainly towards the strut, he floated slowly outwards.

Toller's consciousness was sundered by two focuses of terror. Fear of personal annihilation kept his gaze centred on the smoking patch of fabric until he saw that the flame had extinguished itself, but all the while he was filled with a silent-shrieking awareness of the bright void between Flenn and the balloon growing wider.

Flenn's initial impetus had not been great, but he had drifted outwards for some thirty yards before air resistance brought him to a halt. He hung in the blue emptiness, glowing in the sunlight which the balloon screened from the gondola, scarcely recognisable as a human being in his ragged swaddling of sackcloth.

Toller went to the side and cupped his hands around his mouth to aim a shout. "Flenn! Are you all right?"

"Don't worry about me, captain." Flenn waved an arm and,

incredibly, he was able to sound almost cheerful. "I can see the envelope well from here. There's a scorched area all around the strut attachment, but the fabric isn't holed."

"We're going to bring you in." Toller turned to Zavotle and Rillomyner. "He isn't lost. We need to throw him a line."

Rillomyner was doubled in his chair. "Can't do it, captain," he mumbled. "I can't look out there."

"You're going to look and you're going to work," Toller assured him grimly.

"I can help," Zavotle said, leaving his chair. He opened the rigger's locker and brought out several coils of rope. Toller, impatient to effect a rescue, snatched one of the ropes. He secured one end of it and flung the coil out towards Flenn, but as he did so his feet rose clear of the deck, and what he had intended as a powerful throw proved to be feeble and misdirected. The rope unfurled for only part of its length and froze uselessly, still retaining its undulations.

Toller drew the rope in and while he was coiling it again Zavotle threw his line with similar lack of success. Rillomyner, who was moaning faintly with every breath, hurled out a thinner line of glasscord. It extended fully in roughly the right direction, but stopped too short.

"Good for nothing!" Flenn jeered, seemingly undaunted by the thousands of miles of vacancy yawning below him. "Your old grandmother could do better, Rillo."

Toller removed his gloves and made a fresh attempt to bridge the void, but even though he had braced himself against a partition the cold-stiffened rope again failed to unwind properly. It was while he was retrieving it that he noticed an unnerving fact. At the beginning of the rescue effort Flenn had been considerably higher in relation to the ship, level with the upper end of the acceleration strut—but now he was only slightly above the rim of the gondola.

A moment's reflection told Toller that Flenn was falling. The ship was also falling, but as long as there was warmth inside the balloon it would retain some degree of buoyancy and would descend more slowly than a solid object. This close to the midpoint the relative speeds were negligible, but Flenn was nonetheless in the grip of Overland's gravity, and had begun the long plunge to the surface.

"Have you noticed what's happening?" Toller said to Zavotle in a low voice. "We're running out of time."

Zavotle assessed the situation. "Is there any point in using the laterals?"

"We'd only start cartwheeling."

"This is serious," Zavotle said. "First of all Flenn damages the balloon—then he puts himself in a position where he can't repair it."

"I doubt if he did that on purpose." Toller wheeled on Rillomyner. "The cannon! Find a weight that will go into the cannon. Maybe we can fire a line."

At that moment Flenn, who had been quiescent, appeared to notice his gradual change of position relative to the ship and to draw the appropriate conclusions. He began struggling and squirming, then made exaggerated swimming movements which in other circumstances might have been comic. Discovering that nothing was having any good effect he again became still, except for an involuntary movement of his hands when Zavotle's second throw of the rope failed to reach him.

"I'm getting scared, captain." Although Flenn was shouting his voice seemed faint, its energies leaching away into the surrounding immensities. "You've got to bring me home."

"We'll bring you in. There's. . . ." Toller allowed the sentence to tail off. He had been going to assure Flenn there was plenty of time, but his voice would have lacked conviction. It was becoming apparent that not only was Flenn falling past the gondola, but that—in keeping with the immutable laws of physics—he was gaining speed. The acceleration was almost imperceptible, but its effects were cumulative. Cumulative and lethal. . . .

Rillomyner touched Toller's arm. "There's nothing that will fit in the cannon, captain, but I joined two bits of glasscord and tied it to this." He proffered a hammer with a large brakka head. "I think it will reach him."

"Good man," Toller said, appreciative of the way the mechanic was overcoming his acrophobia in the emergency. He moved aside to let Rillomyner make the throw. The mechanic tied the free end of the glasscord to the rail, judged the distances and hurled the hammer out into space.

Toller saw at once that he had made the mistake of aiming high, compensating for a full-gravity drop that was not going to occur. The hammer dragged the cord out behind it and came to a halt in the air a tantalising few yards above Flenn, who was galvanised into windmilling his arms in a futile attempt to reach it. Rillomyner jiggled the cord in an effort to move the hammer downwards, but only succeeded in drawing it a short distance back towards the ship.

"That's no good," Toller snapped. "Pull it in fast and throw straight at him next time." He was trying to suppress a growing sense of panic and despair. Flenn was now visibly sinking below the level of the gondola, and the hammer was less likely to reach him as the range increased and the angles became less conducive to accurate throwing. What Flenn desperately needed was a means of reducing the distance separating him from the gondola, and that was impossible unless . . . unless. . . .

A familiar voice spoke inside Toller's head. *Action and reaction*, Lain was saying. *That's the universal principle.* . . .

"Flenn, you can bring yourself closer," Toller shouted. "Use the carble! Throw it straight away from the ship, as hard as you can. That will drift you in this direction."

There was a pause before Flenn responded. "I couldn't do that, captain."

"This is an order," Toller bellowed. "Throw the carble, and throw it right *now*! We're running out of time."

There was a further pounding delay, then Flenn was seen to be fumbling with the coverings on his chest. Sunlight flared on the lower surfaces of his body as he slowly produced the green-striped animal.

Toller swore in frustration. "Hurry, *hurry!* We're going to lose you."

"You've already lost me, captain." Flenn's voice was resigned. "But I want you to take Tinny home with you."

There was a sudden sweeping movement of his arm and he went tumbling backwards as the carble sailed towards the ship. It was travelling too low. Toller watched numbly as the terrified animal, mewing and clawing at the air, passed out of sight below the gondola. Its yellow eyes had seemed to be boring into his own. Flenn receded a short distance before he stabilised himself by spreading his arms and legs. He came to rest in the attitude of a drowned man, floating face-down on an invisible ocean, his gaze directed towards Overland—thousands of miles below—which had taken him in its gravitational arms.

"You stupid little midget," Rillomyner sobbed as he again sent the hammer snaking towards Flenn. It stopped short and a little to one side of its target. Flenn, body and limbs rigid, continued to sink with gathering speed.

"He'll be falling for maybe a day," Zavotle whispered. "Just think of it . . . a whole day . . . falling . . . I wonder if he'll still be alive when he hits the ground."

"I've got other things to think about," Toller said harshly, turning away from the gondola wall, unable to watch Flenn dwindling out of sight.

His brief required him to abort the flight in the event of losing a crew member or sustaining some serious structural damage to the ship. Nobody could have foreseen both circumstances arising as a result of one trivial-seeming accident with the galley stove, but he felt no less responsible—and it remained to be seen if the S.E.S. administrators would also regard him as culpable.

"Switch us back to jet power," he said to Rillomyner. "We're going home."

PART III

Region of Strangeness

CHAPTER 16

The cave was in the side of a ragged hill, in an area of broken terrain where numerous gullies, rocky projections and a profusion of spiky scrub made the going difficult for man or beast.

Lain Maraquine was content to let the bluehorn pick its own way around the various obstacles, giving it only an occasional nudge to keep it heading for the orange flag which marked the cave's position. The four mounted soldiers of his personal guard, obligatory for any senior official of the S.E.S., followed a short distance behind, the murmur of their conversation blending with the heavy drone of insects. Littlenight was not long past and the high sun was baking the ground, clothing the horizon in tremulous purple-tinted blankets of hot air.

Lain felt unusually relaxed, appreciating the opportunity to get away from the skyship base and turn his mind to matters which had nothing to do with world crises and interplanetary travel. Toller's premature return from the proving flight, ten days earlier, had involved Lain in a harrowing round of meetings, consultations and protracted studies of the new scientific data obtained. One faction in the S.E.S. administration had wanted a second proving flight with a full descent to Overland and detailed mapping of the central continent. In normal circumstances Lain would have been in agreement, but the rapidly worsening situation in Kolcorron overrode all other consideration. . . .

The production target of one thousand skyships had been achieved with some to spare, thanks to the driving ruthlessness and Leddravohr and Chakkell.

Fifty of the ships had been set aside for the transportation of the country's royalty and aristocrats in small family groups who would travel in comparative luxury, though by no means all of the nobility had decided to take part in the migration. Another two-hundred were designated as cargo vessels which would carry food, livestock, seeds, weapons and essential machinery and materials; and a further hundred were for the use of military personnel. That left six-hundred-and-fifty ships which, with reduced two-man crews, had the capability of transporting almost twelve thousand of the general population to Overland.

At an early stage of the great undertaking King Prad had decreed that emigration would be on a purely voluntary basis, with equal numbers of males and females, and that fixed proportions of the available places would be allocated to men with key skills.

For a long time the hard-headed citizenry had declined to take the proposal seriously, regarding it as a diversion, a regal folly to be chuckled over in taverns. The small numbers who put their names forward were treated with derision, and it seemed that if the skyship fleet were ever to be filled it would only be at swordpoint.

Prad had chosen to bide his time, knowing in advance that greater forces than he could ever muster were on the move. The ptertha plague, famine and the abrupt crumbling of social order had exerted their powerful persuasions, and—in spite of condemnation from the Church—the roster of willing emigrants had swollen. But such was the conservatism of the Kolcorronians and so radical the solution to their problems that a certain degree of reserve still had to be overcome, a lingering feeling that any amount of deprivation and danger on Land was preferable to the near-inevitability of a highly unnatural death in the alien blue reaches of the sky.

Then had come the news that an S.E.S. ship had voyaged more than halfway to Overland and had returned intact.

Within hours every remaining place on the emigration flight had been allocated, and suddenly those who held the necessary warrants were objects of envy and resentment. There was a reversal of public opinion, swift and irrational, and many who had scorned the very notion of flying to the sister world began to see themselves as victims of discrimination.

Even the majority who were too apathetic to care much either way about the broad historical issues were disgruntled by stories of wagons loaded with scarce provisions disappearing through the gates of Skyship Quarter. . . .

Against that background Lain had argued that the proving flight had achieved all its major objectives by successfully turning over and passing the midpoint. The descent to the surface of Overland would have been a passive and predictable business; and Zavotle's sketches of the central continent, viewed through binoculars, were good enough to show that it was remarkably free of mountains and other features which would have jeopardised safe landings.

Even the loss of a crew member had occurred in such a way as to provide a valuable lesson about the inadvisability of cooking in weightless conditions. The commander of the ship was to be congratulated on his conduct of a uniquely demanding mission, Lain had concluded, and the migration itself should begin in the very near future.

His arguments had been accepted.

The first squadron of forty skyships, mainly carrying soldiers and construction workers, was scheduled to depart on Day 80 of the year 2630.

That date was only six days in the future, and as Lain's steed picked its way up the hill to the cave it came to him that he was curiously unexcited by the prospect of flying to Overland. If all went according to plan he and Gesalla would be on a ship of the tenth squadron, which—allowing for delays caused by unsuitable weather or ptertha activity—was due to leave the home world in perhaps only twenty days' time. Why was he so little moved by the imminence of what would be the greatest personal adventure of his life, the finest scientific opportunity he could ever conceive, the boldest undertaking in the entire history of mankind?

Was it that he was too timorous even to allow himself to think about the event? Was it that the growing rift with Gesalla —unacknowledged but ever present in his awareness—had severed a spiritual taproot, rendering him emotionally sere and sterile? Or was it a simple failure of the imagination on the part of one who prided himself on his superior qualities of mind?

The torrent of questions and doubts subsided as the bluehorn reached a rock-strewn shelf and Lain saw the entrance to the cave a short distance ahead. Grateful for the internal respite, he dismounted and waited for the soldiers to catch up on him. The four men's faces were beaded with sweat below their leather helmets, and they were obviously puzzled at having been brought to such a desolate spot.

"You will wait for me here," Lain said to the burly sergeant. "Where will you post your look-outs?"

The sergeant shaded his eyes from the near-vertical rays of the sun which were stabbing past the fire-limned disk of Overland. "On top of the hill, sir. They should be able to see five or six observation posts from there."

"Good! I'm going into this cave and I don't want to be disturbed. Only call me if there is a ptertha warning."

"Yes, sir."

While the sergeant dismounted and deployed his men Lain opened the panniers strapped to his bluehorn and took out four oil lanterns. He ignited the wicks with a lens, picked the lanterns up by their glasscord slings and carried them into the cave. The entrance was quite low and as narrow as a single door. For a moment the air was even warmer than in the open, then he was in a region of dim coolness where the walls receded to form a spacious chamber. He set the lanterns on the dirt floor and waited for his eyes to adjust to the poor light.

The cave had been discovered earlier in the year by a surveyor investigating the hill as a possible site for an observation post. Perhaps through genuine enthusiasm, perhaps out of a desire to sample Lord Glo's noted hospitality, the surveyor had made his way to Greenmount and lodged a description of the cave's startling contents. The report had reached Lain a short time later and he had decided to view the find for himself as soon as he had time to spare from his work. Now, surrounded by a fading screen of after-images, he understood that his coming to the dark place was symbolic. He was turning towards Land's past and away from Overland's future, confessing that he wanted no part of the migration flight or what lay beyond it. . . .

The pictures on the cave walls were becoming visible.

There was no order to the scenes portrayed. It appeared that the largest and flattest areas had been used first, and that succeeding generations of artists had filled in the intervening spaces with fragmentary scenes, using their ingenuity to incorporate bosses, hollows and cracks as features of their designs.

The result was a labyrinthian montage in which the eye was compelled to wander unceasingly from semi-naked hunters to family groups to stylised brakka trees to strange and familiar animals, erotica, demons, cooking pots, flowers, human skeletons, weapons, suckling babes, geometrical abstracts, fish, snakes, unclassifiable artifacts and impenetrable symbols. In some cases cardinal lines had been graven into the rock and filled with pitch, causing the images to advance on the sight with relentless power; in others there was a spatial ambiguity by which a human or animal form might be defined by nothing more than the changing intensity of a patch of colour. For the most part the pigments were still vivid where they were meant to be vivid, and restrained where the artist had chosen to be subtle, but in some places time itself had contributed to the visual complexity with the stainings of moisture and fungal growths.

Lain was overwhelmed, as never before, by a sense of duration.

The basic thesis of the Kolcorronian religion was that Land and Overland had always existed and had always been very much as they were in modern times, twin poles for the continuous alternation of discarnate human spirits. Four centuries earlier a war had been fought to stamp out the Bithian Heresy, which claimed that a person would be rewarded for a life of virtue on one world by being given a higher station when reincarnated on the sister planet. The Church's main objection had been to the idea of a progression and therefore of change, which conflicted with the essential teaching that the present order was immutable and eternal. Lain found it easy to believe that the macrocosm had always been as it was, but on the small stage of human history there was evidence of change, and by extrapolating backwards one could arrive at . . . *this!*

He had no way of estimating the age of the cave paintings, but his instinct was to think in millennia and not in centuries. Here was evidence that men had once existed in vastly different circumstances, that they had thought in different ways, and had shared the planet with animals which no longer existed. He experienced a pang of mingled intellectual stimulation and regret as he realised that here, in the confines of one rocky cavity, was the material for a lifetime of work. It would have been possible for him to complement the abstractions of mathematics with the study of his own kind, a course which seemed infinitely more natural and rewarding than fleeing to another world.

Could I still do it?

The thought, only half serious though it was, seemed to intensify the coolness of the cave and Lain raised his shoulders in the beginnings of a shudder. He found himself, as had happened several times recently, trying to analyse his commitment to flying to Overland.

Was it the logical thing to do—the coolly considered action of a philosopher—or did he feel that he owed it to Gesalla, and the children she was determined to have, to give them a divergent future? Until he had begun examining his own motives the issue had seemed clear cut—fly to Overland and embrace the future, or stay on Land and die with the past.

But the majority of the population had not had to make that decision. They would be following the very human course of refusing to lie down until they were dead, of simply ignoring the defeatist notion that the blind and mindless ptertha could triumph over mankind. Indeed, the migration flight could not even take place without the cooperation of those who were staying behind—the inflation crews, the men in the ptertha observation posts, the military who would defend Skyship Quarter and continue to impose order after the King and his entourage had departed.

Human life was not going to cease overnight on Land, Lain had realised. There could be many years, decades, of shrinkage and retrenchment, and perhaps the process would eventually produce a hard core of unkillables, few in number, living underground in conditions of unimaginable privation. Lain did not want to be part of that grim scenario, but the point was that he might be able to find a niche within it. The point was that, given sufficient will, he could probably live out his allotted span on the planet of his birth, where his existence had relevance and meaning.

But what about Gesalla?

She was too loyal to consider leaving without him. Such was her character that the very fact of their drifting apart mentally would cause her to cleave to him all the more in body, in obedience to her marriage vows. He doubted if she had even yet admitted to herself that she was. . . .

Lain's eyes, darting urgently over the time-deep panorama surrounding him, fastened on the image of a small child at play. It was a vignette, at the triangular juncture of three larger scenes, and showed a male infant absorbed with what appeared to be a doll which he was holding in one hand. His other hand was outstretched to the side, as though carelessly reaching for a familiar pet, and just beyond it was a featureless circle. The circle was devoid of coloration and could have represented several things—a large ball, a balloon, a whimsically placed Overland—but Lain was oddly tempted to see it as a ptertha.

He picked up a lantern and went closer to the picture. The intensified illumination confirmed that the circle had never contained any pigment, which was strange considering that the long-dead artists had shown great scrupulousness and subtlety in their rendering of other less significant subjects. That implied that his interpretation had been wrong, especially as the child in the fragmentary scene was obviously relaxed and unperturbed by the nearness of what would have been an object of terror.

Lain's deliberations were interrupted by the sound of someone entering the cave. Frowning with annoyance, he raised the lantern, then took an involuntary pace backwards as he saw that the newcomer was Leddravohr. The prince's smile flicked into existence for a moment as he emerged from the narrow passage, battle sword scraping the wall, and ran his gaze around the cave.

"Good aftday, Prince," Lain said, dismayed to find that he was beginning to tremble. Many meetings with Leddravohr during the course of his work for the S.E.S. had taught him to retain most of his composure when they were with others and in the humdrum atmosphere of an office, but here in the constricted space of the cave Leddravohr was huge, inhumanly powerful and frightening. He was far enough removed from Lain in mind and outlook to have stepped out of one of the primitive scenes glowing in the surrounding half-light.

Leddravohr gave the entire display a cursory inspection before speaking. "I was told there was something remarkable here, Maraquine. Was I misinformed?"

"I don't think so, Prince." Lain hoped he had been able to keep a tremor out of his voice.

"You don't think so? Well, what is it that your fine brain appreciates and mine doesn't?"

Lain sought an answer which would not frame the insult Leddravohr had devised for him. "I haven't had time to study the pictures, Prince—but I am interested in the fact that they are obviously very old."

"How old?"

"Perhaps three or four thousand years."

Leddravohr snorted in amusement. "That's nonsense. You're saying these scrawls are far older than Ro-Atabri itself?"

"It was just my opinion, Prince."

"You're wrong. The colours are too fresh. This place has been a bolt hole during one of the civil wars. Some insurgents have hidden out here and. . . ." Leddravohr paused to peer closely at a sketch depicting two men in a contorted sexual position. "And you can see what they did to pass the time. Is this what intrigues you, Maraquine?"

"No, Prince."

"Do you ever lose your temper, Maraquine?"

"I try not to, Prince."

Leddravohr snorted again, padded around the cave and came back to Lain. "All right, you can stop shaking—I'm not going to touch you. It may interest you to learn that I'm here because my father has heard about this spider hole. He wants the drawings accurately copied. How long will that take?"

Lain glanced around the walls. "Four good draughtsmen could do it in a day, Prince."

"You arrange it." Leddravohr stared at him with an unreadable expression on his smooth face. "Why does anybody give a fig about the likes of this place? My father is old and worn out; he has soon to face flying to Overland; most of our population has been wiped out by the plague, and the remainder are getting ready to riot; and even some units of the army are becoming unruly now that they are hungry and it has dawned on them that I soon won't be here to look after their welfare—and yet all my father is concerned about is seeing these miserable scrawls for himself. Why, Maraquine, *why*?"

Lain was unprepared for the question. "King Prad appears to have the instincts of a philosopher, Prince."

"You mean he's like you?"

"I didn't intend to elevate myself to. . . .""

"Never mind all that. Was that supposed to be your answer? He wants to know things because he wants to know things?"

"That's what 'philosopher' means, Prince."

"But. . . ." Leddravohr broke off as there was a clattering of equipment in the cave entrance and the sergeant of Lain's personal guard appeared. He saluted Leddravohr and, although agitated, waited for permission to speak.

"Go on, man" Leddravohr said.

"The wind is rising in the west, Prince. We are warned of ptertha."

Leddravohr waved the sergeant away. "All right—we will leave soon."

"The wind is rising quickly, Prince," the sergeant said, obviously deeply unhappy at lingering beyond his dismissal.

"And a crafty old soldier like you sees no point in taking unnecessary risks." Leddravohr placed a hand on the sergeant's shoulder and shook him playfully, an intimacy he would not have granted the loftiest aristocrat. "Take your men and leave now, sergeant."

The sergeant's eyes emitted a single flash of gratitude and adoration as he hurried away. Leddravohr watched him depart, then turned to Lain.

"You were explaining this passion for useless knowledge," he said. "Continue!"

"I. . . ." Lain tried to organise his thoughts. "In my profession all knowledge is regarded as useful."

"Why?"

225

"It's part of a whole . . . a unified structure . . . and when that structure is complete Man will be complete and will have total control of his destiny."

"Fine words!" Leddravohr's discontented gaze steadied on the section of wall closest to where Lain was standing. "Do you really believe the future of our race hinges on that picture of a brat playing ball?"

"That isn't what I said, Prince."

"That isn't what I said, Prince," Leddravohr mocked. "You have told me nothing, philosopher."

"I am sorry that you heard nothing," Lain said quietly.

Leddravohr's smile appeared on the instant. "That was meant to be an insult, wasn't it? Love of knowledge must be an ardent passion indeed if it begins to stiffen your backbone, Maraquine. We will continue this discussion on the ride back. Come!"

Leddravohr went to the entrance, turned sideways and negotiated the narrow passage. Lain blew out the four lanterns and, leaving them where they were, followed Leddravohr to the outside. A noticeable breeze was streaming over the uneven contours of the hill from the west. Leddravohr, already astride his bluehorn, watched in amusement as Lain gathered the skirts of his robe and inexpertly dragged himself up into his own saddle. After a searching look at the sky, Leddravohr led the way down the hill, controlling his mount with the straight-backed nonchalance of the born rider.

Lain, yielding to an impulse, urged his bluehorn forward on a roughly parallel track, determined to keep abreast of the prince. They were almost halfway down the hill when he discovered he was guiding his animal at speed into a patch of loose shale. He tried to pull the bluehorn to the right, but only succeeded in throwing it off balance. It gave a bark of alarm as it lost its footing on the treacherous surface and fell sideways. Lain heard its leg snap as he threw himself clear, aiming for a clump of yellow grass which had mercifully appeared in his view. He hit the ground, rolled over and jumped to his feet immediately, unharmed but appalled by the agonised howling of the bluehorn as it threshed on the clattering flakes of rock.

Leddravohr dismounted in a single swift movement and strode

to the fallen animal, black sword in hand. He moved in quickly and drove the blade into the bluehorn's belly, angling the thrust forward to penetrate the chest cavity. The bluehorn gave a convulsive heave and emitted a slobbering, snoring sound as it died. Lain clapped a hand over his mouth as he fought to control the racking upsurges of his stomach.

"Here's another morsel of useful knowledge for you," Leddravohr said calmly. "When you're killing a bluehorn, never go straight into the heart or you'll get blood all over you. This way the heart discharges into the body cavities, and there is very little mess. See?" Leddravohr withdrew his sword, wiped it on the dead animal's mane and spread his arms, inviting inspection of his unmarked clothing. "Don't you agree that it's all very . . . philosophical?"

"I made it fall," Lain mumbled.

"It was only a bluehorn." Leddravohr sheathed his sword, returned to his mount and swung himself into the saddle. "Come on, Maraquine—what are you waiting for?"

Lain looked at the prince, who had one hand outstretched in readiness to assist him on to the bluehorn, and felt a powerful aversion to making the physical contact. "Thank you, Prince —but it would be improper for one of my station to ride with you."

Leddravohr burst out laughing. "What are you talking about, you fool? We're out in the real world now—the soldier's world —and the pertha are on the move."

The reference to the pertha went through Lain like a dagger of ice. He took a hesitant step forward.

"Don't be so bashful," Leddravohr said, his eyes amused and derisive. "After all, it wouldn't be the first time you and I had shared a mount."

Lain came to a standstill, his brow dewing over with cool perspiration, and he heard himself say, "On consideration, I prefer to make my own way back to the Quarter on foot."

"I'm losing patience with you, Maraquine." Leddravohr shaded his eyes and scanned the western sky. "I'm not going to plead with you to preserve your own life."

"My life is my responsibility, Prince."

"It must be something in the Maraquine blood," Leddravohr said, shrugging as he addressed a notional third party.

He turned his bluehorn's head to the east and urged the beast into a canter. Within a few seconds he had passed out of sight behind a shoulder of rock, and Lain was alone in a harsh landscape which suddenly seemed as alien and unforgiving as a distant planet. He gave a shaky, incredulous laugh as he took stock of the predicament he had placed himself in with a single failure of reason.

Why now? he demanded of himself. *Why did I wait until now?*

There was a faint scraping sound from nearby. Lain wheeled in fright and saw that pallid multipedes were already writhing upwards out of their burrows, disturbing small pebbles in their eagerness to converge on the dead bluehorn. He lunged away from the spectacle. For a moment he considered returning to the cave, then realised it would offer only minimal protection during daylight—and after nightfall the entire hill was likely to be swarming with globes, patiently nuzzling and probing. The best plan was to head eastwards to Skyship Quarter with all possible speed and try to get there before the ptertha came riding down the wind.

The decision made, Lain began to run through the murmurous heat. Near the base of the hill he emerged on an open slope which gave him an unrestricted view to the east. A far-off plume of dust marked Leddravohr's course and a long way ahead of him, almost at the drab boundaries of the Quarter, a larger cloud showed how far the four soldiers had gone. He had not appreciated the difference in speed between a man on foot and one mounted on a galloping bluehorn. He would be able to make better progress when he reached the flat grassland, but even so it would probably be an hour before he reached safety.

An hour!

Is there any hope at all of my surviving for that length of time?

As a distraction from his growing physical distress, he tried to bring his professional skills to bear on the question. The statistics, when looked at dispassionately, were more encouraging than he might have expected.

Daylight and flat terrain were conditions which did not favour the ptertha. They had virtually no self-propulsive capability in the horizontal plane, depending on air currents to carry them across the face of the land, which meant that an active man had little to fear from ptertha while he was crossing open ground. Assuming they had not blanketed the area—something which rarely happened in daytime—all he had to do was observe the globes closely and be aware of the wind direction. When menaced by a ptertha, it was simply a matter of waiting until just before it came within the killing radius, then running crosswind for a short distance and allowing the globe to drift helplessly by.

Lain stumbled to a halt in a gully, his mouth filling with the salt froth of exhaustion, and leaned on a rock to recover his breath. It was vital that he should still have reserves of strength and be nimble on his feet when he reached the plain. As the tumult in his chest gradually subsided he indulged himself in a visualisation of his next encounter with Leddravohr, and—incredibly—he felt his gaping mouth trying to form a grin. This was the irony of ironies! While the renowned military prince had fled to seek refuge from the ptertha, the mild-mannered philosopher had strolled back to the city, in need of no armour but his intellect. This was proof indeed that he was no coward, proof for all to see, proof that even his wife would have to. . . .

I've gone mad! The thought caused Lain to moan aloud in sheer self-loathing. *I have truly lost what used to be my mind!*

I permitted a savage to breach my defences with all his crassness and malice, his celebration of stupidity and glorification of ignorance. I let him debase me until I was prepared to throw away life itself in a weltering of hatred and pride—what laudable emotions! —and now I'm indulging in fantasies of childish revenge, so gratified by my own superiority that I haven't even taken the basic precaution of making sure there are no ptertha at hand!

Lain straightened up and—sick with premonition—turned to look back along the gully.

The ptertha was barely ten paces away, well within its killing radius, and the breeze coursing along the gully was sweeping it closer to him with mind-freezing swiftness.

It swelled to encompass his view, its glistening transparencies tinged with purple and black. In one part of his mind Lain felt a perverse flicker of gratitude that the issue had been decided for him, so quickly and so finally. There was no point in trying to run, no point in trying to fight. He saw the ptertha as he had never seen one before, saw the livid swirlings of the toxic dust inside it. Was there a hint of structure there? A globe within a globe? Was a malign proto-intelligence knowingly sacrificing itself in order to destroy him?

The ptertha filled Lain's universe.

It was everywhere—and then it was nowhere.

He took a deep breath and looked about him with the ruefully placid gaze of the man who has only one further decision to make.

Not here, he thought. *Not in this blind and circumscribed place—it isn't at all suitable.*

Recalling the higher slope which had afforded the good view to the east, he retraced his steps along the bed of the ancient stream, walking slowly now and emitting occasional sighs. When he reached the slope he sat on the ground with his back to an agreeably shaped boulder and arranged his robe in neat folds around his outstretched legs.

The world of his last day was laid out before him. The triangular outline of Mount Opelmer floated low in the sky, seemingly detached from the horizontal ribbons and speckled bands which represented Ro-Atabri and the derelict suburbs on the shores of Arle Bay. Closer and lower was the artificial community of the Skyship Quarter, its dozens of balloon enclosures an illusory city of rectangular towers. The Tree glittered in the southern heavens, its nine stars challenging the sun's brilliance, and at the zenith a broad crescent of mellow light was spreading insensibly across the disk of Overland.

The whole span of my life and work is in that scene, Lain mused. *I have brought my writing materials and should try to make some kind of a summation . . . not that the last thoughts of one who precipitated his own demise in such a ludicrous fashion would be of much interest or value to others . . . at most I could record what is already known—that pterthacosis is not a bad death . . . as deaths go, that is . . . nature can be merciful . . . as the most horrific shark bites are often unaccompanied by pain, so the inhalation of ptertha dust can sometimes engender a strange mood of resignation, a chemical fatalism . . . in that respect at least, I appear to be fortunate . . . except that I am deprived of feelings which are mine by ancient right. . . .*

A burning sensation manifested itself below Lain's chest and spread radial tendrils into the rest of his torso. At the same time the air about him seemed to grow cold, as though the sun had lost its heat. He put a hand into a pocket of his robe, brought out a bag made of yellow linen and spread it on his lap. There was a final duty to be performed—but not yet.

I wish Gesalla were here . . . Gesalla and Toller . . . so that I could give them to each other, or ask them to accept each other . . . irony piles upon irony . . . Toller always wanted to be different, to be more like me . . . and when he became the new Toller, I was forced to become the old Toller . . . to the final extent of throwing down my life for the sake of honour, a gesture which should have been made before my beautiful solewife was ravaged and defiled by Leddravohr . . . Toller was right about that, and I—in my so-called wisdom—told him he was wrong . . . Gesalla knew in her head that he was wrong, and in her heart that he was right. . . .

A stab of pain in Lain's chest was accompanied by a bout of shivering. The view before him was curiously flat. He could see more ptertha now. They were drifting down towards the plain in groups of two and three, but they had no relevance to what was left of his life. The dream-flow of his fragmentary thoughts was the new reality.

Poor Toller . . . he became what he aspired to be, and how did I reward him? . . . with resentment and envy . . . I hurt him on the day of Glo's interment, only able to do so because he loves me, but he responded to my childish spite with dignity and forbearance . . . brakka and ptertha go together . . . I love my "little brother" and I wonder if Gesalla even yet realises that she too . . . these things can take such a long time . . . of course brakka and ptertha go together—it's a symbiotic partnership . . . only now do I understand why it was not in my heart to fly to Overland . . . the future is there, and the future belongs to Gesalla and Toller . . . could that be the underlying reason for my refusing to ride with

Leddravohr, for choosing my own Bright Road? . . . was I making Toller's way clear? . . . was I excising an unbalancing factor from the equation? . . . equations used to mean so much to me. . . .

The fire in Lain's chest was becoming hotter, expanding, causing him to struggle for breath. He was sweating profusely and yet his skin felt deathly cold, and the world was merely a scene painted on rippling cloth. It was time for the yellow hood.

Lain lifted it with clumsy fingers and drew it over his head—a warning to anyone who might come by that he had died of pterthacosis and that the body was not to be approached for at least five days. The eye slits were not in the right place, but he allowed his hands to fall to his side without adjusting them, content to remain in a private universe of formless and featureless yellow.

Time and space ran together in that undemanding microcosm.

Yes, I was right about the cave painting . . . the circle represents a ptertha . . . a colourless ptertha . . . one which has not yet developed its specialised toxins . . . who was it who once asked me if the ptertha used to be pink? . . . and what was my reply? . . . did I say the naked child is not afraid of the globe because he knows it will not harm him? . . . I know I have always disappointed Toller in one respect, by my lack of physical courage . . . my disregard for honour . . . but now he can be proud of me . . . I wish I could be there to see his face when he hears that I preferred to die rather than to ride with . . . isn't it strange that the answer to the riddle of the ptertha has always been visible in the sky? . . . the Tree and the circle of Overland, symbolising the ptertha, co-existing in harmony . . . the brakka pollination discharges feed the ptertha with . . . with what? . . . pollen, green and purple, miglign? . . . and in return the ptertha seek out and destroy the brakka's enemies . . . Toller should be protected from Prince Leddravohr . . . he believes himself to be equal to him, but I fear . . . I FEAR I HAVE NOT TOLD ANYONE ABOUT THE BRAKKA AND THE PTERTHA! . . . how long have I known? . . . is this a dream? . . . where is my lovely Gesalla? . . . can I still move my hands? . . . can I still. . . .

CHAPTER 17

Prince Leddravohr picked up a looking glass and frowned at his reflection. Even when resident in the Great Palace he preferred not to be attended by body servants, and for his morning toilet he had spent a considerable time in honing a brakka razor to a perfect edge and softening his facial stubble with hot water. As a result, annoyingly, he had pared away too much skin at his throat. There were no real incisions, but droplets of blood were oozing through the skin, and no matter how often he dabbed them away more appeared in their place.

This what comes of living like a pampered maiden, he told himself, pressing a damp cloth to his throat and postponing the act of dressing until the bleeding had stopped. The mirror, made from two different kinds of glass bonded together, was almost totally reflective, but when he faced the window he could discern its brilliant rectangles through the glass sandwich, apparently occupying the same space as his own body.

It's only appropriate, he thought. *I'm becoming insubstantial, a ghost, in preparation for the ascent to Overland. My real life, the only life that has any significance, will be over and done with when* . . . His thoughts were interrupted by the sound of running footsteps in the adjoining apartment. He turned and saw in the doorway of the toilet chamber the square-shouldered figure of Major Yachimalt, the adjutant responsible for communications between the palace and Skyship Quarter. Yachimalt's anxious eyes took in the fact that Leddravohr was naked and he made as if to back out of the room.

"Forgive me, Prince," he said. "I didn't realise. . . ."

"What's the matter with you, man?" Leddravohr snapped. "If you have a message for me, spit it out."

"It's a signal from Colonel Hippern, Prince. He says a mob is gathering at the main entrance to the Quarter."

"He has a full regiment at his disposal, hasn't he? Why should I concern myself with the activities of a rabble?"

"The signal says that the Lord Prelate is inciting them, Prince," Yachimalt replied. "Colonel Hippern requests your authority to place him under arrest."

"Balountar! That miserable sack of bones!" Leddravohr threw the looking glass aside and went to the rack which held his clothing. "Tell Colonel Hippern that he is to hold his ground, but to make no move against Balountar until I arrive. I will deal with our Lord Scarecrow in person."

Yachimalt saluted and vanished from the doorway. Leddravohr found himself actually smiling as he dressed quickly and strapped on his white cuirass. With only five days to go until the first squadron departed for Overland the preparations for the migration were virtually complete and he had not looked forward to a span of enforced idleness. When there was no work to be done his thoughts all too easily turned to the unnatural ordeal which lay ahead, and it was then that the pale maggots of fear and self-doubt began the insidious attack. Now he could almost feel grateful to the ranting Lord Prelate for presenting him with a diversion, the opportunity to be fully alive and functional once more.

Leddravohr buckled on his sword and the knife he wore on his left arm. He hurried out of his suite, heading for the principal forecourt, choosing a downward route on which there was little chance of encountering his father. The King maintained an excellent intelligence network and would almost certainly have heard about Lain Maraquine's suicidal behaviour of the previous aftday. Leddravohr had no wish to be quizzed about the absurd incident at that moment. He had given orders for a team of draughtsmen to go to the cave and copy the drawings, and he wanted to be able to present the transcription to his father at their next meeting. Instinct told him that the King would be angry and suspicious if, as was almost certainly the case, Maraquine proved to be dead, but it was possible that the drawings would mollify him.

On reaching the forecourt Leddravohr signalled for an ostiary to bring forward the dappled bluehorn he normally rode and in a matter of seconds he was galloping towards the Skyship Quarter. Emerging from the double coccoon of netting which enveloped the palace he entered one of the tubular covered ways which crossed the four ornamental moats. The sheath of varnished linen was proof against ptertha dust and provided safe passage into Ro-Atabri itself, but the sense of being enclosed and herded was irksome to Leddravohr. He was glad when he reached the city, where the sky was at least visible through the overhead meshworks, and he could follow the embankments of the Borann to the west.

There were few citizens abroad and most of those he saw were making their way towards the Quarter, seemingly guided by an extra sense which told them of significant events taking place far ahead. It was a hot and windless morning, with no threat from ptertha. When he reached the western limit of the city he ignored the covered way which ran to the perimeter of the skyship base, riding south of it in the open air to where he could see a crowd gathered at the main entrance. The side panels of the flimsy tube had been furled, enabling the crowd to form a continuous obstruction across the security gate. On the far side of the gate he could see a line of pikes projecting into the air, indicating the presence of soldiers, and he nodded in approval—the pike was a good weapon for demonstrating to unruly civilians the error of their ways.

As he neared the mass of people Leddravohr slowed his bluehorn to a walking pace. When his approach was noticed the crowd parted respectfully to make way for him, and he was surprised to note how many were dressed in ragged garments. The plight of the ordinary citizens of Ro-Atabri was obviously worse than he had realised. Amid much whispering and jostling, the edge of the crowd flowed outwards to create a semicircular space at the focus of which was the black-robed figure of Balountar.

The Lord Prelate, who had been haranguing an officer on the other side of the closed gate, turned to face Leddravohr. He started visibly at the sight of the military prince, but the expression of anger on his squeezed-in features did not change. Leddravohr rode to him at a leisurely pace, dismounted with a deliberate display of lazy confidence and signalled for the gate to be opened. Two soldiers drew the heavy gate inwards and now Leddravohr and Balountar were at the centre of a public arena.

"Well, priest," Leddravohr said calmly, "what brings you here?"

"I think you know why I am here." Balountar waited a full three seconds before adding the royal form of address, thereby detaching it from his first remark and creating a deliberate insolence. "Prince."

Leddravohr smiled. "If you have come to beg a migration warrant, you are too late—they have all been disbursed."

"I beg for nothing," Balountar said, raising his voice, addressing the crowd rather than Leddravohr. "I come to make demands. Demands which must be met."

"Demands!" Nobody had ever dared use that word to Leddravohr, and as he repeated it a strange thing happened to him. His body became two bodies—one physical and solid, anchored to the ground; the other weightless and ethereal, seemingly capable of drifting on the slightest breeze. The latter self severed the connection between the two by taking a step backwards. He felt as if he were no longer in contact with the surface of the plain, but poised at grass-top height, like a ptertha, with a comprehensive but detached view of all that was taking place. From that vantage point he watched, bemused, as his corporeal self played out an immature game. . . .

"Do not dare speak to me of demands!" the fleshly Leddravohr cried. "Have you forgotten the authority invested in me by the King?"

"I speak with a higher authority," Balountar insisted, yielding no ground. "I speak for the Church, for the Great Permanence, and I command you to destroy the vehicles with which you plan to desecrate the High Path. Furthermore, all the food and crystals and other vital supplies which you have stolen from the people must be returned to them immediately. Those are my final words."

"You speak truer than you know," Leddravohr breathed. He unsheathed his battle sword, but some lingering vestige of regard for the processes of law dissuaded him from driving the black

blade through the Lord Prelate's body. Instead, he moved away from Balountar, turned to the watchful army officers nearby and addressed himself to a stony-faced Colonel Hippern.

"Arrest the traitor," he said sharply.

Hippern gave a low command and two soldiers ran forward, swords drawn. A curious growling, grumbling sound arose from the crowd as the soldiers took Balountar by the arms and marched him, in spite of his struggles, inside the line of the Quarter's perimeter. Hippern looked questioningly at Leddravohr.

"What are you waiting for?" Leddravohr stabbed a forefinger towards the ground, indicating that he wanted the Lord Prelate forced to his knees. "You know the punishment for high treason. Get on with it!"

Hippern, face impassive beneath the rim of his ornate helmet, spoke again to the officers near him and a few seconds later a burly high-sergeant ran towards the two soldiers who were restraining Balountar. The Lord Prelate redoubled his efforts to break free, his black-swathed body undergoing inhuman contortions as his captors forced him to the ground. He raised his face to his executioner. His mouth opened wide as he tried to utter a prayer or a curse, creating a target which the sergeant chose unthinkingly on the murderous instant. The sergeant's blade drove into Balountar's mouth and emerged under the base of his skull, severing the spine, ending his life between heartbeats. The two soldiers released his body and stepped back from it as a moan of consternation went up from the crowd. A large pebble arched through the air and skittered through the dust near Leddravohr's feet.

For a moment the prince looked as though he would launch himself at the mob and attack them single-handed, then he wheeled on the high-sergeant. "Get the priest's head off. Elevate it on a pike so that his followers can continue to look up to him."

The sergeant nodded and went about his grisly work with the unruffled dexterity of a pork butcher, and within a minute Balountar's head had been raised on a pikestaff which was then lashed to a gatepost. Rivulets of blood spead swiftly down the staff.

There was a long moment of utter silence—a silence which

burrowed into the ears—and it seemed that an impasse had been reached. Then it gradually became apparent to those watching from within the base that the situation was not truly static—the semi-circle of ground visible beyond the gate was slowly shrinking. Those on the edge of the mass of human beings appeared not to be moving their feet, but they were advancing nonetheless, like ranks of statues which were being inched forward by an inexorable pressure from behind. Evidence of the tremendous force being exerted came when a fence post to the right of the gate creaked and began to lean inwards.

"Close the gate," Colonel Hippern shouted.

"Leave the gate!" Leddravohr faced the colonel. "The army does not cower away from a civilian rabble. Order your men to clear the entire area."

Hippern swallowed, showing his unease, but he met Leddravohr's gaze directly. "The situation is difficult, Prince. This is a local regiment, mostly drawn from Ro-Atabri itself, and the men won't take to the idea of going against their own."

"Do I hear you properly, colonel?" Leddravohr altered his grip on his sword and a worm of white light coiled in his eyes. "Since when have common soldiers become arbiters in the affairs of Kolcorron?"

Hippern's throat worked again, but his courage did not desert him. "Since they became hungry, Prince. It was ever the way."

Unexpectedly, Leddravohr smiled. "That's your professional judgment, is it, colonel? Now observe me closely—I am going to teach you something about the essential nature of command." He turned, took several paces towards the triple row of waiting soldiers and raised his sword.

"Disperse the rabble!" he shouted, sweeping his sword downwards to indicate the direction of attack against the advancing crowd. Soldiers broke rank immediately and ran to engage the foremost of the intruders, and the comparative silence which had pervaded the scene was lost in a sudden uproar. The crowd fell back, but instead of fleeing in complete disarray its members compacted again, having receded but a short distance, and it was then that a significant fact emerged—that only one third of the soldiers had obeyed Leddravohr's command. The others had

scarcely moved and were gazing unhappily at their nearest junior officers. Even the soldiers who had confronted the mob appeared to have done so in a tame and half-hearted manner. They were allowing themselves to be overcome easily, losing their weapons with such rapidity that they had become an asset to the surging throng. Cheering was heard as a large section of the covered way was pulled to the ground and its framing broken up to provide even more weapons. . . .

The other Leddravohr—cool, ethereal and uninvolved— watched with a mild degree of interest as the body-locked, carnate Leddravohr ran to a fresh-faced lieutenant and ordered him to lead his men against the crowd. The lieutenant was seen to shake his head in argument and a second later he was dead, almost decapitated by a single stroke of the prince's blade. Leddravohr had lost his humanity, had ceased to register on the senses as a human being. Craned forward and shambling, black sword hurling a crimson spray, he went among his officers and men like a terrible demon, wreaking destruction.

How long can this go on? the other Leddravohr mused. *Is there no limit to what the men will stand?*

His attention was suddenly drawn to a new phenomenon. The sky in the east was growing dark as columns of smoke ascended from several districts of the city. It could only mean that the ptertha screens were burning, that some members of the community had been driven by anger and frustration to make the ultimate protest against the present order.

The message was clear—that all would go down together. Rich man and poor man alike. King and pauper alike.

At the thought of the King, alone and vulnerable in the Great Palace, the other Leddravohr's composure disintegrated. Vital and urgent work had to be done; he had responsibilities whose importance far outweighed that of a clash involving a few hundred citizens and soldiers.

He took a step towards his complementary self, and there came a swooping sensation, a blurring of time and space. . . .

Prince Leddravohr Neldeever opened his eyes to a flood of harsh sunlight. The haft of his sword was wet in his hand, and around him were the sounds of turmoil and the colours of carnage. He surveyed the scene for a moment, blinking as he sought to reorientate himself in a changed reality, then he sheathed his sword and ran towards his waiting bluehorn.

CHAPTER 18

Toller stared at the yellow-hooded body without moving for perhaps ten minutes, trying to understand how he was to deal with the pain of loss.

Leddravohr has done this, he thought. *This is the harvest I reap for allowing the monster to stay alive. He abandoned my brother to the pertha!*

The foreday sun was still low in the east, but in the total absence of air movement the rocky hillside was already beginning to throw up heat. Toller was torn between passion and prudence—the desire to run to his brother's body and the need to remain at a safe distance. His blurred vision showed something white gleaming on the sunken chest, held in place by the waistcord of the grey robe and one slim hand.

Paper? Could it be, Toller's heart speeded up at the thought, *an indictment of Leddravohr?*

He took out the stubby telescope he had carried since boyhood and directed it at the white rectangle. His tears conspired with the fierce brilliance of the image to make the scrawled words difficult to read, but at length he received Lain's final communication:

PTERTHA FRIENDS OF BRAK. KILL US BECAU WE KILL BRAK. BRAK FEED PTERTH. IN RETURN P PROTEC B. CLEAR → PINK → PURPLE P EVOLV TOXINS. WE MUS LIVE IN HARMONY WITH B. LOOK TO SKY

Toller lowered the telescope. Somewhere under the thundering turmoil of his grief was the realisation that Lain's message had a significance which reached far beyond the present circumstances, but for the present he was unable to relate to it. Instead he was overwhelmed by a baffled disappointment. Why had Lain not used the dregs of his mental and physical energy to

241

accuse his murderer and thus pave a straight path for retribution? After a moment's thought the answer came to Toller, and he almost managed to smile with affection and respect. Lain, even in death, had been the true pacifist, far removed from thoughts of revenge. He had withdrawn his personal light from the world in a manner befitting his way of life—and Leddravohr still endured. . . .

Toller turned to walk across the slope to where the sergeant was waiting with the two bluehorns. He was fully in control of himself and there were no longer any tears to interfere with his vision, but now his thoughts were dominated by a new question which was raking his brain with the force and persistence of waves clawing at a beach.

How can I live without my brother? The heat reflected from slabs of stone pressed against his eyes, entered his mouth. *It's going to be a long hot day, and how am I going to live through it without my brother?*

"I grieve with you, captain," Engluh said. "Your brother was a good man."

"Yes." Toller stared at the sergeant, trying to suppress his feelings of dislike. This was the man who had been formally entrusted with Lain's safety, and who remained alive while Lain was dead. There was little the sergeant could have done against ptertha in this kind of terrain, and according to his story he had been dismissed by Leddravohr; and yet his presence among the living was an affront to the primitive in Toller's character.

"Do you want to go back now, captain?" Engluh showed no signs of being discomfited by Toller's scrutiny. He was a hard-looking veteran, undoubtedly skilled in the art of preserving his own skin, but Toller could not judge him as being untrustworthy.

"Not yet," Toller said. "I want to find the bluehorn."

"Very good, captain." A flickering in the depths of the sergeant's brown eyes showed his awareness of the fact that Toller had not fully accepted Prince Leddravohr's terse account of the previous day's events. "I'll show you the path we took."

Toller mounted his bluehorn and rode behind Engluh as they worked their way up the hill. About halfway to the top they came to an area of laminated rock bounded on its lower edge by an accumulation of flakes. The remains of the bluehorn lay on the loose material, already stripped to a skeleton by multipedes and other scavengers. Even the saddle and harness had been shredded and gnawed in places. Toller felt a coolness on his spine as he realised that Lain's body would have suffered a similar fate but for the ptertha poison in the tissues. His bluehorn had begun to toss its head and behave nervously, but he guided it closer to the skeleton and frowned as he saw the fractured shinbone. *My brother was living when that happened—and now he's dead.* As the pain raged through him with renewed forced he closed his eyes and tried to think about the unthinkable.

According to what he had been told, Sergeant Engluh and the other three soldiers had ridden to the west entrance of Skyship Quarter after being dismissed by Leddravohr. They had waited there for Lain and had been astonished to see Leddravohr returning alone.

The prince had been in a strange mood, angry and jovial at once, and on seeing Engluh was reported to have said, "Prepare yourself for a long wait, sergeant—your master disabled his mount and now he is playing hide-and-seek with the ptertha." Thinking it was expected of him, Engluh had volunteered to gallop back to the hill with a spare bluehorn, but Leddravohr had said, "Stay where you are! He chose to play a dangerous game with his own life—and that is no sport for a good soldier."

Toller had made the sergeant repeat his account several times and the only interpretation he could place on it was that Lain had been offered transportation to safety, but had wilfully elected to flirt with death. Leddravohr was above the need to lie about any of his actions—and still Toller was unable to accept what he had been told. Lain Maraquine, who had been known to faint at the sight of blood, would have been the last man in the world to pit himself against the globes. Had he wanted to take his life he would have found a better way—but in any case there had been no reason for him to commit suicide. He had had too much to live for. No, there was a mystery central to what had happened on the barren hillside on the previous day, and Toller knew of only one man who could clear it up. Leddravohr may not have lied, but he knew more than. . . .

"Captain!" Engluh spoke in a startled whisper. "Look over there!"

Toller followed the line of his pointing finger to the east and blinked as he saw the unmistakable dark brown shape of a balloon lifting into the sky above Ro-Atabri. A few seconds later it was joined by three others climbing in close formation, almost as though the mass ascent to Overland was beginning days ahead of schedule.

Something has gone wrong, Toller thought before he was stricken by a sense of personal outrage. The death of Lain would have been more than enough to contend with on its own, but to that had been added aggravating doubt and suspicion—and now skyships were rising from the Quarter in contravention of all the rigid planning that had gone into the migration flight. There was a limit to how much his mind could encompass at a single time, and the universe was unfairly choosing to disregard it.

"I have to go back now," he said, urging his bluehorn into motion. They rode down the hill, rounded a briar-covered shoulder and reached the open slope where Lain's body lay. The unrestricted view to the east showed that more balloons were rising from the line of enclosures, but Toller's gaze was drawn to the dappled sweeps of the city beyond. Columns of dark smoke were rising from the central districts.

"It looks like a war, captain," Engluh said in wonderment, rising in his stirrups.

"Perhaps that's what it is." Toller glanced once towards the inert anonymous shape that had been his brother—*You will live in me, Lain*—then spurred his mount forward in the direction of the city.

He had been aware of the growing restlessness among Ro-Atabri's beleaguered population, but he found it hard to imagine how civil disturbances could have any real effect on the ordered course of events within the Quarter. Leddravohr had installed army units in a crescent between the skyship base and the edge of the city itself, and had seen to it that they were controlled by officers he could trust even in the unique circumstances of the migration. The commanders were men who had no personal wish to fly to Overland and were stubbornly committed to preserving Ro-Atabri as an entity, come what may. Toller had believed the base to be secure, even in the event of full-scale riots, but the skyships were taking off long before their appointed time. . . .

On reaching flat grassland he put the bluehorn into a full gallop and watched intently as the base's perimeter barrier expanded across his field of view. The west entrance was little used because it faced open countryside, but as he drew closer he saw there were large groups of mounted soldiers and infantry behind the gate, and supply wagons could be seen on the move beyond the double screens where they curved away to the north and south. More ships were drifting up into the morning sky, and the hollow roars of their burners were mingling with the clacking of the inflation fans and the background shouting of overseers.

The outer gates were swung open for Toller and the sergeant, then slammed shut again as soon as they had entered the buffer zone. Toller reined his bluehorn to a halt as he was approached by an army captain who was carrying his orange-crested helmet under his arm.

"Are you Skycaptain Toller Maraquine?" he said, mopping his glistening brow.

"Yes. What has happened?"

"Prince Leddravohr orders you to report to Enclosure 12 immediately."

Toller nodded his assent. "What has happened?"

"What makes you think anything has happened?" the captain said bitterly. He turned and strode away, issuing angry orders to the nearest soldiers, who had an overtly sullen look.

Toller considered going after him and extracting an informative reply, but at that moment he noticed a blue-uniformed figure beckoning to him from the inner gate. It was Ilven Zavotle, newly commissioned to the rank of pilot lieutenant. Toller rode to him and dismounted, noting as he did so that the young man looked pale and troubled.

"I'm glad you're back, Toller," Zavotle said anxiously. "I heard you had gone out to look for your brother, and I came to warn you about Prince Leddravohr."

"Leddravohr?" Toller glanced upwards as a skyship briefly occulted the sun. "What about Leddravohr?"

"He's insane," Zavotle said, looking about him to ensure the treasonous statement had not been overheard. "He's at the enclosures now . . . driving the loaders and inflation crews . . . sword in hand . . . I saw him cut a man down just for stopping to take a drink."

"He . . . !" Toller's consternation and bafflement increased. "What brought all this about?"

Zavotle looked up at him in surprise. "You don't know? You must have left the Quarter before . . . Everything happened in a couple of hours, Toller."

"*What* happened? Speak up, Ilven, or there'll be more swordplay."

"Lord Prelate Balountar led a citizens' march on the base. He demanded that all the ships be destroyed and the supplies distributed among the people. Leddravohr had him arrested and beheaded on the spot."

Toller narrowed his eyes as he visualised the scene. "That was a mistake."

"A bad one," Zavotle agreed, "but that was only the beginning. Balountar had the crowds worked up with religion and promises of food and crystals. When they saw his head on a pole they started tearing down our screens. Leddravohr sent the army against them, but . . . it was an amazing thing, Toller . . . most of the soldiers refused to fight."

"They defied Leddravohr?"

"They're local men—most of them drawn from Ro-Atabri itself—and they were being ordered to massacre their own people." Zavotle paused as a skyship overhead produced a thunderous roar. "The soldiers are hungry, too, and there's a feeling abroad that Leddravohr is turning his back on them."

"Even so. . . ." Toller found it almost impossible to imagine ordinary soldiers rebelling against the military prince.

"That was when Leddravohr really became possessed. They say he killed more than a dozen officers and men. They wouldn't obey his orders . . . but they wouldn't defend themselves against him either . . . and he butchered them. . . ." Zavotle's voice faltered. "Like pigs, Toller. Just like pigs."

In spite of the enormity of what he was hearing, Toller developed an unaccountable feeling that he had another and more pressing cause for concern. "How did it end?"

"The fires in the city. When Leddravohr saw the smoke . . . realised the pertha screens were burning . . . he came to his senses. He pulled all the men who remained loyal to him back inside the perimeter, and now he's trying to get the whole skyship fleet off the ground before the rebels organise themselves and invade the base." Zavotle studied the nearby soldiers from beneath lowered brows. "This lot are supposed to defend the west gate, but if you ask me they aren't too sure which side they're on. Blue uniforms are no longer popular around here. We should get back to the enclosures as soon as. . . ."

The words faded from Toller's hearing as his mind made a rapid series of leaps, each one bringing him closer to the source of his subconscious alarm. *The fires in the city . . . pertha screens burning . . . there has been no rain for many days . . . when the screens go the city will be indefensible . . . the migration MUST get under way at once . . . and that means. . . .*

"Gesalla!" Toller blurted the name in a sudden accession of panic and self-recrimination. How could he have forgotten her for so long? She would be waiting at home in the Square House . . . still without confirmation of Lain's death . . . and the flight to Overland had already begun. . . .

"Did you hear me?" Zavotle said. "We should be. . . ."

"Never mind that," Toller cut in. "What's been done about notifying the migrants and bringing them in?"

"The King and Prince Chakkell are already at the enclosures. All the other royals and nobles have to get here under the protection of their own guards. It's a shambles, Toller. The ordinary migrants will have to get through by themselves, and the way things are out there I doubt if. . . ."

"I'm indebted to you for meeting me here, Ilven," Toller said, turning to mount his bluehorn. "I seem to remember you telling me when we were up there—freezing to death and with nothing

247

to do but count the falling stars—that you have no family. Is that right?"

"Yes."

"In that case you should get back to the enclosures and take the first ship that becomes available to you. I am not free to leave just yet."

Zavotle came forward as Toller swung himself into the saddle. "Leddravohr wants us both as royal pilots, Toller. You especially, because nobody else has turned a ship over."

"Forget that you saw me," Toller said. "I'll be back as soon as I can."

He rode into the base, taking a route which kept him well away from the balloon enclosures. The ptertha nets overhead were casting their patterns of shadow on a scene of confused and frenetic activity. It had been intended that the migration fleet would depart in an orderly manner over a period of between ten and twenty days, depending on weather conditions. Now there was a race to see how many ships could be despatched before the Quarter was overrun by dissenters, and the situation was made even more desperate by the fact that the vulnerable ptertha screens had been attacked. It was fortunate that there was no perceptible air movement—a circumstance which aided the skyship crews and kept ptertha activity to the minimum—but with the arrival of night the livid globes would come in force.

In their haste to load supply carts workers were tearing down the wooden storage huts with their bare hands. Soldiers belonging to the newly formed Overland Regiment—their loyalty guaranteed because they were due to fly with Leddravohr—roamed the area, noisily exhorting base personnel to make greater efforts and in some cases joining in the work. Here and there amid the chaos wandered small groups of men, women and children who had obtained migration warrants in the provinces and had arrived at the Quarter well in advance of their flights. Above and through everything drifted the racket of the inflation fans, the unnerving spasmodic roar of skyship burners and the marshy odour of free miglign gas.

Toller attracted scant attention from anybody as he rode through storage and workshop sections, but on reaching the covered way which ran east to the city he found its entrance guarded by a large detachment of soldiers. Officers with them were questioning everybody who passed through. Toller moved to one side and used his telescope to survey the distant exit. Compressed perspectives made the image hard to interpret, but he could see massed foot soldiers and some mounted groups, and beyond them crowds thronging the sloping streets where the city proper began. There was little evidence of movement, but it was obvious that a confrontation was still taking place and that the normal route to the city was impassable.

He was considering what to do when his attention was caught by shifting specks of colour in the scrubby land which stretched off to the south-east in the direction of the Greenmount suburb. The telescope revealed them to be civilians hurrying towards the centre of the base. From the high proportion of women and children Toller deduced they were emigrants who had breached the perimeter fence at a point remote from the main entrance. He turned away from the tunnel, located an auxiliary exit through the double ptertha meshes and rode out towards the advancing citizenry. When he got close to the leaders they brandished their blue-and-white migration warrants.

"Keep heading towards the balloon enclosures," he shouted to them. "We'll get you away."

The anxious-faced men and women called out their thanks and hurried on, some carrying or dragging infants. Turning to look after them, Toller saw that their arrival had been noticed and mounted men were coming out to meet them. The sky behind the riders made a unique spectacle. Perhaps fifty ships were now in the air over the enclosures, dangerously crowded at the lower levels and straggling out as they receded into the zenith.

Not pausing to see what kind of reception the migrants would receive, Toller spurred his bluehorn on towards Greenmount. Far off to his right, in Ro-Atabri itself, the fires appeared to be spreading. The city was built of stone, but the timber and rope with which it had been cocooned to ward off the ptertha were highly flammable and the fires were becoming large enough to create their own convection systems, gaining ground with no assistance from the elements. It was only necessary, Toller knew, for a slight breeze to spring up and the whole city would be engulfed in a matter of minutes.

He urged the bluehorn into a gallop, judging his direction from the groups of refugees he met, and eventually espied a place where the perimeter barricade had been pulled to the ground. He rode through the gap, ignoring apprehensive stares from people who were clambering across the stakes, and chose a direct route up the hill towards the Square House. The streets he had roamed as a boy were littered and deserted, part of the alien territory of the past.

A minute after entering Greenmount district he rounded a corner and encountered a band of five civilians who had armed themselves with staves. Although obviously not migrants, they were hurrying towards the Quarter. Toller divined at once that it was their intention to harass and perhaps rob some of the migrant families he had seen earlier.

They spread out to block the narrow street and their leader, a slack-jawed hulk in a cloak thonged with dried pillar snakes, said, "What do you think you're doing, bluecoat?"

Toller, who could easily have ridden the man down, reined to a halt. "As you ask so politely, I don't mind telling you that I'm deciding whether or not I should kill you."

"Kill *me*!" The man pounded the ground imperiously with his staff, apparently in the belief that all skymen went unarmed. "And exactly how . . . ?"

Toller drew his sword with a horizontal sweep which lopped the staff just above the man's hand. "That could just have easily been your wrist or your neck," he said mildly. "Do any or all of you wish to pursue the matter?"

The four others eyed each other and backed away.

"We have no quarrel with you, sir," the cloaked man said, nursing the hand which had been jarred by the fierce impact on his staff. "We'll go peaceably on our way."

"You won't." Toller used his brakka blade to point out an alley which led away from the skyship base. "You will go that way, and back to your dens. I will be returning to the Quarter in a few minutes—and I swear that if I set eyes on any of you again it will be my sword that does all the talking. Now *go*!"

As soon as the men had passed out of sight he sheathed his sword and resumed the ascent of the hill. He doubted if his warning would have a lasting effect on the ruffians, but he had spared as much time as he could on behalf of the migrants, all of whom would have to learn to face many rigours in the coming days. A glance at the narrowing crescent of light on the disk of Overland told him there was not much more than an hour until littlenight, and it was imperative that he should take Gesalla to the base before then.

On reaching the crest of Greenmount he galloped through silent avenues to the Square House and dismounted in the walled precinct. He went into the entrance hall and was met by Sany, the rotund cook, and a balding manservant who was unknown to him.

"Master Toller!" Sany cried. "Have you news of your brother?"

Toller felt a renewed shock of bereavement—the pressure of events had suspended his normal emotional processes. "My brother is dead," he said. "Where is your mistress?"

"In her bedchamber." Sany pressed both hands to her throat. "This is a terrible day for all of us."

Toller ran to the main stair, but paused on the first flight. "Sany, I'm returning to the Skyship Quarter in a few minutes. I strongly advise you and. . . ." He looked questioningly at the manservant.

"Harribend, sir."

". . . you and Harribend—and any other domestics who are still here—to come with me. The migration has started ahead of time in great confusion, and even though you don't have warrants I think I can get you places on a ship."

Both servants backed away from him. "I couldn't go into the sky before my time," Sany said. "It isn't natural. It isn't right."

"There are riots in the city and the perttha screens are burning."

"Be that as it may, Master Toller—we'll take our chances here where we belong."

"Think hard about it," Toller said. He went up to the landing and through the familiar corridor which led to the south side of the house, unable to accept fully that this was the last occasion on which he would see the ceramic figurines glowing in their niches, or his blurred reflection ghosting along the polished glasswood panels. The door to the principal bedchamber was open.

Gesalla was standing at the window which framed a view of the city in which the dominant features were the seemingly motionless columns of grey and white smoke intersecting the natural blue and green horizontals of Arle Bay and the Gulf of Tronom. She was dressed as he had never seen her before, in a waistcoat and breeches of grey whipcord complemented by a lighter grey shirt—the whole being almost a muted echo of his own skyman's uniform. A sudden timidity made him refrain from speaking or tapping the door. How was one to impart the kind of news he bore?

Gesalla turned and looked at him with wise, sombre eyes. "Thank you for coming, Toller."

"It's about Lain," he said, entering the room. "I'm afraid I bring bad news."

"I knew he had to be dead when there was no message by nightfall." Her voice was cool, almost brisk. "All that was needed was the confirmation."

Toller was unprepared for her lack of emotion. "Gesalla, I don't know how to tell you this . . . at a time like this . . . but you have seen the fires in the city. We have no choice but to. . . ."

"I'm ready to leave," Gesalla said, picking up a tightly rolled bundle which had been on a chair. "These are all the personal possessions I'll need. It isn't too much, is it?"

He stared at her beautiful unperturbed face for a moment, battling with an irrational resentment. "Have you any idea where we're going?"

"Where else but to Overland? The skyships are leaving. According to what I could decipher of the sunwriter messages coming out of the Great Palace, civil war is breaking out in Ro-Atabri and the King has already fled. Do you think I'm stupid, Toller?"

"Stupid? No, you're very intelligent—very logical."

"Did you expect me to be hysterical? Was I to be carried out of here screaming that I was afraid to go into the sky, where only the heroic Toller Maraquine has been? Was I to weep and plead for time to strew flowers around my husband's body?"

"No, I didn't expect you to weep." Toller was dismayed by what he was saying, yet was unable to hold back. "I don't expect you to feign grief."

Gesalla struck him across the face, her hand moving so quickly that he was given no chance to avoid the blow. "Never say anything like that to me again. *Never* make that kind of presumption about me! Now, are we leaving or are we going to stand here and talk all day?"

"The sooner we leave the better," he said stonily, resisting the urge to finger the stinging patch on his cheek. "I'll take your pack."

Gesalla snatched the bundle away from him and slung it from her shoulders. "I made it for *me* to carry—you have enough to do." She slipped past him into the corridor, moving lightly and with deceptive speed, and had reached the main stair before he caught up with her.

"What about Sany and the other servants?" he said. "Leaving them doesn't sit easy with me."

She shook her head. "Lain and I both tried to talk them into applying for warrants, and we failed. You can't force people to go, Toller."

"I suppose you're right." He walked with her to the entrance, taking a last nostalgic look around the hall, and went out to the precinct where his bluehorn was waiting. "Where is your carriage?"

"I don't know—Lain took it yesterday."

"Does that mean we have to ride together?"

Gesalla sighed. "I have no intention of trotting along beside you."

"Very well." Feeling oddly selfconscious, Toller climbed into the saddle and extended a hand to Gesalla. He was surprised at how little effort it took to help her spring into place behind him, and even more so when she slipped her arms around his waist and pressed herself to his back. Some bodily contact was necessary, but it almost seemed as though she . . . He dismissed the half-formed thought, appalled by his obscene readiness to think of Gesalla in a sexual context, and put the bluehorn into a fast trot.

On leaving the precinct and turning north-west he saw that many more ships were now in the sky above the Quarter, dwindling into specks as they were absorbed by the blue depths of the upper atmosphere. A slight eastward drift was becoming apparent in their movement, which meant that the chaos of the departure might soon be made worse by the arrival of ptertha. Off to his left the towers of smoke rising from the city were being horizontally sheared and smeared where they reached high level air currents. Burning trees created occasional powdery explosions.

Toller rode down the hill as fast as was compatible with safety. The streets were as empty as before, but he was increasingly aware of the sounds of tumult coming from directly ahead. He emerged from the last screen of abandoned buildings and found that the scene at the Quarter's periphery had changed.

The break in the barricade had been enlarged and groups totalling perhaps a hundred had gathered there, denied entry to the base by ranks of infantry. Stones and pieces of timber were being hurled at the soldiers who, although armed with swords and javelins, were not retaliating. Several mounted officers were stationed behind the soldiers, and Toller knew by their sleeved swords and the green flashes on their shoulders that they were part of a Sorka regiment, men who were loyal to Leddravohr and had no particular affiliations with Ro-Atabri. It was a situation which could erupt into carnage at any moment, and if that happened rebel soldiers would probably be drawn to the spot to turn it into a miniature theatre of war.

"Hold on and keep your head down," he said to Gesalla as he drew his sword. "We have to go in hard."

He spurred the bluehorn into a gallop. The powerful beast responded readily, covering the intervening ground in a few wind-rushing seconds. Toller had hoped to take the rioters completely unawares and burst through them before they could react, but the pounding of hooves on the hard clay attracted the attention of men who had turned to gather stones.

"There's a bluecoat," the cry went up. "Get the filthy bluecoat!"

The sight of the massive charging animal and of Toller's battle sword was enough to scatter all from his path, but there was no escaping the irregular volley of missiles. Toller was struck solidly on the upper arm and thigh, and a skimming piece of slate laid open the knuckles of his rein hand. He kept the bluehorn on course through the overturned timbers of the barricade and had almost reached the lines of soldiers when he heard a thud and felt an impact transmitted through Gesalla's body. She gasped and slackened her hold for an instant, then recovered her strength. The lines of soldiers parted to make way for him and he pulled the bluehorn to a halt.

"Is it bad?" he said to Gesalla, unable to turn in the saddle or dismount because of her grip on him.

"It isn't serious," she replied in a voice he could scarcely hear. "You must go on."

A bearded lieutenant approached them, saluted and caught the bluehorn's bridle. "Are you Skycaptain Toller Maraquine?"

"I am."

"You are to report immediately to Prince Leddravohr at Enclosure 12."

"That's what I'm trying to do, lieutenant," Toller said. "It would be easier if you stepped aside."

"Sir, Prince Leddravohr's orders made no mention of a woman."

Toller raised his eyebrows and met the lieutenant's gaze directly. "What of it?"

"I . . . Nothing, sir." The lieutenant released the bridle and moved back.

Toller urged the bluehorn forward, heading for the row of balloon enclosures. It had been found, though nobody had explained the phenomenon, that perforated barriers protected balloons from air disturbances better than solid screens. The open western sky was shining through square apertures in the enclosures, making them look more than ever like a line of lofty towers, at the foot of which was the seething activity of thousands of workers, air crew and emigrants with all their paraphernalia and supplies.

It said much for the organising ability of Leddravohr, Chakkell and their appointees that the system was able to function at all in such extreme circumstances. Ships were still taking off in groups of two or three, and it occurred to Toller that it was almost a miracle that there had been no serious accidents.

At that moment, as if the thought had engendered the event, the gondola of a ship rising too quickly struck the rim of its enclosure. The ship was oscillating as it shot into clear air and at a height of two-hundred feet overtook another which had departed some seconds earlier. At the limit of one of its pendulum swings the gondola of the uncontrolled ship drove sideways into the balloon of the slower craft. The latter's envelope split and lost its symmetry, flapping and rippling like some wounded creature of the deep, and the ship plunged to the ground, its acceleration struts trailing loosely. It landed squarely on a group of supply wagons. The impact must have severed its burner feed lines for there was an immediate gouting of flame and black smoke, and the barking of injured or terrified bluehorns was added to the general commotion.

Toller tried not to think about the fate of those on board. The other ship's appallingly bad take-off had looked like the work of a novice, making it seem that many of the one thousand qualified pilots assigned to the migration fleet were not available, possibly stranded by the disturbances in the city. New dangers had been added to the already daunting array of hazards facing the interworld voyagers.

He could feel Gesalla's head lolling against his back as they rode towards the enclosure, and his anxiety about her increased. Her lightweight frame was ill-equipped to withstand the sort of blow he had felt at a remove. As he neared the twelfth enclosure he saw that it and the three adjoining to the north were heavily ringed by foot soldiers and cavalry. In the protected zone there was an area of comparative calm. Four balloons were waiting in the enclosures, with the inflation teams to hand, and knots of richly dressed men and women were standing by heaps of ornamented cases and other belongings. Some of the men were sipping drinks as they craned to see the crashed ship, while small children darted around their legs as though at play on a family outing.

Toller scanned the area and was able to pick out a group at the core of which were Leddravohr, Chakkell and Pouche, all standing close to the seated figure of King Prad. The ruler, slumped on an ordinary chair, was staring at the ground, apparently oblivious to all that was happening. He looked old and dispirited, in marked contrast to the vigorous aspect which Toller remembered.

A youngish army captain came forward to meet Toller as he reined the bluehorn to a halt. He looked surprised when he saw Gesalla, but helped her to the ground readily enough and without any comment. Toller dismounted and saw that her face was totally without colour. She was swaying a little and her eyes had a distant, abstracted look which told him she was in severe pain.

"Perhaps I should carry you," he said as the ranks of soldiers parted at a signal from the captain.

"I can walk, I can *walk*," she whispered. "Take your hands away, Toller—the beast is not to see me being assisted."

Toller nodded, impressed by her courage, and walked ahead of her towards the royal group. Leddravohr turned to face him and for once did not produce his snake-strike of a smile. His eyes were smouldering in the marble-smooth face. There was a diagonal spattering of crimson on his white cuirass, and blood was congealing thickly around the top of his scabbard, but his manner was suggestive of controlled anger rather than the insane rage of which Zavotle had spoken.

"I sent for you hours ago, Maraquine," he said icily. "Where have you been?"

"Viewing the remains of my brother," Toller said, deliberately omitting the required form of address. "There is something highly suspicious about his death."

"Do you know what you are saying?"

"Yes."

"I see you have returned to your old ways." Leddravohr moved closer and lowered his voice. "My father once extracted a

257

vow from me that I would not harm you, but I will regard myself as released from that vow when we reach Overland. Then, I promise you, I will give you what you have sought so long—but for now more important matters must engage my attention."

Leddravohr turned and padded away, giving a signal to the launch supervisors. At once the balloon inflating crews went to work, cranking the big fans into noisy life. King Prad raised his head, startled, and looked about him with his single troubled eye. The spurious festive mood deserted the various noblemen as the clatter of the fans impressed on them that the unprecedented flight into the unknown was about to begin. Family groups drew together, the children ceased their play, and servants made ready to transfer their masters' belongings to the ships which would depart in the wake of the royal flight.

Beyond the protective lines of guards was a sea of apparently undirected activity as the work of despatching the migration fleet continued. Men were running everywhere, and supply wagons careered among the lumbering flatbed carts which were transporting skyships to the enclosures. Farther away across the open ground of the Quarter, taking advantage of the near-perfect weather conditions, the pilots of cargo ships were inflating their balloons and taking off without the aid of windbreaks. The sky was now thronged with ships, rising like a cloud of strange airborne spores towards the fiery crescent of Overland.

Toller was awed by the sheer drama of the spectacle, the proof that when driven to the limit his own kind had the courage and ability to stride like gods from one world to another, but he was also bemused by what he had just heard from Leddravohr.

The vow of which Leddravohr had spoken explained certain things—but why had he been asked to make it in the first place? What had prompted the King to single one of his subjects out of so many and place him under his personal protection? Intrigued by the new mystery, Toller glanced thoughtfully in the direction of the seated figure of the King and experienced a peculiar thrill when he saw that Prad was staring directly at him. A moment later the King pointed a finger at Toller, casting a line of psychic force through the groups of bystanders, and then beckoned to him. Ignoring the curious gazes of royal attendants, Toller approached the King and bowed.

"You have served me well, Toller Maraquine," Prad said in a tired but firm voice. "And now it is in my mind to charge you with one further responsibility."

"You have but to name it, Majesty," Toller replied, his sense of unreality increasing as Prad gestured for him to move closer and stoop to receive a private message.

"See to it," the King whispered, "that my name is remembered on Overland."

"Majesty. . . ." Toller straightened up, beset with confusion. "Majesty, I don't understand."

"Understanding will come—now go to your post."

Toller bowed and backed away, but before he had time to ponder on the brief exchange he was summoned by Colonel Kartkang, former chief administrator for the S.E.S. Following the dissolution of the Experimental Squadron the colonel had been given the responsibility for coordinating the departure of the royal flight, a task he could hardly have foreseen carrying out in such adverse conditions. His lips were moving silently as he directed Toller to a spot where Leddravohr was addressing three pilots. One of them was Ilven Zavotle, and another was Gollav Amber—an experienced man who had been short-listed for the proving flight. The third was a thick-bodied red-bearded man in his forties, who wore the uniform of a skycommander. After a moment's thought, Toller identified him as Halsen Kedalse, a former aircaptain and royal messenger.

". . . decided that we will travel in separate ships," Leddravohr was saying as his gaze flickered towards Toller. "Maraquine—the one officer who has experience of taking a ship past the midpoint—will have the responsibility of piloting my father's ship. I will fly with Zavotle. Prince Chakkell will go with Kedalse, and Prince Pouche with Amber. Each of you will now go to his designated ship and prepare to ascend before littlenight is on us."

The four pilots saluted and were about to walk to the enclosures when Leddravohr halted them by raising a hand. He studied them for what seemed a long time, looking uncharacteristically irresolute, before he spoke again. "On reflection, Kedalse has flown my father many times during his long service as an aircaptain. He will fly the King's ship on this occasion, and Prince Chakkell will go with Maraquine. That is all."

Toller saluted again and turned away, wondering what was signified by Leddravohr's change of mind. He had been quick to take the point when Toller had said he was suspicious about Lain's death. *My brother is dead!* Was that an indication of guilt? Had some grotesque twist of thought made Leddravohr unwilling to entrust his father's life to a man whose brother he had murdered, or at least caused to die?

The unmistakable sound of a heavy cannon being fired somewhere in the distance reminded Toller that he had no time to spare for speculation. He looked around for Gesalla. She was standing alone, isolated from the surrounding activity, and something about her posture told him she was still in extreme pain. He ran to the gondola where Prince Chakkell was waiting with his wife, daughter and two small sons. The pearl-coiffed Princess Daseene and the children gazed up at Toller with expressions of wary surmise, and even Chakkell seemed tentative in his manner. They were all deeply afraid, Toller realised, and one of the unknowns facing them was the nature of the relationship to be dictated by the man into whose hands chance had delivered their lives.

"Well, Maraquine," Chakkell said, "are we about to leave?"

Toller nodded. "We could all be safely away from here in a few minutes, Prince—but there is a difficulty."

"A difficulty? What difficulty?"

"My brother died yesterday." Toller paused, taking advantage of the fresh anxiety he had glimpsed in Chakkell's eyes. "My obligation to his widow can only be discharged by bringing her with me on this flight."

"I'm sorry, Maraquine, but that is out of the question," Chakkell said. "This ship is for my use only."

"I know that, Prince, but you are a man who understands family ties, and you can appreciate that it is impossible for me to abandon my brother's widow. If she can't travel on this ship, then I must decline the honour of being your pilot."

"You're talking about treason," Chakkell snapped, wiping perspiration from his bald brown scalp. "I . . . Leddravohr would have you executed on the spot if you dared disobey his orders."

"I know that too, Prince, and it would be a great pity for all concerned." Toller directed a thin smile at the watchful children. "If I weren't here an inexperienced pilot would have to take you and your family through that strange region between the worlds. I'm familiar with all the terrors and dangers of the middle passage, you see, and could have prepared you for them."

The two boys continued to gaze up at him, but the girl hid her face in her mother's skirts. Chakkell stared at her with pain-filled eyes and shuffled his feet in an agony of frustration as, for the first time in his life, he had to consider subordinating himself to the will of an ordinary man. Toller smiled at him, falsely sympathetic, and thought, *If this is power, may I never need it again.*

"Your brother's widow may travel in my ship," Chakkell finally said. "And I won't forget about this, Maraquine."

"I'll always remember you with gratitude too," Toller said. As he was climbing into the pilot's station of the gondola he resigned himself to having hardened the enmity that Chakkell already felt for him, but he could feel no guilt or shame this time. He had acted with deliberation and logic to achieve what was necessary, unlike the Toller Maraquine of old, and had the further consolation of knowing he was in tune with the realities of the situation. Lain—*My brother is dead!*—had once said that Leddravohr and his kind belonged to the past, and Chakkell had just vindicated those words. In spite of all the catastrophic changes which had overwhelmed their world, men like Leddravohr and Chakkell acted as though Kolcorron would be created anew on Overland. Only the King seemed to have intuited that everything would be different.

Lying on his back against a partition, Toller signalled to the inflation crew that he was ready to start burning. They stopped cranking and hauled the fan aside, giving him a clear view of the balloon's interior. The envelope, partially filled with cool air, was sagging and rolling between the upraised acceleration struts.

He fired a series of blasts into it, drowning out the sound of the other burners which were being operated all along the line of enclosures, and watched it distend and lift itself clear of the ground. As it reached the vertical position the men holding the crown lines closed in and fastened them to the gondola's load frame, and others rotated the lightweight structure until it was horizontal. The huge assemblage of balloon and gondola, now lighter than air, began to strain gently at its central anchor as though Overland was calling to it.

Toller leapt down from the gondola and nodded to Chakkell and the waiting attendants as a sign that the passengers and belongings could go aboard. He went to Gesalla and she made no objection as he unslung the bundle from her shoulder.

"We're ready to go," he said. "You'll be able to lie down and rest as soon as you're on board."

"But that's a royal ship," she replied, unexpectedly hanging back. "I'm supposed to find a place on one of the others."

"Gesalla, please forget all about what was *supposed* to happen. Many ships will fail to leave this place altogether, and it's likely that blood will be shed in the fight to get on to some of those that do. You must come now."

"Has the Prince given his consent?"

"We talked it over, and he wouldn't even consider departing without you." Toller took Gesalla by the arm and walked with her to the gondola. He went on board first and found that Chakkell, Daseene and the children had taken their places in one passenger compartment, tacitly assigning the other to him and Gesalla. She winced with pain as he helped her climb over the side, and as soon as he had shown her into the vacant compartment she lay down on the wool-filled quilts stored there.

He unbuckled his sword, placed it beside her and returned to the pilot's station. A heavy cannon again sounded in the distance as he reactivated the burner. The ship was lightly loaded compared to the one he had taken on the proving flight, and he waited less than a minute before pulling the anchor link. There was a gentle lurch and the walls of the enclosure began to slide vertically past him. The climb continued well even when the balloon had fully entered the open air, and in a few seconds Toller had a full-circle view of the Quarter. The three other ships of the royal flight—distinguished by white lateral stripes on their gondolas—had already cleared their enclosures and were slightly above him. All other launches had been temporarily halted, but he still felt the air to be uncomfortably crowded, and he kept a careful watch on the companion ships until the beginnings of a westerly breeze had brought about some dispersion.

In a mass flight there was always the risk of collision between two ships ascending or descending at different speeds. As it was impossible for a pilot to see anything directly above him, because of the balloon, the rule was that the uppermost of a pair had the responsibility of taking action to avoid the lower. The theory was sound as far as it went, but Toller had misgivings about it because almost the only option available in the climb phase was to climb faster and thus increase the risk of overtaking a third ship. That risk would have been minimal had the fleet been able to depart according to plan, but now he was uneasily aware of being part of a straggling vertical swarm.

As the ship gained height the scene on the ground below was revealed in all its astonishing complexity.

Balloons, inflated or laid out flat on the grass, were the dominant features in a matrix of paths and wagon tracks, supply dumps, carts, animals and thousands of people milling about in seemingly aimless activities. Toller could almost see them as communal insects labouring to save bloated queens from some imminent catastrophe. Off to the south, crowds formed a variegated mass at the main entrance to the base, but the foreshortened perspective made it impossible to tell if fighting was already breaking out between newly sundered military units.

Sketchy lines of people, presumably determined emigrants, were converging on the launch area from several points on the field's perimeter. And beyond them the fires were now spreading more quickly in Ro-Atabri, aided by the freshening breeze, stripping the city of its ptertha defences. In contrast to the seething turmoil engendered by human beings and their appur- tenances, Arle Bay and the Gulf of Tronom formed a placid backdrop of turquoise and blue. A two-dimensional Mount Opelmer floated in the hazy distance, serene and undisturbed.

Toller, operating the burner by means of the extension lever, stood at the side of the gondola and tried to assimilate the fact that he was departing the scene for ever, but within him there was only a tremulous void, a near-subliminal agitation which told of suppressed emotions. Too much had happened in the space of a single foreday—*My brother is dead!*—and pain and regret had been laid in store for him, to be drawn upon when the first quiet hours came.

Chakkell was also looking outwards from his compartment, arms around Daseene and his daughter, who appeared to be aged about twelve. Toller, who had previously regarded him as a man motivated by nothing but ambition, wondered if he should revise his opinion. The ease with which he had been coerced in the matter of Gesalla indicated an overriding concern for his family.

Spectators could be seen at the rails of two other royal ships—King Prad and his personal attendants in one, the withdrawn Prince Pouche and retainers in another. Only Leddravohr, who seemed to have decided to travel unaccompanied, was not visible. Zavotle, a lonely figure at the controls of Leddravohr's ship, gave Toller a wave, then began drawing in and fastening his acceleration struts. As his ship was the least burdened of the four he could leave the burner for quite long periods and still match the others' rate of climb.

Toller, who had settled on a two-and-twenty rhythm, did not have the same latitude. As a result of what had been learned from the proving flight it had been decided that the migration ships could safely be operated by unaided pilots, thus freeing more lifting ability for passengers and cargo. During a pilot's rest periods he would entrust the burner or jet to a passenger, though always continuing to monitor the rhythm.

"Littlenight is almost here, Prince," Toller said, speaking courteously to make amends for his earlier insubordination. "I want to secure our struts before then, so I must request you to relieve me at the burner."

"Very well." Chakkell seemed almost pleased at having something useful to do as he took over the extension lever. His dark-haired boys, still shooting timid glances at Toller, came to his side and listened attentively while he explained the workings of the machinery to them. By the time Toller had hauled in and lashed the struts to the corners of the gondola, Chakkell had taught the boys to count the burner rhythm by making a chanting game of it.

Seeing that all three were engrossed for the time being, Toller went into the compartment where Gesalla was lying. Her eyes were alert and the strained expression had left her face. She extended a hand and offered him a rolled-up bandage which must have come from her bundle of possessions.

He knelt beside her on the bed of soft quilts, reviling himself for the flicker of sexual excitement the action brought, and took the bandage. "How are you?" he said quietly.

"I don't think any of my ribs are actually broken, but they'll have to be bound if I'm to do my share of the work. Help me up." With Toller's assistance she gingerly raised herself to a kneeling position, half-turned away from him and pulled up her grey shirt to expose a massive bruise at one side of her lower ribs. "What do you think?"

"You should be bandaged," he said, unsure of what was expected of him.

"Well, what are you waiting for?"

"Nothing." He passed the bandage around her and began to lap it tight, but his actions were made awkward by the constrictions of her waistcoat and gathered shirt. Time after time, in spite of all his efforts to the contrary, his knuckles brushed against her breasts and the sensation darted through him like ambersparks, adding to his clumsiness.

Gesalla gave an audible sigh. "You're useless, Toller. Wait!" She pulled open her shirt and removed both it and the waistcoat in a single movement, and now the slimness of her was naked from the waist up. "Try it now."

A vision of Lain's yellow-hooded body turned him into a senseless machine. He completed the bandage with the efficiency and briskness of a battlefield surgeon, and allowed his hands to fall to his sides. Gesalla remained as she was for a few protracted seconds, her gaze warm and solemn, before she picked up the shirt and put it on.

"Thank you," she said, then put out her hand and lightly touched him on the lips.

There was a blaze of rainbow colours and suddenly the ship was in darkness. In the other passenger compartment Daseene or her daughter whimpered with alarm. Toller stood up and looked over the side. The fringed, curved shadow of Overland was speeding towards the eastern horizon, and almost directly below the ship Ro-Atabri was a tangle of orange-burning threads caught in a spreading pool of pitch.

When daylight returned the four ships of the royal flight had attained a height of some twenty miles—and were accompanied by a loose cluster of ptertha.

Toller scanned the sky all around and saw that one globe was only thirty yards away to the north. He went immediately to one of the two rail-mounted cannon on that side, took aim and released the pin which shattered the bilobed glass container in the gun's breech. There was a brief delay while the charges of pikon and halvell mixed, reacted and exploded. The projectile blurred along its trajectory, followed by a glitter of glass fragments, spreading its radial arms as it flew. It curved down through the ptertha and annihilated it, releasing a fast-fading smudge of purple dust.

"That was a good shot," Chakkell said from behind Toller. "Would you say we're safe from the poison at this range?"

Toller nodded. "The ship goes with any wind there is, so the dust can't reach us. The ptertha are not much of a threat, really, but I destroyed that one because there can be some air turbulence at the edge of littlenight. I didn't want to risk the globe picking up a stray eddy and moving in on us."

Chakkell's swarthy face bore an expression of concern as he stared at the remaining globes. "How did they get so close?"

"Pure chance, it seems. If they are spread out over an area of sky and a ship happens to rise up through them, they match its rate of climb. The same thing happened on the. . . ." Toller broke off on hearing two more cannon shots, some distance away, followed by faint screaming which seemed to come from below.

He leaned over the gondola wall and looked straight down. The convex immensity of Land provided an intricate blue-green background for a seemingly endless series of balloons, the nearest of which were only a few hundred yards away and looking very large. Many others were ranged out below them in irregular steps and random groupings, progressively shrinking in apparent size until they reached near-invisibility.

Ptertha could be seen mingling with the uppermost ships and, as Toller watched, another cannon fired and picked off a globe. The projectile quickly lost momentum and faded from sight in a dizzy plunge, losing itself in the cloud patterns far below. The screaming continued, regular as breathing, for some time before gradually fading away.

Toller moved back from the rail, wondering if the screams had been inspired by groundless panic, or if someone had actually seen one of the globes hovering close to a gondola wall—blind, malignant and utterly invincible—just before it darted in for the kill. He was experiencing relief tinged with guilt over having been spared such a fate when a new thought occurred to him. The ptertha had no need to wait for daylight before closing in. There was no guarantee that one or more of the globes had not driven itself against his own ship during the spell of darkness —and if that were the case neither he, Gesalla nor any of his passengers would live to set foot on Overland.

As he tried to come to terms with the notion he slipped a hand into his pocket, located the curious keepsake given to him by his father, and allowed his thumb to begin circling on the ice-smooth surface.

CHAPTER 19

By the tenth day of the flight the ship was only a thousand miles above the surface of Overland, and the ancient patterns of night and day had been reversed.

The period Toller still tended to think of as littlenight—when Overland was screening out the sun—had grown to be seven hours in length; whereas night—when they were in the shadow of the home world—now lasted less than half that time. He was sitting alone at the pilot's station, waiting for daybreak and trying to foresee his people's future on the new world. It seemed to him that even native Kolcorronians, who had always been accustomed to living directly below the fixed sphere of Overland, might feel oppressed by the sight of a larger planet suspended directly above them and depriving them of a proportionately greater part of their day. Assuming Overland to be uninhabited, the migrants could be disposed towards building their new nation on the far side of the planet, in latitudes corresponding to those of Chamteth on Land. Perhaps a time would come when all memory of their origins had faded and. . . .

Toller's thoughts were interrupted by the appearance of Chakkell's seven-year-old son, Setwan, at the entrance to their compartment. The boy came to his side and leaned his head on Toller's shoulder.

"I can't sleep, Uncle Toller," he whispered. "May I stay here with you?"

Toller lifted the boy on to his knee, smiling to himself as he visualised Daseene's reaction if she heard one of her children address him as uncle.

Of the seven people confined to the punishing microcosm of the gondola, Daseene was the only one who had made no concessions to their situation. She had not spoken to Toller or Gesalla, still wore her pearl coif, and ventured out of the passenger compartment only when it was absolutely necessary. She had gone without food or drink for three whole days rather than submit to the ordeal of using the primitive toilet when near the midpoint of the voyage. Her features had become pale and pinched, and—although the ship had since descended to warmer levels of Overland's atmosphere—she remained huddled in the quilted garments which had been hastily manufactured for the migration flight. She answered in monosyllables when spoken to by her family.

Toller had a certain sympathy for Daseene, knowing that the traumas of recent days had been greater for her than for any of the others on board. The children—Corba, Oldo and Setwan—had not had enough years in the privileged dreamland of the Five Palaces to condition them irrevocably, and they had a natural sense of curiosity and adventure on their side. Chakkell's responsibilities and ambitions had always kept him fully in touch with the everyday realities of life in Kolcorron, and he had sufficient strength and resourcefulness to let him anticipate a key role in the founding of a new nation on Overland. Indeed Toller had been quite impressed by the way in which the prince, after the initial period of adjustment, had chosen to involve himself with the operation of the ship without shirking any task.

Chakkell had been particularly scrupulous as regards taking long spells at the microjets which gave the ship some control over its lateral position. It was expected and accepted that all other ships of the fleet would be dispersed by air currents over quite a large area of Overland after a journey of five-thousand miles, but Leddravohr had decreed that the royal flight should be able to land in a tight group.

Different methods of tethering the four ships had been dismissed as impracticable, and in the end they had been fitted with miniature horizontal jets delivering only a small fraction of the thrust produced by the attitude control jets. When fired continuously for a long time they added a very slight lateral component to a ship's vertical motion, without causing it to rotate around its centre of gravity, and assiduous use of them had kept the four royal ships in close formation throughout the flight.

The proximity of the others had furnished Toller with one of the most memorable spectacles of his life, when the group had passed the midpoint and it came time to turn the ships over. Although he had been through the experience before, he found something awesome and ineffably beautiful in the sight of the sister planets majestically drifting in opposite directions, Overland gliding out from the occultation of the balloon and down the sky while Land, at the other end of an invisible beam, climbed above the gondola wall.

And with the transposition half complete a new dimension of wonder was added. A receding, dwindling series of ships seemed to reach all the way to each planet, visible as disks which progressively shrank to glowing points. Several of those going in the direction of Overland had delayed turning over and could be seen from underneath with their gondolas, attachments and jet pipes scribed in ever finer detail on the shrinking circles.

As if that were not enough to brim the eye and mind, there was also—against deep blue infinities seeded with swirls and braids and points of frozen brilliance—the sight of the three companion ships carrying out their own inversion manoeuvres. The structures, which were so fragile that they could be crumpled by a boisterous breeze, remained magically immune to distortion as they stood the universe on its head, proclaiming that this truly was the zone of strangeness. Their pilots, visible as enigmatic mounds of swaddling, surely had to be alien supermen gifted with knowledge and skills inaccessible to ordinary men.

Not all of the scenes witnessed by Toller had possessed such grandeur, but they were imprinted on his memory for different reasons. There was Gesalla's face in its varied moods and aspects—dubiously triumphant as she overcame the waywardness of the galley fire, wanly introspective after hours of "falling" through the region of zero or negligible gravity . . . the bursting of all the accompanying ptertha within minutes of each other, after a day of climbing . . . the children's looks of astonishment and delight as their breath became visible in the surrounding chill . . . the games they played during the brief period when they could suspend beads and trinkets in the air to sketch simplified faces and build three-dimensional designs. . . .

And there had been the other scenes, exterior to the ship,

which told of distant tragedies and the kind of death which heretofore had belonged to the realms of purest nightmare.

The royal flight had taken off at quite an early stage in the evacuation of the Quarter, and Toller knew that by the time they were a day and more past the midpoint they had above them an attenuated linear cloud of ships perhaps a hundred miles high. Had they not already been screened from view by the sedate vastness of his own balloon most of them would have been rendered invisible by sheer distance, but he had received disturbing proof of their existence. It took the form of a sparse, spasmodic and dreadful rain. A rain whose droplets were solid and which varied in size, from entire skyships to human bodies.

On three separate occasions he had seen crumpled ships plunge down past him, the gondolas wrapped in the slow-flapping ruins of their balloons, bound on the day-long fall to Overland. It was his guess that all vestiges of order had disappeared during the latter hours of the escape from Ro-Atabri, and that in the chaos some ships had been taken up by inexperienced fliers or had even been commandeered by rebels with no aviation knowledge at all. It looked as though some of them had driven far past the midpoint without turning over, their velocity being augmented by the growing attraction of Overland until the stresses in the flimsy envelopes had torn them apart.

Once he had seen a gondola plummeting down without its balloon, maintaining its proper attitude because of the trailing lines and acceleration struts, and a dozen soldiers had been visible at its rails, mutely surveying the procession of still-airworthy ships which was to be their last tenuous link with humanity and with life.

But for the most part the falling objects had been smaller —cooking utensils, ornate boxes, sacks of provisions, human and animal forms—evidence of catastrophic accidents tens of miles higher in the wavering stack of ships.

Not very far past the midpoint, while Overland's pull was still weak and the fall speeds were low, a young man had dropped past the ships, so close that Toller could easily discern his features. Perhaps out of bravado, or a desperate craving for a last communion with another human being, the young man had called out to Toller, quite cheerfully, and had waved a hand. Toller had not responded in a way, feeling that to do so would have been to take part in some unspeakable parody of a jest, and had remained petrified at the rail, appalled and yet unable to avert his gaze from the doomed man for the many minutes that it took him to dwindle out of sight.

Hours later, when darkness was all about him and he was trying to sleep, Toller had kept thinking of the falling man—who by then might have been a thousand miles ahead of the migration fleet—and wondering how he was preparing himself for the final impact. . . .

Comforted by the drowsing presence of Setwan on his knee, Toller was operating the burner like an automaton, unconsciously timing the blasts with his heartbeats, when daylight abruptly returned. He blinked several times and saw at once that something was wrong, that only two ships of the royal flight were holding level with him, instead of three.

The missing skyship was the one in which the King was flying.

There was nothing very unusual about that—Kedalse was an ultra-cautious pilot who liked to slow his descent at night, preferring to keep the other ships a little below him where he could easily monitor their positions—but this time he was not even visible in the upper sweeps of the sky.

Toller swiftly lifted Setwan and had just placed him in the passenger compartment with his family when he heard frantic shouts from Zavotle and Amber. He glanced towards them and saw that they were pointing at something above his ship, and in the same moment a gust of hot miglign gas came belching down out of the balloon mouth, bringing a startled whimper from one of the children. Toller looked up into the glowing dome of the balloon and his heart quaked as he saw the square silhouette of a gondola impressed upon it, distorting the spider-web geometries of the load tapes.

The King's ship was directly above him and had come down hard on his own balloon.

Toller could see the circular imprint of the other ship's jet nozzle digging into the crown of the envelope, endangering the integrity of the rip panel. There was a chorus of creaks from the rigging and from the acceleration struts, and a rippling distortion of the balloon fabric expelled more choking gas down into the gondola.

"Kedalse," he shouted, not knowing if his voice would be heard in the upper gondola. "Lift your ship! Lift your ship!"

The faint voices of Zavotle and Amber joined with his own, and a sunwriter began to flash from one of their gondolas, but there was no response from above. The King's ship continued to bear down on the overloaded balloon, threatening to burst or collapse it.

Toller glanced helplessly at Gesalla and Chakkell, who had risen to their feet and were staring at him in open-mouthed dread. The best explanation he could think of for the crisis was that the King's pilot had been overcome by illness and was unconscious or dead at the controls. If that were the case somebody else in the upper gondola might begin firing the burner and separate the two craft, but it would need to be done very soon. And there was also the possibility—Toller's mouth went dry at the thought—that the burner had failed in some way and could not be fired.

He strove to force his brain into action as the deck swayed beneath his feet and the fabric of the balloon emitted sounds like the cracking of a whip. The pair of ships had already begun to lose height too quickly, as was evidenced by the fact that the other two visible ships had acquired a relative upward movement.

Leddravohr had appeared at the rail of his own gondola, for the first time since the take-off, and behind him Zavotle was still emitting futile blinks of brilliance from his sunwriter.

It was impossible for Toller to get away from the King's ship by increasing his own rate of descent. His craft had already lost gas and was coming perilously near the condition in which the air pressures of an excessive fall-speed could collapse the balloon, initiating a thousand-mile drop to the surface of Overland.

In fact, there was an urgent requirement to fire large quantities of hot gas into the balloon—but doing so, with the extra load imposed from above, was to risk increasing the internal pressure so much that the envelope would simply tear itself apart.

Toller locked eyes with Gesalla, and the imperative was born in his mind: *I choose to live!*

He twisted his way into the seat at the pilot's station and fired the burner in a long thunderous blast, engorging the hungry balloon with hot gas, and a few seconds later he pushed the lever of an attitude-control jet. The jet's exhaust was lost in the engulfing roar of the burner, but its effect was not diminished.

The other two members of the royal flight drifted downwards and out of sight as Toller's ship rotated around its centre of gravity. There came a series of low-pitched inhuman groans and shudders as the King's ship slid down the side of Toller's balloon and came into view above him. One of its acceleration struts tore free of its lower attachment point and began wandering and circling in the air like a duellist's sword.

As Toller watched, frozen into his own continuum, the sluggish movements so characteristic of skyships abruptly accelerated. The other gondola drew level with him and the free end of the strut came blindly stabbing down into the galley compartment of Toller's ship, imparting a dangerous tilt to the universe. The shock of the impact raced back along the strut and its upper end gouged into the other balloon.

A seam ripped apart—and the balloon *died*.

It collapsed inwards, writhing in a perfect simulation of agony, and now the King's ship was falling unchecked. The leverage it exerted through the strut turned Toller's gondola on its side and Overland flashed into view, eager and expectant. Gesalla screamed as she fell against the lowermost wall and the looking-glass she had been holding spun out into the blue emptiness. Toller threw himself into the galley, risking going over the side in the process, gripped the end of the strut and—summoning all the power of his warrior's physique—raised it and cast it free.

As the gondola righted itself he clung to the rail and watched the other ship begin its lethal plunge. At the height of a thousand miles gravity was at less than half strength and the tempo of events had again lapsed into dreamlike slow motion. He saw King Prad swim to the side of the falling gondola. The King, his blind eye shining like a star, raised one hand and pointed at Toller, then he was hidden from view by the swirls of his ship's ruined balloon. Gaining speed as it settled into the fall, still seeking a balance between gravitation and air resistance, the ship dwindled to become a fluttering speck at the limits of vision, and finally was lost in the fractal patterns of Overland.

Becoming aware of a fierce psychic pressure, Toller raised his head and looked at the two accompanying ships. Leddravohr was gazing at him from the nearer, and as their eyes met he extended both arms towards Toller, like a man calling a loved one to his embrace. He remained like that, mutely imploring, and even when Toller had returned to the burner he could almost feel the prince's hatred as an invisible blade knifing through his soul. A grey-faced Chakkell was gazing at him from the entrance to the passenger compartment, inside which Daseene and Corba were quietly sobbing.

"This is a bad day," Chakkell said in a halting voice. "The King is dead."

Not yet, Toller thought. *He still has quite a few hours to go.* Aloud he said, "You saw what happened. We're lucky to be here. I had no choice."

"Leddravohr won't see it like that."

"No," Toller said pensively. "Leddravohr won't see it like that."

That night, while Toller was vainly trying to sleep, Gesalla came to his side, and in the loneliness of the hour it seemed perfectly natural for him to put his arm around her. She rested her head on his shoulder and brought her mouth close to his ear.

"Toller," she whispered, "what are you thinking about?"

He considered lying to her, then decided he had had enough of barriers. "I'm thinking about Leddravohr. It all has to be settled between us."

"Perhaps he will have thought the thing through by the time we reach Overland and will be of a different mind. I mean, it wasn't even as if sacrificing us would have saved the King. Leddravohr is bound to admit that you had no choice."

"I may have felt I had no choice, but Leddravohr will say I

acted too quickly in rolling us out from under his father's ship. Perhaps I would say the same thing if the positions were reversed. If I had waited a little longer Kedalse or somebody else might have got their burner going."

"You mustn't think that way," Gesalla said softly. "You did what had to be done."

"And Leddravohr is going to do what has to be done."

"You can overcome him, can't you?"

"Perhaps—but I fear that he will have already given orders for me to be executed," Toller said. "I can't fight a regiment."

"I see." Gesalla raised herself on one elbow and looked down at him, and in the dimness her face was impossibly beautiful. "Do you love me, Toller?"

He felt he had reached the end of a lifelong journey. "Yes."

"I'm glad." She sat up straighter and began to remove her clothing. "Because I want a child from you."

He caught her wrist, smiling numbly in his disbelief. "What do you think you're doing? Chakkell is on the burner just on the other side of this partition."

"He can't see us."

"But this isn't the way to. . . ."

"I don't care about any of that," Gesalla said, pressing her breast against the hand that was holding her wrist. "I have chosen you to father my child, and there may be very little time for us."

"It won't work, you know." Toller relaxed back on the quilts. "It's physically impossible for me to make love in these conditions."

"That's what you think," Gesalla said as she moved astride of him and brought her mouth down on his, moulding his cheeks with both her hands to coax him into an ardent response.

CHAPTER 20

Overland's equatorial continent, seen from a height of two miles, looked essentially prehistoric.

Toller had been staring down at the outward-seeping landscape for some time before realising why that particular adjective kept coming to mind. It was not the total absence of cities and roads—first proof that the continent was uninhabited—but the uniform coloration of the grasslands.

Throughout his life every aerial view he had seen had been modified in some way by the six-harvest system which was universal on Land. The edible grasses and all other cultivated vegetation had been arranged in parallel strips in which the colours ranged from brown through several shades of green to harvest yellow, but here the plains were simply . . . *green*.

The sunlit expanses of the single colour shimmered in his eyes.

Our farmers will have to start the seed-sorting all over again, he thought. *And the mountains and seas and rivers all have to be given names. It really is a new beginning on a new world. And I don't think I'm going to be part of it. . . .*

Reminded of his personal problems, he turned his attention to the artificial elements of the scene. The two other ships of the royal flight were slightly below him. Pouche's was the more distant, most of its passengers visible at the rail as they journeyed ahead in their imaginations to the unknown world.

Ilven Zavotle was the only person to be seen on Leddravohr's ship, sitting tiredly at the controls. Leddravohr himself must have been lying down in a passenger compartment, as he had done—except during the traumatic episode two days before —throughout the voyage. Toller had noted the prince's behaviour earlier and wondered if he could be phobic about the boundless emptiness surrounding the migration fleet. If that were the case, it would have been better for Toller if their inevitable duel could have been fought aboard one of the gondolas.

In the two miles of airspace below him he could see twelve other balloons forming an irregular line which increasingly flared off to the west, evidence of a moderate breeze in the lowest levels of the atmosphere. The general area into which they were drifting was sprinkled with the elongated shapes of collapsed balloons, which would later be used to build a temporary township of tents. As he had expected, Toller's binoculars showed that most of the grounded ships had military markings. Even in the turmoil of the escape from Ro-Atabri, Leddravohr had had the foresight to provide himself with a power base which would be effective from the instant he set foot on Overland.

Analysing the situation, Toller could see no prospect at all of his living for more than a matter of minutes if he put his ship down close to Leddravohr's. Even if he were to defeat Leddravohr in single combat, he would—as the man charged with the death of the King—be taken by the army. His single and desperately slim chance of survival, for a term to be measured in days at most, lay in hanging back during the touchdown and going aloft again as soon as Leddravohr's ship was committed to a landing. There were forested hills perhaps twenty miles west of the landing site, and if he could reach them with his balloon he might be able to avoid capture until the forces of the infant nations were properly organised in the cause of his destruction.

The weakest point of the plan was that it hinged on factors outside his own control, all of them concerned with the mind and character of Leddravohr's pilot.

He had no doubt at all that Zavotle would make the correct deductions when he saw Toller's ship being tardy during the landing, but would he be sympathetic with Toller's aims? And even if he were inclined to be loyal to a fellow skyman, would he take the personal risk of doing what Toller expected of him? He would have to be quick to pull the rip panel and collapse his balloon—just as it was becoming apparent to Leddravohr that his enemy was slipping out of his grasp—and there was no predicting how the prince might react in his anger. He had struck other men down for lesser offences.

Toller stared across the field of brightness at the solitary figure of Zavotle, knowing that his gaze was being returned, then he put his back against the gondola wall and eyed Chakkell, who was operating the burner at the one-and-twenty rhythm of the descent.

"Prince, there is a breeze at ground level and I fear the ship may be dragged," he said, making his opening move. "You and the princess and your children should be ready to go over the side even before we touch the ground. It might sound dangerous, but there's a good ledge all around the gondola for standing on, and our ground speed will be little more than a walking pace. Jumping off before touchdown is preferable to being in the gondola if it overturns."

"I'm touched by your solicitude," Chakkell said, giving Toller a tilt-headed look of surmise.

Wondering if he had blundered so early, Toller approached the pilot's station. "We'll be landing very soon, Prince. You must be prepared."

Chakkell nodded, vacated the seat and, unexpectedly, said, "I still remember the first time I saw you, in the company of Glo. I never thought it would come to this."

"Lord Glo had vision," Toller replied. "He should be here."

"I suppose so." Chakkell gave him another searching look and went into the compartment where Daseene and the children were making ready for the landing.

Toller sat down and took control of the burner, noting as he did so that the pointer on the altitude gauge had fully returned to the bottom mark. As Overland was smaller than Land he would have expected its surface gravity to be less, but Lain had said otherwise. *Overland has a higher density, and therefore everything there will weigh about the same as on Land.* Toller shook his head, half smiling in belated tribute to his brother. How had Lain *known* what to expect? Mathematics was one aspect of his brother's life which would forever remain a closed book to him, as looked like being the case with. . . .

He glanced at Gesalla, who for an hour had been motionless at the outer wall of their compartment, her attention fully absorbed by the expanding vistas of the new world below. Her bundle of possessions was already slung on her shoulder, giving the impression that she was impatient to set foot on Overland and go about the business of carving out whatever future she had visualised for herself and the child which, possibly, he had seeded into her. The emotions aroused in him by the sight of her slim, straight and uncompromising form were the most complex he had ever known.

On the night she had come to him he had been quite certain he would be unable to fulfil the male role because of his tiredness, his guilt and the unnerving presence of Chakkell, who had been operating the burner only a few feet away. But Gesalla had known better. She had worked on him with fervour, skill and imagination, plying him with her mouth and gracile body until nothing else existed for him but the need to pulse his semen into her. She had remained on top of him until the climactic moment was near, then had insensibly engineered a change of position and had held it, with upthrust pelvis and legs locked around him, for minutes afterwards. Only later, when they had been talking, had he realised that she had been maximising the chances of conception.

And now, as well as loving her, he hated her for some of the things she had said to him during the remainder of that night while the meteors flickered in the dimness all around. There had been no direct statements, but there was revealed to him a Gesalla who, while displaying chilly anger over a fine point of etiquette, was at the same time prepared to defy any convention for the sake of a future child. In the milieu of the old Kolcorron it had seemed to her that the qualities offered by Lain Maraquine would be the most advantageous for her offspring, and so she had married him. She had loved Lain, but the thing which chafed Toller's sensibilities was that she had loved Lain for a reason.

And now that she was being projected into the vastly different frontier environment of Overland, it had been her considered judgment that attributes available through Toller Maraquine's seed were to be preferred, and so she had coupled with him.

In his confusion and pain, Toller was unable to identify the principal source of his resentment. Was it self-disgust at having been so easily seduced by his brother's widow? Was it lacerated pride over having his finest feelings made part of an exercise in eugenics? Or was he furious with Gesalla for not fitting in with his preconceptions, for not being what he wanted her to be? How was it possible for a woman to be a prude and a wanton at the same time, to be generous and selfish, hard and soft, accessible and remote, his and not his?

The questions were endless, Toller realised, and to dwell on them at this stage would be futile and dangerous. The only preoccupations he could afford were with staying alive.

He fitted the extension tube to the burner lever and moved to the side of the gondola to give himself maximum visibility for the descent. As the horizon began to rise level with him he gradually increased his burn ratio, allowing Zavotle's ship to move farther ahead. It was important to achieve the greatest vertical separation that was possible without arousing the suspicions of Leddravohr and Chakkell. He watched as the dozen ships still airborne ahead of the royal flight touched down one by one, the precise moment of each contact being signalled by the shocked contortion of the balloon, followed by the appearance of a triangular rent in the crown and the wilting collapse of the entire envelope.

The entire area was dotted with ships which had landed previously, and already some sort of order was beginning to be imposed on the scene. Supplies were being brought together and piled, and teams of men were running to each new ship as it touched down.

The sense of awe Toller had expected to accompany such a sight was missing, displaced by the urgency of his situation. He trained his binoculars on Zavotle's ship as it neared the ground and risked firing a long blast of miglign into his own balloon. On that instant, as though his ears had been attuned to the telltale sound, Leddravohr materialised at the gondola rail. His shadowed eyes were intent on Toller's ship, and even at that distance they could be seen flaring with coronas of white as he realised what was happening.

He turned to say something to his pilot, but Zavotle—without waiting for ground contact—pulled his rip line. The balloon above him went into the heaving convulsions of its death throes.

The gondola skidded into the grass and was lost from view as the dark brown shroud of the envelope fluttered down around it. Groups of soldiers—among them one officer mounted on a bluehorn—ran to the ship and that of Pouche, which was making a more leisurely touchdown a furlong farther away.

Toller lowered his binoculars and faced Chakkell. "Prince, for reasons which must be obvious to you, I am not going to land my ship at this time. I have no desire to take you or any other disinterested parties—" he paused to glance at Gesalla—"into an alien wilderness with me, therefore I'm going to go within grass level of the surface. At that point it will be very easy for you and your family to part company with the ship, but you must act quickly and with resolution. Is that understood?"

"No!" Chakkell left the passenger compartment and took a step towards Toller. "You will land the ship in full accordance with normal procedure. That is my command, Maraquine. I have no intention of subjecting myself or my family to any unnecessary hazards."

"*Hazards!*" Toller drew his lips into a smile. "Prince, we are talking about a drop of a few inches. Compare that to the thousand-mile tumble they almost embarked upon two days ago."

"Your meaning isn't lost on me." Chakkell hesitated and glanced at his wife. "But still I must insist on a landing."

"And I insist otherwise," Toller said, hardening his voice. The ship was still about thirty feet above the ground and with each passing moment the breeze bore it farther away from the spot where Leddravohr had come down, but the period of grace had to come to an end soon. Even as Toller was trying to guess how much time he had in hand he saw Leddravohr emerge from under the collapsed balloon. Simultaneously, Gesalla climbed over the gondola wall and positioned herself on the outer ledge, ready to jump free. Her eyes met Toller's only briefly, and there was no communication. He allowed the descent to continue until he could discern individual blades of grass.

"Prince, you must decide quickly," he said. "If you don't leave the ship soon, we all go aloft together."

"Not necessarily." Chakkell leaned closer to the pilot's station and snatched the red line which was connected to the balloon's rip panel. "I think this restores my authority," he said, and jabbed a pointing finger as he saw Toller instinctively tighten his grip on the extension lever. "If you try to ascend I'll vent the balloon."

"That would be dangerous at this height."

"Not if I only do it partially," Chakkell replied, displaying knowledge he had acquired while controlling production of the migration fleet. "I can bring the ship down quite gently."

Toller looked beyond him and in the distance saw Leddravohr in the act of commandeering the bluehorn of the officer who had rode to meet his ship. "Any landing would be gentle," he said, "compared to the one your children would have made after falling a thousand miles."

Chakkell shook his head. "Repetition doesn't strengthen your case, Maraquine—it only brings to mind the fact that you were also saving your own skin. Leddravohr is now King, and my first duty is to him."

There was a whispering sound from underfoot as the jet exhaust funnel brushed the tips of tall grass. Half-a-mile away to the east, Leddravohr was astride the bluehorn and was galloping towards the ship, followed by groups of soldiers on foot.

"And my first loyalty is towards my children," the Princess Daseene announced unexpectedly, her head appearing above the partition of the passenger compartment. "I've had enough of this—and of you, Chakkell."

With surprising agility and lack of concern for her dignity she swarmed over the gondola wall and helped Corba to follow. Unbidden, Gesalla came swiftly around the gondola on the outside and aided in the lifting of the two boys on to the ledge.

Daseene, still wearing the incongruous pearl coif like a general's insignia, fixed her husband with an imperious stare. "You are indebted to that man for my life," she said angrily. "If you refuse to honour the debt it can mean but one thing."

"But. . . ." Chakkell clapped his brow in perplexity, then pointed at Leddravohr, who was rapidly gaining on the slow-drifting ship. "What will I say to *him*?"

Toller reached down into the compartment he had shared with

Gesalla and retrieved his sword. "You could say I threatened you with this."

"*Are* you threatening me with it?"

The sound of whipping grass became louder, and the gondola bucked slightly as the jet exhaust made a fleeting contact with the ground. Toller glanced at Leddravohr—now only two-hundred yards away and flailing the bluehorn into a wilder gallop—then shouted at Chakkell.

"For your own good—leave the ship *now*!"

"Something else to remember you for," Chakkell mumbled as he let go of the rip line. He went to the side, rolled himself over on to the ledge and immediately dropped away to the ground. Daseene and the children followed him at once, one of the boys whooping with pleasurable excitement, leaving only Gesalla holding on to the rail.

"Goodbye," Toller said.

"Goodbye, Toller." She continued to stand at the rail, staring at him in what looked like surprise. Leddravohr was now little more than a hundred yards away and the sound of his bluehorn's hoofbeats was growing louder by the second.

"What are you waiting for?" Toller heard his own voice cracking with urgency. "Get off the ship!"

"No—I'm going with you." In the time it took her to utter the words Gesalla had climbed back over the rail and dropped to the gondola floor.

"What are you *doing*?" Every nerve in Toller's body was screaming for him to fire the burner and try to lift the ship out of Leddravohr's reach, but his arm muscles and hands were locked. "Have you gone crazy?"

"I think so," Gesalla said strickenly. "It's idiotic—but I'm going with you."

"You're mine, Maraquine," Leddravohr called out in a strange fervent chant as he drew his sword. "Come to me, Maraquine."

Almost mesmerised, Toller was tightening his grip on his own sword when Gesalla threw herself past him and dropped her full weight on to the extension lever. The burner roared at once, blasting gas into the waiting balloon. Toller silenced it by pulling the lever up, then he pushed Gesalla back against a partition.

"Thank you, but this is pointless," he said. "Leddravohr has to be faced at some stage, and this seems to be the ordained time."

He kissed Gesalla lightly on the forehead, turned back to the rail and locked eyes with Leddravohr, who was on a level with him and now only a dozen yards away. Leddravohr, apparently sensing his change of heart, struck his smile into existence. Toller felt the first stirrings of a shameful excitement, a yearning to have everything settled with Leddravohr once and for all, regardless of the outcome, to know for certain if. . . .

His sequence of thought was broken as he saw an abrupt change of expression on Leddravohr's face. There was sudden alarm there, and the prince was no longer looking directly at him. Toller swung round and saw that Gesalla was holding the butt of one of the ship's ptertha cannon. She had already driven home the firing pin and was aiming the weapon at Leddravohr. Before Toller could react the cannon fired. The projectile was a central blur in a spray of glass fragments, spreading its arms as it flew.

Leddravohr twisted away from it successfully, pulling his mount off course, but shards of glass pocked his face with crimson. He gasped with shock and hauled the galloping bluehorn back into line, rapidly making up lost ground.

Staring frozenly at Leddravohr, knowing the rules of their private war had been changed, Toller fired the burner. The skyship had been made lighter by the departure of Chakkell and his family and had been disposed to rise ever since, but the inertia of the tons of gas inside the balloon made it nightmarishly slow to respond. Toller kept the burner roaring and the gondola began to lift clear of the grass, Leddravohr was now almost within reach and was raising himself in the stirrups. His eyes glared insanely at Toller from a mask of blood.

Is he mad enough to try leaping on to the gondola? Toller wondered. *Does he want to meet the point of my sword?*

In the next pounding second Toller became aware that Gesalla had darted around behind him and was at the other cannon on the windward side. Leddravohr saw her, drew back his arm and hurled his sword.

Toller gave a warning cry, but the sword had not been aimed at a human target. It arced high above him and sank to the hilt in a lower panel of the balloon. The fabric split and the sword fell clear, spinning down into the grass. Leddravohr reined his bluehorn to a halt, jumped down and retrieved the black blade. He remounted immediately and spurred the bluehorn forward, but he was no longer overtaking the ship, being content to pace it at a distance. Gesalla fired the second cannon, but the projectile plunged harmlessly into the grass well clear of Leddravohr, who responded with a courtly wave of his arm.

Still firing the burner, Toller looked up and saw that the rent in the varnished linen of the envelope had run the full length of the panel. The edges of it were pursed, invisibly spewing gas, but the ship had finally gained some upward momentum and was continuing its sluggish climb.

Toller was startled by the sound of hoarse shouting from close by. He spun round and discovered that, while all his attention had been concentrated on Leddravohr, the ship had been drifting directly towards a scattered band of soldiers. The gondola sailed over them with only a few feet to spare and they began to run along behind and below it, leaping in their efforts to grab hold of the ledge.

Their faces were anxious rather than hostile, and it came to Toller that they had only the vaguest idea of what had been happening. Praying he would not have to take action against any of them, he kept on blasting gas into the balloon and was rewarded by an agonisingly slow but steady gain in height.

"Can the ship fly?" Gesalla came to his side, straining to make herself heard above the roar of the burner. "Are we safe?"

"The ship can fly—after a fashion," Toller said, choosing to ignore her second question. "Why did you do it, Gesalla?"

"Surely you know."

"No."

"Love came back to me." She gave him a peaceful smile. "After that I had no choice."

The fulfilment Toller should have felt was lost in black territories of fear. "But you attacked Leddravohr! And he has no mercy, even for women."

"I don't need reminding." Gesalla looked back at the slow-moving, attendant figure of Leddravohr, and for a moment scorn and hatred robbed her of beauty. "You were right, Toller—we must not simply surrender to the butchers. Leddravohr destroyed the life in me once, and Lain and I compounded the crime by ceasing to love each other, ceasing to love ourselves. We gave too much."

"Yes, but. . . ." Toller took a deep breath as he strove to accord Gesalla the rights he had always claimed for himself.

"But what?"

"We have to lighten the ship," he said, passing the burner control lever to her. He went into the compartment vacated by Chakkell and began hurling trunks and boxes over the side.

The pursuing soldiers whooped and cheered until Leddravohr rode in among them, and his gestures showed that he was giving orders for the containers to be carried back to the main landing site. Within a minute the soldiers had turned back with their burdens, leaving Leddravohr to follow the ship alone. The wind speed was about six miles an hour and as a result the bluehorn was able to keep pace in a leisurely trot. Leddravohr was riding slightly beyond the cannons' effective reach, slouched in the saddle, expending little energy and waiting for the situation to turn to his advantage.

Toller checked the pikon and halvell magazines and found he had sufficient crystals for at least a day of continuous burning —the ships of the royal flight having been more generously provided than the others—but his principal concern was with the ship's lack of performance. The rip in the balloon was showing no sign of spreading past the upper and lower panel seams, but the amount of gas spilling through it was almost enough to deprive the ship of its buoyancy.

In spite of the continuous firing of the burner the gondola had gained no more than twenty feet, and Toller knew that the slightest adverse change in conditions would force a descent. A sudden gust of wind, for example, could flatten one side of the envelope and expel precious gas, delivering Gesalla and him into the hands of the patiently stalking enemy. Alone he would have been more than prepared to contend with Leddravohr, but now Gesalla's life also depended on the outcome. . . .

He went to the rail and gripped it with both hands, staring back at Leddravohr and longing for a weapon capable of striking the prince down at a distance. The arrival on Overland had been so different to all his imaginings. Here he was on the sister planet—*on Overland!*—but the malign presence of Leddravohr, embodiment of all that was rank and evil in Kolcorron, had degraded the experience and made the new world an offshoot of the old. Like the ptertha increasing their lethal powers, Leddravohr had extended his own killing radius to encompass Overland. Toller should have been enthralled by the spectacle of a pristine sky bisected by a zigzag line of fragile ships which stretched down from the zenith, emerging from invisibility as they sank like windborne seeds in search of fertile ground—but there was Leddravohr.

Always there was Leddravohr.

"Are you worried about the hills?" Gesalla said. She had sunk to a kneeling position, out of Leddravohr's view, and had one hand raised to work the burner's lever.

"We can lash that down," Toller said. "You won't need to keep on holding it."

"Toller, are you worried about the hills?"

"Yes." He took a length of twine from a locker and used it to tie down the lever. "If we could get over the hills there'd be a chance of wearing Leddravohr's bluehorn out—but I don't know if we can gain enough height."

"I'm not afraid, you know." Gesalla touched his hand. "If you would prefer to go down and face him now, it's all right."

"No, we'll stay aloft as long as possible. We have food and drink here and can keep up our strength while Leddravohr is slowly losing his." He gave her what he hoped was a reassuring smile. "Besides, littlenight will be here soon, and that's to our advantage because the balloon will work better in the cooler air. We may yet be able to set up our own little colony on Overland."

Littlenight was longer than on Land, and by the time it had passed the gondola was at an altitude of slightly more than two-hundred feet—which was a better gain than Toller had expected. The lower slopes of the nameless hills were sliding by beneath the ship, and none of the ridges he could see ahead seemed quite high enough to claw it out of the sky. He consulted the map he had drawn while still on the skyship.

"There's a big lake about ten miles beyond the hills," he said. "If we can fly over it we should be able to. . . ."

"Toller! I think I see a ptertha!" Gesalla caught his arm as she pointed to the south. "Look!"

Toller threw the map down, raised his binoculars and scanned the indicated section of sky. He was about to query Gesalla's remark when he picked out a hint of sphericity, a near-invisible crescent of sunlight glinting on something transparent.

"I think you're right," he said. "And it has no colour. That's what Lain meant. It has no colour because. . . ." He passed the binoculars to Gesalla. "Can you find any brakka trees?"

"I didn't realise you can see so much with glasses." Gesalla, speaking with childish enthusiasm, might have been on a pleasure flight as she studied the hillside. "Most of the trees aren't like anything I've ever seen before, but I think there are brakka among them. Yes, I'm sure. Brakka! How can that be, Toller?"

Guessing she was purposely distracting her mind from what was to come, he said, "Lain wrote that brakka and ptertha go together. Perhaps the brakka discharges are so powerful that they shoot their seeds up into . . . No, that's only for pollen, isn't it? Perhaps brakka grow everywhere—on Farland and every other planet."

Leaving Gesalla to her observations with the binoculars, Toller leaned on the rail and returned his attention to Leddravohr, the relentless pursuer.

For hours Leddravohr had been slumped in the saddle, giving the impression of being asleep, but now—as though concerned that his quarry could be on the point of eluding him—he was sitting upright. He had no helmet, but was shading his eyes with his hands as he chose the bluehorn's path through the trees and patches of scrub which dappled the slopes he was climbing. Off to the east the landing site and the line of descending balloons had been lost in blue-hazed distance, and it was as though Gesalla, Toller and Leddravohr had the entire planet to themselves. Overland had become a vast sunlit arena, held in readiness since the beginning of time. . . .

His thoughts were interrupted by a sudden flapping sound from the balloon.

The noise was followed by a downward rush of heat from the balloon mouth which told him the ship had blundered into turbulent air flung up from a secondary ridge. The gondola abruptly began to yaw and sway. Toller fixed his gaze on the main crest, which was now only about two-hundred yards away on the line of flight. He knew that if they could scrape over it there might be time for the balloon to recover, but in the instant of looking at the rocky barrier he realised the situation was hopeless. The ship, which had been so reluctant to take flight, was already abandoning the aerial element, sailing determinedly towards the hillside.

"Hold on to something," Toller shouted. "We're going down!"

He tore the extension lever free of its lashings and shut the burner off. A few seconds later the gondola began swishing through treetops. The sounds grew louder and the gondola bucked violently as it impacted with increasingly thicker branches and trunks. Above and behind Toller the collapsing balloon tore with a series of groans and snaps as it entangled itself with the trees, applying a brake to the ship's lateral movement.

The gondola dropped vertically as it took up the slack in its load cables, broke free at two corners and turned on its side, almost hurling its two occupants clear amid a shower of quilts and small objects. Incredibly, after the jolting and dangerous progression from treetop height, Toller found himself able to step down easily on to mossy ground. He turned and lifted Gesalla, who was clinging to a stanchion, and set her down beside him.

"You must get away from here," he said quickly. "Get to the other side of the hill and find a place to hide."

Gesalla threw her arms around him. "I should stay with you. I might be able to help."

"Believe me, you won't be able to help. If our baby is growing in you, you must take this chance for it to live. If Leddravohr kills me he may not go after you—especially if he is wounded."

"But. . . ." Gesalla's eyes widened as the bluehorn snorted a short distance away. "But I won't know what has happened."

"I'll fire one of the cannon if I win." He spun Gesalla around and pushed her away with such force that she was obliged to break into a run to avoid falling. "Only come back if you hear a cannon."

He stood quite still and watched until Gesalla, with several backward glances, had disappeared into the cover of the trees. He had drawn his sword, and was looking about him for a clear space in which to fight, when it came to him that ingrained behaviour patterns were causing him to approach the clash with Leddravohr as though he were entering a formal duel.

How can you think that way when other lives are at stake? he asked himself, dismayed by the extent of his own naivety. *What was honour got to do with the plain task of excising a canker?*

He glanced at the slow-swinging gondola, decided on Leddravohr's most probable line of approach to it, and stepped back into the concealment of three trees which grew so closely that they might have sprung from the same root. The same excitement he had known before—shameful and inexplicably sexual—began to steal over him.

He quieted his breathing, ridding himself of his humanity, and a new thought occurred: *Leddravohr was nearby a minute ago —so why have I not seen him by now?*

Knowing the answer, he turned his head and saw Leddravohr about ten paces away. Leddravohr had already thrown his knife. The speed and distance were such that Toller had no time to duck or move aside. He flung up his left hand and took the knife in the centre of the palm. The full length of the black blade came through between the bones with so much force that his hand was driven back and the knife-point tore open his face just below the left eye.

A natural instinct would have been to look at the injured hand, but Toller ignored it and whipped his sword into the guard position just in time to deter Leddravohr, who had followed up on the throw with a running attack.

"You have learned a few things, Maraquine," Leddravohr said, as he too went on guard. "Most men would be dead twice over by this time."

"The lesson was a simple one," Toller replied. "Always prepare for reptiles to behave as such."

"I can't be goaded—so keep your insults."

"I haven't offered any, except to reptiles."

Leddravohr's smile twitched into existence, very white in a face made unrecognisable by traceries of dried blood. His hair was matted and his cuirass, which had been blood-stained before the migration flight began, was streaked with dirt and what looked like partially-digested food. Toller moved away from the constriction of the three trees, turning his mind to combat tactics.

Was it possible that Leddravohr was one of those men, fearless in all other respects, who were laid low by acrophobia? Was that why he had been seen so little throughout the flight? If so, Leddravohr could hardly be fit enough to embark on a prolonged struggle.

The Kolcorronian battle sword was a two-edged weapon whose weight precluded its use in formalised duelling. It was limited to basic cutting and thrusting strokes which could generally be blocked or deflected by an opponent with fast reactions and a good eye. All other things being equal, the victor in single combat tended to be the man with the most physical power and endurance. Toller had a natural advantage in that he was more than ten years younger than Leddravohr, but that had been offset by the disablement of his left hand. Now he had reason to suppose that the balance was restored in his favour—and yet Leddravohr, vastly experienced in such matters, had lost none of his arrogance. . . .

"Why so pensive, Maraquine?" Leddravohr was moving with

Toller to maintain the line of engagement. "Are you troubled by the ghost of my father?"

Toller shook his head. "By the ghost of my brother. We never settled that issue." To his surprise, he saw that his words had disturbed Leddravohr's composure.

"Why do you plague me with this?"

"I believe you are responsible for my brother's death."

"I told you the fool was responsible for his own death." Leddravohr made an angry stabbing movement with his sword and the two blades touched for the first time. "Why should I lie about it, then or now? He broke his mount's leg and he refused a seat on mine."

"Lain wouldn't have done that."

"He did! I tell you he could have been at your side at this minute, and I wish he were—so that I could have the pleasure of cleaving both your skulls."

While Leddravohr was speaking Toller took the opportunity to glance at his wounded hand. There was no great pain as yet, but blood was coursing steadily down the handle of the knife and beading off it to the ground. When he shook his hand the blade remained firmly in place, wedged to the hilt between the bones. The wound, though not a crippling one, would have a progressive effect on his strength and fighting capability. It behoved him to get the duel under way as soon as possible. He forced himself to disregard the lies Leddravohr was uttering about his brother, and to seek a reason for the noteworthy fact that a man whose potency must have been diminished by twelve days of dislocation and illness appeared overweeningly confident of victory.

Was there a significant clue he had overlooked?

He studied his opponent again—tenths of a second passing like minutes in his keyed-up state—and saw only that Leddravohr had sleeved his sword. Soldiers from some parts of the Kolcorronian empire, principally Sorka and Middac, had the practice of covering the base of a blade with leather so that on occasion one hand could be transposed ahead of the hilt and the sword used as a two-handed weapon. Toller had never seen much merit in the idea, but he resolved to be extra wary in the event of an unexpected variation in Leddravohr's attack.

All at once the preliminaries were over.

Each man had circled to a position which materially was no better than any other, but which satisfied him in some indefinable way as being the most propitious, the most suitable for his purpose. Toller went in first, surprised at being allowed that psychological advantage, starting on the backhand with a series of downward hacks alternating from left to right, and was immediately thrilled with the result. As was inevitable, Leddravohr blocked every stroke with ease, but the blade shocks were not quite what Toller had expected. It was as though Leddravohr's sword arm had given way a little at each blow, hinting at a serious lack of strength.

A few minutes could decide everything, Toller exulted as he allowed the sequence to come to a natural end, then his survivor's instinct reasserted itself. *Dangerous thinking! Would Leddravohr have pursued me this far—alone—knowing he was unequal to the struggle?*

Toller disengaged and shifted his ground, holding his dripping left hand clear of his body. Leddravohr closed in on him with startling speed, creating a low sweep triangle which almost forced Toller to defend his useless arm rather than his head and body. The flurry ended with a mighty backhand cross from Leddravohr which actually fanned cool air against the underside of Toller's chin. He leapt back, chastened, reminded that the prince in a debilitated condition was a match for an ordinary soldier in his prime.

Had that resurgence of power represented the trap he suspected Leddravohr of preparing for him? If so, it was vital not to allow Leddravohr breathing space and recovery time. Toller renewed his attack on the instant, initiating sequence after sequence with no perceptible interludes, using all his strength but at the same time modifying fury with intelligence, allowing the prince no mental or physical respite.

Leddravohr, breathing hard now, was forced to yield ground. Toller saw that he was backing into a cluser of low thorn bushes and forced himself closer, awaiting the moment when Leddravohr would be distracted, immobilised or caught off balance. But Leddravohr, displaying his genius for combat, appeared to sense the presence of the bushes without having to turn his head.

He saved himself by gathering Toller's blade in a circular counter parry worthy of a smallsword master, stepping inside his defences and turning both their bodies into a new line. For a second the two men were pressed together, chest to chest, their swords locked at the hilts overhead at the apex of the triangle formed by their straining right arms.

Toller felt the heat of Leddravohr's breath and smelled the foulness of vomit from him, then he broke the contact by forcing his sword arm down, making it into an irresistible lever which drove them apart.

Leddravohr aided the separation by jumping backwards and quickly sidestepping to bring the thorn bushes between them. His chest was heaving rapidly, evidence of his growing tiredness, but—strangely—he appeared to have been buoyed up rather than disconcerted by the narrowness of his escape from peril. He was leaning forward slightly in an attitude suggestive of a new eagerness, and his eyes were animated and derisive amid the filigrees of dried blood which covered his face.

Something has happened, Toller thought, his skin crawling with apprehension. *Leddravohr knows something!*

"By the way, Maraquine," Leddravohr said, sounding almost genial, "I heard what you said to your woman."

"Yes?" In spite of his alarm, a part of Toller's consciousness was being taken up by the odd fact that the disgusting odour he had endured while in contact with Leddravohr was still strong in his nostrils. Was it really just the sourness of regurgitated food, or was there another smell there? Something strangely familiar and with a deadly significance?

Leddravohr smiled. "It was a good idea. About firing the cannon, I mean. It will save me the trouble of going looking for her when I have disposed of you."

Don't waste breath on a reply, Toller urged himself. *Leddravohr is putting on too much of a show. It means he isn't leading you into a trap—it has already been sprung!*

"Well, I don't think I'm going to need this," Leddravohr said. He gripped the leather sleeve at the base of his sword, slid it off and dropped it to the ground. His eyes were fixed on Toller, amused and enigmatic.

Toller looked closely at the sleeve and saw that it seemed to have been made in two layers, with a thin outer skin which had been ruptured. Around the edges of the split were glistening traces of yellow slime.

Toller looked down at his own sword, belatedly identifying the stench which was emanating from it—the stench of whitefern—and saw more of the slime on the broadest part of the blade, close to the hilt. The black material of the blade was bubbling and vapouring as it dissolved under the attack of the brakka slime, which had been smeared there by Leddravohr's sword when the two were crossed at the hilts.

I accept my death, Toller mused, his thoughts blurring into frenzied battle tempo as he saw Leddravohr darting towards him, *on condition that I don't journey alone*.

He raised his head and lunged at Leddravohr's chest with his sword. Leddravohr struck across it and snapped the blade at the root, sending it tumbling away to one side, and in the same movement swept his sword round into a thrust aimed at Toller's body.

Toller took the thrust, throwing himself on to it as he knew he had to were he to achieve life's last ambition. He gasped as the blade passed all the way through him, allowing him to drive on until he was within reach of Leddravohr. He gripped the throwing knife and, with his left hand still impaled on it, ran the blade upwards into Leddravohr's stomach, circling and seeking with the tip. There was a gushing warmth on the back of his hand.

Leddravohr growled and pushed Toller away from him with desperate force, simultaneously withdrawing his sword. He stared at Toller, open-mouthed, for several seconds, then he dropped the sword and sank to his knees. He pitched forward on to his hands and remained like that, head lowered, staring at the pool of blood gathering below his body.

Toller worked the knife free of the bones clamped around it, mentally remote from the pain he was inflicting on himself, then clutched his side in an effort to stem the sopping pulsations of the sword wound. The edges of his vision were in a ferment; the sunlit hillside was rushing towards him and retreating. He threw the knife away, approached Leddravohr on buckling legs and picked up the sword. Forcing all that remained of his strength into his right arm, he raised the sword high.

Leddravohr did not look up, but he moved his head a little, showing he was aware of Toller's actions. "I have killed you, haven't I, Maraquine?" he said in a choking, blood-drowning voice. "Give me that one consolation."

"Sorry, but you hardly scratched me," Toller said as he cleaved downwards with the black blade.

"And this is for my brother . . . *Prince!*"

He turned away from Leddravohr's corpse and with difficulty steadied his gaze on the square shape of the gondola. Was it swinging in a breeze, or was it the one fixed point in a see-sawing, dissolving universe?

He set out to walk towards it, intrigued by the discovery that it was now very far away . . . at a remove much greater than the distance from Land to Overland. . . .

CHAPTER 21

The rear wall of the cave was partially hidden by a mound of large pebbles and rock fragments which over the centuries had washed down through a natural chimney. Toller enjoyed gazing at the mound because he knew the Overlanders lived inside it.

He had not actually seen them, and therefore did not know if they resembled miniature men or animals, but he was keenly aware of their presence—because they used lanterns.

The light from the lanterns shone out through chinks in the rock at intervals which were not attuned to the outside world's rhythm of night and day. Toller liked to think of Overlanders going about their own business in there, secure in their tumble-down fortress, with no concern for anything which might be happening in the universe at large.

It was the nature of his delirium that even in periods when he felt himself to be perfectly lucid one tiny lantern would sometimes continue to gleam from the heart of the pile. At those times he took no pleasure from the experience. Afraid for his sanity, he would stare at the point of light, willing it to vanish because it had no place in the rational world. Sometimes it would obey quickly, but there were occasions when it took hours to dim out of existence, and then he would cling to Gesalla, making her the lifeline which joined him to all that was familiar and normal. . . .

"Well, *I* don't think you're strong enough to travel," Gesalla said firmly, "so there is no point in carrying on with this discussion."

"But I'm almost fully recovered," Toller protested, waving his arms to prove the point.

"Your tongue is the only part of you which has recovered, and even that is getting too much exercise. Just be quiet for a while and allow me to get on with my work." She turned her back on him and used a twig to stir the pot in which his dressings were being boiled.

After seven days the wounds on his face and left hand needed virtually no attention, but the twin punctures in his side were still discharging. Gesalla cleaned them and changed the dressings every few hours, a regimen which necessitated re-using the meagre stock of pads and bandages she had been able to make.

Toller had little doubt that he would have died but for her ministrations, but his gratitude was tinged with concern for her safety. He guessed that the initial confusion in the fleet's landing zone must have rivalled that of the departure, but it seemed little short of a miracle to him that he and Gesalla had since remained unmolested for so long. With each passing day, as the fever abated, his sense of urgency increased.

We are leaving here in the morning, my love, he thought. *Whether you agree or not.*

He leaned back on the bed of folded quilts, trying to curb his impatience, and allowed his gaze to roam the panoramic view which the cave mouth afforded. Grassy slopes, dotted here and there with unfamiliar trees, folded gently down for about a mile to the west, to the edge of a large lake whose water was a pure indigo seeded with sun-jewels. The northern and southern shores were banked forests, receding and narrowing bands of a colour which—as on Land—was a composite of a million speckles ranging from lime green to deep red, representing trees at different stages of their leaf cycles. The lake stretched all the way to a western horizon composed of the ethereal blue triangles of distant mountains, above which a pure sky soared up to encompass the disk of the Old World.

It was a scene which Toller found unutterably beautiful, and in the first days in the cave he had been unable to distinguish it with any certainty from other products of his delirium. His memory of those days was patchy. It had taken him some time to understand that he had not succeeded in firing a cannon, and that Gesalla had made an independent decision to go back for him. She had tried to make little of the matter, claiming that had Leddravohr been victorious he would soon have advertised the fact by coming in search of her. Toller had known otherwise.

Lying in the hushed peace of early morning, watching Gesalla go about the chores she had set for herself, he felt a surge of admiration for her courage and resourcefulness. He would never understand how she had managed to get him into the saddle of Leddravohr's bluehorn, load up with supplies from the gondola, and lead the beast on foot for many miles before finding the cave. It would have been a considerable feat for a man, but for a slightly-built woman facing an unknown planet and all its possible dangers on her own the achievement had been truly exceptional.

Gesalla is a truly exceptional woman, Toller thought. *So how long will it be before she realises I have no intention of taking her off into the wilderness?*

The sheer impracticability of his original plan had weighed heavily on Toller after his rationality had begun to return. Without a baby to consider it might have been possible for two adults to eke out some kind of fugitive existence in the forests of Overland—but if Gesalla was not already pregnant she would see to it that she became pregnant.

It had taken him some time to appreciate that the core of the problem also contained its solution. With Leddravohr dead Prince Pouche would have become King, and Toller knew him to be a dry, dispassionate man who would abide by Kolcorron's traditional leniency with pregnant women—especially as Leddravohr was the only one who could have testified about Gesalla's use of the cannon against him.

The task ahead, Toller had decided—while doing his best to ignore the gleam of the single, persistent Overlander's lantern in the mound of rubble—was to keep Gesalla alive until she was demonstrably with child. A hundred days seemed a reasonable target, but the very act of setting a term had somehow increased and aggravated his unease about the fleeting passage of time. How was he to strike the proper balance between leaving early and only being able to travel slowly, and leaving late—when the swiftness of a deer might prove insufficient?

"What are you brooding about?" Gesalla said, removing the boiling pot from the heat.

"About you—and about preparing to leave here in the morning."

"I told you, you aren't ready." She knelt beside him to inspect his dressings and the touch of her hands sent a pleasurable shock racing down to his groin.

"I think another part of me is starting to recover," he said.

"That's something else you aren't ready for." She smiled as she dabbed his forehead with a damp cloth. "You can have some stew instead."

"A fine substitute," he grumbled, making an unsuccessful attempt to touch her breasts as she slid away from him. The sudden movement of his arm, slight though it was, produced a sharp pain in his side and made him wonder how he would fare trying to get astride the bluehorn in the morning.

He pushed the worry to the back of his thoughts and watched Gesalla as she prepared a simple breakfast. She had found a flattish, slightly concave stone to use as a hob. By mingling on it tiny pinches of pikon and halvell brought from the ship, she was able to create a smoke-free heat which would not betray their whereabouts to pursuers. When she had finished warming the stew—a thick mixture of grain, pulses and shreds of salt-beef—she passed a dish of it to him and allowed him to feed himself.

Toller had been amused to note—echo of the old Gesalla he thought he had known—that among the "essentials" she had salvaged from the gondola were dishes and table utensils. There was a poignancy about eating in such conditions, with common-place domestic items framed in the pervasive strangeness of a virgin world; with the romance which could have suffused the moment abnegated by uncertainties and danger.

Toller was not really hungry, but he ate steadily with a determination to win back his strength as quickly as possible. Apart from occasional snuffles from the tethered bluehorn the only sounds reaching the cave from elsewhere were the rolling reports of brakka pollination discharges. The frequency of the explosions indicated that brakka were plentiful throughout the region, and were a reminder of the question which had first been posed by Gesalla—if the other plant forms of Overland were unknown on Land, why did the two worlds have the brakka in common?

Gesalla had collected handfuls of grass, leaves, flowers and berries for joint scrutiny, and—with the possible exception of the grass, upon which only a botanist could have passed judgment—all had shared the common factor of strangeness. Toller had reiterated his idea that the brakka was a universal form, one which would be found on any planet, but although he was unused to pondering such matters he recognised that the notion had an unsatisfactory philosophical feel to it, one which made him wish he could turn to Lain for guidance.

"There's another ptertha," Gesalla exclaimed. "Look! I can see seven or eight of them going towards the water."

Toller looked in the direction she was indicating and had to change the focus of his eyes several times before he picked out the bubble-glints of the colourless, near-invisible spheres. They were slowly drifting down the hillside on the air flow generated by the night-time cooling of the surface.

"You're better at spotting those things than I am," he said ruefully. "That one yesterday was almost in my lap before I saw it."

The ptertha which had drifted in on them soon after littlenight on the previous day had come to within ten paces of Toller's bed, and in spite of what he had learned from Lain the nearness of it had inspired much of the dread he would have experienced on Land. Had he been mobile he would probably have been unable to prevent himself from hurling his sword through it. The globe had hovered nearby for a few seconds before sailing away down the hillside in a series of slow ruminative bounds.

"Your face was a picture!" Gesalla paused in her eating to parody an expression of fear.

"I've just thought of something," Toller said. "Have we any writing materials?"

"No. Why?"

"You and I are the only two people on the whole of Overland who know what Lain wrote about the ptertha. I wish I had thought of telling Chakkell. All those hours together on the ship—and I didn't even mention it!"

"You weren't to know there would be brakka trees and ptertha here. You thought you were leaving all that behind."

Toller was gripped by a new and greater urgency which had nothing to do with his personal aspirations. "Listen, Gesalla, this is the most important thing either of us will ever have the chance to do. You have got to make sure that Pouche and Chakkell hear and understand Lain's ideas.

"If we leave the brakka trees alone, to live out their time and die naturally, the ptertha here will never become our enemies. Even a modest amount of culling—the way they did it in Chamteth—is probably too much because the ptertha there had turned pink and that's a sign that. . . ." He stopped speaking as he saw that Gesalla was staring at him, her expression of odd blend of concern and accusation.

"Is there anything the matter?"

"You said *I* had to make sure that Pouche and. . . ." Gesalla set her dish down and came to kneel beside him. "What's going to happen to us, Toller?"

He forced himself to laugh then exaggerated the effects of the pain it caused, playing for time in which to cover up his blunder. "We're going to found our own dynasty, that's what is going to happen to us. Do you think I would let any harm come to you?"

"I know you wouldn't—and that's why you frightened me."

"Gesalla, all I meant was that we must leave a message here . . . or somewhere else where it will be found and taken to the King. I'm not able to move around much, so I have to turn the responsibility over to you. I'll show you how to make charcoal, and then we'll find something to. . . ."

Gesalla was slowly shaking her head and her eyes were magnified by the first tears he had ever seen there. "It's all unreal, isn't it? It's all just a dream."

"Flying to Overland was just a dream—once—but now we're here, and in spite of everything we're still alive." He drew her down to lie beside him, her head cushioned on his shoulder. "I don't know what's going to happen to us, Gesalla. All I can promise is that . . . how did you put it? . . . that we are not going to surrender life to the butchers. That has to be enough for us.

Now, why don't you rest and let me watch over you, just for a change?"

"All right, Toller." Gesalla made herself comfortable, fitting her body to his whilst being careful of his injuries, and in an amazingly short time she was asleep. Her transition from anxious wakefulness to the tranquillity of sleep was announced by the faintest of snores, and Toller smiled as he stored the event in his memory for use in future bantering. The only home they were likely to know on Overland would be built of such insubstantial timbers.

He tried to stay awake, to watch over her, but the vapours of an insidious weariness were coiling in his head—and the last Overlander's lantern was again glowing in the rock pile.

The only way to escape from it was to close his eyes. . . .

The soldier standing over him was holding a sword.

Toller tried to move, to take some defensive action in spite of his weakness and the encumbrance of Gesalla's body draped across his own, then he saw that the sword in the soldier's hand was Leddravohr's, and even in his befuddled state he was able to assess the situation correctly.

It was too late to do anything, anything at all—because his little domain had already been surrounded, conquered and overrun.

Further evidence came from the shifting of the light as other soldiers moved around beyond the immediate area of the cave mouth. There were the sounds of men beginning to talk as they realised that silence was no longer required, and from somewhere nearby came the snorting and slithering of a bluehorn as it made its way down the hill. Toller squeezed Gesalla's shoulder to bring her awake, and although she remained immobile he felt her spasm of alarm.

The soldier with the sword moved away and his place was taken by a slit-eyed major, whose head was in near-silhouette against the sky as he looked down at Toller. "Can you stand up?"

"No—he's too ill," Gesalla said, rising to a kneeling position.

"I can stand." Toller caught her arm. "Help me, Gesalla—I

304

prefer to be on my feet at this time." With her assistance he achieved a standing position and faced the major. He was dully surprised to find that, when he should have been oppressed by failure and prospects of death, he was discomfited by the trivial fact that he was naked.

"Well, major," he said, "what is it you want of me?"

The major's face was professionally impassive. "The King will speak to you now."

He moved aside and Toller saw the paunchy figure of Chakkell approaching. His dress was subdued and plain, suitable for cross-country riding, but suspended from his neck was a huge blue jewel which Toller had seen only once before, when it had been worn by Prad. Chakkell had retrieved Leddravohr's sword from the first soldier and was carrying it with the blade leaning on his right shoulder, a neutral position which could quickly become one of attack. His swarthy well-padded face and brown scalp were gleaming in the equatorial heat.

He came within two paces of Toller and surveyed him from head to toe. "Well, Maraquine, I promised I would remember you."

"Majesty, I daresay I have given you and your loved ones good cause to remember me." Toller was aware of Gesalla drawing closer to him, and for her sake he went on to rid his words of any possible ambiguity. "A fall of a thousand miles would have. . . ."

"Don't start rhyming at me again," Chakkell cut in. "And lie down, man, before you fall down!"

He nodded to Gesalla, ordering her to ease Toller down on to the quilts, and signalled for the major and the rest of his escort to withdraw. When they had retreated out of earshot he squatted in the dirt and, unexpectedly, lobbed the black sword over Toller and into the dimness of the cave.

"We are going to have a brief conversation," he said, "and not a word of it is to be repeated. Is that clear?"

Toller nodded uncertainly, wondering if he dared introduce hope to the confusion of his thoughts and emotions.

"There is a certain amount of ill-feeling towards you among the nobility and among the military who completed the crossing," Chakkell said comfortably. "After all, not many men have committed regicide twice in the space of three days. It can be dealt with, however. There is a great air of practicality in our new statelet—and the settlers appreciate that loyalty to one living king is more beneficial to the health than a similar regard for two dead kings. Are you wondering about Pouche?"

"Does he live?"

"He lives, but he was quick to see that the subtleties of his kind of statesmanship would be inappropriate to the situation we have here. He is more than happy to relinquish his claims to the throne—if a chair made from old gondola parts can be dignified with that name."

It came to Toller that he was seeing Chakkell as he had never seen him before—cheerful, loquacious, at ease with his environment. Was it simply that he preferred supremacy for himself and his offspring in a seedling society to preordained secondary role in the long-established and static Kolcorron? Or was it that he possessed an adventurous spirit which had been liberated by the unique circumstances of the great migration? Looking closely at Chakkell, encouraged by his instincts, Toller experienced a sudden upwelling of relief and the purest kind of joy.

Gesalla and I are going to have children, he thought. *And it doesn't matter that she and I will have to die some day, because our children will have children, and the future stretches out before us . . . on and on . . . on and on, except that. . . .*

One reality dissolved around Toller and he found himself standing on a rocky outcrop to the west of Ro-Atabri. He was gazing through his telescope at the sprawled body of his brother, reading that last communication which had nothing to do with revenge or personal regrets, but which—as befitted Lain's compassionate intellect—addressed itself to the welfare of millions as yet unborn.

"Prince . . . Majesty. . . ." Toller raised himself on one elbow the better to confront Chakkell with the truth which had been placed in his keeping, but the incautious torsion of his body lanced him with an agony which stilled his voice and dropped him back into his bedding.

"Leddravohr came very near to killing you, didn't he?" Chakkell's voice had lost all of its lightness.

"That doesn't matter," Toller said, smoothing Gesalla's hair as she bent over the renewed fire of the wounds in his side. "You knew my brother and what he was?"

"Yes."

"Very well. Forget all about me—my brother lives in my body, and he is speaking to you through my mouth. . . ." Toller went on, battling through riptides of nausea and weakness to paint a word-picture of the tortured triangular relationship involving humankind, the brakka tree and the ptertha. He described the symbiotic partnership between brakka and ptertha, using inspiration and informed imagination where real knowledge failed.

As in all cases of true symbiosis, both parties derived benefit from the association. The ptertha bred in high levels of the atmosphere, nourished—in all probability—by minute traces of pikon and halvell, or miglign gas, or brakka pollen, or by some derivation from the four. In return, the ptertha sought out all organisms who threatened the welfare of the brakka. Employing the blind forces of random mutation, they varied their internal composition until they chanced on an effective toxin, at which point—the path having been signposted—they concentrated and refined and *aimed* it to create a weapon capable of scourging the scourge, of removing from existence all traces of that which did not deserve to exist.

The way ahead for mankind on Overland lay in treating the brakka with the respect it deserved. Only dead trees should be used for their yield of super-hard materials and power crystals, and if the supply seemed insufficient it was incumbent on the immigrants to develop substitutes or to modify their way of life accordingly.

If they failed to do so, the history of humanity on Land would, inevitably, be repeated on Overland. . . .

"I admit to being impressed," Chakkell said when Toller had finally finished speaking. "There is no real proof that what you say is true, but it is worthy of serious consideration. Luckily for our generation, which has seen its full share of hardships, there is no need to make any hasty decisions. We have enough to worry about in the meantime."

"You must not think that way," Toller urged. "You are the *ruler* . . . and you have the unique opportunity . . . the unique responsibility. . . ." He sighed and stopped speaking, yielding to a tiredness which seemed to dim the very heavens.

"Save your strength for another time," Chakkell said gently. "I should let you rest now, but before I leave I'd like to know one more thing. Between you and Leddravohr—was it a fair contest?"

"It was almost fair . . . until he destroyed my sword with brakka slime."

"But you overcame him just the same."

"It was required of me." Toller was experiencing the mysticism which can come with illness and utter weariness. "I was born to overcome Leddravohr."

"Perhaps he knew that."

Toller forced his gaze to steady on Chakkell's face. "I don't know what you. . . ."

"I wonder if Leddravohr had any heart for all of this, for our brave new beginning," Chakkell said. "I wonder if he pursued you—alone—because he divined that you were his Bright Road?"

"That idea," Toller whispered, "has little appeal for me."

"You need to rest." Chakkell stood up and addressed himself to Gesalla. "Look after this man for my sake as well as your own—I have work for him. I think it would be better not to move him for some days yet, but you seem quite comfortable here. Do you need any supplies?"

"We could use more fresh water, Majesty," Gesalla said. "Apart from that our wants are already satisfied."

"Yes." Chakkell studied her face for a moment. "I'm going to take your bluehorn because we have only seven all told, and the breeding must begin as soon as possible, but I will post guards nearby. Call them when you deem you are ready to leave here. Does that suit you?"

"Yes, Majesty—we are indebted."

"I trust your patient will remember that when his health is

recovered." Chakkell turned and strode away towards the waiting soldiers, moving with the energetic assurance peculiar to those who feel themselves to be responding to the calls of destiny.

Later, when silence had again returned to the hillside, Toller awoke to see that Gesalla was passing the time by sorting and arranging her collection of leaves and flowers. She had spread them on the ground before her, and her lips were moving silently as she thoughtfully placed each specimen in an order of her own devising. Beyond her the vivid purity of Overland sparkled and advanced on the eye.

Toller cautiously raised himself in the bed. He glanced at the mound of rocky fragments in the rear of the cave, then turned his head away quickly, unwilling to risk seeing the tiny lantern gleaming at him. Only when it had ceased to shine altogether would he know for certain that the fever had entirely left his system, and until then he had no wish to be reminded of how close he had come to death and to losing all that Gesalla meant to him.

She looked up from her emergent patterns. "Did you see something back there?"

"There's nothing," he said, mustering a smile. "Nothing at all."

"But I've noticed you staring at those rocks before. What is your secret?" Intrigued, and playing a game for his benefit, Gesalla came to him and knelt to share his line of sight. The movement brought her face very close to his, and he saw her eyes widen in surprise.

"Toller!" Her voice was that of a child, hushed with wonder. "There's something shining in there!"

She rose to her feet with all the speed of which her weightless body was capable, stepped over him and ran into the cave.

Prey to a strange fear, Toller tried to call out a warning, but his throat was dry and the power of speech seemed to have deserted him. And Gesalla was already throwing the outermost stones aside. He watched numbly as she put her hands into the mound, lifted something heavy and bore it out to the brighter light at the entrance to the cave.

She knelt beside him, cradling the find on her thighs. It was a large flake of dark grey rock—but it was unlike any rock Toller had ever seen before. Running across and through it, integral to and yet differing from the stone, was a broad band of material which was white, but more than white, reflecting the sun like the waters of a distant lake at dawn.

"It's beautiful," Gesalla breathed, "but what is it?"

"I don't. . . ." Grimacing with pain, Toller reached for his clothing, found a pocket and brought out the strange memento given to him by his father. He placed it against the gleaming stratum in the stone, confirming what he already knew—that they were identical in composition.

Gesalla took the nugget from him and ran a fingertip across its polished surface. "Where did you get this?"

"My father . . . my real father . . . gave it to me in Chamteth just before he died. He told me he found it long ago. Before I was born. In the Redant province."

"I feel strange." Gesalla shivered as she looked up at the misty, enigmatic, watchful disk of the Old World. "Was ours not the first migration, Toller? Has it all happened before?"

"I think so—perhaps many times—but the important thing for us is to ensure that it never. . . ." His weariness forced Toller to leave the sentence unfinished.

He laid the back of his hand on the lustrous strip within the rock, captivated by its coolness and its strangeness—and by silent intimations that, somehow, he could make the future differ from the past.

Here is an excerpt from the sequel to The Ragged Astronauts,
to be published in hardcover by Baen Books in July 1988:

THE WOODEN SPACESHIPS
Bob Shaw

The alien skyship was being borne eastwards on the
lightest of breezes, but the ground over which it was
drifting was uneven and covered with scrub, which
meant that the mounted soldiers had some difficulty in
keeping pace with their quarry.

Colonel Mandle Gartasian, riding at the head of the
column, kept his gaze firmly fixed on the ship and for
the most part trusted his bluehorn to find its way
around obstacles. The sight of the vast balloon and
its room-sized gondola was activating bleak memories,
causing a degree of pain he had not experienced since his
first years on Overland, and yet he was unable to look
elsewhere.

He was a tall man, with the powerful build typical of
the Kolcorronian military caste, and showed few signs
of his fifty years. Apart from a dusting of grey in his
cropped black hair and a deepening of the lines on his
square face, he looked much as he had done at the time
of the hasty evacuation of Ro-Atabri. He had been an
idealistic young lieutenant then, and had unhesitatingly
taken his place on one of the first military ships to
depart the doomed city. Thousands of times since that
day he had cursed the naive trust in his senior officers
which had led him to take off ahead of his wife and
infant son.

Ronoda and the boy had been assigned places on a
civilian ship, and he had left them in the belief that the
army was in full control of the situation, that the
embarkation schedules would be maintained, and that

the separation would last just for the duration of the flight. Only when his binoculars revealed the growing chaos far below had he felt the first pangs of fear, and by then it had been much too late. . . .

"Look, sir!" The words came from Lieutenant Keero, who was riding at Gartasian's side. "I think they're preparing to land!"

Gartasian nooded. "I believe you're right. Now, remember to keep your men from crowding in on the ship after it touches down. Nobody is to go closer than two hundred paces, even if the ship appears to have landing difficulties. We don't know what the crew's intentions are—and they may have powerful weaponry."

"I understand, sir. I can hardly believe this is happening. Can they really have flown all the way from Land?" Keero was infringing field discipline by making inessential remarks, but it was explained by the excitement on his pink-cheeked face. Gartasian, normally strict on such points, decided the lapse was excusable in the unique circumstances.

"There can be no doubt that they have come from the Old World," he said. "The first question we have to ask is . . . *why?* Why after all these years? And *who?* Are we dealing with a small group who managed to survive the pertertha attacks, and finally succeeded in making an escape? Or. . . ?" Gartasian left the question unspoken. The idea that the pterthacosis plague might have abated—sparing enough of the population to rebuild an organised society—was too far-fetched for words. It certainly was not the kind of fanciful speculation to be voiced before a junior officer, especially as concealed within it were the seeds of a far wilder notion. Was there the remotest possibility that Ronoda and Hallie were still alive? And had all his years of guilt and remorse been a self-indulgent waste? With sufficient vision, enterprise and courage could he have instigated a return flight to Land?

The torrent of questions, a distillation of fantastic wish-fulfilment dreams, was the last thing Gartasian needed if he were to function well as the commander of a military operation. He gave himself a mental shake and forced his mind to concentrate on the palpable realities of the situation. It had been more than a minute since he had heard the hollow, echoing roar of the skyship's burner as it discharged hot gas into the balloon—an indication that the crew had selected a suitable landing site. The gondola was now a mere twenty feet above the ground, and at its sides he could see the silhouettes of several men who appeared to be working with rail-mounted cannon. He was beginning to wonder if two hundred paces was a good enough margin of safety for his own force when the cannon fired. Four harpoon-like anchors speared into the ground, each trailing a line, and at once crewmen began hauling the lines in, thereby drawing the gondola into a controlled touchdown. The balloon above it remained inflated, swaying ponderously.

"We have learned one thing," Gartasian said to his lieutenant. "Our visitors never had any intention of staying for long—otherwise they would have vented their balloon."

His only answer was a hurried salute as Keero wheeled away with a sergeant beside him to deploy the soldiers in a circle around the skyship. Gartasian took a pair of binoculars out of his saddle pouch and trained them on the gondola.

He could see the heads of the four crewmen as they went about the work of securing the ship, but something else in the magnified image attracted his attention. The gondola was of basically the same design as those used in the Migration, and yet had no anti-ptertha cannon on the sides. In spite of the weight penalty imposed by such weapons, they had been deemed necessary for the passage through Land's lower atmosphere, and Gartasian found their absence intriguing. Could it really be a sign that the ptertha—the airborne globes whose poison had all but annihilated Kolcorron—had ceased their onslaught on humanity? Gartasian's heart lurched as he again considered the possibilities. A civilisation which embraced two worlds . . . a mass return to Land for those who were discontent on Overland . . . miraculous reunions with loved ones who were believed to be long-dead . . .

"Remain here," he said to Lieutenant Keero, who was just returning to his starting point. He nudged his bluehorn into a walk which he deliberately kept slow, demonstrating to the visitors that his intentions were not hostile. As he neared the ship he was uneasily aware that his cuirass, moulded from boiled leather, would provide little protection if he were to be fired upon, but he remained upright in the saddle, presenting the appearance of one who was satisfied with his ability to deal with the situation.

Those aboard the ship, observing his approach, ceased their activities and came to stand at the near side of the gondola. Gartasian looked for an identifiable commander, but the crew all seemed to be of an age—not much more than twenty—and were wearing identical brown shirts and jerkins. The only visible insignia were small circles of different colours sewn to the lapels of the jerkins, but the variations had no significance for Gartasian.

He was surprised to note that the men were sufficiently alike to have been mistaken for brothers—each with a narrow forehead, close-set eyes and narrow jutting jaw. As he entered the shadow of the ballon he saw, with a sudden sense of disquiet, that the four had dark jaundiced complexions and a peculiar metallic sheen to their skins. It was an appearance which would have suggested a recent brush with some cruel disease, except that the men also exuded that unconscious arrogance which can arise from being superbly fit. They regarded Gartasian with expressions which to him seemed both amused and contemptuous.

"I am Colonel Gartasian," he said, halting his bluehorn a few yards from the gondola. "On behalf of King Chakkell, the planetary ruler, I welcome you to Overland. We were greatly surprised by the sight of your ship, and many questions clamour in our minds."

"Keep your questions and your welcome to yourself." The man on the right, tallest of the four, spoke in oddly accented Kolcorronian. "My name is Orracolde, and I am the commander here, but I also have the honour of being a royal courier. I come to this world with a message from King Rassamarden."

Gartasian was shocked by the speaker's immediate and overt hostility, but he decided to control his temper. "I have never heard of a King Rassamarden."

"That is hardly surprising under the circumstances," Orracolde said, smiling disdainfully. "Now, I expected that Prad would be dead by this time, but how did Chakkell become King? What of Prad's son, Leddravohr? And Pouche?"

"They too are dead," Gartasian said stiffly, realising that the deliberate challenge in Orracolde's manner would have to be taken up for the sake of honour. "And for your further enlightenment, I intend that this meeting will henceforth be conducted along different lines. I will provide the questions, and you the answers."

"And what if I decide otherwise, *old* warrior?"

"My men have your ship surrounded."

"That fact had not escaped my attention," Orracolde said. "But unless their flea-infested mounts can soar like eagles they pose my ship no threat. We can be airborne in an instant." He turned away from the rail and a second later the skyship's burner discharged a burse of hot gas into the balloon which loomed overhead. Gartasian's bluehorn, startled by the echoing blast, half-reared and he had to act quickly to bring it under control, much to the amusement of the four onlookers. It came to him that for the present the visitors were in a greatly superior position, and that unless he devised a better method of dealing with them he could be humiliated. He glanced at the sparse circle of mounted soldiers, now seeming so distant, and chose new tactics.

"Neither of us has anything to gain by quarreling," he said reasonably. "The message you spoke of can be relayed to the King through me, or—if you would prefer it—you can wait until his Majesty arrives in person."

Orracolde tilted his head. "How long will that take?"

"The King is already on his way and could be here within the hour."

"Giving you ample time in which to draw up long-range cannon!" Orracolde scanned the brush-covered terrain as though expecting to find evidence of troop movements.

"But we have no reason to bear you ill will," Gartasian protested, dismayed by the other man's irrationality. What kind of envoy was this? And what kind of a ruler would entrust such a man with diplomatic responsibility?

"Do not take me for a fool, *old* warrior—I will deliver King Rassamarden's message without delay." Orracolde stooped, momentarily disappearing behind the gondola's side, and when he came into view again he was removing a yellowish scroll from a leather tube.

Gartasian had time in which to find his thoughts seizing on a triviality. Orracolde derogated him with every sentence he spoke, but he uttered the word "old" with a particular venom, as though it was one of the most insulting in his vocabulary. It was a minor mystery compared to the other puzzling aspects of what was happening, even though Gartasian had never considered himself as being old, and he resolutely pushed it aside as he saw Orracolde unroll a square sheet of heavy paper.

"I am an instrument of King Rassamarden, and the following message must be regarded as issuing directly from his lips," Orracolde said.

"I, King Rassamarden, am the rightful sovereign of all men and women born on the planet of Land, and of all their offspring, wherever they may be. In consequence, all new territories on the planet of Overland are considered to have been occupied on my behalf. I therefore proclaim myself sole ruler of Land and Overland. Be it known that I intend to exact all tributes which are rightfully mine."

Orracolde lowered the paper and stared solemnly at Gartasian, awaiting his response.

Gartasian gaped at him for a few seconds, then began to laugh. The sheer preposterousness of what he had heard, combined with the pompous style of the delivery, had abruptly translated the entire scene into farce. Release of the tension which had been growing inside him fueled his mirth, and he had genuine difficulty in bringing his breathing back under control.

"Have you lost your reason, *old* man?" Orracolde leaned over the rail, bronzed face thrusted forward, like a snake spitting venom. "I see nothing to laugh at."

"Only because you can't see yourself," Gartasian said. "I don't know which was the greater fool— Rassamarden for issuing that ridiculous message; or you for undertaking such a long and hazardous journey to deliver it."

"Your punishment for insulting the King will be death."

"I tremble."

Orracolde's mouth twitched. "I will remember you, Gartasian, but for now I have more important concerns. Littlenight will soon be upon us. When darkness falls I will take my ship aloft—rather than give you the chance to launch a sneak attack—but I will pause at a height of one thousand feet and wait for aftday. Chakkell will no doubt be with you by that time, and you will communicate his response to me by sunwriter."

"Response?"

"Yes. Either Chakkell bows the knee to King Rassamarden willingly—or he will be compelled to do so."

"You truly *are* mad—a madman speaking for a madman." Gartasian held his bluehorn steady while one of the crewmen fired another burst of gas into the balloon. "Are you talking of war between our two worlds?"

"Most certainly."

Struggling with his growing incredulity, Gartasian said, "And how would such a war be prosecuted?"

"A fleet of skyships is already under construction."

"How many?"

Orracolde produced a thin smile. "Enough."

"There could never be enough," Gartasian said calmly. "Our soldiers would be waiting for each ship as it landed."

"You don't really expect me to swallow that, *old* warrior," Orracolde said, his smile widening. "I know how thinly your population must be scattered. With informed use of wind cells we can put down almost anywhere on this planet. We could land under cover of darkness, but there will be little need for stealth, because we have weapons the like of which you have never imagined.

"And on top of everything else—" Orracolde paused to glance at his three companions, who gave approving nods as though knowing what he was about to say— "there's the natural and undeniable superiority of the New Men."

"Men are men," Gartasian said, unimpressed. "How can there be *new* men?"

"Nature saw to that. Nature and the ptertha. We have been created with total immunity to the ptertha plague."

"So that's it!" Gartasian ran his gaze over the four narrow faces which, with their inhuman metallic sheen, could almost have belonged to four statues cast from the same mould, and understanding began to flicker in his mind. "I thought that . . . perhaps . . . the ptertha might have ceased their attacks."

"The attacks continue unabated, but now they are futile."

"And what about . . . my kind? Are there any survivors?"

"None," Orracolde said, smugly triumphant. "The old have all been swept away."

Gartasian was silent for a moment, saying a final goodbye to his wife and son, then his thoughts were drawn back to the problems of the present and the need to learn all he could about the interplanetary visitors. Implicit in the few words Orracolde had already spoken was a dreadful scenario, a vision of a civilisation in its death throes. The drifting globes of the ptertha had swarmed in the skies of Land, hunting down their human quarries without mercy, driving them closer and closer to extinction, until their numbers were so . . .

My stomach is on fire!

The burning sensation was so severe that Gartasian almost doubled over. Within seconds the heat center beneath his chest had spread tendrils into the rest of his torso, and at the same time the air about him seemed to cool a little. Unwilling to show any sign of discomfort, he sat perfectly still in the saddle and waited for the spasm to come to an end. It continued unabated and he realised he would have to try disregarding it while he gathered precious information. He had not seen a case of pterthacosis since his youth on Land, but nobody of his generation could ever forget the symptoms— the burning sensation in the stomach, the copious sweating, the chest pains and the bloating of the spleen. . . .

"You grow pale, *old* warrior," Orracolde said. "What ails you?"

Gartasian held his voice steady. "Nothing ails me."

"But you sweat and shiver and . . ." Orracolde leaned forward across the rail, his gaze hunting over Gartasian's face, and his eyes widened. There was a moment of near-telepathic communion, then Orracolde drew back and gave a whispered order to his crew. One of them stooped out of sight and the ship's burner began a continuous roar while the other two men hurriedly began releasing the anchor lines from the downward-pointing cannon.

Gartasian had a pure, clear understanding of what he had read in the other man's eyes, and in the instant of accepting his own death sentence his mind had vaulted far beyond the circumscribed present. Earlier Orracolde had boasted of weapons outside the Overlanders' imaginings, but even he had been taken by surprise, had not sensed the dreadful truth foreshadowed by his own words. He and his crew were weapons in themselves— carriers of the ptertha plague in a form so virulent that an unprotected person had only to go near them to be smitten!

Their king, though apparently insane by Gartasian's standards, had been prudent enough to send a scout ship to gauge the opposition the invading force would meet. If he received word that there could be very little effective resistance, that Overland's defenders would be annihilated by pterthacosis, his territorial ambitions would be even further inflamed.

The skyship must not be allowed to depart!